# Nana's Niece

① pg 125

② 1st time placement?
which WW?
1st hint not autobiographical
pg 168 } pet or vet
197

### H Horace Broomes

227 - How does she do this whilst on a phone

Copyright © 2018 H Horace Broomes
All rights reserved
First Edition

PAGE PUBLISHING, INC.
New York, NY

First originally published by Page Publishing, Inc. 2018

ISBN 978-1-64350-255-7 (Paperback)
ISBN 978-1-64350-345-5 (Digital)

Printed in the United States of America

For Clarisa

# Chapter 1

Reason, as it happens, refuses me permission to accept the validity of the star sign readings. But reason, as ever showing keenness to consign my mind to a state of chaos for good, would offer me no room to deny the singularity of the girl, or of the woman, Shirley Wilson, or yet any justification ever to have declined any of Vanessa's gifts.

So it is that, just as, in the end, she wanted it to be, today and for all time, Vanessa, who bestowed me with my baptism around the time of her July 27 birthday so many years ago, remains family—you may even say twice family. My life could very easily have followed a different course had she and Shirley not been the women that they were and have been. The thing was, as I discovered after Vanessa died, if you engaged with me for a time in the glory of the ultimate intimacy, in repeated experiences of quality, you could make your claim, if you wished, and become simply family for good.

That way of seeing and of feeling could, even otherwise, even without Vanessa and Shirley, very easily have eluded me, though. From my early days, there was for long a deep, deep sensation floating about in my head that could, as I grew older, easily have possessed me fully—an uneasy feeling that it was an essential, existential even, duty to keep a close eye on the women about and around you.

Altogether to my distress, it had started with Gra'ma. The sensation was born, so far as I can make out, one impressionable day just outside the sturdy wooden kitchen that dutifully shouldered the Cocoa House. The kitchen stood on its concrete base, which itself firmly embraced at its perimeters eight crabwood pillars at their roots, stoically bearing this burden, a few yards distant from the cedarwood house her husband, Karsy, had left behind when he died in March 1939. A mere three-bedroom though the house was, it was the ancestral home, the home in which Gra'ma and Karsy's four boys and three girls had grown up. The house had stood there untroubled for long: cedarwood had a bitter taste that the wood lice did not like.

The reverence you felt in the presence of the house seemed to come by command—command brooking no question, but coming out from somewhere right inside of you. It was not just that it was the house built by grandparents whom you were taught to revere and to regard with something akin to awe, or that it was the place where they had raised your father and his siblings; there was an unmistakable mystique in its location itself. It stood on a kind of subpromontory, halfway down the slope sliding—now gently, now sharply—away from the boundary with Mayor Short's estate down to Level Bottom, where the breadfruit trees flourished among the coconuts and the seashore was nearer, and the lazy, beckoning roll of the waves more insistent.

It was a late-August afternoon, during the long school vacation, one of those days, no doubt about it, when it had rained in the morning, or Pappy had opted to do a *daywork* instead of a *task*, playing laborer on Mayor Short's estate, and we, the two eldest siblings of our family, were spared the rigors of the farmland or the Cocoa Piece, many miles away in the Woods. It had been my turn to do the dishes—or the wares, as we called them—and I had dutifully attended to that chore, half-filling the two plastic buckets with water from the concrete cistern standing in the shade of the giant bamboo patch constantly swaying in the sea breeze at the edge of the subpromontory just beyond the cedarwood house, and washed the wares in one bucket and rinsed them in the other and turned them down on the wooden draining board waiting on the dresser in the kitchen. In the warm glow of a deep sense of fulfilment, I rushed into the wide-open space outside to join my siblings and first cousins in whatever game was in progress at that time on that day.

Soon enough, Gra'ma emerged from the kitchen, where, engaged with mortar and pestle, she had been pounding half-ripe boiled plantain for her deft conversion into some delicacy fit for dinner, and as ever not daring to do otherwise whenever she appeared, we paused and gave her our full attention.

"Who wash up dem wares deh so good?"

Breathlessly striving to imagine what my reward could be, I gushed, "Is me, Gra'ma, is me!"

"Well, yuh haf to stap doin' w'ateva yuh doin' right now an' go een back een deh an' wash dem over: dey nat clean, dey nat clean at arl!"

The deflation was swift, immediate and painful, and more than a little subversive of my ability to trust her fully afterward.

\* \* \* \* \*

We, my siblings and I, did not have the normal two grandmothers: we had three. The second one was, simply, *Gran*. She lived in Glamorgan, the little village where we attended church and elementary school, both housed in the same building, the church, quite properly, above on the first floor and the school on the ground floor. As was proper, too, Sabbath school, for the children, was also held on the ground floor, on Saturday mornings. It was a building central to the cultivation of my psyche and one that seems, in some peculiar way, never to have ceased to have a certain power over my nervous system. I shiver in apprehension of some unholy act of God every time I pass by it now and bear witness to the unclean, commercial fate that has befallen it. No saint I, still I ask myself, Who will drive the money changers out of the temple? Who, wielding the whip of the Son, will try to persuade them to choose the path of righteousness? And my wandering mind would sometimes wonder who was desecrating that place and muse about whether Jesus's whip would have compared favorably with a quailed sibyl-jack or a bull-pistle duly soaked for days in grown men's urine and then put out to dry in the midday sun. And at times, assailed by thoughts of the renowned efficacy of a properly prepared bull-pistle, I would find certain possibilities for corrective action I could personally take suggesting themselves to me. But I would resist such temptations, not even bothering to find out who the money changers were.

Running along the eastern and southern perimeters of the building was a paved L-shaped walkway from which you entered the classrooms through the ground floor's northeastern, southeastern, and southwestern doors. Beyond the southern extremity of the walkway lay the latrines. Beyond the eastern part of it was the flower garden, bordered by George Street. The land lying to the east of the latrines rose sharply away from them to meet George Street and provide space for the school's vegetable garden. George Street ran away from the Windward Main Road right down to Gran's house, which stood on a high rock-based hill shooting sheerly up out of the sea below, where she lived with her husband, Jonathan, before he was hanged for killing my uncle, my father's elder brother, Egbert.

Like their late father, our uncles from the other side, our mother's half brothers, were fishermen, and no fry-fish tasted half as good as Gran's, as we discovered when, in course of time, we eventually decided we could partake of it. I was seven years old when my favorite uncle died. He was the one who would gather us together on many of those Sabbath Days when, for one reason or another, we were able to escape the drudgery of church, and tell us, after his inimitably gripping fashion, stories from the Bible, a book that would otherwise not necessarily be our own priority read. His outstanding narrative skills were lagniappe to the escape from church. Up until then, much as we loved Gran, defying the best efforts of our mother, we tried to keep our visits to the cliff-top house to a minimum, for whenever we visited her, as any island grandmother would do, she would offer us food, and that was a problem. Never were we hungry, and in time, we determined to ensure that that statement, whenever we made it to her, was always true—by being sure to eat just before we went. Needless to say, neither Gran nor Mammy was ecstatic over this, but they persevered with their invitations to us to "come arn, eat somet'ing." The real problem for us, however, was pork and crab.

Karsy, who died a couple of years before I was born, hailed from Barbados but was brought to Tobago as a child. He was an Anglican then, as were Gra'ma and Gran. At some time after he married Gra'ma, they became Seventh-Day Adventists, and being converts, they took the matter of their new state and condition extremely seriously. The way we were brought up made us want to eruct at the thought of pork or crabmeat in or near our mouths—and even at the thought of lifting to our lips this slice or that of obviously fantastic fried fish, if the frying had been done in those same iron pots that had been, at one time or another, warm, caressing homes to heathen spareribs or satanic gundy.

The problem surrounding visiting was compounded by the murder of Uncle Egbert. I can still see through seven-year-old eyes the dark, stilled flood of caked bloodstains looking up pleadingly from the *teleleh* shirt, set to become, in time, a screaming item of evidence come to life in the trial at the Assizes in Scarborough. The hands that helped to cuddle and nurture the pig ribs and the crab fins in their fiery, iron pot homes now bore, in the vivid, undiscriminating imaginations of our childhood, bloodstains caked and purple, and crying. Dearly did we love our grandmother, whose feelings toward us we knew, with the unerring instinct of the innocent, were ones of boundless adoration, yet we could not, for a long time, bring ourselves to savor her heartfelt offerings of food at the cliff-top house.

By and by she figured it out, did Gran. She cornered us one Sabbath Day after church, in the evening after the sun had set. Up to this day, I don't know still if she and Mammy had cooked up something. But at the end of the church day, Mammy told me and Gobo and Doodoo that she was going to see Paapa Milton, her father, who lived on Tambran Tree Road, which branched off from George Street about a half-mile east of the cliff-top house overlooking the sea. She told us to go by Gran and wait there for her until she came. As usual, Gran was all over us the moment she laid eyes on us, or, to use her own words, the moment she "bless mih eye 'pan al-yuh." She grabbed and squeezed each of us in turn and, as usual to our utter dismay, kissed us.

"Weh al-yuh modda, shi garn to see shi faada?"

"Yes, Gran," we confirmed in unison.

"Mih know, mih know, she an' shi faada, dey have t'ing to tark. Come, come, al-yuh mus'-be hungry."

"No, Gran!" we all but screamed in a hurried, desperate chorus.

"Look here, mih ketch up wid al-yuh. Mih know exac'ly w'a' 'appenin' arl dis time al-yuh ain' want to eat mih food: al-yuh 'fraid de pork-pat. Buh good news! Mih jes' buy a new iron pat jes' fooh al-yuh."

And she showed us the new iron pot with the coconut oil left back in it after she had fried the fish. We did not speak as we ate; the fry-fish was like no fried fish we had ever tasted before, and we reveled with no little fervor in the pit-roasted sweet potatoes, the boiled half-ripe plantains, and the garlic-lime sauce. I was about twelve then, and for long, very long, thereafter, we kept stringently shelved our old habit of arriving well-fed on any visit to Gran's. Then the day came when Gobo and I overheard a fateful conversation between mother and daughter.

"Gyul," Gran said in the course of it, "t'ree-fowre time, by accident, mih cook pork eena dat pat. Even yuh sister Fancilla does forget an' du dat sometimes. Mih cyahn le' yuh picknee dem fin' out dat at-arl, at-arl."

Mammy had, of course, been born an Anglican, and Granny and Grampa, the couple with whom she had grown up, had found their way late to the one true church (as we knew it). Her father, Paapa Milton, like her mother, was an Anglican. But she herself was the most flexible, the most liberated of them all. She told her mother, "W'a' nah kill ah fatten."

Gobo and I said nothing about that conversation to Doodoo or anyone. But we talked quite a bit about it. I told Gobo I had been doing a bit of reading on religion in order to try to clear up my confusion over all sorts of things. I told him I was sure I would never knowingly put a morsel of pork or crabmeat to my lips but that if Gran cooked pork or gundy in a pot and then she washed it out thoroughly and then made that tantalizing fry-fish, well... hmmm!

"Furthermore," I told him, "this Adventist Church was invented only around 1830, just about forty-something years before Karsy was born, by a conflicted Jewish lady called Ellen G. White, and, in an instant or two, became the one true church and the only one that says you can't eat great fry-fish prepared by your grandmother if your grandmother had fried it in an iron pot that pork had ever touched."

"Fooh true?"

"Which means that Karsy's grandfather, our great-great-grandfather, never had even a snowball's chance in hell of making it to heaven."

"Fooh true!"

"Buh Gran still shouldn' ah fool ahwi. Dat baad, dat rayl baaad!"

"Fooh true."

\* \* \* \* \*

Granny was our third grandmother. She and Grampa had one child of their own, a son, and they informally adopted two girls, Mammy and Vicki. Their son, before he later married and sired many more children with Andy's mother, had a son named Andy, whom my siblings, my first cousins, and I regarded as highly pampered and more than a bit of a softie. For that we nicknamed him Butter.

Granny was not easy. We used to say she made Grampa *"come-roun',"* our expression for *dizzy*. That expression was born out of a game we played sometimes, involving a spinning wheel contraption we constructed ourselves from discarded wood lying about our expansive living spaces. Sturdy old nails would be driven into the circular deck at three points, and pieces of rope would be attached to the nails. Three of us at a time would each grab ahold of one piece of the rope and run around spinning the deck as fast as we could. Each would let go of the rope in his own time, fall to the ground, rise to his feet as fast as he could, dizzy with the sensation of the continuing spin. Granny did not need a spinning wheel to make anyone *come-roun'*: she was a master of words and heart-stopping imagery. She and Grampa, it seemed to us, were engaged in an unending, if good-natured, verbal battle. Because her tongue was as devastating as it was, we were always on Grampa's side, supporters of the underdog, although, innocent as parents and elders mostly are about the capacity of little children to hear and grasp and talk about their wiles, they little knew what fun it was for us to take their battles all in and talk and laugh about them when we were safely out of their hearing.

For years on end afterward, we had fun talking about one such battle. You didn't try to recall what any particular battle had really been about, because that never mattered; in any case, whenever it suited Granny, she seamlessly changed the subject matter without poor Grampa even noticing. But today, to us, Grampa had triumphed, and we didn't wait to hear the end, but reaching the decision to do so by means of winks and nods, we ran all the way out of their hearing to recount and savor Grampa's unprepossessing, decisive blow.

"Grampa"—she, too, called him that, at least when we were around—"Grampa, is better yuh jus' shet yuh mout'." She paused but perhaps was so gleeful at the thought of the presumed conclusive, Hiroshimic effect of the blow she was about to deliver that she didn't notice the sound of the silence that instantly took the place of the cesser of our erstwhile continuous pretense of intense chatter.

Granny's trump was skid marks. "Grampa," she repeated, "is better yuh jes' shet yuh mout'," with a lush smile of deep satisfaction taking over her face. "*You* caaall yuhse'f ah man, yet every day ah haf to wash shit fram yuh drawers!"

During the seeming eternity of that silence's lifetime, I was certain that, one more time, Granny had made mincemeat of him. How could any mortal man recover from such a blow administered by his woman? Miraculously, Grampa was right up to the task. Putting an end to the said eternity, he smiled and then languidly made his pronouncement. "Granny," he said with lament in his voice, "I *surprise* at you!" He paused and then repeated himself, with more emphasis. "I *totally* surprise at you. Simple, simple t'ing yuh doh know: if a man doh put shit on 'e drawers for de *'ooman* to wash, he ain' no man at arl—no man at arl, at arl!" It was during Granny's wholly unwonted speechlessness (presumably uneverlasting), which, up to the time we left, was her only offering in response, that we went away to savor Grampa's moment.

Granny was opinionated, but you hardly saw it: you just knew it and felt it. She was deft and unobtrusive and in charge. And she seemed to know everything—excepting only, perhaps, that simple thing that Grampa had seen fit to bring so lucidly to her attention. In our own childhood simplicity, we did not realize she knew the name we had bestowed upon Andy, Uncle Dolly's first son, or how long she knew it. You never knew what she knew or when she had come to know it. You knew what she knew only when she pounced. Everybody else would spank us or use harsh words to us, but not Granny: she took neutral or gentle words, somehow equipped them with razor-sharp arrowheads, and unobtrusively administered them to you, with mortal effect.

"Andy rayly nat as tough as al-yuh fooh-true," she suddenly said to us once, the *fooh-true* sneakily implying a concession on her part, which immediately alerted us to impending trouble. "He was sickly as a baby… an' he is al-yuh cousin." We would never dare make fun of Butter in front of her, and we thought he, on the other hand, wouldn't have the guts to tell her about it and seem defenseless, a crybaby unable to handle his stories, and thereby prove us right. Scylla and Charybdis. How did she know? Then again, how did she always know everything? Never mind, we knew a warning when we saw one. But for us, that did nothing to interfere with Butter's name.

On another day, we went by Granny's house (somehow we never called it Grampa's house), hoping to climb up the *doux-douce* mango trees and the sapodilla trees and enjoy some of those delicious fruits, perhaps even taking away some soursop fruits in the bargain. Granny greeted us warmly and gave us lemonade and biscuits.

"So, al-yuh good?" she inquired as we enjoyed her offerings.

"Yes, Granny."

"So where al-yuh goin' now?"

"Now'ere."

"Wait, deh have a place name' Now'ere?"

"Granny, we come fooh mango and sapodilla." I thought it best to get straight to the point and tell her what she almost certainly already knew.

"Eh-heh? Bad. Baad, baad, baad! Al-yuh know Andy cyahn climb. He deh down de hill, down ah battam deh, tryin' to pick some fruit wid de bamboo rad. Suh al-yuh cyahn goh down deh today, al-yuh goh trouble 'im tumuch, al-yuh goh provoke 'im an' make 'im sickly again. Al-yuh haf to come back ah nex' day." We fully understood all that she was saying with these innocent words.

Her house was the first one on the promontory (which we ordinary folk called *the Pint* and some others called *a delightful piece of real estate*) that ran away southward from the Windward Road, starting from Mango Tree—the everlasting landmark standing on the side right at the bend in the road, two hundred yards or so from where a four-hundred-yard driveway began to meander northward before swinging back west toward *the Great House*, in which Mayor Short and his two sons lived, and where, as if peering down with a slight frown over the lenses of gold-rimmed spectacles, the mango-*vert* tree that gave the location its name stood tall and imperious, magisterially scouring the blind corner, to the east and to the west, for careless drivers, until, a mile and a half or so later, it jutted out into the sea, at our private, nameless beach, where the waters of Belle Garden Bay and Richmond Bay gently met night and day, fondling each other unceasingly.

Her house, as I have said, was the first one from Mango Tree. Two hundred yards or less along the seemingly endless dirt track that led from Mango Tree to the ancestral home that Karsy had left to Gra'ma, a subtrack v-shaped its long, unhurried way down toward Granny's house, where it stood, at the lowest point, a hundred feet below. With its earthen ground floor and extensive yard, beyond which there was only flora and fauna in interminable abundance, it imbued you with a heady feeling of living safe and secure in the wild, yet indoors. There was the stream that we called *the Gully*, where we caught crayfish; there were the coconuts and the bamboos, with their tops forever swaying in the breeze; there were the parrots and the bluebirds and the ground doves; there were the fruit trees—the sapodillas, the soursops, the mangoes, the pommecytheres, the sugar apples, the pommeracs, the oranges, the tangerines… the everything. And there was Granny's cooking. It was not a place you wanted to be barred from. But we understood her fully: she was saying that if we wanted to continue to savor all that, we had to treat Butter better; we were to stop calling Butter *Butter*.

We didn't stop calling Butter *Butter*, and for a while, nothing changed. We accepted that she somehow always knew everything, and we could never figure out how. It wouldn't remotely occur to us to call Butter *Butter* anywhere that we thought she could possibly overhear. But she used to say, "Bush have ears and bush have mout' and I have ears fooh bush mout' to full up." And Gobo said to me one day, "Buh, Jakey, how shi could know everyt'ing suh? Suppose bush does tark to shi in trut'?"

"Gobo, nuh tark chuppidness nuh bway!"

"Yeah, well *you* tell mih how she does always know t'ing suh, *you* tell mih!"

One day not long afterward, we sat at a table on the earthen ground floor of Granny's house, enjoying one of our favorite meals. We loved it there. There was something almost magical about that earthen ground floor, and to have paved it over would have been to drive away, to send floating away in the wind, an intangible, invisible, irretrievable something of immense value. There is where Granny cooked and where everybody ate: it was the kitchen, it was the dining room, it was the informal living room for family. The *chocolate tea* and *fry-bake* and *yard-fowl egg* sunny-side up were going down well, and we were wordless as we dug in. When we finished and noticed Granny coming toward the table with no smile on her face, we felt sure her purpose was to assign the responsibility for washing up the wares. But what she did instead was pull a bamboo chair and sit down. For a time, she merely scrutinized us.

## Chapter 2

During the period of silence that the scrutiny brought forth, I briefly recalled to mind an earlier time when she had sat herself down something like that, right there, at that very table. Mammy and Pappy had not long before taken me and my siblings for a short holiday with relatives in Manzanilla in Trinidad. It was my second visit to the big island. I can keenly recall and cannot forget one detail of an even earlier visit to some vague relative, perhaps a great-aunt, when I couldn't have been very much more than a toddler. We had stayed then at the relative's home at Prizgar Road in San Juan, and it still troubles me that I don't seem ever to have seen her or even heard of her at any time since. What I remember, though, is that on the street outside her house one moonlit night, I found myself in a group of four or five boys my age liming, and that as soon as I opened my mouth to enter the chat for the very first time, they all laughed at me and ran away, and that it took me many hours to realize that it was not necessarily any perceived stupidity on my part but rather my *Tobago twang* that had caused the administration to my psyche of that swift and brutal bruising. It was the uncompromising cruelty of tactless innocents. Later, as I ripened into early manhood and reflected, I would find myself thinking sometimes that women could be like that, too.

Our tiny, little world seemed then to be a very large place, and I don't remember the Manzanilla relatives, either: theirs remained another world away, and them, too, I don't recall having ever seen or heard of after the holiday at their home. I was impressed that they had a little driveway to their house coming off the *pitch road*—reminiscent of Mayor Short's leaving the Windward *pitch road* just before Mango Tree—more impressed by that than by the fact that, like Mayor Short, they actually had a motorcar, even if the car was a banged-up, old Zephyr. At that time, though, fearing the ruthless wrath of those of superior *twang*, I mostly tamed my tongue and was inhibited, though a little more so then than I was ten years or so later in the Sixth Form at St. Mary's College in Port of Spain, where not even the priests showed empathy in that regard. But in Manzanilla, Gemma was different with me, and we were uninhibited, and we chatted a lot and did exploratory things.

They said she was my second cousin, and I felt free to risk writing to her after we returned to Tobago at the end of the vacation, but not without taking the precaution of alleging in the letter that the reason I was addressing that letter of gratitude to her in particular was that hers was the only name I remembered. I had written love letters to girls before and had been, in retrospect, to my consternation and amusement, severely reprimanded by my father when recipients' fathers had complained to him about that. So when the Manzanilla moment of truth came, even faced with the most incontrovertible evidence to the contrary, I repeatedly denied authorship of the letter I had written to Gemma. But I was a mere child, and unsworn, and I know now that nowadays you can witness countless adults, most of them claiming to be God-fearing, and supposedly intelligent, routinely doing that kind of thing, the Koran or the Gita or the Bible held piously in their right hands.

"So *yuh* write Gemma?" my father half-inquired, half-declared.

I saw the letter in his hand, and in less than an instant, I could feel the back of my neck and my shoulders and my face all ablaze with extreme discomfort. I knew instinctively that the smart-ass name-recall excuse that I had built into the letter would avail me nothing. *How come neither Mammy nor Pappy neva did hear from me even one blessed word about the letter? And I could'na jes' arks Mammy or Pappy for Tanty's name? And, come to t'ink of it, what Gemma and I was really doin' dem moon-light night an' dem when we was playing hide-and-seek? Eh-ehn! No, sah! Dat cyahn save yuh, bway!* My thoughts were feverish.

"Ah nuh *me* weh write dat, Pa."

It was sheer desperation. After that, and as you grew older, you became more and more keenly aware of how lies simply demeaned their tellers, especially stupid ones that nobody would pause to consider. But they had warned you so often and with such great passion not to interfere with girls, people's daughters. "Doh' trouble people darta, yuh hayr me; doh bring trouble home-yah fooh mih!" Better deal with two sets of applied *sibyl-jacks* later than take a single flogging right now when your mind was not prepared. Experience had taught that, somehow, when you were resigned to the inevitability of the *cut-arse*, as we called it among ourselves, out of hearing of adults, your skin had time to toughen as you waited, and the sting of the whip was blunted, and you wailed mainly to try to touch the heart of the administerer.

"Ah nuh me write dat, Pa."

"Oh mih gard! Emmy, come, come quick. Ahwi have jumbie eena de house. Come!"

My father emphatically did not believe in ghosts and apparitions, and my mother had a good idea of the state of mind that would lead him to speculate with such urgency and passion that one or more of them had invaded his home, and then, in a tone of desperate helplessness, to call upon her to come and help him deal with the necessary exorcism. He and I were, as a matter of fact, below our wooden house that stood on pillars of crabwood (like steel to wood lice, the same way that cedar was aloe vera to them), on foot on the earthen floor of what now I call his workshop, next to his workbench, his carpenter's tools neatly arranged on a shelf in one corner of the ground floor. She was in the kitchen, a separate outbuilding set away a few yards from the house itself, and she couldn't simply switch off the burning firewood as you would a stove.

"Wait, m'ah come jes' now," which, translated into "foreign," could be said to mean, in free translation, "Gimme a minute, please." But she was soon there.

"Emelina Brougham, yuh big son jes' tell mih ahwi have jumbie in dis house."

Mammy looked at me, and I was relieved to sense the empathy, and the terror eased a little bit. She looked back at my father. "The letter?" she asked.

"'E seh is nat he write it, so is jumbie. Jumbie arl over mih house now… Bway, yuh showre *you* nuh write dis letter?"

I made no reply.

"Okay, ah will give yuh time to t'ink about it. W'enever yuh ready, jes' tell mih."

He wheeled around and went away.

"Yuh have corn to weed," Mammy said as she looked me up and down and turned and headed back to the kitchen.

A day or so later, Granny sent for me.

It was a holiday morning, and there was no school, and for once in such circumstances, we were not headed to *the Bush* at Little River or Big River or Cocoa Piece. She made her delicious flatbread, coconut bake, and fried eggs and *buljol,* and you could see the satisfaction on her face as she stood by and watched *Butter* and me eat. Then came that moment when she pulled the chair and sat down by the table.

"Andy, you goh up an' study yuh book. Ah want to tark to dis one."

There is a sense of dark foreboding, and you want to get up and run away, but you know you can't. You think feverishly and come up with what little you can in the circumstances.

"Ah want to help Andy wid 'e homework."

"No, *you* stayin' wid Granny."

"I stayin' wid Granny?"

"Yep!"

I turned and twisted, twisted and turned, and twirled.

"Granny, ah haf' to go to the latrine?"

"Goh an' come back. Ah waitin' fooh yuh."

As could confidently be anticipated, nothing happened in the latrine, but I stayed there as long as I reasonably could, and then, with much deliberation, I washed my hands twice and, in time, returned to the table.

"Siddong, siddong. Pigeon come here an' tell mih yuh put jumbie in yuh poopa house! Ah true?"

"No, Granny."

"Nuh true?"

"No, Granny."

"Yuh like de coconut bake?"

"Yes, Granny."

"And w'at about de egg and de *buljol*?"

"Yes, Granny."

"Well, before yuh eva come back to see yuh Granny, tell yuh poopa that it ain' have no jumbie in 'e house… an' den tell 'im somet'ing about the letter. Be a good boy!"

And she got up, wheeled around, and went back to the fireside in the kitchen.

I wondered for years afterward whether there was no means I could have found by which to forego, to live without forever, Butter's imposed company and the delight of Granny's coconut bake and the yard-fowl eggs and the *buljol*. Grandfathers and fathers and uncles somehow seemed more respectful and more trustworthy. That was the first time Granny had pulled a chair and sat down at that table with obvious intent.

This second time, as we all sat there, waiting with bated breath, Granny conspicuously settled herself into the bamboo chair and cleared her throat.

"Al-yuh enjay de chaacolate tea an' everyt'ing?"

"Yes, Granny," we chorused.

"Good, good. Very good. But arl de time ah slaving over de fireside deh, mekking arl ah dat fooh al-yuh, somet'ing ah badder mih, badder mih, badder mih."

She paused, and I wondered what could be bothering her that much, especially in the midst of the joy I'd always sensed she got from cooking. I raised my head to find that she seemed somehow to be looking directly into my eyes.

"A little bluebird tell mih al-yuh still carlin' 'im *Borta*, still carlin' Andy *Bertha*." Just as she could say *calling* if she chose to, she could, as she chose to now, say *Bertha* with consummate ease.

We were stunned, shaken. Where did this *Bertha* allegation come from, when the boy's name was *Butter*, as everybody knew? Where was Granny going with this one? We could never trust her, trust the way she spun her balls, bowled her googlies. We waited in heart-racing silence.

"Yuh know weh de bluebord tell mih? De bluebird tell me al-yuh jes' want to disrespec' *me*. He is Anderson Alexander, and I is Albertha Alexander, and only big people does carl me *Bertha*. Al-yuh tekking trick to mek luck. W'at al-yuh really warnt to do is carl me *Bertha* too. Al-yuh jes' want to disrespec' al-yuh gran'mother, an' ah cyahn stan' fooh dat!"

In the family circles, all the possible penalties for disrespecting an elder, not to say so venerable an elder as a grandmother (more so than a grandfather), were extremely unattractive. And if a grandmother expressed the view, or indeed gave the slightest indication that she was of the view, that you had disrespected her, one of those penalties immediately became applicable.

Fearing bluebirds and pigeons, we never called Butter *Butter* again. The wily Granny had us completely cornered.

And afterward, we lived by the motto "When Granny give yuh sweetie, suck it slow, slow—an' cayful-cayful."

## Chapter 3

Pappy was straightforward. If he considered it necessary in all the circumstances of a case to administer corporal punishment, he explained that to you, almost apologetically; but he was careful to let you know that he was the only judge in the matter and that he had already given it full and mature consideration, in which case, as experience showed, even maternal intervention would be futile. When I summoned up the mountain of courage required to do so, I went to him one afternoon as he sat on his carpenter's bench underneath the house, using his plane and his level to help straighten replacement floorboards.

"Well, son, dat was ah big one yuh t'row at mih, ah big, big one. Yuh know w'a' dat mean?"

"Yes, Pa."

"Well, wait here. Ah coming." He was, of course, off to select an appropriate instrument of correction.

Mammy, passing by on her way to the kitchen from the house, overheard the exchange. "But," she pleaded as she veered toward us, "he jes' tark de troot. doh' beat 'im dis time nuh."

"Hi' punishment is nat for nat tarking de troot, is for lyin'—big difference."

Pappy always puzzled Mammy, and us (and, in fact, everybody), with his fine distinctions, which he made with great passion and total commitment. Mammy stared at him in blank frustration, regarded me with sadness in her eyes, and continued on her way to the kitchen and the three-stone *fireside*. It had taken me days to make the confession, and I had steeled myself for the spanking I knew to be inevitable, but I had judged that the instrument of application would be the leather belt, so when I saw the *sibyl-jack* swinging from his right hand in the distance, I began to run. I ran past the papaya and the banana and the plantain trees, past the ochroes and the tomatoes, through the coconuts, up the hill, through the sweet potato area.

Every time I looked back, he was there behind me. It had always worked before: he would run after me a bit, stop after a while, shout at me that he was turning back and that I could feel free to postpone the inevitable until whenever I came back, and half the time, he would never revert to the matter, so it was a good gamble. But not today. I kept on running—out of our own lands, across Grampa Bolkan's lands, across Short's lands—until I could envisage starkly the hurdle of the mouth of Richmond River, with its wide and luscious lips kissing the waters of Richmond Bay. Beyond there I would be able to run no farther. I made and implemented a swift decision: I stopped.

"Well, boy," he said, blowing hard, "yuh rayly make me wuk hard today, yuh know dat?"

"Yes, Pa."

Even to the attentions of the *sibyl-jack*, I was now resigned.

"Yuh si how mih blowin'?"

*Please get it over and done with*, I thought.

"Well, is two cut-tail fooh you, yuh hear?"

It clearly was not as cut-and-dried a matter as I had imagined. *Two sibyl-jack cut-arse!* I thought to myself before he addressed me again.

"Yuh anderstan'?"

I did not understand and communicated that fact by means of fidgeting in complete silence.

"The *fus* one yuh gettin' right yah, pan dis same spat, fooh mekking mi run arl de way yah and blow breat'less. The *secan'* one yuh will get pan de spat below de house by mih wukking-bench from w'ere yuh start to run from. Yuh ready?"

After that experience, I deleted running away from my mental manual of techniques for avoiding what, when within the actual or apprehended hearing of adults, we called *cut-tails*, but otherwise *cut-arses*.

## Chapter 4

Alejandro Moreno, although he never made any reference to attendance at Mass, by either word or deed, was as good a Catholic as the next one, being no saint but enamored of the concept of purgatory and the purifying propensities of the place. So student infractions at Elizabeth's College at Roxborough and, later, at Scarborough and, in course of time, Port of Spain attracted not what in other schools was called detention, but penance. Like Pappy, Al, as grown-ups called him, always explained apologetically the need for and claimed sole and full responsibility before carrying out a sentence.

To this day, I have never ceased praising him for the memorable eighteen-month one he once awarded me. He didn't call it that, and indeed, specifically told me it was not that, and it was probably true. In any event, in a year-and-a-half I thoroughly learned—even mastered, I would dare to hazard—the necessary art of turning the other cheek in order to save my life, even if to no one to this day have I ever been able to explain satisfactorily how I could maintain my friendship with the lady who became my ex-lover on the day that she told me, "No, just leave me alone. You just don't know how to do it. Look, believe me, whenever I want a good one, I just go elsewhere." In frustration, I would simply say to friends who became insistent in their demand for an explanation, "Blame Al," and then you could see on their faces, especially the faces of the ones who had never heard about Alejandro Moreno, that they were then almost fully satisfied that I ought to be committed without delay.

Morro and Morgan took themselves far too seriously for nonsense (meaning by *nonsense* almost all, if not all, the pranks that fourteen-year-old lads would likely engage in), by dint of which the one did not complete even his first degree and the other obtained and greatly relished his doctorate. But Pepe and Tapo (also known as Mango-Head, for a reason that stood out starkly whenever he had just had a haircut) and Doyle and Danny-Boy delighted in mischief of every conceivable sort. Pepe's mind was undoubtedly the sharpest and most impish, and without sign of effort, it spat out idea after idea that led you to wonder if the lad's entire cranium was constructed of unrelenting wickedness; Tapo and Doyle were the master finishers and fine-tuners of the product, and Danny-Boy, a worthy amalgam of them all, would every now and then deploy a devastating stealth-bomb.

"Brougham!" screamed Pepe, completely out of the blue. "Why yuh oil-up de desk so, bwoy?"

It would have been about half past twelve on what I recall was one of those hot, dry March days when, away from schools, away from churches, away from cedarwood houses on their crabwood stilts, away from the refuge of buildings of every kind, Pappy and Uncle Jimmy (Uncle Egbert now seven years dead) and Grampa, toiling underneath the searing sun, would be clearing and plowing up the lands in anticipation of the teasing April showers, John the Baptists of the rains of May. The coconuts, the cocoa, and the coffee seemed to be always there, everlasting and immovable, like the fruit trees, which simply stood there, silent, majestic, and self-assured, bearing from season to season; the root crops—the sweet potatoes and the dasheens and the tanias—that were yet unreaped, now withered but, alert to the distant sound of refreshing showers, ready, not to breathe their last, but, given half a chance, to spring up again, would be hauled out of the parching earth, disinterred to deliver up their life's work and reunite with, and be replaced there (on that part of those lands forming part of that particular piece of earth) by a rudimentary speck of, the infinite flora. The banana and the plantain trees, which would have surrendered their output and faithfully installed their successors, their *suckers*, and then shriveled to the verge of nothingness, would be cut away and dismembered for compost, as would the okra trees and the cornstalks that stoically grew up, presented their produce for the taking, then peacefully dried and died, died erect, standing at their full height, waiting resignedly for oblivion, seeking no reprieve. Sometimes on a quiet, sunny day, lying in the shade of coconut trees swaying in the breeze, I would think of all of them and about the infinite fauna and wonder what would happen, how the world would be different, if humans were like them.

"Brougham! Yuh sleepin' or w'at?" Pepe continued. "Mih arks yuh ah question! W'y yuh oil up the desk so?"

Almost in chorus, Doyle and Tapo said, "Brougham, de man arks yuh ah question. Answer!" as they grinned with teenage malice. Danny-Boy was mum.

By this time, Alejandro Moreno, the principal, was standing over us and the two school desks we had, as usual, pulled together to form our lunch table, and I immediately understood my predicament: I was going to be the fall guy for the grease that had oozed out of Doyle's and Pepe's and Tapo's brown paper bag lunch carriers onto the desks. Like me, Danny-Boy was far too finicky and far too rule-abiding to let himself fall into the error of that infraction; all the same, he would, as I knew only too well, even in the teeth of the malice deployed against me, settle for silence.

"So, boys, oil on my desks again, eh? Guess that's how you do it at home, eh?"

"Sir, ask Brougham!" said Tapo, not only he, whose father was the head teacher at the school standing at the corner of the Windward Road and George Street in Glamorgan, but all of us, knowing full well in whose presence we were never to pronounce *ask* as *arks*.

"Yes, sir, ask Brougham," Doyle and Pepe complemented, casting a sharp eye each at a taciturn Danny-Boy, through whose teeth and lips there managed to ease forth now a barely audible repetition of the unjust accusation: "Sir, ask Brougham."

Just as he did with his ungovernable passion for punctuality, a veritable scourge in a lawless and disorderly society, Pappy inflicted me with an abiding sense of a duty to reject and repel what he called *carnfulniss*. He could well say *scornful*, and even *scornfulness*, whenever he wanted to, but for him, *carnful* and *carnfulniss*, for being fractured verbalizations, gave more satisfaction as truer representations of what he wished to convey. Especially so was that as he viewed the very concept of scorn in his own peculiar way and in that way exclusively. To be scornful was to have a deep-seated aversion to repelling constantly or, failing that, to taking by the scruff of their necks dirt and filth and muck and decisively removing every trace of them from your surroundings. Thus his motto, "Carnful people are nasty people," was constantly ringing in your ears. For me to soil our make-do lunch table with oil from my *fry-bake* or *fry-egg* was a virtual impossibility; for me, if, by some accident, the virtually impossible happened, to fail to take instant remedial action would be unthinkable.

"Get to it, then, Brougham… and I'm disappointed in you. I thought that you, of all—"

"Sir, it wasn't me…," I said slowly and with superb articulation.

"You mean to say…"

"Sir," I said, and paused. "Sir," I slowly repeated, "*it was not me!*"

"So you want me to believe that all these four boys…"

It may be that the greatest advantage of cedarwood is that it is bitter and enjoys inherent protection from the ravages of voracious termites, but another great advantage, highly valued in circumstances such as these, is that, while being quite sturdy, it is much lighter than mahogany or *crapaud* or *crab*. All the school furniture, including the chairs on which we sat, were made of cedar and were relatively easy to lift.

He disappointed me: he stood there seeming to wait for me to do the cleaning-up. Had he not noticed how my jawbones had tautened, how my voice had dropped, how my speech had slowed and become excessively modulated and deliberate, how my tone burned? Nothing at all happened for a very, very little moment that, perhaps, remained an untroubled bubble ensconced in a minute space in the endlessness of time, forever unsullied by human verbal or other contamination. Then they watched me as I rose and, in what even now I can recall only as one smooth, swift, and polished action, stepped to one side and grabbed my chair, lifted it over my head, and hurled it with all my might at Alejandro Moreno.

"The four of you," said the principal calmly, breaking the deathly silence that ensued, "will do penance for ninety minutes every afternoon for four weeks."

Danny-Boy began to protest. "But, sir—"

"The upholder is worse than the thief," the principal said, shooting him down.

I stood there now shivering on a hot March afternoon, scarcely able to believe that I had done what I had done: if they were going to do thirty hours of penance for *their* sin, surely, I, who had tried to redesign the principal's face with my cedarwood chair, was going to be expelled, or at least suspended for an entire term. Suspension would be bad enough in itself, but it was a *bagatelle* compared to the concomitant requirement of explaining to Pappy how I had earned it in the first place. The difficulty of putting such an explanation together would not be made easier against the background of the family rule that we children must show respect to every older person, no matter who he might be, leaving any advantage taken of us by such a person to Pappy's notoriously rigorous and uncompromising attention. Expulsion would be easier to deal with: all I would have to decide would be whether to go down to Belle Garden Bay and swim far out into the ocean until I was completely exhausted and had no means of returning to shore or simply to stow away on the boat to Trinidad and take it from there.

"You!" said the principal, startling me out of my clinical analysis of my predicament.

He was a short brown-skinned man of Venezuelan ancestry, with a little slanted splice of gold running away southeastward down one of his upper front teeth and a ready smile. Almost parallel to that splice of gold, there lingered, near the beginnings of his nose bridge, tickled by the lower lashes of his left eye, a slightly darkened scar, doubtlessly a memento of some childhood battle, evidence that, his physical stature notwithstanding, he probably never ran away from a fight. His round head stood steady on his shoulders, and his piercing brown eyes, now unaccompanied by his ready smile, engaged me frontally.

"I'm not going to punish you."

I gasped all but audibly and pressed my palms onto the desk for support, not daring to take my eyes off him, hardly able to breathe.

"What I have to do is save you from the hangman's noose. I have to teach you to control your temper. No matter how well you may do in whatever examinations, no matter what else you learn here, nothing is more important."

He paused and looked at me, and I could almost hear his mind fine-tuning the exact terms of his decision.

"Starting tomorrow, you will spend one hour with me every afternoon. It will take eighteen months by my estimate. Don't take it as penance. I mean that. I *have* to save you. That is my primary duty."

## Chapter 5

There were times afterward when I wondered if Teacher Aaron, too, had had a nasty temper in his youth. After the previous head teacher, Teacher Buddy, got married and left to attend the SDA university in Michigan in the United States, Teacher Aaron took over on transfer from the Seventh-Day Adventist primary school in Moriah. He was a man of dark complexion, just under medium height and just over medium build, with eyes that took their time to search you and a smile that not infrequently flickered to displace his poker mien—not that he played poker, as card games were on the list of Mrs. Ellen G. White's forbidden pastimes when, conflicted and half-deserting Judaism, she had, on her second try some ninety years earlier, founded the new Christian denomination, careful to stay close to roots, unsettling her core as little as possible, and he was a good Seventh-Day Adventist, whether his wife, Genevieve, believed it or not.

He got us to replace the plants in the flower garden that lay between the eastern section of the school's L-shaped walkway and George Street, each class in turn, on a Thursday afternoon, having the gardening assignment for its last period. Right at the beginning, two students of the class showed reluctance. He told them it was a request in the interest of the surroundings and that he would not insist but that what he was about to put forward to resolve the matter was not a request but a decision.

"I was planning to be the overseer and guide you all, but now I will do the work of you two and you two will be the overseer. You will have to guide us as we work, observe how we work, and on Monday morning, make a report to the whole school about how well or how badly we worked."

They begged to do the work instead. He told them that the decision had already been made but that they would be free to work when the turn of their class came around again. No one ever demurred after that, and the flower garden flourished. Later, he introduced a similar program for the vegetable garden, and soon we were able to mount a vegetable stall at the annual Harvest Festival organized by the church elders at the school ground at crop-over time every year, a festival that, there in Glamorgan—as in the cases of the similar ones that took place in just about every village throughout the island—we simply called Harvest.

Teacher Aaron seemed to have an aversion to belts. There was one hanging by a nail in the corner of the schoolroom, where the head teacher's desk stood, next to it a three-drawer steel cabinet. That corner was the head teacher's office, without walls. More than once I heard adults saying they agreed with him that the school board could put curtain runners on the ceiling and buy some curtains, which he could draw and get some privacy as needed; the school board should do that as soon as they had the money. The nail with the cowhide leather belt running down sheer from it was on the northern wall of the building, behind the head teacher when he sat at his desk, facing the entire schoolroom. If that northern corner was the source or symbol of authority in that place, it was not to escape your notice that there was nothing there north of the belt. But Teacher Aaron never gave it glory, never used it, never needed it, reducing it to the level of a ceremonial figurehead.

After a time, I observed that he didn't use a belt to hold up his trousers either. It was a cardinal rule all over the island that children must never "get into big-people business." By breaking that rule, whether *in flagrante* or on the balance of probabilities, a child would, in an instant, earn a sound cut-tail. Like so many of my contemporaries, I developed to a fine point the art of gathering information while feigning innocence and disinterest—as we put it in the villages, playing dead to catch *corbeaux* (our scavenging birds) alive.

Depending on the particular circumstances, I could be chatting with another lad without hearing a word he said, or I could be reading a book upside down, or I could be on the verge of applying black polish to Pappy's brown shoes: I would nonetheless be all ears, gathering information without, in any way, alerting "big people." And that was how I discovered why Teacher Aaron didn't use a belt to hold up his trousers.

It was at a Sunday-night service in the church upstairs that I first noticed the necktie in the trouser loops around his waist. I paid little attention to it at first: church services were held, apart from the entire day on Saturdays, on Sunday and Wednesday evenings, and the regularity of your attendance at all of them was a main measure of the degree of your devotion. Pappy always displayed a keen awareness of this yardstick and liked to have his family with him in church. Yet I had never before noticed this necktie running through Teacher Aaron's loops. And it was nighttime to boot. If I could see it in the night, surely, I would have seen it if he had ever worn it in the daytime. Still, I wondered and was not satisfied; so the thing to do was gather information from big people, which I did.

"Dat man nat easy," cousin Sydney said, "'E tek arf 'e belt fooh dem!"

"Yuh haf to anderstan' de man," Pappy cautioned. "He nat a simple man."

"Suh, Sydney," Uncle Jimmy put in, "yuh rayly t'ink a man like he plannin' to cut de board backside?"

The morning services at church would end at around twelve thirty, and sometimes, going Dutch, we would go off to Tanty Etho's to have lunch together—Pappy, Mammy, and children and Uncle Jimmy (the eldest of Gra'ma's offspring) and his wife and children. Lunch would be corn bread or cassava bread, followed by, for dessert, coconut drops or pone made most times of sweet potatoes, but often of corn or cassava, the preparation of all of which had to be completed before sundown on Fridays, work, including the preparation of meals, being prohibited on Saturday, the Sabbath. The meals were washed down with lime juice made of plain water and limes picked and freshly squeezed before sunset on Friday and sweetened with brown sugar and set down on the kitchen counter, without refrigeration, of which, in any event, we knew nothing, to await the Sabbath lunch. During lunch, the grown-ups would sit at the table, critiquing the preacher's sermon, with Sydney, the host, trying to prove himself erudite to the scarcely concealed irritation of Uncle Jimmy and Pappy. We children, sitting, some on chairs, some on old bedsheets spread on the floor, having all too often been reminded that such was our station, that we were to be "seen but not heard," would tackle our bread and homemade butter in silence and feigned innocence and hone into fine art our ability to speak to one another with our eyes alone.

After lunch, the younger children would go out into the yard and play, while we, the older ones, would have to sit around, reading the Bible or the quarterly or one of Mrs. Ellen G. White's books. For the adults, still sitting at the table, this was time for serious gossip, an activity that was not specifically identified and prohibited either in the Word or in any of the many authoritative writings of Mrs. White. When I heard Uncle Jimmy engaging cousin Sydney on the matter of the probability that Teacher Aaron would administer a cut-arse to the members of the school board, my ears caught fire, but I managed to grab back my quarterly before it hit the floor.

"I never seh anyt'ing about cutting de board backside," Sydney announced. "Aaron too smart for dat. He smarter dan arl al-yuh put together."

"And of course," Uncle Jimmy shot back, "you smarter dan he, right? You is de smart one in dis family, right?"

"Aaron doh cut nobady backside," Sydney resumed, clearly not interested in a fight. "He doh even use de belt wid de children and dem in de school, he goh use it on de board? Is tac' de man using, de man usin' 'e head to tackle de board."

"Mek sense nuh, Sydney, mek sense!" Pappy said impatiently, while Uncle Jimmy glowered. "W'a' tac' yuh tarking 'bout?"

"Al-yuh fooget how long de man arksin' fooh a raise 'a salary an' 'e cyahn get none? Wid me own two ears mih hayr 'im tell John-Boy how 'e goin' an' demonstrate quietly, an' how he ain' haf to use no placard fooh dat."

Pappy seemed to turn his head in my direction, and my eyes, smoothly returning to the quarterly, empathetically permitted me to read the upside-down page with a straight face until it was safe to bring a halt to that feat.

"Suh de tie is de placard?" Pappy asked rhetorically.

"No," Sydney replied, "e seh he ain' usin' no placard!"

"Suh de belt is de placard!" Pappy seldom lost an opportunity presented to him by Sydney to subvert the notion of Sydney's self-supposed erudition. Sydney's jaw fell away a little, and he briefly bit his lips. But he loved the sound of his voice and he could never bear not to have the last word.

"Suh, doh t'ink is because he ain' have belt dat 'e tyin' up 'e trousers wid tie," he declared as no one listened. "'E tek arf 'e belt fooh dem!"

I liked that about Teacher Aaron. He was, in so many ways, like Pappy, like Uncle Egbert, like Uncle Jimmy, even like Uncle Eddy, who mostly lived in a world of his own and unceasingly argued aloud with himself, sometimes even appealing to anyone of us children who might happen to be nearby to support him in some argument he had just been having against himself. Teacher Aaron was cool, calm, and collected and had a preference for quiet, telling action over loud, aggressive words. It was why he always gave every opportunity to you to come good. It was why he always strove to give you the benefit of the doubt. It was why he sometimes purposefully tilled the soil in the school's flower garden or vegetable garden and manned a stall at Harvest. It was the reason he had no use for the ceremonial figurehead hanging on the northern wall behind his desk at the school. It was how he was able to watch the board cave in at last and give him the pay raise he deserved. As on Pappy and on my uncles, and as I would, later, on Alejandro Moreno, unknowingly to my consciousness, I modeled part of myself on him.

In time, I could feel that he sensed the admiration I had for him and, no doubt, the reason for it. It didn't hurt either that I seemed very far from being the dullest lad in the upper school. Willy-nilly, I became a bit of a favorite, an outcome that brought with it its own downside.

I became, in practice, if not in name, the supervisor of the gardens. Whether what we were tending were flowers or vegetables, I would put my happy hands into the soil only when overcome (as happened often enough) by irrepressible love for the land or driven (as happened often, too) to demonstrate to one of my erring charges the proper way in which to plant this Joseph's coat or mold that cornstalk. If there was some item urgently needed for the school during teaching hours, I would be the one entrusted with the money to go across the road to cousin Derrick's shop or go three hundred yards westward along the Windward Road to cousin Conrad's parlor for it. If Teacher Aaron wanted the blackboard partially dusted so that certain specified parts were left intact as needed for continuation of the lesson, unlike when he simply wanted the blackboard cleaned completely, I would be the one chosen to do that intelligent dusting. If he had to leave the school compound for a while, he would let the senior teacher know that I was the pupil to supervise his class in his absence. Through all this preferment I maintained, or hoped I maintained, a bland and equable disposition. But I reveled in it inside.

I didn't feel the same about the post office trips, especially about how Genevieve damaged me along the way. For some reason, there was no post office in Glamorgan. There was none in Richmond either, but I could forgive that because Richmond (of which *the Pint* was a kind of subvillage) seemed, itself, more like an orphan stepvillage of either Glamorgan or Belle Garden (you couldn't quite make up your mind which), because the church and the school and cousin Derrick's shop (across the Windward Road from the school) were in Glamorgan, as was Gran's house, overlooking the cliff where George Street, as if tired of traveling or fed up with the pounding of footsteps, jumped off into the sea far down below and, committing suicide, met an abrupt and unholy end; while all our paternal relatives lived in Belle Garden but, like Gran and Paapa Milton, Mammy's father, were not Seventh-Day Adventists, but had been baptized in, and attended, other Christian churches and were, therefore, heathens, they were tolerated (and, at the same time, passionately loved) only because they were blood relatives. And the only people who lived in Richmond were the Broughams, Granny and Grampa and

Butter, and Mr. Pilgrim with his *cork-foot* and his pretty granddaughter, whom, later, I had the pleasure of teaching things. You could understand why Richmond might not have merited its own post office, but Glamorgan's situation was a puzzle. Some adult might have declared it somewhere at some time, I can't say I'm sure, but deep inside my mind, there dwelled an apprehensive half-certainty that Glamorgan's (if not Richmond's) punishment was for harboring too many Seventh-Day Adventists, the Christian's "God's chosen people," as proclaimed by the conflicted Jewish lady, of whose irrepressible self-assuredness and bombast I continue in everlasting awe and admiration. Belle Garden, lying just east of Richmond, had its post office; Pembroke, immediately west of Glamorgan, also had its own.

It is to the Pembroke Post Office, three-quarters of a mile away from the school—past cousin Conrad's parlor on the left; past Lammie Nurse Variety Store and Grocery, standing invitingly on a little incline, on the right; past the unpaved side road leading to the Depot, where we would temporarily house, carefully packed in crocus bags, our properly danced and dried cocoa and our copra and our plantains and dasheens and sweet potatoes, ready for shipment to Trinidad on steamer days—that, on foot in the ten o'clock sun, during the recess period, I made the post office trips. I didn't too much mind the relatively gentle heat of the midmorning sun, or even the perspiration itself, while it was fresh and cool and trickling down my face and back and legs, but it was quite a different story when the freshness and the cool gave way to stickiness and clam and drove my body to yell, in anguish all unheard, for breeze and nakedness and water. Nor did my encounters with Genevieve help matters.

In the beginning, I used to wonder, Why me? I would ask myself, Why not Mango-Head? I slowly began to appreciate, however, that being favorite had, perhaps, no more advantages than disadvantages. But it was clearly all a matter of trust: just as you could be trusted to oversee the garden works or to go to the shop or parlor with the school's money or to supervise the head teacher's class in his absence, so, too, could you be trusted to collect the school's mail and, of equal importance, the head teacher's personal mail and bring it safely back to the northern corner. It was Genevieve, in the end, who made me come to appreciate that and abort the embryonic resentment sucking sustenance from all about within me.

As I made my way eastward, heading back for the school, the old khaki bag with the mails slung by its handle over my right shoulder and hanging down my left side, I glimpsed, on the other side of the bridge that straddled the stream running parallel to the unpaved side road leading load-bearing donkeys and little lorries and purposeful pedestrians to the Depot by the sea, the figure of a woman who seemed to be doing nothing in particular. I had just gone past Sammy's Food-and-Booze store and taken a breath or two of the commingled aroma of imported Canadian salt fish and Trinidad Angostura rum, which always exhilarated me in a strange, exciting way which, little Seventh-Day Adventist lad that I was, I had had meticulously to conceal. Added to that, just then, was the arresting horn of the interisland steamer announcing its arrival, on its way back from its Roxborough and Charlotteville stops, to collect the produce from the Pembroke Depot, before the Scarborough stop and the return trip to Port of Spain, all of which made me feel that the world was alive and well and that important things were happening everywhere, even the branches of the coconut palms on either edge of the earthen side road, as well as of those forming a canopy over the Depot building on the seashore, swaying in the incessant breeze as if in multiple Japanese bows, not merely of welcome to the ship, but more so of eternal deference to the building's importance to the economic well-being of all the surrounding villages. I did a double take and let my eyes confirm that the woman looking hard at me from the other end of the little bridge was none other than Genevieve, Teacher Aaron's wife, Mrs. Millington.

Forgetting clean the approaching interisland steamer and my suppressed objections to the voluminous black smoke rising up out of its chimney, I kept my eyes fixed upon *Mrs. M* as she keenly observed me pensively covering the ten-yard span of the baby bridge, making my way toward her with unclarified reluctance.

I could see her more clearly as I got nearer. I thought how she was no typical Tobago woman. She was not very dark or deep, dark brown; she was not manifestly robust in physical structure and expression of self-assuredness. She did not wear the aura of the resolute matriarch. Her complexion was too light, and her nose was too straight-ish, and her hair was too flimsy, fluttering in the wind when the hair of a real Tobago woman stood unmoved in the eye of any storm that came along. What on earth was she doing standing there?

In spite of myself, I arrived. I found myself face-to-face with her and managed to fight off an almost completely overwhelming, if inexplicable, urge to run back across the baby bridge and go and hide in a dark corner of the Depot at the end of the side road, by the seashore, until I was found by somebody I felt I could trust. But it was too late now. If I was going to do that, I should have done it at least before I crossed the baby bridge.

"Mor-morning, Mrs. Millie."

The khaki bag with the letters I had collected from the Pembroke Post Office hung by its long handle about my neck, just where the neck met with the right shoulder, the handle draped across my upper back and chest, the bag itself nestling by my side, just beneath my left armpit.

"Oh, you poor boy!" she exclaimed in her strange accent, her voice swimming in a sea of concern and seeming tenderness. "Loook 'ow you arre sweating. You must be tired, *non*?"

"Nuh! No, no, I nat tired, nat tired. I nat tired!" My determination always to try to speak proper English to teachers and pastors and their wives had dissipated before I knew it.

"Vell, vell! So vhat do you 'ave zere for us? Vhat's in zee leetle bag today?"

I fled.

I had run all the way back to the school, but when Teacher Aaron asked me how come I was bathed in so much perspiration on that particular day, my poverty-stricken answer was that it was a very hot day. And then I proceeded forthwith to cower under his searching eye examination.

"Permission, please, sir, to go to the latrine?"

I didn't invent the urgent need to pass the urine, but I was grateful for its timely assistance.

"Suuure," he replied slowly. "Sure." He was directly engaging my eyes with his, which were wordlessly telling me that I could trust him with my troubles. "You must never keep these things in."

*These things? What things?* I desperately asked myself.

It was not until the fourth such encounter that I caved in and gave her the bag, and looking back now, I have a strong sense that she very likely is one of the many persons whose lives Alejandro Moreno has saved by teaching me the importance of adhering to his highly recommended rule of putting at least a ten-second space firmly between the selection and the actual application of a satisfactory act of suitable retribution for hurt administered to me. It was a well-learned rule, the lifelong obedience to which has inflicted much pain on my baser self but has brought even greater joy to the higher. I was to see or think of Mrs. M countless times for many years right into adulthood, but for injury to my childhood psyche (which, throughout my life, I have borne in silence, alone), she forever escaped the application of many a subconsciously selected act of retribution by reason of the existence of an equivalent number of ten-second spaces.

On the day of the second encounter, it was raining slightly, and when I spotted her, I turned around, headed back westward, and escaped into Sammy's Food-and-Booze, where it stood on the left-hand side forty yards from the bridge as you abandoned your journey toward the school and briskly began to proceed as if your destination were an imminent meeting of the greatest importance in the capital city, Scarborough. The only Indian-origin people I knew then (not counting Gokool, who loved the bottle and drove an invisible motorcar) were Mr. Sammy and, to a lesser extent, his wife and three children, and Rookmin, Nessa's friend from Trinidad, who, with her parents and siblings, lived on Mayor Short's Richmond Estate, and Mr. Powder, the primary school inspector. Rookmin was more or less my age, and with Nessa's active, if not, at times, aggressive, encouragement, I soon began to take a liking to her, at first gradually, and then rapidly and intensely, which seemed to please Nessa quite a bit. Mr. Sammy, too, always was kind to me whenever I went to his shop to "mek message," which was what we children did when, having memorized the list, we faithfully bought and took back with us every item we had been sent to a shop to buy.

Today, Mr. Sammy quickly observed my hyperventilation, regarded me with considerable concern, and asked me what was wrong.

"Not'ing, Misser Sammy."

"How yuh mean 'nutten'? Look how yuh shakin'!"

Thus dismissing me, he nonetheless turned to the display shelf behind him, took down and opened a bottle of cream soda, and handed it to me.

"Heh, drink dis befo' yuh farl down an' dead on mih han' right hayre."

Between him and Rookmin—not forgetting Mr. Powder, the primary school inspector—they made me inculcate a very good disposition toward Indian-origin people, which set me up to keep Rookmin in my mind for long after she was spirited back to Trinidad and her fate at the hands of an uncle.

"Yuh good now?"

He had seated and left me there on a stool in a corner of the shop, slowly sipping the cream soda (after gobbling, and nearly choking on, a first mouthful), and attended to four or five customers who had come in and made their purchases and left without even noticing me, one of them being Gokool, who went off with a *petit-quart*, a small bottle manufactured to hold 25 percent of the contents of a full bottle of Old Oak rum, concealed in a brown paper bag he had brought with him, having saved it up through his last four such purchases in order to avoid unnecessarily paying the one-cent cost of a new one. Gokool would invariably do that until time disintegrated a paper bag before his very eyes or a sudden, unkind shower made pulp of it, surprising him on his way to whichever rum shop was nearest to him when the nectar in the current petit-quart was no more. And draining the last drop from the petit-quart, once Gokool had straightened up and pulled himself and his thoughts together and, turning his head slowly from side to side, expertly sniffed the air about him, he would unerringly go, practically as the crow flies, directly to the nearest rum shop.

"Yes, Misser Sammy. I good now."

"Arright, mih si de shakin' stap. Goh-arn back to school."

To my great relief, Mrs. M was gone by the time I was looking across again to the far end of the little bridge, and I resolved to tell Teacher Aaron, when he asked about the delay, that there had been a queue at the post office.

"It had a long line at the post office," I lied.

"*There was, there was!*" Teacher Aaron frustratingly corrected.

"There was a line at the post office." I left out the *long* in an illogical effort to decrease the size of the lie and make it easier to quiet my conscience and to try to control the pace of my heartbeat. I didn't think it worked, though.

He presented me with a look that said, "Why on earth aren't you telling me the truth?" And he accepted the khaki bag with the mail from me, took a deep breath, pulled out the spacious bottom right-hand drawer of his desk and put the bag in there, and then turned back to the papers on the desk before him. You felt that you preferred to be beaten with many stripes, as once had happened to some people referred to in the Holy Book, than to be proclaimed a liar in such a loud and piercing silence.

The third encounter with Mrs. M came less than a week later, when she held on to and, as if lovingly, squeezed my hand and slid her fingers onto and caressed, but at first did not grease, my palm, but then, becoming suddenly definitive and purposeful, all but buried a five-cent piece under the skin of it, insisting that the coin was mine. "Furr you, all furr you!"

Without further word, she let my hand into an abrupt free fall, briskly walked past me, and headed across the baby bridge. I looked around and watched her wide-eyed until she turned south onto the earthen side road leading to the Depot, but no load-bearing donkey beside her, on her head no crocus bag of cocoa or copra, dasheen or sweet potato, traversing quasihallowed ground with un-Tobagonian purposelessness.

All that controlled me as I made my way back to the school was confusion. What was Mrs. M trying to do to me?

Nessa had made me experience a certain feeling some three years before, and the repetitions of that experience had gone on for a good time. After a while, she had become Rookmin's friend and had told Rookmin and me that we looked "nice together." All that time, whenever she could, Nessa would give me a penny to "buy somet'ing fuh" myself. After the first two or three occasions of experiencing that certain feeling, I had come to like it rather much, not to discount the feel of the special secret relationship itself and the pennies that happened to come with the relationship.

But the first experience of that feeling had been mysterious and overwhelming, and afterward, I had suffered from a hot fever and a persistent, vague headache for the rest of the weekend. It was a Sabbath Day, and everybody else had gone to church, leaving me in her care, doubtless because for some good (and welcome) reason, I was not in a position to go to church that day and, either by coincidence or by design, she was the one old enough and available to take care of me.

For us as children growing up, churchgoing was not a favorite activity, and I clearly recall—indeed, can never forget—one Sabbath morning when Gobo began to bawl like a cow being slaughtered because Mammy had just reversed an earlier decision, made by sunset the day before, to allow him to miss church. The basis of the earlier decision, as articulated by Mammy, had been that his "head too shabby," by which she meant that his hair had not been cut for some considerable time and, though in a passable condition for church up to and including the previous Saturday, could in no way, that day, be helped into nearly such condition, with or without extreme coiffeuring, and rendered even barely presentable for exposure in the holy place. Gobo, who had, no doubt unwittingly, let slip some aspect of the plans he had carefully designed for the day, stoutly opposed the reversal, making it clear that in his view a reasoned decision made on impeccable grounds many hours earlier could not be discarded at the whim and fancy of the decision maker, especially at the expense of the duly named, specific individual who had a legitimate expectation to benefit from it. Disconsolate, he bawled, "Mammy seh dat mih na'ah goh ah chu'ch arready. Mammy seh dat mih head too shabby!"

Crying long tears, he repeated this protestation ceaselessly and was becalmed only when Mammy, surely worn down by logic and interminable reaffirmation, relented.

It was not, let me clarify, that we hated church, and we, indeed, regarded the relative brevity of the Sunday- and Wednesday-evening services as a veritable blessing from above, even if the logic of Sunday escaped us clean. We could understand Wednesday: that was the midweek day, and the conscientious faithful would surely not want to take the chance of seeming to forget to praise God completely between Saturdays. Saturday itself was, however, long and dreary, and Sunday followed rather sharply on its heels. But then again, the heathen Christian churches met on Sundays, and it might have seemed important to prevent them from having God all to themselves on that day.

If what we had against Saturdays was length and dreariness, what bothered us about Sundays and Wednesdays was the long walk home in the ten o'clock dark after the service, although we often enjoyed it when there was moonlight. Electricity was an entirely alien idea to the Pint and the Windward Road villages, and at night we read our Bibles by our faithful *bols de fer*, which we called *bulldifay*. So it was not, as I have said, that we did not like church: transfer to the Sabbath Day itself the brevity (or anything resembling it) of Sunday and Wednesday, and all would be well with our endurance and our fledgling souls.

Some three years had gone by since that fateful Sabbath Day, and Nessa was now encouraging the sparks of attraction she saw beginning to fly between Rookmin and me. She was going on nineteen now, and I could sense that she was setting me free. It was something I had wanted: I had started to feel myself developing a keen interest in girls my own age as well as an understanding that she herself must need somebody closer to hers. Still, to this day, involvement in that experience of the ultimate intimacy on a Saturday remains special for me.

Here is how it all began. I was sitting in the drawing room, reading an illustrated story in the Sabbath school quarterly, when she called out to me from the bedroom. "Come, Jakey, yuh hayr want combin'. Come, lemme comb yuh hair." I put down the quarterly on the center table and went to her, where she was sitting at the edge of the low bed, wearing her panties and a well-worn but clean bodice. In her hand was what we called a fine comb, a comb for short hair, men's freshly cut hair, not the big-teeth kind used for combing the long, thick hair that so many true Tobago women boasted. "Come, siddong hayre," she directed as she guided me to sit on the floor with my back to her, my legs stretched straight out in front of me, my head held firmly by her between her open thighs. As she combed my hair, she gradually, by voluntary or involuntary motion, brought her buttocks forward to the edge of the bed until I could feel her whole pelvic area rubbing against my neck with every movement of the comb in her hand. I felt that my hair had long been properly combed, but she combed on and on, and I really did not dislike that. In any case, I always liked someone to go on combing my hair once it was recently cut or, else, the stage of all the tugging at the knots had passed and that certain feeling akin to ecstasy had set in. Up to now, in fact, I have never stopped liking that. As the Americans would say, I am still a sucker for that.

Presently, though, she stopped the combing. She told me to stand. She herself stood up and looked me in the eye.

"Leddong pan de bed, m'ah come back."

For a minute or two, I lay on the bed with my eyes shut, only then fully realizing how much I had been enjoying the combing and wishing that it wouldn't stop. She interrupted the reverie, saying, "Heh, look some lemonade," tickling my palm as she handed me a plastic glass with the drink. Fixing her glistening gaze on me, she drank off hers in a single gulp, and her hand seemed to be shaking as she set down the glass on the bedroom dresser; and then, to my astonishment and horror and excitement and trepidation, she took off her panties and placed them next to the empty glass on the dresser and came onto the bed and lay beside me. Her hand was clearly shaking now as she handed me the fine-tooth comb. "Comb me here," she said softly, pointing to the center of her pubic area. "Comb me here… please!"

The vivid recollection of all these things was a considerable component of the source of the confusion that engulfed me as I headed back to the school to declare my innocence—in the throes of an uncomfortable silence fueled by unfounded feelings of guilt—to Teacher Aaron, the husband of Mrs. M.

"Long queue again?"

Why couldn't Teacher Aaron be like normal people? Why did he have to have those piercing eyes set back in that smooth black face, at once kindly and expressionless? How could he be so able obviously to love you and clinically to dissect you, like some unique biological specimen, at one and the same time? Still, I had to say something in reply.

"Yes, Teacher Aaron."

I could hear the hollowness in my own voice and feel myself violently cringing. So robust did that cringe feel that I could swear it was visible to him.

"Well, we'll have to look into that, won't we?"

I sought and got permission to go to the outdoor latrine on the south side of the school. That brought me physical relief, but the rest of the school day was pure torture as I tried and tried to avoid making contact with the searing eyes set back against the calm, assured mien of Teacher Aaron. When the last bell mercifully rang and the closing prayers were over, I made my way home together with my siblings Gobo and Doodoo, and we did our weeding and molding of the cornstalks and fed the cows before darkness fell.

But I did not sleep well that night. Sometimes, after attending to such after-school chores, I had, at dusk, to turn to the task of preparing dinner in the wooden kitchen standing a few yards away from the house itself. Unlike the house, it did not stand on crabwood stilts rooted in concrete bases but on four-foot cedar logs half-buried in their graves, wide holes in the ground, surrounded by sand and gravel to promote their longevity. The kitchen enclosure proper was a ten-by-twelve-foot affair with a four-by-four ground-provision storeroom under a counter across from the window that opened onto the fireside. The entrance to the kitchen was through a door two feet wide on the eastern twelve-foot side. As you entered through the door and went down two steps, you found yourself at ground level, facing the *fireside*, itself two feet wide, imperious at the western extremity. Once in, you could now climb the two steps to your left and enter the kitchen proper or go through the two-piece door/window on your right leading to the tapia oven outside or continue straight ahead to the fireside. On its northern side, the kitchen boasted both an inner and an outer wall, both of cedarwood, running for six feet from the entrance, and then, for the rest of its length, of *tapia*—that formidable material made of rich dark-brown clay and *mattress grass* mingled and mixed together with water and danced like cocoa beans to perfection—the poor man's cement, to be set into and be combined with scrap iron to yield the final product, the wall, no less easily breached than its cousin, cement fashioned with sand and gravel into concrete. Like its three sides, the mound of the fireside, rising three feet off the ground, was made of tapia too. On the mound stood nine stones, in three triangular arrangements, to accommodate the iron pots and the wood fire fuel underneath them, the main triangle, for the big iron pot, consisting of large stones configured in the center at the back and the two supplementaries, smaller triangles more forward, to the left and to the right, yielding untrammeled access to the main one. I was the eldest of the siblings and the one having quasiparental responsibilities, and it was at that fireside that sometimes, my outdoor after-school chores done, I would find myself preparing dinner. But today was one of my fairly frequent lucky days. Mammy had not gone with our father to the Woods, where, on a much larger scale than we did on the expansive grounds on which the house stood almost forlornly, we grew food of every description, mostly for shipment on sale to Trinidad; nor was it a washday, when she would have been on a bank of the Richmond River, armed with her *jooking board* (*jooking stone* nearby, too, to deal with the heavier trousers material, such as khaki and dungaree) and her blue soap, toiling till nightfall to keep our clothes clean. So not only would I not have to cook, I could also look forward to a better-tasting dinner and, at the same time, escape some relentlessly candid, if largely good-natured, commentary on the perceived rate of improvement of my culinary skills. I wished, though, that it were cooking and commentary that were the worry on my mind now, in place and instead of the moves of Mrs. M.

What could she really want of me? In my innocent, child's eyes, she was an extremely old woman, at least thirty-five or thirty-six, older than Mammy—how old was Gra'ma, I wondered, or Granny, or Gran? Whatever the case, this Mrs. M was an old woman. *Older than your mother!* I thought, thinking I heard myself whispering to myself. Yet when she'd been pressing the five-cent piece into my palm, the excitement I had felt had not been excitement over the money; it was an excitement more closely resembling the excitement that would take ahold of me and make volcanic quicksands of my insides during the several weeks following Nessa's third engagement with my youthful body after she had first introduced me to the joys and concomitant delights of hair combing. How had I dreamed of and breathlessly awaited the fourth Sabbath Day that I would be alone with her! It was that kind of excitement that decidedly displaced any lurking joy of lucre. Still, Mrs. M was definitely more than twice Nessa's age and, worse still, older than Mammy, and married—and not just married, but whose wife? Teacher Aaron's wife! And when and where and how would we get the privacy to do that, anyway? *Nah,* I told myself, *impossible, completely impossible!*

In any case, by this time, Nessa had more or less put me together with Rookmin and had gone further to tell me that I could do even better and check out Shirley, one of her nieces on her mother's side, who was my age and who, without quite realizing she was doing so, had told her a lot about things that she did and who, she was sure, could show me one or two things that I would like a lot. I knew for sure what I did not want Mrs. M to want from me, and looking at the whole picture, I had a feeling that my prayers in that regard were likely to be answered. Having reached this impeccably logical conclusion, I promptly felt cowered and unsure again and gave in to the insistence of my meticulous and demanding innards that I should start all over again, from the beginning, and analyze the whole thing one more time. At that, I hurriedly experienced calm again.

When the calm came, it was around 4:00 a.m.; it was always around 4:00 a.m. when the large cock with the menacing red comb and the long multicolored feathers boisterously gracing its neck crowed. That was the hour at which the other, minor cocks dutifully followed suit and crowed their more subdued and respectful crows and at which Gobo and I had to leap out of bed—or, more specifically, leap off our bedding of old clothes spread on the floor of the two-bedroom house—and put on our *bush clothes* and head out into the darkness bound for the Belle Garden or, sometimes, the Richmond Estate, our grass knives in hand, to get additional feed for the cows. Pappy would already have been duly attired in his bush wear, his heels hot and at the ready to set out for the Woods, where he would give his fully committed attention to the commercial crops. And if, on occasion, by then, by 4:00 a.m., by any accident we seemed to be still in a horizontal position, he would declaim, "Al-yuh! Al-yuh know de time? Sun naly down an' al-yuh nuh get up yet? *Me* know *fooh-me rispansability*: *me* garn, al-yuh hayr me? Me *garn*!" We never had any difficulty whatsoever grasping the full import of those words. And hearing them this morning, we responded without demur.

"Yuh rayly quiet dis marnin, bredder," Gobo probed.

"Ah guess" was all I offered in response.

We were out of the house and, in pursuit of the sweet-tasting guinea grass that our cows loved so much, heading for an area inside Belle Garden Estate, perhaps eight hundred yards northeastward from its boundary with the Brougham family lands.

It is amazing how, especially when your head and your feet know every slope, every sharp drop, every bend along a dirt road trampled into being over time by feet that came and went before yours, you need no light beyond that offered by the dimming morning stars to make a near-mile-long trip to an unwelcoming estate to cut grass for your cows. For nearly half the journey, after we exited the intimate grounds of the house, the road sped downhill and, willy-nilly, we half-ran that portion of the way if for no other reason than that it was simply easier to run than walk. We did not tire ourselves by talking as we half-ran, and for me, Gobo's energy-preserving silence was infinitely more than golden.

When we reached Level Bottom, we set down our plastic milk pails at the root of a convenient coconut tree and, grass knives in hand, went after the cow feed. As was the case most mornings, we encountered no shotgun-waving estate watchman and did not have any need to escape leaving the animals' meals behind. We carefully tied our grass into bundles with the cords made of the spines of dried banana leaves (which we always carried along with us), placed the bundles on the bare crowns of our heads, and made our quick way back to the safety of Brougham ground. We recovered our plastic pails, milked a cow each, put the precious liquid aside, fed the four cows and the bull, and made our way back up the hill to the house.

As we would on most such days, we each got ourselves a plastic bath bucket of water from the cistern, had a quick wash, dressed for school, and hurriedly had the breakfast Mammy by then had waiting for us. For lunch, she would have on hand for each of us either a brown paper bag with an egg or okra or tomato or cucumber sandwich—or else, a penny to "buy something," or perhaps two things, a glass of maubey and a rock cake. This morning we had the egg for breakfast and went off with the penny.

We sometimes got a lift in a vehicle. It could be the "health van" driven by Tallboy or the Works and Hydraulics truck driven by Sweetman or the lorry for hire owned and driven by Mr. Lenny Job, who would die years later when the lorry fell a hundred feet down the cliff at Bad-Rock as he headed west toward Belle Garden, driving his son Winston home from the high school at Roxborough. When we thanked them or spoke of them in the presence of other adults, the expressions we used were *Mr. Tallboy*, *Mr. Sweetman*, and *cousin Lenny*, but in the privacy of our children's conversations, we did not employ any of the prefixes. In our rural village on a little island itself almost wholly rural, being the driver of a vehicle—not to speak of actually being the owner—conferred a hushed status. There were unspoken privileges attaching to the status enjoyed by the three, and out of the mouths of unsuspecting adults, we had heard stories about their exploits. Cousin Joshua Bishop also had a lorry for hire, just like Lenny's, and we got lifts from him too, but there were no stories about him, as his huge frame and enormous belly almost certainly served to shield him from temptations of the flesh. This morning, we got a lift from Tallboy and got to school well on time.

"You do understand, don't you, Jacob?"

I jumped. Only now, in rear view, could my mind's eye see the faces of Teacher Aaron and my twenty-odd classmates trained on me. And had I not heard a pin drop on the concrete floor somewhere along the line? I shifted on my little school bench and grinned weakly. There was nothing I could say. You couldn't ever explain to anyone who had any inkling of Teacher Aaron's commitment and dedication how you could be absentminded in Teacher Aaron's class, least of all when it was the first class of the morning. In any case, what was I doing trying to imagine what he and Mrs. M did last night? And how could I tell anybody that that was exactly what I was doing?

"We were all looking at your body for a while," he told me, "but you were not there, not in it, not in it at all… Anyhow, let's move on."

*Not in what?* I quizzed myself briefly before I could figure out what he was saying. I promised myself to pay rapt attention in class for the rest of the day.

An awkward feeling of the kind that followed all this was, of course, to repeat itself years later when I was a student at the high school at Roxborough. But there is a difference between an occasion on which you are not guilty and one on which you are. One such occasion of innocence was when Pepe and Doyle and Tapo tried to frame me during the lunchtime break at the school and, in so doing, exposed, as much to me as to the principal and others, my latent capacity for firm and definitive responses heedless of the possible cost, that capacity that the principal had later spent so many generous after-school hours dampening and taming. Another such, but of the guilty kind, was when it dramatically came to light that I had "interfered with" Mr. Pilgrim's granddaughter Jacinta. Thoughtless and cruel as children can be, because of his artificial leg (which we callously called his *cork-foot*, given that in the language of Tobago, together all the parts of the body located below the knee constitute the *foot*, north of which there is located the *leg*), our name for this alien resident of the Pint was *One-Foot Pilgrim*, a fact that, to this day, makes me cringe in quiet, undemonstrated shame each time the thought of it crosses my mind. Not that adults were any better in that regard: they always warned that if we were disrespectful to Mr. Pilgrim, he would beat us with his (and this was the expression they used) *cork-foot*. In those situations, the common feature was the glare of every pair of eyes present fixed on you. You had an overwhelming feeling of being set upon—in the one case, by a pack of hungry stray dogs greedily sniffing at your body as if to certify that you were untainted meat but, at the same time, though with teeth unsheathed, growling only barely audibly so as to avoid the possibility of others of your kind coming to your aid, and in the other case, by a swarm of purposeful, avenging angels intent upon exacting retribution. In either kind of case, forcibly shoved into acute self-doubt, you are cowering in a corner of an open field, on a moonless night, futilely willing your body to grow small, your arms crossed in defense in front of your face, and all at once several pairs of glistening torchlights, out of the blue, come on together, like so many electric bulbs controlled by a single switch set in the wall of the darkness, all of them resolutely trained upon you now, their owners secure in the safety of the sturdy dark hanging about them, keeping them secure.

This time there were, arithmetically speaking, and also by any objective analysis, four pairs of torchlights; but arithmetic and objective analysis were of no relevance when the bearers of the torchlights were Pappy and Mammy and Gra'ma and Granny: in point of effective fact, there were forty pairs of glistening torchlights burrowing through my hapless body. Mammy was to tell me weeks later that, fearful of the kind of reaction to be expected from my father, having found the pair of bloodstained short pants where I had hopelessly hidden it under their bed (anywhere else would have been even more inadequate), she had taken it from the bottom of the basket and concealed it in the belly of the bundle of dirty laundry waiting for the day when, on a fine laundry day, on a bank of the Richmond River, she could wash away my sin. But the rains of May had already set in, and laundry day had twice been postponed, when the river had *come down* and, with its dirty brown water, overflowed its banks. Sometimes when this happened, when these postponements occurred, you would run out of clean clothing and would—especially for the purpose of ignoring ceaseless showers to go out and feed the animals or tend the crops—extract a shirt from the laundry bundle. Thus it was that Pappy had happened upon the smoking gun, in the shape of my bloodied pair of short khaki pants. Pleading guilty to the unverbalized charge of accessory after the fact, Mammy had promptly agreed to the current inquisition.

"Suh, bway," said Pappy, "yuh mean somebady chap yuh an' yuh nuh tell nobady nutten?"

It was typical of the kind of question with which he approached you to start his interrogation of you regarding any suspected wrongdoing. Mostly, by the time the examination began, you had a reasonably good idea of exactly which sin of omission or commission was under reference, and if you had had enough sixth-sense notice, you would be ready with some sort of quasifeasible response. Experience had taught you that trying to buy time by dissembling, with a contrived look of astonishment on your face, would only attract the all-too-gentle concession to you to "tek yuh time to 'member, buh nat too much," as he was busy. In time, you would have come to abandon the tactic of dissembling—except in the gravest of circumstances. The present circumstances were grave in the extreme and fully met the requirements for dissembling.

"Pappy?"

Nor were the requirements just barely met either: it would have been manifest even to that forlorn figure we so often cited to emphasize a point—the blind man in a dark room wearing wooden spectacles—that these were extremely grave circumstances. It was near to midday on a Sunday morning, under a cloudless sky, and it was by no means a cool day; but I was shivering, and the perspiration snaking down my back felt quite as cold as the thick rectangular block clothed in saw-dust lying serenely in the box on the workbench below the house, innocent of the coming vicious, if bloodless, attack upon it by a thirsty ice pick. Yet my mind, recklessly or in a death dance, meandered its way back to that memorable evening with Jacinta.

Nearly two years after Mr. Moreno had seen the need for a high school at Roxborough and left the relative comfort of life as a teacher employed at Osmond High School in Port of Spain to start Elizabeth's College there, in the heart of a rustic community, living with gas lamps for light and outhouses for toilets and for bathrooms, and without running water—nearly two years after that—a certain long-resident priest *from foreign*, who was careful to live in Scarborough, and whose allegiance lay with a denomination of Christianity different from that of Mr. Moreno, no doubt guided by a much-delayed memorandum from *above*, set up a rival institution, housing it in an old-ish building located a few hundred yards to the east along the never-ending Windward Road. Jacinta was a student at that new school. Jacinta, at that stage of her life, was addicted to breaking rules and was, as a consequence, a fixture in the detention room of the Star of Hope College for Tobago East. So it was that when my principal embarked upon the after-class program to retool and redirect my innate capacity for firm and definitive responses without thought of consequence, Jacinta and I began walking the three-mile journey home together, and sometimes, during the rainy season, we would have to put off our departure from Roxborough until the weather had cleared, only to find, now and then, when we got home to the Pint, that it had not rained there at all.

Whenever we got a lift from Mr. Tallboy in the health van, we would have to sit at the back of the van, on the straight bench seat; according to him, the front-passenger bucket seat was "fuh big people." We didn't mind that in the least: since in Tobago in that era children were, by big-people edict, to speak only when spoken to, we could sit there quietly, as Mr. Tallboy drove along, touching forbidden parts of each other's bodies. Nessa had taught me a lot, and Shirley, who was two years my junior but whose know-how had, in the beginning, more than once rendered me speechless and would probably have blown the mind of Nessa, had patiently passed on to me all that she had learned from her elementary school teacher. I would, in time, make sure that Jacinta benefited fully from all my experiences, which, much later on, I would find myself trying to share with Rookmin too.

"No, wait!" Jacinta said on the fateful evening. "Mih nuh ready fooh goh 'ome yet. L'ahwi goh by Bamboo Patch."

"W'a'? Gyal, yuh know weh y'ah seh deh?"

"Mmm-hmm, mih know good, good."

"Bamboo Patch? Yuh showre, gyul?"

"Showre, showre, sugar."

There has always been, for me, something almost ethereal, something idyllic about a bamboo patch. That was why I found it completely natural that the patch near to Gra'ma's house was a place, a location, in its own right called, simply, Bamboo, itself reminiscent of that spot where the Windward Road still watched running away from it the endless dirt track that took you to the Pint proper—and, beyond that, to the sea—that portion of, that spot upon, Eastern Tobago land known to all and sundry on our island as, simply, Mango Tree. The tall bamboos clustering at their roots bent over and caressed one another at their skyward extremities, forming a high-ceilinged tent that provided to its floor below protection from the sun and from the rain. The floor of the tent was not bare earth, but earth adorned with a mattress of dried bamboo leaves waiting to welcome the adventurous, the lovers of the great outdoors. Much as if I were the younger one, Jacinta gently held my hand and led me off the dirt track onto the patch, and the barely audible crackling of the mattress, stealthier by far than the heartbeats of its throbbing guests, was a muted, moaning sound. She let go of my hand and, removing her book bag from where it hung across her shoulder, spoke to me in a trembling whisper.

"Ahwi cyah tek out de book an' dem fram de bag an' dem an' me cyah leddong down pan de two book bag dem."

"Okay… buh yuh showre yuh… ?"

"M'ah goh keep arn mih skyurt an' mih badize. M'ah goh put mih panty eena mih book bag befo' mih leddong pan am."

She lay on her back, her upper body on one book bag, her lower body on the other. I lay on my side next to her on the bamboo-leaf mattress, and she, in turn, rolled onto her side to face me. We had kissed in the van a few times not many minutes before, but this kiss was special, and our bodies became two gigantic *bols de fer* burning with relentless fury, driven by some single-minded force unseen to merge and become one raging flame that would soon leave behind it when it subsided the still-smoldering ashes of our ardor.

"We doh have plenty time," she warned, lifting her skirt tails to the level of her taut and anxious nipples. "Touch me, touch me there."

And I touched her there. I touched her there again. Then I touched and touched her there again. When the moment came and then the blood spurted and madly rushed out, in our innocence, we were shocked. This was an entirely new phenomenon, and it was sobering in the extreme. Nothing of the sort had happened with Nessa or Shirley, and although, listening in to the conversations of older boys, I had heard a lot about "*bussin' shi maid*" and formed a kind of rudimentary notion about it, nothing at all had prepared me for this.

*She* was lucky: her panties had been securely put away in her bag, on which she had rested her upper body, and her skirt had been lifted up to the safety of the level of her breasts; in case of emergency, it would, we had calculated, be a simple matter to pull the skirt into position, and no one would lift it up to check for her panties or search for them in her book bag. Me now, I wasn't wearing jockey shorts, and there, at Bamboo Patch, in the open, on the bamboo-leaf mattress, I had had to keep my short trousers on. True, her lower body had been resting on my book bag, but I was able to remove from it most of the more visible red stain by the vigor of desperate application of dried bamboo leaves; as for my trousers, they seemed to have been dipped into some malicious plastic basin full of red dye and to be now looking up at me, grinning through their open fly. Darkness had already fallen when I got home, and Mammy was in the kitchen, preparing dinner, two *bols de fer* for light. Pappy, whose unrelenting policy was that when working the land your day ended only when you could no longer see your outstretched palms in the darkness, was not yet home, and I had no fear about my undoubtedly innocent siblings. I sneaked into my parents' bedroom and buried the dyed trousers at the bottom of the dirty-clothes basket that they kept underneath their bed. I knew I was merely postponing D-day, for by what miracle would Mammy fail to discover my pants as they screamed out with all that loud color?

"Tark fas' bway. Mih hurry, arl-ahwi hurry. Ah who chap yuh? Which part ah yuh bady dey chap yuh?" Pappy persisted.

"Pa…"

"Mih warn' fooh know ah who chap yuh!"

I knew that he knew what the blood was all about; they all knew, and that was the reason they were all there together, the reason all those forty pairs of torchlights were skinning me alive with their steadfast glare, leaving me exposed like a careless *soucouyant*, that well-known night creature of our mythology, atypically caught at dawn awakening from an unwonted nighttime nap, rendered nude by the first light of the morning sun. It began to feel like oppression and abuse: they knew very well that no one had chopped me. I felt a surge I could not control, of more than embryonic defiance.

"Nobady nuh chap mih. Ah Jacinta, ah me an' Jacinta: ahwi behn ah do rudeness an' blood come out!"

I had gotten it all out in one go, and that was a great relief. Up to that day—and to this—I had never unequivocally admitted that I had written the letter to Gemma, my cousin in Manzanilla, and it is a thing that had never ceased to haunt me, that still haunts me. Nearly all lies, I decided, if not altogether all, are disreputable to tell, such telling being acts of frightened subordination to the other and of compliant enslavement of the teller's soul; but the transparent ones, the transparent lies—except when served up with the acrid sauce of cynical intent—are doubly disreputable. I am forever aware of that component of lying: far less bad to seek refuge in silence, if silence seems an option.

I began to repeat, "Nobady nuh chap mih. Me an' Jacinta behn—"

"Wait, wait!" Granny screamed, clearly in terror, completely uncharacteristic, at the prospect of having to listen in the raw to what was possibly going to be now a detailed description of what Jacinta and I had done.

The old cliché coming to life like Adam in the garden of Eden when the breath was first breathed into his inert earthen form, the truth had set me free, had in fact done so in so extraordinary, so unplanned, and so uncalculating a manner that it was an earth-shattering discovery to me and made me feel I could fly. The moment I had owned up to the origins of the blood and heard their hush and seen the looks of powerlessness on their faces and observed the futility of their search in one another's torchlights for some sign of direction, I had succumbed to perverse feelings of almost-uncontrollable exhilaration. Inebriation fueled by alcohol you can begin to tame by sealing your lips or biting your tongue; inebriation engendered and given ceaseless sustenance by the air about you that you have no choice but to breathe is substantially more difficult to rein in. It was only for fear of the immediate loss of many front teeth as a direct result of a lightning backhand coming out of nowhere that I feigned a frightened face and did not giggle.

After a medium-size eternity, which, from all appearances, only I enjoyed, Pappy, no doubt assuming responsibility as senior progenitor of the miscreant, stepped back in.

"Maa," he said to Gra'ma, his mother, who was widely believed to regard me as her favorite grandson, many of whose transgressions she had in fact shown over time some tendency to downplay, "mih t'ink ahwi betta le' Granny handle dis t'ing yah wid dis bway—weh yuh t'ink, Maa?"

If sex had not been involved at all, or if I had not confessed and shown myself ready to provide the full details of the crime, they would solemnly have, there and then, considered the case and determined my punishment. But like all the parents and grandparents we knew, they were, to a man (and to a woman), mortally afraid of using, or appearing to be thinking of, or even being suspected of thinking of, the word *sex*—or anything related to it—if they knew, or feared, that there was any child within a certain radius from where they stood. We, for our part, living as we were in the rural areas of an island itself wholly rural, without electricity but with trees and shrubs and bushes of all descriptions, and with countless moonlit nights, began, in all natural innocence, to explore the thing as soon as we could barely walk and talk, although the name we had for it, the origin of which I do not quite know, was *rudeniss*. Joy of joys, though, we males, after a time, as we grew older, would, mischievous glint in our eyes, exhort one another from time to time that "whatever else you do, make sure you get some *rudeniss*," and we would laugh heartily, leaving each little man to comply with the injunction how he would.

In their predicament now, my judges, espying a little crack in the wall of their prison of helplessness, turned their torchlights away from me, everyone, and firmly grabbed ahold of Pappy's suggestion with all their fingers and their purposeful nails and, in a chorus drowning out Gra'ma's quiet attempt to respond to her son's appeal, all but sang out, as if prerehearsed, "Good p'int, Manny. Good p'int, Manny."

Then Granny, taking no chances with what she viewed as the entirely unpredictable life span of the little crack, brought the proceedings to a close. "And I will do my duty," she announced, employing, as was her wont in circumstances in which she desired to imprint the stamp of her authority, the kind of syntax, vocabulary, and elocution appropriate to the solemnity of the assignment. It was an unwritten rule that when Granny spoke like that, the only person who could offer further comment was, by reason of seniority, Gra'ma, and Gra'ma gave no indication that she had anything to add.

# Chapter 6

Inquisitions of this kind were not unusual in the family, and anybody, be it child or adult, could, at any time, find himself at the uncomfortable end of one of them. As children, we could sense, with the certainty conferred by our well-exercised innate instincts, that it was not us alone who were subject to that peril; as young adults, we came to know it as fact. There were times, I recall, when Pappy or Mammy barely escaped, and I remember two such occasions in particular.

There were rough times when the founder, Alejandro Moreno, had just started the high school at Roxborough in 1952, soon after the coronation of Queen Elizabeth II, by the grace of God, queen of Great Britain and Northern Ireland and monarch of the British Empire (upon which the sun never set). At primary school, not so long before the coronation, we had been awarded a holiday on the death of Her Majesty's father, King George VI, and had properly been guided into appropriate mourning mode by our teachers and loyal elders. Now, similarly guided, we were rejoicing at the ascension to the throne of our brand-new owner. "The king is dead!" "Long live the queen!" Alejandro Moreno, not yet the implacable enemy of colonial rule, duly christened the new school Elizabeth's College. The brand-new high school students, most of whom never, without Mr. Moreno's enterprising move, might even have heard of Shakespeare or Cicero or calculus, would now make their way to school on foot from as far west as Goodwood Village and as far east as Speyside Village. We from Richmond and Belle Garden, eastward of Glamorgan and

Pembroke and Goodwood, were among the lucky ones: our daily trudge was only six miles, three to go and three to come.

Some early, some late, some dead on time, we would reach school one by one or in little groups. On the way home at day's end, however, we would move in bigger groups. No penance for late-coming hung over our heads now, and the walk tended to be leisurely and replete with opportunities for many teenage things to happen. Threats and insults, veiled or otherwise, would not go unattended after a victim had been queried, in mock astonishment, "Bway, yuh tekking dat?" A less than supremely respectful reference to a schoolmate's mother or sister would educe a response such as, "Eh-eh, eh-eh, doh go home, doh go home. Doh go home at-arl," followed by a rapid flow of fisticuffs and/or head butts, whether or not the outcome of the ensuing scuffle could, by reason of the comparative sizes and skills of the combatants, be easily foretold, the matter at issue being strictly one of honor to be defended at all costs.

If no one did cross the line and "go home" and traded threats and insults were less unpardonable and were indeed equally bruising and entertaining, then there might be no *cuffs* or *butts* and there could be, rather, an afternoon on which matters would simply be left unresolved or be settled without resort to force. It was not an afternoon of the latter sort when Andrew Martin of Goodwood, a physically insufficient lad, facing defeat in an unequal engagement with me, completely surprised me by throwing himself onto the roadway, pulling off my right shoe and, leaping to an upright position, hurling the shoe down the steep cliff at Bad-Rock, near where Lenny Job's truck would later go down and our schoolmate Winston, luckier than his father, would miraculously escape death. To stay steady as I walked on home, I put away the other shoe into my schoolbag.

"Dem ah badda yuh tuh-much? Yuh warn' to stap de high school?" Were my schoolmates bothering me too much, and did I prefer to give up high school?

At the SDA elementary school in Glamorgan, they had taught us that in nature, there were warm-blooded animals and cold-blooded animals and that reptiles, such as snakes and iguanas, were cold-blooded animals and unfit for human consumption. Iguanas flourished in the Pint, where, except for One-Foot Pilgrim and his family, we were all Seventh-Day Adventists and did not eat them or their eggs: like web-footed birds and fish without scales, cold-blooded animals were prohibited food sources, and the grass-green iguana was, in any case, nothing if not an overgrown lizard. You often could not easily see one as it lay asleep in the shade nestled in between the abundant flora or resting in the hammock of a still branch well concealed and canopied by the ruggedly verdant leaves of some thriving tree. But for it no less than for you, when you happened upon it and it awakened with a start much like yours, there materialized a deer-in-a-headlamp moment. I was an iguana in a motionless hammock at the moment in which those words had fallen from my mother's lips. Less deer than wordless reptile, I said nothing—well, not right away. I listened to them over and over for many days as they lingered in the wind about my ears, and each time my blood ran cold once more, as if, I sometimes thought, to mimic what must surely have been, at that hurtful point, the state of my progenitor's. I had had that kind of feeling before, at the time when Gra'ma had enticed me to expect praise, believing her word that the wares were spotlessly clean, only to receive cavalier punishment instead. A certain perception of what seemed to be the way of women had begun to form itself.

"No, Mammy, mih like school!"

Feigning deep concentration on one matter or another—reading the Bible or the quarterly, making a kite out of kite paper and the spines of coconut tree branches and homemade glue, fashioning a spinning top out of guava wood with the aid of a sharp cutlass—I had often absorbed every word of her extremely vigorous discussions with my father over the five-dollar-per-month school fees and the additional costs of uniforms and books. She would praise to high heavens the virtues of my parallel apprenticeship to Darwin, the tailor at Sheep-Pen Ridge in Glamorgan, and the money I could make with the use of a good sewing machine once the apprenticeship ended and I was a trained tradesman. Luckily for all concerned, Pappy seldom lost his temper, as on the rare occasions that he did, all persons and sensitive animals (such as dogs and cats and goats) instinctively took cover in dedicated pursuit of their own longevity. The less patient he became with what he regarded as stupidity (an ailment he had long rechristened *chuppidniss*), the calmer he was on the surface and the more misleading the teeth he showed.

"Gyal," he would say with a benign-looking smile, "mih sarry, but ah fooh-*me* money an' ah fooh-*me* picknee, yuh hayrr mih good? Fooh-*me* money an' fooh-*me* picknee!" What might appear to be proclamation of new dogma was merely a reminder that the matter had been discussed time and again, and at great length, and a declaration that the chairman was exercising his right to reregister his casting vote and bring the matter to a close.

What I viewed as my mother's shortcoming in this area, this area of the relevance of a secondary education to our rustic existence, was not by any means a thing I held strongly against her. It was what it was: her view of life and my father's were different in that respect. But I was severely troubled by, and have never stopped feeling pain at, the memory of what seemed a somewhat sneaky attempt to contrive, by a fake fair choice and election seemingly made by me, an outcome she had failed to achieve through discussions with my father. That was one occasion on which, if the matter had come to the attention of my father, experience warned me, there would without doubt have, at some point, been an inquisition. But I never breathed a word of it to him.

On the other occasion that remains ingrained in my memory, the subject matter did reach Granny's ears, but not from the lips of any *big people* (as opposed to children), and the rule in the Pint, which I had learned only by keen observation, was clear: the occurrence of undesirable incidents between and among grown-ups would not be formally acknowledged unless brought to the attention of one of the elders by some adult, which is not to say that the "guilty" ever escaped the sly, unrelenting torment of the knowing elders.

The morning of this memory-ingrained occasion was a good one for Gobo and me. It had rained quite a bit during the night, and the showers, though considerably lightened, had not altogether ceased by 4:00 a.m. On days like that, if, by Pappy's acquired meteorologist's skill, he knew that there would be more rain during the course of the day, he would get the cows' grass from the estate himself and also do the milking. Those were days when he would not go to our lands miles away in the Woods, which you couldn't get to without having to cross both the meandering Big River and Little River at several points. After he had had something to eat, he would go to Mr. Short's overseer at Richmond Estate to see if he could get a *task*, an assignment to clear a designated area of the estate's land for an agreed price. What we would have to do on such days before getting ready for school was weed and mold crops as necessary, which meant we could enjoy the warmth of our bedding spread out on the floor until nearer daybreak. The rule as to starting time for this duty was clear: at day-clean, that precise moment at which the darkness lifted enough for you to be able to see your outstretched hand, you must begin the act of weeding, removing weeds and other miscreant plant growths from the environs of the crops.

We had completed our morning chores, Gobo and I, and I was in the kitchen, watching Mammy hustle to finish the breakfast fry-bake and eggs before Pappy got back, but before we knew it, he appeared, panting from his usual brisk walk up the hill from Level Bottom, the two plastic milk pails hanging from his fingers one each at his sides. All that stood between him and breakfast, he would expect, was the pouring of milk into the pot of chocolate tea waiting on one of the two smaller three-stone formations of the fireside and fanning the flames between the stones to burn ever more ardently until the chocolate tea, now a lighter, creamier brown, began to bubble again. But there she was, still struggling with the fry-bake and the eggs, no potful of chocolate tea in sight.

"Gyal, ah weh mih tea?" he demanded, looking over her shoulder at the fireside. "Wait, wait, wait! Gyal weh de… weh de hell yuh been doin' whole marnin'?"

"Well, the col' Doodoo have… an' mih had was to iron wah shurt…"

"Look, gyal, lakka arl yuh du yah whole marnin' ah 'pin-'pin, 'pin-'pin, 'pin-'pin an' nat wan damn t'ing moe. Move! Get outta mih way!" In the heat of intense emotion, Pappy's initial esses mostly disappeared from his speech. He pushed her aside and took charge of the fireside as she sat on the mortar stool and wept, silently at first, and then, painfully for me, aloud.

All this struck me quite a lot and made me see that women could also be made to suffer unfairly, and that now began to complicate the view of them that had been taking shape in my mind: they were not, after all, just hovering there, engaged in an unceasing search for the actions and words they needed to design, with your unknowing help, the world that they determined you should live in.

She had not been articulate—in fact, had uttered not a single word—in her own defense: she had been permitted no opportunity to do so. Doodoo, our younger brother, had for days been suffering with a rather nasty cold. That sort of thing happened to us frequently during the rainy season, when a hot, sunny spell could pull down a heavy shower of rain as if out of nowhere and your body, caught outdoors far away from sufficient shelter, could succumb to the assault of the extremes. The sound of your cough, when you had a nasty chest cold, was thunder itself, and it could lead a sensitive mother to drop whatever she was doing and dedicate important morning minutes to preparing for you a severe concoction of honey, large quantities of fresh lime juice, and crushed gum of aloes. As I had personally observed at close quarters, attending to Doodoo was the first thing that had slowed down Mammy that morning.

The second thing that had undermined her productivity by the fireside was Gobo's *teleleh* school shirt. You didn't, in the world of effortless elegance and class overlaid with genuine rusticity and *faux* poverty in which we lived, go to school wearing a shirt that remotely looked as if you might have slept in it, and Gobo was noticeably less particular than I was about the matter of hanging up school clothes shed on afternoons after school. She had had to find the time, from somewhere or other, to "pass ah iron pan" Gobo's shirt.

Finally, even while she had been ironing the *teleleh* shirt, I had gone to her asking her to use the sharp end of some pin or needle or other to get out a quarter-inch piece of *picker*, or thorn, broken off and lodged and visible just underneath the skin running southward from the tip of my right middle finger.

## VANESSA'S NIECE

I knew well why Mammy was weeping, and inside, I wept with her; she was weeping because, while she had been carrying out a multiplicity of tasks, much as if she had been blessed with more arms than a senior Hindu deity, she had kept whispering, in tones of prayer, to herself or to one or other of us, it was never clear, "Mih haffoo finish *brockfus* befo' Manny come back. Mih *haf* to finish *brockfus* befo' *aryuh* dardie come back!" I felt very, very deeply for her, and immersed in her pain and her sorrow, I quietly wept with her, as I have said, even while being yet unable, despite my best efforts, to discover anywhere inside of me the will fully to forgive her for having tried to snare me into giving up high school.

Sunday came four days later. While at the lunch break from church on Sabbath Days, all the other families from the Pint (barring the Pilgrims, who, being members of another Christian denomination, were heathens who went to church on the first day) would gather at Tanty Etho's house on George Street—where Pappy and his other brothers, interacting with their sister's husband, cousin Sydney, remained determined, most of the time successfully, to maintain at all cost a spirit of brotherly love on the Holy Day, developed to an extremely fine point the art of biting their lips—Granny and Grampa would go to Sister Kate's house right next to the church. So it was following the afternoon session at church that Sabbath that, as I was walking toward the exit, Granny drew me aside by the ear—gently on this occasion, as she was not particularly disturbed about anything—and ordered, for me alone to hear, "Eight a'clack tamarrow marnin', come eight a'clack tamarrow mornin'. You an' me haf to tark about Pilgrim an' dem gyal-picknee."

Yet another night of horrors lay in wait for me, in addition to all those I had had after hiding my blood-drenched school pants under the bed, when I well knew that the day of its discovery could not be far away; in addition to those I had had, and continued to have, wondering if Mrs. M wanted me for the same kind of doings as had Nessa and how, even in my total innocence, I could face the head teacher if I felt that he thought that any of such thoughts were alive in anybody's head. Some of the horrors danced about before my eyes like evil, taunting fairies as I lay awake in the darkness; some made me active in the dance, in nightmares convincingly mimicking reality, while I slept. Tonight I would lie awake for long and then briefly fall asleep, until I lived the nightmare in which Mr. Pilgrim's cork-foot kicked me decisively out of the semiconsciousness of slumber. Awake or asleep, I would hear the voice of Granny, calm, controlled, and authoritative, saying, as she joined me at the little table in its special place on the earthen ground floor of her house, "Suh, what yuh have to say? Why yuh interfayre wid de little heathen gyurl?"

From small, and, indeed, all along the tortuous way as you go through life, there are nights you spend a great part of pleading with the Almighty to let day never come. But in spite of my many prayerful exertions, Sunday came. By six thirty, Gobo and I had fed the animals with the guinea grass from Mr. Young's estate and were heading up the hill from Level Bottom, carrying our plastic pails of milk. Now, not only had Sunday seen the light of its own day, but it was also nearly seven hours old, and the walk to Granny's house would be twenty minutes or so. I got ahold of my plastic bath bucket, filled it with water from the cistern, and washed myself. I had none of Mammy's corn-bake and roasted *smoke'-herrin'*; for one thing, overfed with fear, I wasn't hungry at all, and for another, I knew that, before anything else, Granny would have required a proper explanation as to why I had had breakfast before coming to meet with her, practically inside her kitchen, at eight o'clock in the morning. And I felt no passion at all for compounding the misery of the main examination that awaited me.

I knew better, when I arrived, than to be fooled by the warm hug with which she greeted me. I was not going to let down my guard. I wasn't going to forget matters like Grama's alluring suggestions that I was worthy of praise for having done a good job washing wares, only to be punished, or that I should make an independent decision to give up high school, or that Mrs. M had one day, clean out of the blue, taken a special, selfless liking to me that she could, somehow, not control. My unresponsiveness to Granny was noticeable, and I could see that she had sensed it as she loosened her embrace abruptly and drew back.

"Come, come," she said, softening, resting her right hand on my shoulder and guiding me to the little table. "Mih know yuh like *fry-breadfruit* an' *bwyail'-egg* wid tomato an' cucumber. Mih mek dat fooh yuh. Siddong, siddong, m'ah bring it fooh yuh."

As I sat there in my unrelenting straightjacket, forged from nothing if not from tensile apprehension, they seemed like hours, those three or four minutes before she returned with that delightful food combination and an enamel cup of chocolate tea. In spite of my worry, I relaxed a little as she swiftly left and came again, her own enamel plate and cup in hand, and sat down. For ten or twelve minutes, we half-pretended that it was only the goodness of the meal that demanded our complete and silent dedication. Soon, however, there was nothing left on our plates, and we had to lift our heads.

"Me an' you haf to tark about w'at yuh do to dat gyurl," she said, in a tone that brought me some relief. "Mih sen' Grampa down de hill to do some wuk suh me an' you wan cyah tark praparly. Dis ah wah seriaus t'ing, yuhnuh, wah rayl seriaus t'ing."

She rose and placed the plates one inside the other and then slipped her left middle finger through the handle of each cup before folding her fingers into a fist; then she took up the plates with her right hand and made her way back to the kitchen.

When Granny returned from the kitchen, she relocated her chair, and now, instead of having to look across the table into my eyes, she was sitting beside me. It was very, very heart-calming, this reassuring display of a softer side.

"Mih son," she all but whispered, "gyurl is trouble." Then, putting her left arm around me, she added, "Yuh haf to be cayful. Yuh have to be very cayful, yuh hayr mih, son?"

I had never quite seen this side of her before, and her embrace and her quiet tones and her almost-conspiratorial demeanor delivered relaxation I had not felt since the previous evening in the church, when she had issued me with her summons. She was a brown-complexioned woman of above-average height and substantial girth, with silvery hair on her head and a distinguishing black mole on her left cheek, who seldom smiled with children—so as not to cause disruption to their proper upbringing. All the same, I had an urge to climb up onto my chair and hug her in gratitude for her understanding. But just then, she rose and turned toward the kitchen, saying, "Ah comin' back now." Her action terminated the urge to hug and spared me the agony of deciding if to give in to it.

For the first time since my arrival at her house that morning, my ears could hear the parrots on the trees outside chattering among themselves in words I did not know but joining me into their festivities through the universal medium of communicable elation; for the first time, too, I could hear the musical whirring of sky-scraping bamboo leaves, turned instruments powered by unceasing, joyful breeze.

"Firs' to begin," Granny said, returning from the kitchen and resuming her place beside me, "people doh like bways intafayrin' wid dere dartas—mih showre yuh know dat. Secand of arl, an' even mo' seriaus, yuh interfayre wid gyal and nex-t'ing yuh know, gyal ah mek baby, gyal belly big!"

Shifting her body in her chair, she turned toward me. "How ol' yuh is again, bway?" she asked rhetorically. "Yuh wukking anyw'ere, yuh have money to min' baby?"

As I sat there mute, her piercing brown eyes locked onto mine, I could feel pure terror claim my entire body and communicate to me its altruistic preference to whisk me away to some place of escape from the dark images that Granny's words had conjured up and that now were in exclusive possession of my chastened mind.

She was merciful. "You don't have to answer," she said in officialese, while permitting herself a half smile. "Jes' doh eva forget one single word ah w'at mih seh to yuh hayr dis marnin'—an' behave yuhself to suit."

*That is it?* I silently asked myself. I couldn't believe that the grand ordeal I had so dreaded was over. What was it, I wondered incredulously, that made my very magisterial granny so lenient in this case? It could just as easily have been Gra'ma. But I was far too happy to go dwelling upon such matters and gleefully answered yes when, getting up and heading for the kitchen again, she asked me if I would like some fresh guava juice.

## VANESSA'S NIECE

It was when she returned with the two plastic glasses of juice, rested them down on the table, relocated her chair, and looking at me from across the table again, took a sip of her own juice before motioning me to have mine—it was then that, taking my first sip, I told her how Pappy had treated Mammy that sad morning by the fireside. But Granny would never acknowledge receipt of reports made by children against big people. She listened intently, her eyes fixed upon mine, while sipping her own juice to the end, and I could sense that she did not miss a single word; but then, without comment, she rose and dismissed me. "Grampa comin' jes' now. An' doh forget, always be obedient to yuh mooma an' yuh poopa."

# Chapter 7

Receipt of the report that, driven by gratitude for her unexpected leniency, I had made to Granny would never be acknowledged, and there would accordingly be no inquisition. But Pappy would come to understand everything in time. The day would come when Granny would detain him briefly as they were about to walk past each other at a point, not far from One-Foot Pilgrim's gap, along the dirt track that led away from Mango Tree right down to Level Bottom, where the cows waited patiently each morning to yield up their precious white liquid and, in return, receive their guinea grass rations reaped from the adjacent estate.

"Manny bway," she said, resting her open right palm on his left shoulder as they stood on the dirt road, facing each other, "mih sid-dong right home eena mih house de-adda-day an' hayr mih picknee ah cry!"

Over the years, beginning with the days of his courtship, Pappy had grown to know Granny reasonably well. "Manny bway," she had once said to him, "yuh want to co'tn Emmy? Yuh have house?" He had quickly grasped and digested then the entire ten paragraphs compressed into those two brief queries that Granny had just gently uttered. He was no less astute now, and he knew immediately what subject matter she was inviting him to address.

"W'at picknee?" he countered in a desperate effort to buy some time in which he could work out how to deal with her unwanted attentions. Worst of all, it was nearing dusk on a Wednesday evening, and he was hurrying to a committee meeting at the church in Glamorgan, which had to finish in time for the start of the seven thirty service. Even without constraints of that, or any, nature, Pappy disliked to the point of resentment every attempt to hold him up when he was on his way to keep an appointment of whatsoever kind. It mattered not to him that nobody else in the villages cared a hoot about punctuality and that, almost without fail, upon arrival at the appointed place, he would have to wait at least thirty minutes for sight of the next earliest participant in whatsoever was the matter at hand. Being on time was an obsession, which, in that regard, made him completely out of place in that society, and for that he suffered all his life, his ailment proving to be incurable.

Granny gloried now in his obvious discomfort, regarding it as just punishment for what he had done according to the report the existence of which she refused to acknowledge, except to herself. She well knew where he was going, and she was totally familiar with his dedication to punctuality. But she would play the innocent, and when she was done with him, he would be wishing he had been subjected to an inquisition instead. She let go of his shoulder and, pulling her body upright, put her hands about her hips.

"How yuh mean *w'at picknee*? Yuh mek somebady beside Emmy cry?"

"Oh-ho, you mean… ? Well, just a little misunderstanding…" His language was already in church-committee mode.

"Bway, wid mih own two aze an' dem mih hayr de baad, baad boofin'-up yuh gi' shi. Mih hayr de shoutin'. Mih hayr de anger eena yuh vaice… Mih siddong right home deh eeena mih house an' hayr arl ah dat! Ah weh mih picknee do yuh suh, bway?"

He knew Granny well, as I have said, and he knew for sure that, while she might, indeed, have heard some such things with her own two ears, she had not heard them as they were happening. He fully understood that the information that she clearly had had reached her from a source she would not ever openly recognize, and further, he quickly deciphered the identity of that source. And she, for her part, knew that he knew and understood and had worked it all out. That was the way in which Granny and the rest of the adult family communicated. For him now, there was no point in dissembling anymore: to do that would be to make himself even later for the committee meeting than he now already was, and it would not buy him any grace with Granny.

"I'm sorry," he said simply, looking away.

"Manny, you must tell me if yuh rayly sarry or if yuh jes' sayin' suh!" She was not going to let him off as easily as he no doubt would have liked.

"Mih sarry, mih tell yuh mih sarry!" He was trying in vain to hide his irritation.

"Yuh really mean it, then?" The rising resentment he was experiencing was clear and obvious to Granny, but Granny pretended not to notice it, because for him to become very irritated and for her to pretend she didn't know it was part of his punishment—that irritation that must intensify as he got later and later for his committee meeting.

"Yes!" Even he was startled by the sharpness in his voice, but Granny paid it no mind, instead remaining placid and setting a smile of satisfaction about her lips.

"So you will tell her when you go back home?" she asked in officialese.

"Yes!"

"You are sure you will tell her?"

"Yes!"

"Enjoy your meeting, then."

"T'anks!"

If he had had time to spare, he would have prolonged the joust by pointing out that he had not uttered a single word about any meeting, but by now, inside, he was almost apoplectic at the inevitability of his impending late arrival at the church.

# Chapter 8

By now, Vanessa, who would tell me and Rookmin sometimes that there was nothing like the sweetness of the times that a boy and a girl could spend alone together, had eased herself almost completely out of our secret relationship. But whenever she could find a way for us three to be by ourselves—at home in the house, or at the quiet beach we could reach by the short track running briefly from our land through Mr. Young's adjacent estate, or on the leafy carpet in the shade of the luxuriant mango-*vert* tree—she would go and fetch Rookmin and we would eat and drink and talk, and Nessa would miss no opportunity to tell us two that we didn't always have to have her around when we were together and that a boy and a girl needed to spend time alone together to get to know each other better, with nobody else around. I would study Rookmin's facial responses, trying to unravel whether she understood as well as I did what our mentor was saying. I knew deep inside me that if it had been Shirley, I would have been faced with no such question.

Neither of them knew that I had become the object of Shirley's unmistakable, if in no way unwelcome, aggression. True, Vanessa had, at some stage before I met Rookmin, promised to introduce me to her little niece, but that idea seemed somehow to have gone out of her mind. Since that promise, however, and sometime after I had met Rookmin, Shirley had come a few times from the little subvillage of Zion Hill to visit her young auntie and had seemed to become excited as she observed the warm relationship between Nessa and me. It was only on the second occasion that we'd found ourselves alone together for a minute or two that she'd confronted me with the sharp stroke of a few alarming words: "Hmmm! Look like mih tanty like you rayl baad, bway."

I shivered. I had been sworn to secrecy by Nessa and hadn't done and would never have done anything to betray her trust, even if I had had anything to gain by doing so. And to me, Nessa was nothing if not expert at concealing our secret when there were others around. What was it that this little girl—at just around twelve a little less than two years my junior—could see? It was not just her words: there was mischief in her tone and a knowing glint in her eyes that, at once, accused and offered forgiveness. I felt an almost-overwhelming sense of inadequacy in the face of her deft self-assuredness.

"Wehmek yuh seh dat?" Was it my imagination, or was my voice in fact a little faint and trembly?

As I sat in the Morris chair, wondering if Shirley had noticed the unsteadiness I was certain I had detected in my own voice, Vanessa came back into the drawing room and saved the day. Barely two weeks earlier, she had also reentered the drawing room in the nick of time after Shirley had gotten up from where she sat, come across to my Morris chair, kissed me on my lips, grabbed, gently squeezed, and then rapidly let go of my crotch, and calmly gone back and sat down and was looking at me with a blank, innocent stare, waiting for, indeed demanding, a response. As Nessa entered the drawing room now, Shirley looked at me and said, adeptly and to my complete amazement, "Yeah, I like to pitch marble too." I saw nothing on Nessa's face to suggest that she had seen through Shirley's ruse.

The last time Nessa and I savored the pleasures of the combing of the hairs was, she told me, to celebrate her twenty-first birthday. The rainy season had already set in, and it was a wet day toward the end of May. Somehow, everything was cozier and sweeter if you did certain things to the ecstatic sound of conspiratorial raindrops making music on the galvanized roof. As usual, it was a Sabbath Day. In fact, it was almost always a Sabbath Day. To be alone with her on any other day was practically impossible, and I often feigned illness or conjured up some situation that allowed me to escape going to church on a Sabbath Day. The lead-up was always delightful. I would know she was ready when she got her plastic bucket and drew water from the cistern and showered and then refilled the bucket for me. When we were both showered and dried and she was powdered, she would sit at the edge of the bed and I would sit on the floor while she combed my hair, the back of my neck nestled in her crotch; then, in time, she would hand me the comb and lie on her back on the bed and beckon me to comb her hairs. That time, it was more pleasurable than ever, though in the end, I realized it was not only to celebrate her birthday but also to bid a fond farewell to those same pleasures.

I should have known, because she had not cut me loose suddenly and without a life raft on the stormy seas of great emotional loss. She had done all she could beforehand to ensure that, as she let go of me, I could float and I could swim and that on my own I had what it took to derive and manage and enhance my pleasure. Always she had been firm that people who tried to play down the beauty of engagement in such recurring sessions of ultimate intimacy were only trying, for reasons of their own sorry sense of insecurity, to keep ordinary, peace-loving folk away from nature's greatest gift. "Arl yuh haf to do is mek showre you rule it an' doh le' it rule you," she would say.

I remember well the two occasions, months before that farewell, on which she had steered Rookmin and me into it. The first time was on that very bed, and the second was on the leaf-made carpet below the huge mango-*vert* tree down at Level Bottom. Rookmin did not, as a rule, come to visit on a Saturday, as the rules prohibited entertainment of any sort on the Holy Day. But if persons belonging to other Christian denominations were heathens, it followed relentlessly that persons who were not Christians at all were even more so. And as Teacher Aaron had, in his time, drilled into our consciousness, it was the duty of every Seventh-Day Adventist, each one being, by definition, one of God's chosen (or elect), to convert as many nonbelievers, as many heathens, as possible and thereby save that many souls from eternal damnation. Vividly do I still recall his insistence, as we sang one of his favorite hymns, upon our substituting the word *many* for the word *any* in the lines "Will there be any stars, any stars in my crown / When at ev'ning the sun goeth down?" According to that Teacher Aaron of yore—the one in being before, frustrated, he quit the job as head teacher and started his own business as a driving instructor, discarding all neckties and buying half a dozen stylish Italian-made leather belts to hold up his trousers—the reference to sunset was a reference to the darkness that fell at the final closing of your eyes and your subsequent arrival in heaven and the award of a star for every soul that you had saved; but a necessary precondition for any arrival in heaven at all, once the sun had gone down on you, was the previous saving of at least one soul, which meant that the word *any* appearing in the hymn was a complete oversight. Thus, for soul-saving purposes, it would, according to Nessa, be very much in order for Rookmin to be invited on a Saturday for a study of the lessons in the quarterly. And on the Sabbath Day in question, the visit of Rookmin did indeed begin with a swift review of the most important in the lessons in the current edition of the quarterly.

As was the case with our house, it was not that there was no shower room. Just as the appurtenances of the living compound included a latrine, so, too, there was a wooden outhouse for showering, to which you repaired once you had drawn your plastic bucket of bathwater from the cistern. The difference was that these latrines, as my mind's eye still sees them, were a quarter mile away from the immediate vicinities of the houses and kitchens, while the bathrooms stood in the yards but a few arm's lengths from the cisterns, turning their backs on these water stores, their entrances to the south looking out onto the sea. It was not a windy day, and I could hear the gentle rolling of the waves as, obedient to Nessa's command, I entered the bathroom and set down two plastic buckets on the floor, the only part of the bathroom that was made of concrete. I heard their footsteps right outside the still-open door and turned. Rookmin seemed a little bewildered, but Nessa looked me smilingly in the eye and announced, "Wih doin' somet'ing special today."

"Rooks," she went on, turning to the fourteen-year-old standing beside her, "ah hope you will like it. In fac', gyurl, mih showre yuh goh like it... go inside an' tek arf yuh clothes."

Rookmin was more than hesitant, and she awkwardly looked down at her prospective nakedness, then at me, then at Nessa, then, with a lightning glance, back at her pubic area—and then back at us again, as if pleading with all three of us (Nessa and me and the area) to not let her have to do a thing like that. But Nessa, though gentle, spotting through the genuine apprehension more than a hint of equivocation, was relentless. For my part, it was only a stubborn little streak of shyness that made me behave as if I were really trying to temper the fire beginning to blaze inside me.

"Goh-arn, go een an' tek dem arf. Jakey, yuh haf fooh tek arf fooh-you own, too."

Colluding only through our eyes, Rookmin and I, without more coaxing, decided against resistance and, by now with rapidly receding reluctance, did as we'd been directed. Nessa it was who thought to close the door behind us. For clothes hangers, there were nails driven all around into the wooden walls of the bathroom. Rookmin and I had hardly finished hanging up our clothes and begun to stare with determination directly over each other's heads, just so as not to let our eyes wander, or seem to wander, toward our pubic areas, when, to our consternation and consummate unease, Nessa pulled open the bathroom door and came in, all her clothing in her hand.

"Doh panic," she urged us gently. "Mih only come een yah fooh guide ar-yuh. Is a t'ing ar-yuh haf to know how fooh enjay."

Gra'ma's house, left to her by my grandfather Karsy, as I have said, stood upon a unique flat plot of the family lands in the Pint. It began, this plot, just as you came down the hill southward from Uncle Jimmy's house, past Uncle Egbert's on the right—later on, also past Tanty Etho's little one that her brothers had built for her after cousin Sydney, having blessed her with five children in the fifty months their marriage lasted, disappeared, never to be seen or heard of again. In shape, Gra'ma's house was almost a perfect oblong, five hundred feet long from north to south and a hundred feet wide. At the southern end, looking out onto the sea, was the everlasting bamboo patch. To the west of it, the land sloped gently down to Pappy's house and remained a gentle slope all the way to the point where it encountered one of the seemingly innumerable extremities of Richmond Estate, but not before it decided to turn sharply south and fall away sheerly to become home to the little track that carried us to Level Bottom, Belle Garden Estate (that mostly supplied the sustenance for our cows), and eventually, the sea. On the east, the land, just past the space commandeered by the sprawling Jamaica plum tree seemingly from the beginning of time, dropped sharply at first and then sloped down onto Cocoa Piece. It was at the northern perimeter that stood the huge imperious calabash tree that would warn the alert stranger that what he was embarking upon was entry onto the quasisacred domain of the matriarch.

The calabash tree was the source of our homemade utensils. When we were going to the Woods, walking for miles, crossing both Little River and Big River at several points to get to our provision grounds or our other Cocoa Piece, we would cut mature bamboo trunks for use as water bottles, to be filled at the last river-crossing point, to quench our thirst throughout the working day. But when Pappy was doing a task on one of the two neighboring estates (almost always Mr. Short's) and when we were working on the Cocoa Piece or the fields nearer home, it was the calabash goblet that held our drinking water. The calabashes were pear-shaped, and what we did was excise from the narrower extremity, the top, a round piece that, cured in the sun, would later serve as the cap for the goblet. The excised piece would be of a size sufficient to leave behind an opening large enough to provide relatively easy access to the belly, the innards, of the calabash, which, with our inborn dedication and commitment to homely imagery and the economical use of words, we simply called the calabash-guts. We did the excision of the future cap while the calabash was green and more responsive to the attentions of our basic tools. After the excision, we would gut the calabash and, with the aid of brushes made from coconut husks pounded into submission and tied with sibyl-jack cords onto short lengths of dried guava wood for handles, wash the insides of the calabash clean and then expose it to bake and harden in the tropical sun.

Our soup bowls, too, we made from the calabash, and we made them in various sizes to cater for the needs of little children and big people and the others in between, a determining production factor being the ages and sizes at which the calabashes were picked from the tree. The procedure for making soup bowls was quite similar to that for making the water goblets, except that for making the bowls, we would cut the calabash into two pear-shaped halves and gut and clean the halves before offering them up to the sun for finalization of the manufacture.

The water-scoops we used in the bathroom were in nearly all respects like little soup bowls. As Nessa entered the bathroom, she hung her clothes on one of the clothing nails protruding from its wooden walls dutifully awaiting its turn to be of service. Stark naked, she hugged me close and kissed me on the forehead. And I shook and shivered.

The noticeable difference between a bowl and a scoop was that, before a scoop was put out under the rays of the sun, with the aid of a hot nail held between the jaws of a pair of pliers, a hole would be punched in it at its narrower end so that when not in use it could hang from one of the smaller nails jutting out from the bathroom's wooden walls. Nessa kissed me again and then, releasing me from her firm embrace, turned and took ahold of one of the two scoops hanging from the wall. Then, turning back to me, right hand outstretched with the scoop in it, she said with a sweet smile and in a near whisper, "Bathe her."

It was a lot for me to handle all at once—her nude embrace of me, with Rookmin standing right there next to us, an embrace of a kind I had never experienced before (with us upright, our genitals pressing against each other), her urging me to wash Rookmin right there before her, all this time thoughts of Shirley's aggressiveness on my unwarrantedly guilty mind. I demurred.

Nessa dipped a scoopful of water from one of the plastic buckets and threw it onto Rookmin's body, letting it run from her shoulders down; then, dipping another scoopful, she half-whispered to Rookmin, "Stoop down and open your legs." To my surprise, Rookmin promptly obeyed, and Nessa threw the water up into her genitals. And Nessa, reaching now for the soap shelf that extended four or five inches outward from the wooden wall, handed me the Lux bar and, bending her head slowly forward and backward to urge me on, told me, "Wash shi *pupu*. Wash shi *pupu* nice-nice. Keep yuh leg an' dem open, Rooks. Leh 'im wash yuh pupu good an' nice."

When I completed what had, rather quickly and a little to my surprise, become a rather pleasant task (all too soon for Rookmin, I thought I sensed), Nessa finished bathing the girl and had her dry herself and dress and go out of the bathroom. Then she quickly, almost clinically, bathed all of me herself and told me as I was leaving to hand her the third plastic bucket of water, which I had not realized before was patiently waiting its turn just outside the bathroom door. Rookmin and I waited outside the bathroom door as Nessa did her own bathing. We hardly spoke; in fact, we were very quiet, surely just grappling with our own thoughts, for practically the whole time that elapsed before Nessa emerged. But by then we had had a solitary intense exchange that settled an important matter.

"Yuh did like it?" I asked, seeking confirmation.

"W'a'?" she feigned.

"How mih wash yuh pupu."

"Yeah," she sheepishly confessed, without hesitation, "mih did like it." She paused, let an earnest smile light up her face, and then, looking dreamily skyward, repeated in a soft, controlled semiscream, "Mih did rayly like it!"

Vanessa was fully dressed when she came through the bathroom door. She smiled and winked at us and, having hung her towel next to ours on the clean-teeth-bush hedge, beckoned us to follow her to the outdoor kitchen nearby. The hedge was on the southern side of the house, yards away from the bathroom, a mere foot behind the line from which the land began to fall away from it, heading for Level Bottom. Five or six yards from where the western extremity of the house rested on the shoulders of its confident, almost arrogant, crapaud wood pillars, the hedge made a ninety-degree turn northward and traveled for a few yards, coming to a halt where the track leading to Level Bottom lay. It probably was not coincidence, and I never found out why, but while the hedges at Uncle Egbert's house and at ours were the same, in the case of Uncle Egbert's house, the hedge ran first along the northern side, standing up in quiet defiance to the boundary with Richmond Estate, and made the sharp right-angle turn southward along its western perimeter. The fourth brother, Uncle Eddie, who, never married, liked, instead, to conduct heated, often bitter, debates with himself and, in the course of the conduct of such debates, would often appeal to the nearest one of us nephews to help him knock some sense into the head of his opponent and thereby encourage him to see the error of his ways and acknowledge the obvious flaws in his arguments, and lived, until his death, a bachelor and outstanding debater, basking in the glory of winning almost all his important arguments, at the ancestral home, having first shared it with Gra'ma until she passed away in 1968.

I have never bothered to find out, and, to this day, do not know, the scientific or any other name of the clean-teeth-bush. It is willful ignorance, I suppose; as with all, or nearly all, our innumerable other "bushes," I have felt that to sully the wholesome simplicity of our delightful, rustic lives by replacing with the cold objectivity of science the magic names so cozy, comfortable, and reassuring in my memory could easily turn out be an act of unspeakable violence to my psyche. Who, anyway, reading this selected account of my rural life, would be better off for knowing the scientific name of the clean-teeth-bush? The bush earned its name from its special utility to us: it provided us with our toothbrushes. You would cut a piece from a mature branch and, resting one end of it upon the smooth side of a stone, pound it with a hammer or another stone to produce the bristles, thereby completing the manufacture of this important, though rudimentary, bathroom utility.

Obedient to Nessa's beckoning, we followed her for the few yards to the kitchen, where it stood, on baby stilts of wood half-buried in the ground protected by sand and gravel, a little distance away from the bathroom and the house proper. There she lifted a calabash lid to expose a pear-shaped cake pan, one of many that Uncle Egbert had fashioned in his shortened time with us by soldering together bits of galvanized sheets left over from this or that roofing work that he or Uncle Jimmy or Pappy had, in some near or distant past, completed. Taking three half-size enamel plates and three plastic glasses out of the wares cupboard above the kitchen dresser, she cut three slices off the sweet potato pone waiting in the cake pan, put each slice on a plate, and handed a plate and an empty glass each to me and Rookmin. She replaced the calabash lid and, wordlessly, led us out of the kitchen toward the house, but stopping by the cistern to remove its wooden lid and then the fine-wire meshing set in place beneath it, unhook the wire cord from the nail jutting out of the wooden lid, and draw out the bottle of ginger beer secured at the far end of the wire cord sunk earlier in the day into the cool waters always waiting at the underground bottom of the cistern, the household's concrete reservoir. She loosened the insistent grasp of the wire cord on the neck of the bottle and, with her free hand, picked up and handed her plastic glass to me and then took ahold of the plate with her pone.

"Come," she said to us simply, continuing the little trip toward the house.

We had our pone and ginger beer sitting on the edge of the bed, but no conversation came to interrupt the snacking, which did not take us long.

"Good?" Nessa inquired when it was clear that we were all done.
"Yes."

Nessa rested her enamel plate on the bed then took Rookmin's and mine in turn and settled them into hers; then, methodically, she slid the glasses into one another, bottoms down, and lay them horizontally onto the packet of plates. She rose from the edge of the bed, went to the bedroom dresser, and returned with the fine-tooth comb. Handing the comb to me and winking with one eye, she said, "Enjoy!" Then, turning toward Rookmin, she said, "'E goin' to comb yuh small fine hair. Trus' mih, yuh goh like it, Rooks." And then she picked up the package of plates together with the glasses and disappeared, closing the bedroom door behind her.

## Chapter 9

It was not long before the day of my fourth encounter with Mrs. M came. As usual, I was headed east on my way back to the school at Glamorgan, the khaki bag slung over my shoulder with the mail I had collected from the post office in Pembroke. As not infrequently happened, a light midmorning shower sent me to seek refuge in Mr. Sammy's shop. As I was about to go through the door of the shop, Gokool pulled up and carefully parked his invisible car on the side of the road just outside before reaching across to the front passenger seat of the car and grasping an imaginary brown paper bag with his left hand. He exited the car and, facing west, let his left hand pass the paper bag to his right hand, which slid it into the right-side pocket of his trousers. With his now-free left hand, he slammed shut the driver's door of the car, wiped his pursed lips with the back of his right hand as he salivated at the sight and the nearness of the rum shop's door, and hurried in at my heels. He went straight to the counter, glinting eyes fixed upon the Old Oak section of the shelf.

"Marnin', Misser Sammy," he greeted the shopkeeper, who stood behind the counter, facing his faithful customer, the liquor shelf behind and a bit above him. Already in Mr. Sammy's hand was the petit-quart that Gokool would inevitably requisition. Seeing it, Gokool became emotional and swallowed hard and wiped his lips with the back of his right hand; then, taking the brown paper bag from his pocket, he turned back to the other two morning customers sitting at a table in the corner, with a dying flask, and said, "Marnin', genklemen. Look lakka mih fooget mih manners. Marnin', marnin'."

Hardly had he uttered his apology and, as clear compensation for his default, tripled his greetings to his fellow patrons than there came through the door of the shop none other than Mrs. M. Recognizing the presence of the head teacher's wife in the rum shop, Gokool drew himself to attention, looked straight at her, and bowed exaggeratedly from the waist.

"Good morning, ma'am," he welcomed her in language appropriate for a head teacher's wife. "Good to see you here!"

Either I was badly mistaken or he had somehow managed, in the spoken word, to paper-clip a little giggle onto the word *here*. Giggling was all well and good for someone with a car, invisible or not, parked just outside the shop. For me, the sight of her in there was the source of sheer terror.

Gokool paid for the petit-quart, took it out of Mr. Sammy's hand, emitted a slurping sound, and securing the petit-quart in his brown paper bag, headed for the door. John-Boy, one of the two patrons at the little table in the corner having rum for breakfast, called out after him.

"Bway, yuh nuh si rain ah farl, ah weh y'ah goh?"

"Min' yuh own business, sah… in any case, dat nuh no rain, ah jes' wah likkle drizzle."

"Rain goh wet yuh paper bag an' yuh rum battle goh drap an' brok!"

"Oh gard, nuh seh dat nuh, man. Nuh put goat-mout' 'pan mih rum nuh. M'ah beg yuh!" Gokool pleaded as he vanished into the now-abating rain.

"'E ah wah true-true rummy, eh," a sighing John-Boy commented aloud as he and his friend at the little table in the corner turned back to their breakfast.

Almost immediately, Mrs. M briskly made her way out through the door, having politely declined Mr. Sammy's offer of a towel to dry her hair. Not only her hair but also her dress offered evidence that she had not reached the shop and safety from the attention of the brisk shower, quite as speedily as she might have liked. I felt sure that she had been standing at the eastern end of the little bridge when the shower started and had misjudged the timing of her scamper or, else, had deliberately postponed to the very last moment a decision as to the point at which she should seek shelter. Now that she was leaving, Mr. Sammy and his two faithful breakfast patrons would have no doubt that she was going to go straight home to change her dress and dry her hair. But I felt I knew better.

I stood awkwardly in what felt like the middle of the shop, and I could sense the six torchlights shining on me, and I thought I could hear three weary brains ticking, looking for lips through which to ask if the boy didn't know the rain had stopped and that he manifestly had no further business being in a rum shop, especially at that time of a school day, and wearing his school uniform to boot. How I wished Gokool's car had been real and another shower had come down and Mrs. M, not wanting to come back into the rum shop, had demanded that Gokool drive her home. Pressured by my unwholesome circumstances into briefly mistaking my wishes for reality, I actually peered through the doorway to see if Gokool's car was still parked outside. I do not think I need report that I found the spot on which Gokool had parked his car to be vacant. For a fleeting moment, I, too, became vacant. But I couldn't afford to remain that way for too long, as there was an urgent necessity for me to free my mind and make room in it for thoughts about how to confront effectively the matter of my imminent meeting with Mrs. M at the spot where she inevitably stood waiting for me at the eastern extremity of the baby bridge. In my desperation as I eventually approached the spot, I imagined that, with her wet hair and dampish dress, she had decided to go home, planning to meet me again on some other day, and that what I had just heard her say was "Morning dew!" in dismissive reference to the rain. That bothered me for quite a while afterward, remaining a puzzle to be solved entirely by myself much later on, sometime after I got into my French classes at the college at Roxborough.

"Mon dieu!" she had exclaimed when I'd gotten close enough to her. "Eet got you too, ze rain!"

You would have sworn she was seeing me for the first time for the day.

At all events, the illusion that she would now tell me to hurry back to school and that she was going home to dry her hair and change into a dry dress and would see me some other time did not last long. Eyes fixed on the khaki bag hanging from my shoulder, she moved closer to me with outstretched arms, and before I could make any sense of those happenings, she took ahold of me and kept me briefly captive against the pulsating wall of her determined bosom.

"You need a leetle hug, my son."

It did not matter that the period of my captivity was short: when she set me free, I was hyperventilating and cold-sweating all the same, and my heart was trying to hammer its fearful way out of my chest. As I struggled to bring these responses under control, she slid the handle of the khaki bag with the mail off my shoulder, over my head, into her eager embrace, where it changed places with my body. Since then, nothing has served to silence the unrelenting little voice hiding somewhere inside my head that keeps reminding me that I put up no resistance.

"Here," she said, having rapidly gone through the contents of the khaki bag and selected one letter addressed, with beautiful penmanship, to Teacher Aaron. "Zis eez furr you." She buried another five-cent piece into my palm, slid the bag back over my head onto my shoulder, and with a smirk of satisfaction clothed in contempt, said, "Sanks, sank you," and turned and disappeared into the newly reappearing morning sunlight.

She had sunk me indeed; willy-nilly, I had let myself be bribed, head spun. I had fallen prey to the skillfully executed design of an own-way woman. And the unrelenting prosecutorial voice, without letup, added another count that stated, "And further did in return from the said own-way woman knowingly receive and did fail and refuse to return certain monies, namely the sum of five cents, Trinidad and Tobago currency." At church and elsewhere, mostly at a reasonably safe distance, I saw Mrs. M from time to time afterward—in Glamorgan or in one or the other of the little neighboring villages that, one after the other, dotted the sides of the east-west Windward Road—until Teacher Aaron gave up the head teachership (and, indeed, classroom teaching altogether) and then divorced Mrs.

M soon after starting his driving school; but never again in Tobago were we face-to-face at close quarters, until at Teacher Aaron's funeral years later. In between, however, before and after my divorce from Shirley, and what with the relationship that had grown up between her and Jacinta, we did not, in Trinidad, manage to avoid each other.

* * * * *

When I reached back to the school that day of my last mailbag encounter with Mrs. M, Teacher Aaron asked me if the post office queue had been long again and inquired how I had managed with the little shower of rain. Then, curiously, he asked me if everything had gone well all along the road on my way back to the school, and after a split-second's hesitation, I said yes; but it seemed crystal clear to me that he did not believe me and that I might have lost his trust forever. For me, that was a loss of catastrophic proportions. It was a deeply painful feeling that I felt. I was now nothing but the plaything of Mrs. M, methodically made so by her. She had systematically upset my equilibrium, sneakily deceiving me to achieve her own perverse ends, and then she had bribed me into a shameful silence that I was, in any case, too fearful to break. To myself I vowed that thenceforth a person who as much as tried to bribe me in any way, of the female gender or not, would, in my mind, for the trying, stand guilty of a crime worthy of capital punishment.

Before John-Boy's liking for rum had grown beyond his effective control, he was the one in Glamorgan and environs who taught people to drive. In fact, cousin Sydney had, for some time, been one of his students but had suffered from a severe lack of clarity as to which of them was instructor and which the learner-driver. That lack of clarity fatally impeded his progress, and he had, in the end, given up after failing the driving test a large number of times, although it must be said that, to his credit, he hadn't suffered the fate of Denny Roberts, who, at his sixth failure, had torn his learner's permit to bits and slapped the examiner so hard across his cheek that one of his teeth had left his jawbone and flown some distance away at a very remarkable speed, after which Denny was officially banned from ever attempting the driving test again. John-Boy had previously been a good Seventh-Day Adventist who, back then, like others of his kind who attended church regularly, didn't drink a lot of rum and certainly was very careful where and with whom he drank some. But he had left the church altogether after Othnel Nurse died and begun to approach the consumption of alcoholic beverages with less restraint.

## Chapter 10

The circumstances surrounding Othnel's death and burial left a lasting impression on me. Already I had been struggling with many questions about the church that I could not let people know had as much as entered my mind, a location from which I made sure that the notion of articulating them resolutely steered clear. He was my cousin, was Othnel, and it is important to record, my real cousin; *important* because, as it seemed, everybody in Glamorgan, where the church and the school and Derrick's shop and Lammie's variety store were all located, was your cousin, some your real cousins, the others your sort-of-circumstantial cousins. In Othnel's case, not only was he my real cousin, but also, for a man in his midtwenties, he had an exceptionally kind and caring way about him that was particularly noticeable in his interactions with old people as well as with younger ones like myself. Even if one of the village bullies was around scouting, as our bullies would, for any opportunity that might present itself to inflict some distress on somebody or another, you felt safe if Othnel happened to be nearby. So it was a sad day when Othnel died.

"What happen, w'a' 'appen?" Pepe shouted at the crowd rushing westward toward Argyle as we came out of the high school compound at the end of the school day, after the afternoon shower that had detained us had briefly subsided. At first, no one responded, but soon somebody, taking pity, turned his head backward as he ran and provided the answer.

"Man dead down ah road deh!"

Pepe and Tapo and I joined the moving crowd, but Morro and Danny-Boy, older than we were, took the news in stride and did not quicken their pace. Just past the motorcar mechanic shop at the junction of Northside Road and the Windward Road, the crowd had gathered on the right-hand side and was looking past the parallel wastewater drain, out onto the clearing beyond, at the lifeless body unnecessarily kept captive by the teak-hard electric company pole serenely at rest on its head and, about the greater part of its frame, some of the transmission wires still passionately hawking and spitting sparks.

Ever since the murder of Uncle Egbert by my maternal step-grandfather, followed by the deaths, from pneumonia and cancer respectively, of my paternal aunt, Agnes, and my maternal aunt, Fancilla, I have always regarded death as an awesome and rather unpleasant occurrence. I often thought of how, as a child, I had seen cars and vans and trucks shut down and refuse to move, but they would come back to life after some attention at the mechanic shop. Yet there appeared to be no effective mechanic or other shop for human beings who shut down and would not move. I peeped past the drain to the body and the pole and the wires and closed my eyes to absorb the chill that ran down my tautened spine. I did not turn my head to look at this man or that woman but kept my eyes fixed on the inert frame that once housed a live person, perhaps, as I told myself, a perfectly nice person for all I knew.

"Ah who?" I asked. "Ah who dead?"

"Ah Ort'nel."

"Who Ort'nel?" It was not simple stupefaction at all; it was the demonstration of a calm, unquestioning certainty that there had always been, without my knowledge, some other Othnel somewhere.

"Ah ho' much Ort'nel yuh know!"

"Oh gard, oh gard, oh gard!" I did not give in to the temptation to jump the wastewater drain and go across to the clearing to be near him. I held on to a shoulder that turned out to be Pepe's and let my tears have their way through my briny eyes.

By then, the minute hand of the clock, just beyond the hour hand, was making its measured way down the hill to half past four.

By nightfall the body would be lying at the Nurses' house at Sheep-Pen Ridge in a bath pan full of ice, and people would soon afterward begin to gather to pay their respects and express their condolences. Only on the following day would serious trouble intrude.

Even so, there was a little bit of trouble that very evening. It was not a traditional, heathen-type wake with the hymn-singing being generously supplemented by rum-drinking and card-playing; there would, of course, be plenty of hymns, but proper Seventh-Day Adventists did not, except in carefully vetted company, drink rum or play cards, nor did they encourage callers to do so. Persons attending the house of mourning, often insensitively referred to by the unpolished as *the dead-house*, especially where the death was sudden and unexpected, would, in village solidarity, carry appropriate supplies, which, for heathens, would include rum, coffee, and biscuit and cheese and, for Seventh-Day Adventists, *sweet drinks*, biscuit and cheese, and Milo. Thus, it was that Gokool, arriving with some biscuits and some cheese, had in advance fortified his body with a sufficient helping of his favorite beverage and had taken the additional precaution of carrying with him, for later, a petit-quart secured in the trademark brown paper bag and hidden away in the inner left breast pocket of an old jacket that he wore for the convenience. Having thus carefully prepared himself and come and properly paid his respects, Gokool felt free to pull up anyone whose behavior fell short of the required standard.

"Yuh mean yuh nuh wark wid nutten, bway?" he accosted Tallboy, the health van driver, who had just entered the premises *sans* sweet drink *sans* biscuit and cheese and *sans* Milo. "Yuh jes' come wid yuh two lang han'?"

Well-oiled by the earlier application of its owner's favorite beverage, Gokool's voice rang out loud and clear, yet the health van driver looked about the surroundings in terror, ridiculously hoping to be assured that nobody had heard a word of what Gokool had said. Finding no solace in the faces of those present, he mumbled, "M'ah come back now-now," and fled and did not return. Word of what had befallen the health van driver quickly spread by means of what the villagers self-deprecatingly called *niggergram*, and no one else was seen that evening going to the house of mourning with their two long hands swinging.

So much for the early trouble. The really serious trouble came when Othnel's elder cousin, Darwin, went to see the pastor at his home in Roxborough, near midmorning the following day, to discuss arrangements for the funeral.

"But he's on suspension!" Pastor Ramrod said in heartfelt alarm. "We can't do that. We can't have him in the church!"

The look of terror on Pastor Ramrod's face was such as to suggest to Darwin that there burned in the heart of the holy man intense fear that even by entertaining a discussion of the matter at all, he was displeasing God, who might well, as a consequence, by then already be queuing up his soul for a rapid descent into the everlasting fire about which he himself had so often, in graphic, rapturous detail, dutifully warned the flock.

"But 'e dead arready," Darwin protested. "Ort'nel dead. 'E done pay de highes' price!"

"No, no, no, no, no! I can't, I can't. He is on suspension! You have to understand!"

Pastor Ramrod's voice was crackling like a hurry bushfire, and he was cold-sweating and shaking violently and hyperventilating. Not wanting to cause him further distress, Darwin bit his lip and took his leave.

It had otherwise been his lucky day: When he had walked out of the house on his way to the pastor's, he had gotten to the Windward Road just in time to be able to wave down the health van and secure a ride. The van was headed for the health center at Bay Road in Belle Garden, but Tallboy, the driver, agreed that, in the tragic circumstances, he would take Darwin straight to Roxborough before going to the center. In their conversation on the way, he conveyed apologies to the Nurse family for having left the house abruptly the previous evening and not gone back.

"Ah dat wehmek mih boun' fooh kerry yuh straight weh y'ah goh now—mih haffoo show yuh how sarry mih sarry."

"Okay, buh yuh din' rayly haf to tek arn Gokool. Gokool was clean outta place!"

"Ah true dat eh, buh mih behn feel shame, bway, mih behn rayly feel shame. Nat a cent eena mih packet, buh mih still come deh, two lang han' o' no two lang han'… an' den dat drunken jackarse!"

"Yuh till nuh behn haffoo tek arn Gokool!"

Now, as he exited the pastor's house, there was Lenny Job's truck, laden though it was with gravel from the quarry at Betsy's-Hope. What a godsend! In truth, he would still have to either walk the remaining three-quarter-mile distance between the site of the works at the Richmond Bridge and the junction with the church/school and the rum shop and George Street in Glamorgan or wait for Lenny Job's truck to discharge its load by means of a single workman's shovel. But not only was he not a man of great patience, he could and would also use the walking time to think things through, the pressing fact of the matter being that the family had a dead to bury.

By the time he arrived at the junction, he had decided to go and see cousin Sydney, Tanty Etho's husband, a relative who shared the Nurse surname. This gentleman was not a relative of whom he was particularly fond; indeed, out of his presence and hearing, he, like many others, often referred to him as *Kia* or, sometimes, with a certain sarcasm, *Mr. Kia*, a name deriving from the expression *know-it-all*. Still, he knew that every now and then a flow of Kia's words would, by some unheralded miracle, transform themselves into good advice as soon as they escaped his lips. So it was that, as he reached the junction, instead of turning north onto Sheep-Pen Ridge to go home pointlessly, without result to report, he took George Street to the south and, following it as, in time, it wound its way westward, soon found himself at the relative's house. Cousin Sydney, an unhurried man who was not partial to hard work, was seated at the wooden table in the kitchen, facing an enamel plate with fried bake and fried yard-fowl eggs and a large enamel mug of chocolate tea.

"Mornin', cousin Sydney."

Kia arrested the movement of the mug toward his lips, rose from the cedarwood stool Pappy had made for Tanty Etho when she had become weary of waiting on her husband to do it, and embraced Darwin.

"My condolences," he offered. "In fact, condolences to all of us, de grieving family… de arrangement an' dem goin' good?"

"Not too good. In fac', mih come fooh arks fooh yuh advice."

Kia covered the *fry-bake an' egg* with another enamel plate, threw a kitchen towel over the mug with the chocolate tea, and led Darwin to the stairs leading up to the rented first floor of the house he and Tanty Etho and their children shared with the widowed, childless landlord, who lived alone downstairs. Kia sat on a step and motioned Darwin to sit on the next one below it. It was, he knew with confidence, in the natural order of things that people should turn to him when they needed advice on any matter, and it disturbed him that so many people not only showed no grasp of this simple fact, but even made fun of him when, every so often, out of his usual kindness, he would try to bring it to their attention. These people seemed to feel that the fact that a man was not crazy about hard work—tilling soil in the hot sun with rudimentary agricultural tools, cutting cow-feed grass under surprise "fo-day-mornin" showers—made him less than a man and indeed marked him out as a person of little or no value to the community. But one thing was for sure; he knew his own worth, and he would do the appropriate job that he knew in his heart the Good Lord had ordained for him.

"Suh w'at is our little problem now?" They each sat sideways, on one buttock, on their respective steps, in such a way that they could face each other in a diagonal sort of way, Darwin on the lower step, looking up to Kia, as was proper.

"Is nuh w'a's de problem, cousin Sydney. Is *who* is de problem! An' dat is Ramrad!"

"Ramrad? The pastor? Pastar Ramrad? Wehmek? W'y? Wwhhyy?"

Even grappling with the existing grave circumstances relating to Othnel's funeral service and burial, Darwin allowed a faint half smile of amusement to hustle at breakneck speed across his lips. He chuckled to himself. Imagine Kia couldn't figure dat out: Kia did not know it all.

"Yuh fooget Ort'nel breed Verna, Sister Kate gran'darta? Chile nuh even barn yet, de gyal still ah tote big belly—"

"Suspension!" Kia cried, in agony at the blinding light, startling Darwin, who thought for a moment that, for some unambiguous wrong he had just unwittingly committed, his elder cousin, though unordained as pastor, was nevertheless pronouncing sentence upon him. But it was only a *eureka*, he very soon realized with great relief.

"Yes, coz," he answered when he came to, "'e seh 'e nat buryin' 'im. 'E definitely nah bury am!"

The rules of the church were clear: fornication, any form of sexual activity between persons other than two persons duly joined in holy matrimony (provided, even then, that the activity took place on the marital bed itself), was a serious sin, the commission of which, if proven—by confession of one or other or both of the miscreants, or by acclamation of the village, or most painfully, by failure of the reclusive village old lady's potion—attracted the dreaded penalty of suspension, a period of separation from the church, during which the sinner was denied access to every one of God's mercies. The final, crucial mercy, the one that, with all your heart and soul, you did not want to forfeit, was that mercy on your soul that the pastor, every pastor, would ordinarily dutifully pray for on behalf of the departed in the last moment before the definitive disposal of the husk. All the villages were full of fornication—all the villages along the Windward Road, which, as the decades slowly rolled by, had remained untroubled by the intrusion of a supply of electricity or of running water and been proud hosts to the magic of innumerable moonlit nights—and even little children knew it; but action had to be seen to be taken when the evidence was clear, coherent, and cogent and, especially, visible.

"Da' is weh 'e seh, eh? Da' is weh 'e seh?"

"Yes, coz, da' is weh 'e seh!"

"Wait right here. Ah goin' an' put arn clothes." It was not, of course, that cousin Sydney was naked: it was that what you wore at home was simply called *something* and not *clothes*. In a jiffy, the elder relative emerged from the insides of the flat dressed for public consumption. He could clearly see the question marks fluttering about Darwin's lips, and he spared him the effort of uttering the words.

"Ahwi ah goh ah Raxborough, *now*—Ramrad!" he succinctly decreed.

"W'a's de use?" Darwin protested.

"Ahwi ah goh ah Raxbara!" cousin Sydney emphasized.

Pastor Ramrod was no longer in a complete mental and physical mess; he was on the horns of no dilemma. And he was as adamant as he was calm and sure-footed.

"Can't be done, gentlemen, simply can't be done. Clean against the rules."

"Pastar, yuh suspen' Ort'nel an' Ort'nel dead—dead an' garn. Garn! Yuh wuk wid Ort'nel sin over, done. Punishment of man by man done when man dead. Now ah dead man an' Gard to bargain!" Kia was hoping to conjure up a dawn of reason or a spring of compassion.

"So?"

"We doh have Otr'nel here, yuh-nuh pastar. We have 'e bady. Ort'nel deh up deh ah tark to Gard arksin' 'im to let 'im in." Darwin was delighted to see that Kia was thinking his thoughts.

"Brethren, I have prayed about this, and God has given me my answer. The answer is no. I—"

"Jes' lemme finish, Pastar. Arl ahwisuh ah arks fa' ah fuh you to 'llow de bady in the chu'ch—de bady, nat Ort'nel, becaw Ort'nel done garn arready—'llow een de bady, gi' it a service, then arks Gard fuh mercy 'pan Ort'nel soul!"

When cousin Sydney wanted to sound respectful to people who spoke standard English, he made a concerted attempt, no matter how alarming the result, to do likewise; similarly, the depth of his contempt for an interlocutor could be measured with some precision by the purposefulness with which he jettisoned all such attempts. On the evidence, it was clear that cousin Sydney was not happy with the pastor.

"Brethren, I prayed about this. God says *no*. There really is nothing—"

"Look, yuh jes' irritatin' mih, yuh hayr mih, sah? Yuh jes irritatin' mih! Mih garn!"

Cousin Sydney rose and headed for the door, Darwin determinedly in train.

John-Boy's driving-instructor car was parked on the left-hand side of the Windward Road, just beyond the magistrates' court and just before the little police station, facing west. All the windows were down, but there was no sign of John-Boy's head or arms popping up from a sitting or supine position. The windows were down, and not wound up for any fear of theft—an act that, in Roxborough, as indeed in any Tobago village at that time, would, as rare occurrences attested, attract a near-death experience occasioned by a beating (often described in subsequent recounting, in gatherings in the open air under a moonlit sky, as *a sound cut-arse*) administered by any random group of villagers—obviously only because there was no sign of any impending tropical downpour. Darwin and cousin Sydney glanced at each other quickly, and cousin Sydney nodded in the direction of the car. Doing as thus directed, Darwin went up to the car and, bending forward a little, peeped inside to make sure that a so-far invisible John-Boy was not, by any chance, merely taking a midday siesta, perhaps stretched out on the back seat. Straightening up again, Darwin shot a negative shake of his head in the direction of Kia.

# Chapter 11

Years later, in a pleasing Catholic backyard in London, there would come back to intrigue and lightly disturb my mind Pastor Ramrod's earlier predicament. But that was not altogether the first time I was remembering it: there was the time two years or so after Othnel's death when I was compelled to miss the *Spanish orals* section of the Cambridge University school certificate examinations and, around that same time, watch Vicki, Mammy's stepsister (informally adopted like herself), though carrying the suitor's baby, bludgeoned by the gum-of-aloes outpourings of well-meaning parents into turning down an earnest proposal of marriage. It had all been a lot for my whirling head to handle, for it was not long after that time, too, that Nessa perished in childbirth.

Second only to Nessa's going away for good just like that, the ice-cold denial of Vicki's chance at happiness ceaselessly shook me. It may or may not be true that *when beggars die, there are no comets seen*, yet of every such noteworthy occurrence, time must surely pause to make at least a miniscule fine-print footnote. What is beyond dispute, though, is that nowhere in the march of time was there a blink to mark a marriage of Vicki, for no one ever asked for her hand again; and after serving out her inevitable suspension, she continued to raise her daughter alone, if with a little help still from Granny and Grampa. The erstwhile suitor, an Anglican from Pembroke, married a Methodist girl from Mt. St. George and, from all accounts, lived with her a reasonably happy life. Months before that marriage, Morro had told me about the relationship that led up to it, when I had gone, as I did from time to time, to spend a Saturday night at his family home at Mt. St. George. We talked about many things, and I could not leave out Vicki's situation, which had left a deep impression on my mind.

"Weh yuh t'ink 'bout dat, bway?" I asked Morro.

He had been a pupil-teacher—his coveted apprenticeship a just reward for having topped the postprimary standard 7 class at the Scarborough Methodist School—before, like the rest of us, and a little bit to his annoyance, he entered at the form 1 level at Elizabeth's College, with his age two years and a bit above the average of the class, but to us his classmates, notwithstanding certain thoughts about him that we lavishly expressed in his absence, much more than the two years and a bit if measured by what seemed the maturity gulf. He knew it and was suitably magisterial in his dealings with us, indeed quite often only minutely short of condescending. For me personally, it was secretly a source of no little satisfaction to be regarded as intelligent enough and mature enough to merit the odd complete conversation with him. To be invited time and again to spend a Saturday night (Friday night and Saturday would have been included if it had been possible, he assured me) at his family home, perched on the hill rising sharply northward from the edge of the winding Windward Road and looking down imperiously at the silvery sea whose shorebound waves in turn lashed and gently lapped at the rocky coastline to the south—to be so invited was scarcely short of honor.

"Eh?" I pressed as, after his usual fashion, he stayed silent and garnished his countenance with an aspect of deep thought as he smirked and scratched his head with his left middle finger while stroking his little teenager's beard with his right index finger, conspiring with his thumb.

"Chupidniss," he pronounced at last. "Doltishness!"

*Ah*, I thought as I uncritically awaited his profound response, *'e ah goh tark now.*

"Me ah wah Met'odis', an' w'eneva mih ready m'ah married anybody mih want… well, any Christian, becarze mih nuh know nutten 'bout de res' ah dem."

"Mih 'gree," I supported. "Dis t'ing…"

"*You* cyahn know dis, buh de fella who breed yuh auntie Vicki, 'e deh wid a gyal fra' fooh-me chu'ch now. Mih hayr dem ah married nex' couple month. Mih glad fooh shi."

It had been mere weeks before that when I had discussed with him how I had no choice but to miss the Spanish orals and lose the marks attaching to them, perhaps to the detriment of my final grade. The times in which we were growing up were times less tolerant and less accommodating of other people's religious beliefs, and the orals had been unchangeably scheduled for a Saturday, a Sabbath Day, and Pappy saw in the resulting clash of hopes and aspirations no occasion for soul-searching as there was no question of risking offense to God just for the sake of getting a few more marks and, perhaps, an outstanding final grade. "*You* tell me," he had said rhetorically, "*what does it profit a man if he gain the whole world and lose his own soul?*" It seemed a lot like what, in years much later, I would come to know as a do-you-still-beat-your-wife type of question, a formulation that delivered knowledge and understanding that would, however, not have helped me then, even if I had had it, as I would yet have divined no suitable reply and, accordingly, still have held my peace. Morro was sympathetic when I told him about it, but uncharacteristically, he seemed to have no piece of practical wisdom to offer.

"Bway, arl mih cyah tell yuh ah weh mih tell yuh w'en yuh dardy stap yuh fram goin' t'eatre fooh si *Julius Caesar*. Yuh 'member dat?"

As a matter of fact, the *Julius Caesar* matter, too, had scarred me not long before. Except for the fledgling offerings of the odd school or church performance, we didn't at all have theater on our little island. The show that I had had to forego was a movie at our lone cinema, in the faraway capital of Scarborough. *Julius Caesar* was the Shakespeare play on the English literature syllabus for the Cambridge school certificate examinations for that year, and the cinema owners had smartly programmed the screening of the movie for three consecutive Friday evenings to accommodate a captive high school audience of students and teachers. The school principal, Mr. Moreno, who was buying all the tickets for us students, took some time to realize that it was doubly impossible for me to attend the show: not only was attendance at a cinema prohibited altogether, but so, too, between Friday's sunset and Saturday's, was any activity save, in one form or another, worship.

"No, sir," I had advised the principal with complete confidence, "I don't think your going to see my father would not help. More than that, it would simply be completely useless."

"Oh no, no," he said, smiling with confidence sufficient to match mine, "I have met your father, and he's a very sharp man—it's for your exam, you know!"

Alejandro Moreno was, of course, perfectly correct. Pappy, who had never quite finished primary school, was blessed with keen intelligence and an impressively logical mind. There could be little doubt that he would at once perceive the tremendous advantage to be gained from my seeing the movie, especially given his notorious determination and commitment to the project of my secondary and, indeed, further, education. But Mr. Moreno had no insight, could have no insight, where what was in play was Pappy's relationship with the Sabbath.

"I failed you," the principal reported back. "You must be very upset, very disappointed."

"No, sir. It is what I expected, sir. I have a great and loving father."

But it was the Catholic priest in the backyard in London many years later who brought back Pastor Ramrod most vividly to my mind. I had called for an appointment, and Father O'Mally's secretary had returned to the telephone with the news that he would receive me at the Dwellings the following Saturday, at a place and time that took me to St. John's Wood on a beautiful sunny morning in late spring. The little secondhand red car I was driving looked completely out of place when I glanced back at it parked in a Visitor slot on the far, northern, side of the road, but I wasn't fazed. I'd bought it for a few hundred quid, and it was working like a dream, so much so that, years later, when I had finally bought the Mercedes Benz I had always craved, I refused to get rid of it. Still, that Benz, if I had had it then, would have fitted in better, parked in that Visitor slot in St. John's Wood. I faced the house again, unlatched and pulled open the little gate, and climbed the three small steps to the front-door bell. At my second press, a uniformed woman in her midfifties opened the door.

"Mr. Brougham?" she half-asked and half-declared. "Please come this way."

I had long learned, with some surprise, not only not to expect anything remotely resembling *BBC English* all about on the streets of the ancient capital city, but also, on those streets, as well as all over the city, and all over England, and all over the United Kingdom as a whole, to be on the lookout for English in all the glory and the delight of her varied and ubiquitous forms and manifestations. Though she must have lived in England for quite long, this housekeeper was not English, as I could readily discern. She led me into the house, through the living room, with two of its four walls fully commandeered by elegant, overpopulated bookshelves rising from floor to ceiling, just past the dining room, down whose southern side ran railings for the ones who needed them for aid to get down the to the study or the guidance room.

"Come on," she urged as I hesitated at the top of the stairway, "Father is in the garden. He's waiting for you."

I passed by the open door of the study and, peering through it, noticed that to there, too, the simple elegance of the house and the surroundings extended. My mind constructed for priest a self-confident, committed, earnest humanist averse to inflexibility, for I had met ones like that before. My mind gladdened itself and began to bathe in a sea of satisfaction, riding on its languid waves, when the priest, almost immediately, offered me a choice between lager and bitter, for the fruit of its anticipation clearly was not Babel.

The table, castled by four chairs, stood in the shade of a breezy willow tree, a huge garden umbrella planted watchfully nearby, keeping an eye on the subtly changing angles of the sun's rays and on any darkening intentions that the sky's clouds might betray.

"Welcome, Mr. Brougham. Wonderful morning, wonderful morning. Do have a seat. Sit down, please have a seat. Would you have a bitter... a lager?"

As Seventh-Day Adventists, we couldn't go to the cinema—the t'eatre, as the heathens who did go called it—thanks to one of the numerous arcane conceptualizations of evil espoused by our church, but we had heard of that famous moviemaker of our times, Metro-Goldwyn-Mayer, MGM for short. MGM was a name with which we would christen a person, of whatever generation, who, mouth once triggered, could not, or would not, allow anybody else to get a word in edgewise, a name that meant, not moviemaker, but *machine-gun-mouth*.

Father O'Mally did not rise to greet me but, as he spoke, held the mug with his bitter firmly between the fingers of his right hand while liberally gesturing me with his expansive right arm toward the chair, that section of the castle, directly opposite him. While the expanse of his girth and the industriousness of his right hand satisfied me that I could scarcely have expected him to rise and welcome me with a handshake, it came as a surprise to me that (on the evidence before me) he was an MGM. Still, it may well be that I had been myself the proximate cause of the word-rush, for, on the back of my surprise itself, I had hesitated and not sat down at Father's first bidding.

"Good morning, Father. It's a beautiful day. I wouldn't mind a lager, thank you." I did not feel in any way bound, even being in Britain as I was, to do like the British.

"Sean," he called out, "please bring a lager for Mr. Brougham." Then, turning to me, "Mrs. O'Reilly's husband," he explained, "my total household staff."

I raised an eyebrow.

"Of course, Mrs. O'Reilly is—"

"Yes, the housekeeper."

"So," Father said, taking a sip from the mug, "what brings you here, Mr. Brougham? Where do you attend Holy Mass? Or are you new to London?"

There was nothing particularly holy about the performances of barely clad masqueraders—nearly all the female ones—in Port of Spain and San Fernando on a Carnival Tuesday afternoon, and those performances were the only mas' that that question brought immediately to my mind, but I left that automatic response unspoken.

I thought now that the initial gunfire had had nothing to do with me at all: the man was an inherent MGM.

Sean turned out to be a tall, slim man with a congenial rum-face (or, perhaps more appropriately, Guinness-face) reminiscent of Gokool's, and he looked elegant in his uniform.

"Would this be suitable, sir?" he asked as he set down my drink on the table, showing no particular interest in any reply I might choose to make.

"Thank you." I wasn't concerned with responding to his purely perfunctory inquiry, but idly marveling at how often opposites do indeed seem to attract, I reflected on the dexterity of the descent of his right arm from the serving tray to the table, where he rested the beer mug.

The frost on the skin of the mug, ephemeral though it might be, combined and conspired now with the silently purring froth within it (a fetal snowcapped mountain that rose above the level of the mug's rim) to make my throat burn a bit while my unruly mouth watered. I restrained myself and ignored the absurd urge to grab the mug with both hands and take in a good mouthful; instead, I lifted the mug to my lips in a proper manner, sipped, and in an achievement that I viewed with some satisfaction, did not follow up with any application of the back of my right hand to the froth on my fledgling moustache. In any event, Sean, doubtless a man who in an instant became one and kindred with any person treating a splendid drink with due appreciation, did the job for me as, quite without being conscious of it, he drew the back of his right hand across his mouth, wiping imaginary froth from his own lips.

"Cheers!" Father put in, highlighting my omission, sipping at his own mug again.

"Thank you, Father." I was somewhat dismayed that I hadn't cheered him before greedily taking ahold of my own mug, but now I wondered what I would have said anyway: I had never had a drink with a priest (or pastor) before, and even now, after he had done it, I had found myself unable to respond to him with a "Cheers!"

"So what can I do for you today, Mr. Brougham?"

"My son, I would like to arrange his baptism."

He took a rather decent mouthful of his bitter. "Where do you live? Where do you attend Holy Mass?"

I paused long enough to wonder a little if he couldn't just leave the *holy* alone for a bit.

"Father, I'm new to London... and in any event, I'm not a Catholic."

He coughed violently and spilled bitter on the glass-topped table. He looked me over with disbelief on his face. He shook his head and said something inaudible and then finished the rest of the bitter in two substantial mouthfuls before putting the mug down on the table's glass top with an unintended bang.

"Sean!"

Almost immediately the houseman appeared, carrying another mug with bitter, having put down which, he lifted his eyebrows and looked first at me and then at his master, who instantly understood.

"Another?" the master inquired of me.

"Not just yet. Thanks, Father."

"Not a Catholic, you said? I did hear you right, that's what you said?"

"That's correct, Father."

"Well, I can't help you. I can't help you! I cannot help you, sir."

I remembered at once both Pastor Ramrod and the brilliant young priest at St. Mary's College back home who, when I had finally found the courage to ask him if he truly believed every word of what he taught the flock, paused for a moment before replying, "That's none of your business!" and briskly striding away. One way or the other, there seemed to be nobody you could confidently turn to in times of a certain kind of need.

"Father," I said, using a little mouthful for pause, "this has to do with my son's soul!"

"Is your wife a Catholic?"

"'Fraid not, Father."

"I can't, I can't—"

"Father—"

"I can't baptize somebody when there's nobody to guarantee he will be brought up as a good Catholic... simple as that, Mr. Brougham!"

"*Somebody*, Father? He's not just a somebody, he's a baby!"

"Isn't a baby somebody? Isn't even a fetus somebody, never mind what the pro-abortionists say?"

"Father! Father, isn't a heathen like myself bringing a soul to you to be baptized in the hope of salvation a kind of fetus, a fetal Catholic, to be nurtured?"

"Mr. Brougham, are you prepared to become a Catholic before I baptize your son?"

"No."

"Your wife, would she be prepared to do it?"

"Very, very unlikely, Father!"

"Well, then, that's it, Mr. Brougham. Would you like another lager before you go? *I'm* having another bitter."

"No, thanks, Father," I returned as I rose to take my leave.

"One last thing, Mr. Brougham, do you even believe in God?"

"Father, I'm sure it cannot be your intention to suggest that to not be a Catholic, even if you're otherwise a Christian, is to be an atheist!"

"No, but—"

"I'm anxious to give you my answer, Father, and it is this: 'The fool hath said in his heart that there is no God.' I'm not that brave, Father, and I don't count myself a fool... and I never doubt that the fool was probably just whistling in the dark."

I relished his response—a momentary look of utter bemusement that hugged him and squeezed him and seemed to want to suffocate him.

He briefly enveloped my right hand tightly with both of his before releasing one of his own and lightly tapping mine as he spoke.

"I'm truly sorry it can't be done. It was really a pleasure meeting you. In fact, I think... I can't say I'm sure... I think I can probably learn as much from you as you can from me! Perhaps you can come again some time."

"Thank you, Father." I was at once upset, bewildered, and amused and could not think of anything else to say.

He let go of my hand and called out Sean's name, and Sean appeared as if by magic and led me away from the glass-topped table and the shade of the willow tree, past the study, and up the stairs, past the dining room, to the door opening out onto St. John's Road, where my little old red car was waiting for me on the far side of the street.

As we already know, some years after the fateful trip to Pastor Ramrod's house to try again to persuade him to give Othnel a proper funeral, John-Boy would come to develop a clear preference over the driving instructor's calling for the joys of that special corner at Sammy's Food and Booze. But even as a churchgoing SDA then, he had always liked, especially when stressed, what was, in the language of all the neighboring villages, *his waters*. So when Kia, exiting the pastor's house at Roxborough on that occasion, had approached the car parked on the roadside near to the magistrates' court and verified that John-Boy was not indeed stretched out on the back seat, with Darwin in tow, he headed straight for the shop standing on the same side of the street as the pastor's house, but a few hundred yards west of it; and there they found their benefactor swilling Carib lager the way in which it should be swilled, that is to say, directly from the frosted bottle. Having made sure that he had seen them, they turned and headed back to the car and were not surprised to find that they had to wait scarcely half a minute for his arrival right on their heels.

There was stillness in the car all the way until they were beyond the borders of Roxborough and into Argyle. It was John-Boy who broke the silence.

"Suh wha'-'appen, nutten doin' wid Ramrad?"

Neither Kia nor Darwin made any reply. Although John-Boy was not a saintly Seventh-Day Adventist and had never pretended to have anything against drinking (as opposed to excess drinking), the two nonetheless disapproved of his lager-swilling and used silence to censure him—more so Kia, who, being a relatively recent convert, was full of passion for the faith. John-Boy pretended he did not know the meaning of their silence and, with his left hand, playfully patted the convert's right knee as he addressed them again.

"Ramrad even sew-up ar-yuh mout' or w'a'?"

"Be serious, man!" Kia snapped, in a modulation of which he was often more than capable. "Dis is seriaus business. Ramrad warnt ah-we-suh fooh dig wa'n hole an' drap Ortnel een deh lakka wah dead crapaud an' cover 'am up an' goh'ome. Ramrad mus-be drink rum!" In our Seventh-Day Adventist circles, it never was that a person was eccentric or was behaving strangely or irrationally; it was always that he must have drunk rum.

"Mih have ah suggestion," John-Boy persisted. "Teacher Aaron! Leh ahwi get 'im to tark to Ramrad."

That suggestion served to lift some of Kia's gloom. Sitting in the front passenger seat, he swung his knees to the right and looked directly at John-Boy.

"Yuh head full ah liquor, buh y'ah tark sense," he said.

"Great idea!" Darwin chimed in with unaccustomed vigor.

# Chapter 12

By now Teacher Aaron had already cleared his land for the rains of May and was holding discussions with the credit union about funding for the secondhand car he had in mind, but as always, he was available to render assistance wherever it seemed he could make a useful contribution.

The letter Mrs. M had taken out of the khaki mailbag at our last encounter had been frustrating: she had worked so hard to lay her hands on it, and now that she had it, she could find no trace in it of the evidence she had so confidently anticipated. All that Wilhelmina could find to write about was the satisfaction she derived from her job as a teacher and the wonderful readings in the latest edition of the quarterly. That woman couldn't be any Goody Two-Shoes: she had simply found some way to make a complete fool of her. That was very irritating, and she was going to make an example of her—in fact, of both of them.

"Aaron," she called out to him with mock tenderness one afternoon three days after she had burned the letter in a little fire in the yard at the back of the house, symbolizing somebody's pyre, "how is Leetle Willy? No leetle love-notes lately?"

"Pleeasee, not again! I'm up to here with your foolishness," he scolded as he tapped his crown with his right index finger, "and I've had a long day."

"Eets ze only thing long you—"

"Don't, Jenny! Not again! Please, I beg you." Teacher Aaron was exceedingly angry and felt himself atypically on the verge of losing his self-control. Recognizing this, Mrs. M, in a fit of wisdom, turned sharply and hustled out of his presence.

Tobago, the island, lies east-west upon the waters of the Caribbean Sea, but the east-west is not a simple east-west, because as you move eastward from Crown Point, you are due east-northeast as the land gradually shifts its shoulders toward Northside. While Teacher Aaron grew up in Glamorgan, Wilhelmina hailed from Buccoo, Lowside, and they had first met, he pushing twenty-one and she in her midteens, at a Young People's Convention hosted by the church in Scarborough. After that, although they had exchanged many a platonic letter, they had met only a few times, at similar functions organized by the church for the benefit of the youth, she all the while struggling valiantly to conceal her deep attraction to him. It was written in the Holy Book that husband and wife should not be "unequally yoked," and she had not, as he had, received a secondary education at the Harmon School of Seventh-Day Adventists, at that time in the heart of the town, but nowadays located at Government House Road on the way out of Scarborough toward Moriah and Northside. She would just have to manage all her deep longings and keep them to herself.

The young Aaron Millington was not yet twenty-two when he went off to Trinidad to train as a teacher at the Caribbean Union College of Seventh-Day Adventists. Sometimes he attended church at San Juan, but it was at a youth conference at the Caribbean Union Headquarters at St. Augustine that he met the future Mrs. M, at that time Mlle. Genevieve La Roque, daughter of a francophone family from Dominica who had come to Trinidad for the occasion and was staying with the Lestrades of Curepe, a family that had emigrated from Dominica to Trinidad many years before. In the meantime, Mina, as she was generally known, was receiving her training in the pupil-teacher system at the Moriah Seventh-Day Adventist Elementary School.

The St. Augustine conference took place over the Easter weekend, and Jenny would be staying over with her host family at Curepe for ten days afterward. The young Aaron took quite a liking to her and felt a desperate need to abandon the family plan for him to return to Tobago for the three-week school break in order to assist in the preparation of the land for planting as the May rains came. To stand any chance of convincing the family to allow him to remain in Trinidad, he would at least have to be able to say that he had secured a job. It wouldn't have mattered to the family that they might still have to supplement his earnings so he could meet his living expenses, as long as they could, while suppressing their grins of pleasure and delight, tell the folks in Glamorgan and the surrounding villages that "de bway ge' wah good, good jab ah Trinidad yuh-nuh" and listen to the music of their replies, "W'a'! De bway ah du good. 'E ah du good, good. Buh e behn always bright, eh, bright like a bulb!" Aaron could run through the entire scenes in his mind in advance, and he grinned with satisfaction when, after the interview at the Imperial College of Tropical Agriculture, located just south of the Union Headquarters, they told him he was hired as temporary substitute for the filing clerk, who would be proceeding on fifteen working days' vacation the following day. He did not even hear when the bursar later informed him that his salary would be "four pounds ten per month," since the salary was in no way whatsoever a detail that concerned him.

Aaron worked during the brief Easter break and again for most of the long vacation (which, later, in our tropical isles—as the years rolled by and the world grew smaller and we lost our grip on our little corner of it—became the *summer vacation*). With his inborn thrift, he was in time able to live and save enough to get to Dominica by boat and spend four days there, happy to sleep on a cot in the La Roque living room. The family took to him.

"So vhen zu you feenish ze training?"

"It's two academic years. I've just completed the first. I'll finish in May… next year."

"You go back to Tobague to teach."

"Ye-yes. Er, that's the plan…"

"Your fadda eez a farmer."

Aaron said yes but felt uncomfortable, guilty even, as if he had just lied: farmers, from what he had read, were men with tractors and other machinery, not poor folk in rural Tobago laboring with cutlasses and hoes, when not their bare hands. He paused. *Ah, but come to think of it, it was not a lie at all: peasant farmers are farmers too.* He felt far less guilty.

Without prompt, and almost as if talking to himself, he said, barely aloud, "Yes, my pappy is a farmer."

Before his trip to Trinidad the September gone, Aaron had never left Tobago. Now, in no time at all, he had moved farther afield and spent a very enjoyable four days in another Caribbean island altogether. He was on top of the world as he landed back on Trinidad and Tobago (well, strictly speaking, Trinidad) soil. He made his way straight to the college and checked in. As he turned to go to his room, the accommodations officer called out, "Oh, wait a minute, there's mail for you." It was a sealed envelope of greeting card size bearing his name in outstanding penmanship that seemed somehow familiar, and he decided he would open it after the shower that he could not wait any longer to have.

Sitting at the edge of the bed later, scratching his head with all his right-hand fingers, he felt no compulsion to go to Tobago for the October wedding. Not only was there no money available for a trip for that kind of purpose (if, indeed, for any purpose at all), but also, he was determined to give his full attention to his studies during the new term: he wanted to make sure and keep his grades up in order to seal graduation in June, not with a bare pass, but at a level that would allow his parents and relatives, as they went about their daily business in Glamorgan and the adjacent villages for months to come, to mention, with feigned reluctance, but at every conceivable opportunity, how surprisingly well the boy had done at CUC. He knew well that to fall short of their expectations in that regard and deny them the pleasure of recounting, over and over, their joyous surprise at his achievement would lead to their everlasting distress, a distress that would be all the more painful to him for remaining unspoken. Also at the back of his mind was the possibility of working for three weeks or so during December and then spending Christmas in Dominica. In any event, whether he made it to Dominica or not, it would be good to earn some money during the December holidays. It was true that the only holiday jobs available at that time of year might be clerical or porter positions in hardware and grocery and general dry-goods stores, but even if he had to be a porter, the family didn't necessarily have to be made aware of that inconvenient detail.

Between the time he resumed at CUC and December's arrival, he and Jenny exchanged three or four letters. Considering the way she vocalized her English, he was delighted with the way she wrote it—not that if it had been otherwise, that would, in any particular, have interfered with his ever-deepening feelings for her. The proximity of the Caribbean islands to one another did not mean that the delivery time for mail as among them was shorter than for mail between one or the other of them and, say, the mother country. And to communicate by telephone required meticulous advance planning and stringent synchronization. The letters took, on average, twelve days either way, and they managed two telephone calls during the entire period. With these telephone calls, it was touch-and-go each time as the particular letters, the one to the other, had crossed each other on the way. In fact, they had had to set up the second call twice.

"Oh, mon dieu!" she cried at the start of the third call. "You *zid* get my letter ziss time, I'm so glad. 'Ow are you?" All seemingly in a single breath.

"Yes, yes. You mean you didn't get mine yet! Twelve days now I posted it!"

"Vell, zoz it matter now? Vit some luck, I may even get it tomorrow before I leave."

"You're right. The important thing is that we're going to meet for Christmas. Which Lestrade is meeting you?"

"Eustace. Ze boat should arrive around midday… Oh, and zay 'ave agreed vit my parents zat you are invited for one o'clock Chreesmas Day."

He had indeed secured a holiday job as a porter at a supermarket. He had not regarded it as really and truly a lie to tell his parents that it was a clerical position. If you thought about it, it was not a simple case of lifting up customers' Christmas purchases and toting them in trolleys to their cars in the parking lot: to sort out the varying types of groceries and bag them appropriately in the separate plastic shopping bags before packing them intelligently in the carts was clearly a clerical thing. Besides, look at the tips that came with doing what he was doing and which would not come with a conventional clerical job! If what he had told his parents was a lie at all, it was a white one, and therefore not a bad one, which made him feel better about himself. As his thoughts wandered along that path, he fleetingly wondered if the fact that Jenny, being mulatto-ish, was what they called a high-color woman had anything to do with the way he felt about her.

"Perhaps not!" He meant to say that quietly to himself and was startled by the sound of it coming out loud and by the reaction of Telco's (the telephone company's) other customers in the phone booth room.

"What does it matter, anyway?" he asked himself, silently this time. "It's part of who she is, part of the whole appealing package… I dunno!"

He had not had the heart to tell his parents he would rather go back to Dominica than come home for Christmas. It was true that as Seventh-Day Adventists, they were ambivalent about Christmas celebrations and dealt with their dilemma by celebrating half-joyously. Their objection was that there was no evidence in the Good Book that Christ was born on December 25, and there was no record anywhere of his true date of birth. Admittedly, it would, in those circumstances, be no bad thing to pick a day and celebrate on it the fact that he had been born at all: the problem was December 25 itself, which, as records showed, had in fact been an ancient pagan holiday, and the choice of it, in all probability, somewhere, somehow, involved carefully concealed mockery.

There had been a similar problem relative to meat-eating. It is something that had originally been forbidden, but way back in the 1860s, when the church was first beginning to be firmly established, there were important members who found the prohibition against the consumption of meat to be contrary to the spirit and intent of the Scriptures. The argument was that there were specific strictures against consuming the mortal remains of pigs, cold-blooded animals, and web-footed birds: if it had been the will of God to ban all meat-eating, the Scriptures would surely have said so in blanket fashion. In a commendable act of atypical compromise, the church made meat-eating optional and urged those members who felt they must have meat to commit themselves to consuming as little of it as possible. He would not have the inevitable ham offered at the Lestrade house on Christmas Day, but he certainly expected to relish the turkey and the beef or chicken pastelles. As things turned out, Dominica had been ruled completely out of the question. It was not that he had never begun writing the letter indicating to the family that he proposed spending the Christmas in that island; in fact, he had done so three times, but each time he had, at some uneasy point, consigned his effort to the wastepaper basket and, in consequence, had, in his second telephone call, suggested to Jenny that, as he would have to work until late on Christmas Eve and could thus not possibly have time for the journey, she might try to persuade her folks to allow her to spend the holidays with the Lestrades.

He couldn't visit her at Curepe on Christmas Eve: that was one of the most profitable business days for supermarkets, and as usual, they had, each and every one, persistently advertised in advance that they would remain open long enough on that day to serve every customer who walked through their doors before 10:00 p.m. As it turned out, it was almost midnight when he got back home to the furnished room he had rented from an elderly couple at St. Joseph, not far from the convent, the prestigious girls' high school, less than a mile away from the supermarket at St. Augustine. He was tired but happy that he had had the foresight to alert Jenny in good time that that was how his working day was likely to end.

As was the common style in the country in those days, the room available for rent—or, supposedly, for the accommodation of grown-up, unmarried male children of owner-families—was the kind that the well-oiled stealth of effective marketing would, as the years rolled by, come to rechristen studio apartment, and was completely walled off, the only door leading from it into the rest of the house being permanently locked, with the studio dressing table jammed against it and the matriarch of the house in clenched, non-negotiable possession of all related keys; and it boasted its separate entrance leading into it from the common veranda. And although, in towns like St. Joseph, Trinidad's original capital city, houses were built with indoor bathrooms, the relevant facilities for this kind of extramural room in a house were located at some discreet and inconspicuous nearby spot, in the open air. To that outdoor place at that house, Aaron now repaired, exiting the room onto the veranda, then down the four-step stairs, his towel wrapped around him, to think of Christmas Day and Jenny as he showered.

\* \* \* \* \*

The big day was slightly more than eight hours old when he was surprised by a knock at his door. He'd been awake for more than an hour, but his still-tired body kept him lying in bed, his mind, now deliciously lazy, now jubilant, caressing Jenny's mulatto curls in daylight dreams.

"Good morning. Merry Christmas!" came a voice clarifying the meaning of the knock.

"Good morning," Aaron returned, rubbing his eyes with the back of his hand. "Merry Christmas. Just a minute, please."

He hurriedly pulled a pair of short pants over the jockey shorts in which he had slept and pulled a polo shirt over his head down onto his trunk, feeling fully as awake as the stoic mannequins with wooden shotguns in hand as they took imaginary aim, designed by clever Tobagonian villagers to scare away from their cornfields those voracious yellow-tail birds they mysteriously called *poggohs*.

He got to the door as fast as he could in the circumstances and instantly felt as alive as a poggoh exiting its pear-shaped nest to sway alone in the breeze, where it hung in space from a branch of an immortelle tree aiming to descend in delight upon the rewards of an unmannequinned cornfield, for before him stood a lady of an attractiveness noticeably beyond average, bearing Christmas breakfast on a tray.

"Mer-Merry Christmas… I-I mean… again!"

For perhaps the thousandth time in her life, she smiled with satisfaction at the uncontrived, unarticulated compliment of an appreciative man whom her good looks and alluring shapeliness had surprised. But her mother and a little experience had taught her that good looks and alluring shapeliness, like any other kind of riches, could be a curse, if you let them fashion the insides of your head. She had never let her particular riches overwhelm her. She took in stride all shows of recognition of them, subduing externally the considerable pleasure they in fact brought her. This Christmas morning it was no different.

"Again?" The innocence in her voice was feigned, but without malice, because all she wanted to do was prolong his awkwardness for one or two more delicious seconds.

"Well... well, when you called out my name..."

As soon as he heard himself say that, and even before he beheld her facial expression of mild surprise and total empathy, he knew his claim was wholly inaccurate and, further, that it constituted a broadcasting of the effect her beauty was having on him. That realization was strangely liberating: at the end of the day, we all liked to be loved, and she might well regard it as a just reward for her thoughtfulness in bringing him breakfast. She, for her part, felt just then that he had fully paid for his breakfast in the highly convertible currency of awkwardness born of genuine appreciation. And she had no wish to overcharge.

"Oh, I just came by to bring Christmas breakfast for my parents, and my mum said there was quite enough to share with you... Must get back before the rest of the family starve to death."

Taking the tray from her extended arms, he said, "Mer-Merry... have a great day!"

"You, too! Oh, by the way, I'm Sonya."

"Aaron... Aaron Millington."

"I know."

Forgiving Sonya, he immediately removed the two slices of ham from the plate, soaked a paper napkin with water from the sink tap, rubbed the napkin on his bar of bath soap, and proceeded to scrub with passion the spot on the plate where the ham had lain. The purification duly done, he enjoyed fully the two buttered slices of bread fresh from the overnight Christmas oven, the sunny-side-up egg, the cheese slices, and the little mug of chocolate tea. The awkwardness he had endured at the sight of Sonya was a small price to pay for that breakfast. But what was he saying, anyhow, when the sight of her was not price but rather lagniappe?

Why did some Tobago people delight in calling it *niggeritis* when, in truth, the surreptitious stream on which your consciousness, under certain circumstances, glides away, way out of your reach, after a good meal, into the temporary death of uninvited slumber, must, without doubt, lurk and lie in wait somewhere inside all creatures that ever doze? Of course, he mused, their reference could be to mere special tendency or predilection, in which case, applying a similar consideration, a former secretary for agriculture in the then United States cabinet (long before the era of Trump, when euphemism lost its way completely) might well have found a way to avoid loss of office if he had had the good sense to omit the *all* from his lofty, confident *ex-cathedra* declaration that *all a nigger wants in life is comfortable shoes, a tight pussy, and a warm place to shit*, making it, perhaps, a little less easy to justify the immediate indication he received from the president that an appropriate letter from him was being very anxiously awaited.

All the same, it was already past eleven when Aaron was conscious again. The last thing he recalled doing was placing his open right palm over his mouth and, without deliberate intent, looking about him sharply in expectation of a tongue-lashing from one or other of his parents—or, indeed, from any *big person* native of Glamorgan, or of some adjacent village, who happened to be nearby—because he had just belched audibly. Now his eyes, even if still half asleep themselves, darted about him as, without his permission, they sought out any *big people* who might somehow happen to be there. But the result of this spatial examination, authorized or not, brought him welcome relief, and he leaped out of bed.

He did not expect, on Christmas Day, to find at the bottom of the Abercromby Street hill that took him to the Eastern Main Road any form of public transportation, be it bus or *route taxi*, there to spare him the pain of legging it to Curepe. He had no time to lose. True, it was December, and if he was lucky, he could encounter a temperature below seventy-five degrees and he would not sweat too much as he walked. Still, he needed time to shower, much more diligently than usual, and to apply his antiperspirant and cologne with care sufficient to ensure preemptive strike against unwelcome body odor while, at the same time, preventing a possible perception of over-exuberant splashing. Presenting his person in proper light was particularly important as he had not had the foresight or the good sense to get, at whatever cost, a present for the Lestrade household, not to mention Jenny.

He considered taking Farm Road, which ran somewhat diagonally from the Eastern Main Road in St. Joseph to the Southern Main Road and his destination in Curepe, but abandoned the idea as the Farm Road option would kill any chance of access to public transportation and diminish the possibility of the offer of a ride from some considerate private vehicle driver. He made himself ready in good time, headed east, and getting to Curepe Junction, turned right onto the Southern Main Road. Presently, he rang the doorbell and waited.

"Merry Christmas, ma'am," he greeted Mrs. Lestrade as she opened the door.

"And to you, Aaron. Do come in."

She led the way into the living-dining room, and as he entered it, his eyes could not help catching, at the far end bordering on the kitchen, the sight of the colorful, Christmassy paper napkins lying neatly on the table, seemingly set for eight; and after what it had taken him to get there on foot, that sight and the aroma coming from the kitchen first gladdened his heart a great deal and then made him hungry. Mrs. Lestrade's voice refocused his attention upon the more immediate requirements.

"Mr. Lestrade," she said, gesturing, right arm outstretched with palm facing upward, toward the head of the family, "I don't think you met him last time."

"Merry Christmas, sir."

"Have a seat, young man," replied the father, who seldom paid any notice to perfunctory expressions of any kind.

Recalling that there were two brothers abroad, Aaron greeted the three sisters and Eustace before settling himself into the proffered sitting room chair.

"Rum? Whiskey?" Eustace inquired.

"No, thanks. But anything soft would be okay." It was not that he was unlike John-Boy and scrupulously and at all times observed the church's strict prohibition against the consumption of alcohol, but he knew well how he felt about Jenny and that some sort of report would at some stage reach back to her people in Dominica. They, like the Lestrades, were, of course, with their historical French influences, Catholics and, always delighting in the enjoyment of a glass of good wine, had never found anything wrong either with the savor of a properly mixed alcoholic beverage; but he had to mind his image until they knew him better, lest he unwittingly gave them early cause to wonder about his commitment to the rules under which he had been raised.

## Chapter 13

Besides, he had no intention of denying himself the pleasure of the inevitable black cake with its delightful core ingredient of fruits, erstwhile fresh, but in time sliced up and soaked for many patient months in some choice blend of rum, or of the subtle smoothness of the rum-based *ponche-a-crème* drink gliding down his gullet, the taste of its rum ingredient, mingled with the beaten, rind-flavored egg white, lingering on his gleeful tongue while its aroma flitted playfully around and about his nostrils as they flared in deep appreciation. Thinking about all this, he was soon pleased with himself again.

"Sorrell, then?" asked Eustace, waking him up afresh.

"Oh, yes. Capital! That would be very good, thanks."

The words had barely escaped his lips when he saw Jenny appear at the bottom of the stairs, elegantly dressed in an ankle-length skirt, fitting neatly on her slender hips but flaring near the floor, and a bodice of pale orange. Although his knees were shaking more than a little bit and he felt certain that it was in his interest not to trust them, he immediately rose to greet her. She walked straight over to where he stood, and he said, "Merry Christmas," in a weak voice, and then extended his right arm toward her. She, in turn, ignored the outstretched arm and proffered her left cheek, and only after he had kissed it did she say "Merry Christmas" in return. By now to him it felt as if the shaking of his knees had grown exceedingly violent, and by the time she had taken her seat and he could properly do the same, he could feel the dampness of the sweat on his back.

He did not dare to take the glass of sorrel into his hand when Eustace handed it to him, because there was absolutely no guarantee that he could hold it firmly in his unsteady grasp, and Eustace, sensing his predicament, obligingly set it down on the side table. Aaron was happy to join the three sisters and Jenny in the relish of that irresistible, mauve-colored, alcohol-free drink made from those faithful sorrel tree flowers that would, time after time, dutifully appear at that season of the year.

"Mum, scotch and coconut water for you, eh?" Eustace half-inquired, receiving for reply superfluous confirmation from Carmen's faint smile and her silence. He fixed that drink and then, without unnecessary reference to his dad, mixed a scotch and soda each for the master and himself.

"Merry Christmas!" they wished one another in a chorus, raising their glasses, this time Edouard, Lestrade *pere*, gladly acknowledging a rare occasion fit for measured exclamation.

The meal was delicious, his enjoyment of it, though, slightly diminished by a touch of guilt brought on by nagging thoughts of the inevitably less elaborate table being enjoyed by his folks in Glamorgan and by a feeling not quite of nausea, but all too closely resembling it, at the sight of ham slices, pared from the bodies of swine, right there before him as he ate.

Although coffee, like tea, was on the church's prohibition list, he accepted the demitasse presented on the tray after the dessert of black cake and ponche-a-crème, unwilling to decline the offer of a drink, any kind of drink, a second time and look like what growing boys in Tobago used to call a Mr. No-Man. On the same ground, he also said yes to the *crème de menthe*. *You know you really want this woman*, he thought to himself as he sipped, *so you have to project a reasonable image*.

The crowning delight of the occasion came at around half past three as he was at the door, about to take his leave. He had been pleasantly surprised at her self-confidence, if not brazenness, when, entering the living room area soon after he arrived, she had, for all the world to witness, ignored his outstretched arm and offered him her cheek. Now she bolted ahead of Carmen and Edouard and did it again—twice; she offered first the left and then the right. This time he threw caution to the wind, as the saying goes, and let his pursed lips linger on the right cheek for an extra split second or two. Feeling, though not really caring, that he might have crossed some boundary, he briskly said the last goodbye and turned and left.

This time he took Farm Road, because he knew well that the probability of finding transportation of any sort at that hour of a Christmas Day was of a decidedly unattractive degree. But his entire body was in the grip of a great exhilaration brought on by the kisses he had been invited to plant, and he had to will his knees not to let him down but to stop the shaking, at least long enough to take him home.

He visited her once again before December 29, joining Eustace and his mother on that day as they saw her off at the Islands Wharf in Port of Spain, where she boarded the ferry for the trip back home.

The following morning at around six thirty, as he lay in bed thinking of Jenny, there was a knock on his door. Rubbing his eyes with the back of his right hand, he peeped through the wooden jalousies at the upper end of the doorframe and thought he saw his mother. He pulled himself back and rubbed his eyes with the heel of his left hand. Opening the eyes as wide as he could now, he ventured up to the jalousies afresh. Peering through, he considered with alarm that the figure at his door was indeed that of his mother. He opened the door.

"Mammy? You in Trinidad? How?"

"Well, mih nuh rayly t'ink mih deh ah Tobago right now, suh mih mus' be deh ah Trin'dad. How? By the grace of God and the TGR, by the SS *Tobago* and the train… well, an' mih foot an' dem too."

The ferries that carried goods and people between the two islands, the SS *Tobago* and the SS *Trinidad*, moved by night and arrived at their destinations, whether at Port of Spain or Scarborough, at approximately four in the morning. Like the trains, they were owned by Trinidad Government Railways, and the costs of freighting goods and of traveling by them were not unreasonable. Aaron viewed his mother's answers to his rather rapid questions as ominously and unduly comprehensive, and he immediately abandoned that line of inquiry.

"Suh, w'a' 'appen, Mammy, everyt'ing arright, everybady arright?"

"Excep' me. Man doh t'ink tuh-much, suh yuh farda accep' dat yuh decide to spen' Christmas ah Trin'dad jes' fooh suh. *He* accep' dat. *Me*? Mih come down yah fuh arks yuh wehmek yuh stap down yah fooh Christmas. W'a' 's de rayl stowry?"

He was at one and the same time relieved and uneasy: there was no catastrophe in the family, but he had been caught lying by commission and omission. Still, to him the lies were mere white lies, and if he took his time and pulled himself together, he would be able to handle the whole situation.

"Come, Ma, come in and sit down," he said gently, coaxing her.

"Mih-ah goh siddong de minute yuh gimme ah answer!"

"Ma, come in. Please!"

She relented and went into the room and sat down.

"Some Milo or chocolate tea, Ma?"

"Look yah, bway, nuh provoke me dis Baxing Day marnin', yuh hayr me. Mih nuh lef' Tobago an' come down yah fooh drink fooh-you charclit-tea or yuh Milo or yuh Ovaltine. Mih cyah ge' arl dem t'ing deh ah Tobago. Buh nobady ah Tobago cyahn tell me wehmek yuh stap down ah Trin'dad fooh Christmas."

Quietly Aaron sat down and related to his mother the details of his original meeting and of his whole relationship with Jenny.

"Suh y'ah tell mih she is a high-calar woman an' she nice, good-looking?"

"Yes, Ma!" He sensed that he might be home high and dry.

"She have lang hayr?"

"Yes, Ma, lovely long hair," he enthused.

"Bway, fooh get 'way an' come down yah mih behn haffoo tell yuh dardy seh mih dream yuh sick. Someti'ng eena mih head bin ah badda mih, badda mih, badda mih. Yuh coulda save mih plenty headache: yuh coulda seh someti'ng to *me*, becarze after arl I is yuh modda... Buh mih satisfy now. Mek some charclit-tea deh fooh mih."

## VANESSA'S NIECE

In the upshot, Jenny was invited to visit Tobago for Easter, staying, officially, at the Miranda Guesthouse in Scarborough. The Easter long weekend was hectic as usual, what with thousands of visitors going up from Trinidad. Although in theory the weekend ran until Monday, it always, in fact, culminated on Tuesday with the unique spectacle of the goat and crab races at Buccoo, which few wanted to miss. Like so many others who shad seen those races for the first time, Jenny found them engagingly quaint but highly enjoyable. Her accent had a similar effect on the people of Glamorgan, who loved her good looks and her long, flowing hair and, most of all, her high color. Friends and mere acquaintances alike, from all the nearby villages, could hardly hide the fact that they would be on the lookout for the wedding announcement.

The announcement finally came toward the end of September, not long after the start of the World War. In the interim, they had managed to exchange a couple of letters and had successfully connected for just about as many telephone calls. Europe was the world. Even before the dark clouds of war had begun to hang about the European sky, the sweethearts as well as relatives on both sides had been thinking that that unearthly long-distance approach would not do and that it was perhaps time to seal the deal. With the coming of the war, they were sure, letters would take an eternity to arrive and attempts at telephone calls would likely never succeed. The wedding took place in Glamorgan on the first Sunday in December, and it was an unusually joyful one, conducted by Pastor Preston Buddy, one of Pastor Ramrod's predecessors, a man who had been very well-liked by the congregation, not least of all for being full of compassion and wholly without airs.

All these occurrences were unknown to me during the time that Mrs. M, as I knew her to be, would waylay me and, in time, give me money, small change, to overcome me and induce me to let her rummage through that precious khaki mailbag that had been entrusted to me, heedless of the damage she was inflicting upon my seedling soul. It was only long after I had graduated from the school in Glamorgan to Mr. Moreno's high school at Roxborough and the years went by and I grew older that I heard of and understood certain things.

Now after all these years, there was this same Jenny, still with her alluring accent and her flowing hair, but now, by self-torture, rendered haggard and miserable-looking, with nothing at all to recommend her; there was this same Jenny pushing Aaron, Teacher Aaron, to fracture his long-admired calm and lose his temper as she nagged him about the letter from Wilhelmina that she had fished out of my little khaki mailbag when she had last ambushed me and bribed me into an everlasting shame, the pain of which I can barely endure, up to this day.

## Chapter 14

It was a Thursday, the day Mrs. M had accosted Teacher Aaron about the letter from Mina that she had extracted from my mailbag. The days on which Teacher Aaron would send me off at recess time to the post office in Pembroke were Tuesdays and Thursdays, but on that Thursday, there had, to my great relief, been no sight of my tormentor. The following day at school, Teacher Aaron had twice found occasion during the course of the day to say to me, "Remember, God is always watching," but both times the admonition seemed more than half out of context. And it perplexed me. It happened again on Monday, and I became all nerves. Come recess time on Tuesday, however, my eyes opened and I could see clearly that my betrayal of trust had been exposed.

"I'll come with you today," he said gently, handing me the khaki mailbag. "You need protection."

My heart began to pound without mercy against the wall of my chest, and it was only with the most extraordinary effort that I managed to suppress the incipient heaves of aggressive hyperventilation. I thought it oppressive and unfair that to bolt and run away as fast as my legs would go did not look like a smart option in all the circumstances.

"How did she do it?" Those were the first words he uttered as we headed westward to the post office, and uncannily, he spoke them just as we were about to cross the little bridge as we neared Sammy's Food-and-Booze. Did he know or sense that that was the very spot upon which I had been disgraced, or had it all happened just like that by chance? No words of possible response came together in my head, so my lips felt no need to part for speech. What I felt was a sudden chill and a recognition that my imprisoned teeth were rattling.

"Was it violence, cuddling, money?"

"Money!" I screamed out the word, startling myself but thinking, later that night as I lay awake in bed, that it had been nothing short of an involuntary act of casting out of a demon.

"All right, it's all right," he replied calmly, adding, correctly, "I'm certain that, with this, you'll never in life allow yourself to be bribed again. Think of this old saying: 'Out of evil cometh good.'"

These exchanges constituted the whole of the conversations we had on our way to the post office and back to the school. On Thursday, he sent me to the post office alone, as usual.

To my great relief and eternal gratitude, I never afterward heard anyone speak as if he knew anything about my shame, and Teacher Aaron, over all the succeeding years, never treated me other than as a good student whom he liked and trusted, just as if I had never sinned.

On Friday afternoon that same week, the church board secretary went to the school and delivered to Teacher Aaron a notice regarding a meeting of the board scheduled for the upcoming Sunday at 5:00 p.m. Two of the items on the agenda were Teacher Aaron's outstanding application for a pay increase and consideration of a certain complaint of infidelity made against him. He was being invited to make representations to the board, if he so desired, in respect of either or both matters. He asked the secretary to wait for a reply and sent back to the board by her hand two handwritten notes, one declining the offer to make representations, the other being his notice of resignation from the teaching post with immediate effect. He wasn't going to go before the board to explain to those idiots that Jenny's head was thoroughly screwed where sex was concerned; that, having been sexually abused by close relatives as a child and been unfairly blamed for it, she had a deep loathing for the idea of having sex with anyone close to her, including him, and would have preferred occasional *ad hoc* satisfaction; and that, yes, he had from time to time been unfaithful, but never with Mina and, in any event, never in Tobago.

# Chapter 15

HAVING BOUGHT THE IDEA COMING out of John-Boy's beer-lubricated mind that an approach to Teacher Aaron could yield a solution to the problem of Othnel's funeral service, Kia asked John-Boy to take them directly to Sheep-Pen Ridge, where Teacher Aaron now lived. His father had passed away the year before, and mere months afterward, his younger brother, a Works and Hydraulics inspector who had never married and liked to test the performance limits of his souped-up motorbike, had met his end in a road crash. Their mother then lived alone in the old house on the ridge surrounded by the lands her husband used to cultivate. She had long since, ruing the day that, long before she had actually met her, she had bestowed her with blessings and accepted her for daughter-in-law, written Jenny off as a "bard red 'ooman" and was glad when Teacher Aaron returned home for good.

"Good afternoon, Teach!" Kia called out when they got to the house.

Looking out through the open window, Teacher Aaron saw the three men leaning against the car and immediately went out to join them.

"Gimme a minute," he said after listening to Kia recount their tribulations and describe their encounter with Pastor Ramrod. "I'll just run inside and change quickly."

All the way to Pastor Ramrod's house at Roxborough, there was silence in John-Boy's car.

As John-Boy's faithful old Zephyr went past the little inconspicuous Roxborough Police Station on the right, a little ahead of them, the four occupants could see Pastor Ramrod's brand-new Hillman Hunter coming to a stop on the street, just past his house, on the left, obliquely opposite the dilapidated wooden courthouse standing on the right mere yards from Roxborough Bay's high-water mark, where the waves took turns lashing its protective concrete wall when the tide was in. Kia, who had been furious ever since the preacher had bought that new vehicle, once again made his feelings known at the sight of it.

"Look, Teacher Aaron! Look, Darwin!" he exclaimed, a chilling bitterness in his voice. "Look how ahwisuh tithes and afferins tu'n new an' nice an' shiny fooh Ramrad to drive!"

"Gentlemen," Teacher Aaron said, "we are here for a purpose, a very solemn purpose—to see that Othnel gets a decent funeral service. We must be cool, calm, and collected. I will handle this."

As they pulled up behind the Hunter, the pastor emerged from it, shut the driver's door, and turned toward them, where they now stood on the pavement next to the Zephyr. Curious to see Teacher Aaron in the group, he removed his spectacles with his left hand and, with the right, plucked a handkerchief from his left breast pocket. Studiously cleaning the glasses as if attempting to rid them of large volumes of indeterminate miniscule particles barely visible to the naked eye, he nonchalantly, and without looking up, thrust some words in the direction of his visitors.

"Othnel Nurse again, I suppose—and with reinforcements! Good day, Mr. Millington."

Mr. Millington! It used to be Teacher Aaron or, less informally at times, Brother Millington. The logic of the present was loud. Now that he had left his good job and become a peasant farmer and, if the village-grams were correct (as they usually were), an aspiring driving instructor (like John-Boy, who had, he understood, never even finished elementary school) and been removed from the membership roll of the church based on the undefended infidelity charges, he was no longer qualified for the honor of those or any comparable forms of address.

"Good day, sir. May I have a word with you?"

"About the body, the mortal remains, of Othnel Nurse? Is it about that?"

"No, sir! It is about the mercy of God that he has promised to all his children—and promised especially to sinners—and about the duty of those of his servants who have vowed to dispense that mercy in his name and on his behalf!"

"Nice try, but rules are rules, and the rules of the church were made under the direction of God himself and in the throes of much prayer and fasting, and I assure you that if God did not like them, he would not have allowed us to make them. And I think that, disfellowshipped though you have been, you should know better than to lead these innocent, God-fearing men astray! May God have mercy on your soul. Good day, Mr. Millington!"

Teacher Aaron said nothing more. He opened the door and lowered his body into the front passenger seat of the Zephyr, and the other three followed him into the car, Kia last of all as he paused to cast a final searing glare at the holy man.

After the echo of Kia's slammed-shut door died, away somewhere in the distance, the same old silence fell again. John-Boy used the gateway leading into the courthouse grounds to turn the Zephyr around to face west. As they were getting to the end of Argyle Village and could see the road ahead of them gradually rise to reach Bad-Rock, Kia spoke, but as if mumbling to himself.

"Dat man heart harder dan Bard-Rack boulder. Dah man is Satan se'f... nuh, nat Satan nuh, nat Satan at arl, Satan coach!"

"Weh we goh do now, Teach?" Darwin asked the peasant farmer.

"Goodwood," replied Teacher Aaron.

"Goodwood? We doh have no chu'ch dere!"

"Reverend Wentworth Granderson, that's our man. Good friend of mine."

"Buh, Teach," Kia came in, "is no' ah Metadis' chu'ch he have?"

"He is a good man... good priest, good..."

Reverend Granderson had opted for celibacy in order to devote his life not so much to the pursuit of holiness itself as to the task of helping communities structure and organize themselves for self-upliftment. He lived a simple life in the presbytery behind the church in Goodwood and took great pride in the kitchen garden he tended there, in the spare time he made for himself. Once, when a primary school girl had gotten pregnant, he had overruled the school board and insisted that the girl be allowed to continue her attendance until time for delivery and to return to continue preparation for the school leaving examination afterward. That had led to strident calls from many scandalized villagers for him to be replaced as he seemed to have no respect for the laws of God and was encouraging little girls to think it was all right to have sex and get pregnant, but he had weathered that storm as he had weathered so many others of that and other kinds in his pastoral life. When the four arrived at the presbytery, they were informed by the housekeeper that the reverend had gone into Scarborough but that she expected him back in about half an hour. They took the opportunity to drive back to Sammy's Food-and-Booze, where Kia and Darwin each had a rock cake and a Solo soft drink and Teacher Aaron had six Crix biscuits, a slice of cheese, and a glass of maubey with a couple drops of condensed milk.

The Reverend Granderson was very welcoming on their return and more than once apologized for his absence when they had first come.

"Good to see you, Aaron. Been some time. To what do I owe this pleasure?"

"Rev, we need your help urgently. If you don't mind, I'll let Sydney here tell you."

"The Nurse boy… the funeral service! Small place, Tobago. I've heard. I'll do it. You know me, Aaron. My business is serving… serving God directly and serving God through service to my fellow men. You know, we're all just passing through, you know… together. Passing through, together!"

"Mih heart satisfy!" Othnel's mother pronounced as she turned to walk away after the final rites at the graveside following the service inside the church. "Everybady come ah de fineral excep' Ramrad." And every single soul within sight and hearing of her said, in unison, "Amen!"

Me, though, I did not say "Amen" or anything else. I had not uttered many words since my acceptance on my way from school on that fateful day that the dead body lying on the ground on the other side of the drain was indeed Othnel's—and that no, there was no other Othnel that we knew of. I did not sing along in the church and had not listened to Reverend Granderson's presumably consoling words. I thought of how good the dead man had been, and I thought about the fatal cutlass wound inflicted upon Uncle Egbert's neck (his neck!) some seven years earlier, a time, too, when I had for long afterward lost all urge to speak. Death was completely as awesome as birth: the latter filled me with explosive wonder and joy and expectation, the former took ahold of me and deposited me into the swirling and unyielding grip of a belittling incomprehension and of a struggle with the notion of an abrupt return to nothingness. And for good people like Uncle Egbert and Othnel, both of whose mothers were still alive? Later on, there would, of course, be Vanessa.

# Chapter 16

Vanessa! Never can I forget the day that she withdrew from the bedroom, leaving me and Rookmin alone there, but not before she had snacked with us and handed me the fine-tooth comb, telling Rooks that she would like the way I was going to use it.

It was very awkward for both of us when Nessa left us like that. It was really strange to me how, for a long time by then, just like many of my male cousins, I used to be on the lookout for any opportunity when I could be alone with one of the girls, when, for excitement securely wrapped up in a certain unmistakeable innocence and a wild curiosity, we would touch each other's "things" and sometimes even savor the thrill of trying on each other's underwear.

In the Pint, as in all the villages around, having a supply of electricity was still a utopian pipe dream, if dream there was at all, and the acme of achievement in that respect was to own a gas lantern with a power pump instead of having to rely on a *bulldifay*. Of course, at the two great houses, homes of the respective British owners of the two huge coconut and cocoa estates that, in response to petitions duly presented, had been granted to them gratis by edict of the British Sovereign, there were battery-powered *delcos* that generated the electricity needed for basic civilized living. You could very reasonably be envious, or even full of hate, about that. But for little boys and girls curious and excited about making special acquaintance with *pu-pus* and *dingalings*, the cover of darkness, broken sometimes only by the gentle, mischievously winking light of a soft moon, was a gift from heaven. It helped, too, that at nights our favorite game was hide-and-seek, and you hid in pairs and could choose your own partner, and the perfectly legitimate aim was to hide so well that you could not be found. The eventual outcomes in these circumstances were in their own way altogether innocent and made no way for awkwardness. To be left alone with a girl deliberately on a bed with a fine-tooth comb you had been taught to use in a certain way was, however, a horse of a significantly different color.

"Suh yuh did like de ginger-bayr shi gi' ahwi?" Looking not at Rooks but at the ceiling, I could muster no more than that as the moments, seemingly hastening to multiply and become forever, went by as we each fidgeted.

"Yeah."

"Suh de ginger-bayr behn good, den?" I said stupidly after another eternity in the making.

"Yeah."

Sitting at the edge of the bed, I observed that the palms of my hands were open and rubbing my knees, and I wondered when and where I had rested down the comb. That gave me something fairly constructive to say next.

"Eh-eh! Weh de comb garn?" I exclaimed, looking about me. "Gyal, yuh si de comb anyw'ere?"

"No, mih nuh si am noway," she replied, glancing around in search of it, and even sounding a little relaxed.

Presently, turning my head backward, I could see the comb at the other side of the bed, jammed up against the wooden wall of the bedroom. Feet still planted on the floor, I lay on my back and was happy that even so, I could not reach the comb with my outstretched arm. Obviously, then, I had no choice but to use my right elbow as a fulcrum and swing my legs around and lie on my back on the bed within reach of the comb, and of her.

"Ah get it!" I announced and, turning onto my left side, began to move the fine teeth gently upward through the hair at the back of her neck left exposed by the bundle combed-up and held by hairpins at the top of her head.

"Yuh like dat?"

"Eh-eh." The negative words themselves notwithstanding, the tone and texture of her voice conveyed only a half-hearted, perfunctory, and unconvincing denial, and in any event, I could clearly see the goose bumps on her back. And I would see those goose bumps a few times in later years, before as well as during our short marriage. Still, she remained sitting on the edge of the bed, her feet hovering just above the level of the floor.

"Come an' lie down wid mih, nuh."

"No!"

"Come nuh, gyal," I persisted, if a little gently, emboldened by her undeniable ambivalence.

"Why?" she all but whispered. She was, in her heart, quite ready to lie beside me but needed to be pushed a little, needed me to provide the justification her mind demanded.

"Because...," I said unhelpfully, placing my left arm around her as she fell back onto my right side, making believe that I had applied force sufficient to pull her down onto me. I moved away to make room for her and did not even notice when she swung up her legs to help her lie flat on her back on the bed.

That day she did not let me use the fine-tooth comb in the proper place. I used it on the little hairs at the back of her neck, and I discovered that the goose bumps that my combing gave her were infectious, and we both thoroughly enjoyed the mutual condition thus induced. Moreover, eventually, modestly placing the pillow over her eyes and insisting on keeping her panties firmly in place, she let me touch her intimately through the cotton. She liked the stroking with the fine-tooth comb at the back of her neck and delighted in the feel of the goose bumps that the stroking fathered, and she asked me to do it many more times afterward (so much so that I bought my own comb specially for that); soon, however, her relatives seemed to smell a rat, and first, they stopped the visits to Vanessa and then sent her away to live with relatives in Trinidad, where, unfortunately, she endured molestation and abuse by an uncle. It was not until I met her living alone in Trinidad more than a dozen years later that we eased into a full relationship, and then into marriage.

By this time, Vanessa had been long dead. Only Shirley, her niece, and Cork-Foot Pilgrim's daughter Jaccinta understood why I had wept almost uncontrollably on the day of the funeral, although all and sundry must surely have wondered if I hadn't cried quite enough on the awful day of her death and the following, intervening day.

One day soon after she had left me and Rooks alone together in the bedroom, she had made me go with her to Level Bottom on the pretext that she wanted me to help her pick and take back home some "good roas'in' breadfruit." I was a little excited when she told me I had to go with her, because there had been times when we had done things at Level Bottom lying on a crocus bag under the enormous mango-vert (long-mango, we mostly called it) tree that thrived there, but something in her voice and her demeanor told me that this time it wasn't about such things. And I wasn't misled even when she spread the crocus bag under the mango tree, sat on it, and beckoned me to do likewise. Settling myself down, I turned to look at her.

"Yuh like Rooks?" she asked with an encouraging smile, our eyes making four.

I felt uncomfortable. I hadn't quite expected that. True, she had all but clamped us together, but there she was, my mentor, my teacher, asking me this question. The answer was, of course, yes; but wouldn't it be disloyal to give it voice, make it official? But she saved me.

"Nice gyurl," she encouraged. "Nice gyurl fooh you. Yuh like shi?"

"Mm-hmm, mih like shi."

"Mih glad. Mih glad becarze me an' you haffooh stap do weh ahwi does be doin'."

I felt a tinge of sorrow. I was definitely going to miss what we had to stop doing. Still, it was not as if I hadn't seen it coming. I had noticed her getting ever closer to Jeremiah Reid, a man of her own age, a Sabbath school teacher in the church, who had lost his job as a junior front desk clerk at a hotel in Scarborough for refusing to work on Saturdays before sunset and was now hoping for an early selection as a pupil-teacher. Also, we were almost never alone together now, and whenever it seemed that that could happen, she would go to great lengths to invite either Shirley or Rooks to come by and then leave me alone with whichever one of them came.

"Wehmek?" I asked, dissembling.

"Me an' Jerry does get together a likkle bit… yuh anderstan'?"

"Or-huh!"

"Buh Rooks is a nice likkle gyurl fooh you… an' even Shirley too, in case yuh like Shirley betta."

"Okay, is arright. Mih goh be arright, mih goh be arright."

With all that, I was still heartbroken at the open mutual acceptance that that very special, intangible thing between us was now at an end, and I could feel my eyes moisten.

She put her right arm around me and stroked me intimately with her left hand.

"Wan las' time," she said softly, "wan las' time. After dis, yuh have Rooks, or if yuh prefer Shirley, yuh have Shirley."

She lay backward onto the bed of dry mango leaves and lifted up her dress to reveal that she had come without underwear.

"Come, l'ahwi enjay it wan las' time."

# Chapter 17

Just as in the case of Othnel, I absolutely refused to believe it when I first heard of her death. It was a Thursday afternoon, late afternoon, perhaps past five. Tallboy, the ever-accommodating health van driver, had allowed six of us to be crammed into the vehicle when he picked us up just as we were about to enter Argyle as we legged it on our way home from school. As he was about to turn onto Bay Road to drop off some items at the Belle Garden Health Center, he let out the three of our colleagues who lived in Belle Garden proper (the Pint, as always, being seen as merely a subvillage of BG), leaving Jacinta and me more comfortably seated in the van. He parked the van outside the center and got ahold of his official document leather case and stepped out of the vehicle.

"Gimme wan minute," he said briskly and soon disappeared into the belly of the building.

Looking at each other and saying yes only with our eyes, Jacinta and I hugged each other tightly and locked our lips together. We didn't know how long Tallboy was going to be, so we didn't let our feverish embrace last for too long. Instead, we sat there looking straight ahead out through the van's windscreen, waiting for him while, through our clothing, we touched each other's burning organs. And all this time, as I would often scold myself afterward, Vanessa was already dead and I did not know it! I definitely wouldn't have been doing what I was doing if I had known then that Nessa was dead. Presently, Tallboy came back and soon dropped us off at Mango Tree, from where we set out on the dirt road home. When we reached her gap, the turnoff to her grandfather Cork-Foot Pilgrim's house, she pulled her left hand out of my clammy grasp and, book bag still slung over her shoulder, turned sharply, hugged me hard, and planted a brisk kiss on my lips.

"Yuh t'ink 'e suspeck anyt'ing?"

"Who, Tarlbway?"

"Yeah. Mih fin' e' behna watch mih funny."

"Eh, eh. Mih feel yuh jes' imagine dat... nuh, mih nuh t'ink suh."

"Arright, if *you* seh suh!" She turned and headed down the track to the old man's house.

I was in really good spirits as I continued on my walk home: a full kiss in the van and a quick one by the gap. And boy, the intimate touches! The touches had been carried out through our clothing and not on the fiery flesh itself, so when the time came, I would wash my hands as usual and not keep my happy fingers safe from water so I could sniff them overnight. What would girls do or say if they knew how we boys treasured that scent, always saving it up overnight! They little understood the lure of it for us and our helpless enslavement to its promises and mysteries.

I was brought brusquely down to earth by the sight of the solemn women in the gallery, the porch of the house where Nessa lived. It was a time of day when the men had not yet come home from their labors on whatever lands they were tilling or preparing for tilling, and the boys were still on their way home from school or had gone out already to attend to their chores and feed the animals. The women never hung about like that, doing nothing, during daylight hours unless a most serious development demanded it. What could have happened? I asked myself. Then I saw Nessa's mother lying on the floor on her back, with white cloth on her forehead, and one of the other women pouring bay rum onto the cloth, while yet another one was putting a smelling-salts phial to her nostrils. In proper response to that spectacle, the feelings of ecstasy I had been savoring took to their heels and vanished, and quite in spite of myself, I began to tremble.

You didn't, as a child big enough to know better, enter the presence of a group of grown-ups, especially grown-ups of a gender different from yours, without invitation. I approached the group of grown-up women tentatively. To my great relief, they took no notice of me.

"Bring a nex' pillow!" one of them said intensely. "Leh wi raise shi head. Mih feel dat jes' now she goh come-to."

Just then, from among the women, Mammy turned and spotted me standing there, eyes wide open in incomprehension, still shaking.

"Vanessa dead," she said simply.

She and Jeremiah, the Sabbath school teacher, had been *bway-fren-an'-gyal-fren* for just under two years. Three months into her pregnancy, when she had begun to show, they had both stopped going to church, and even though the new pastor, Pastor Anatol Leonce, had taken the position that the doors of the church were open to all, especially those who had fallen short of the glory of God, and had urged Jerry and Vanessa to come back to God's house and constantly seek God's grace, shame had kept them away. Now she was dead!

He had reached out and tried to be kind to Pastor Ramrod, too, even after the latter had refused to receive from his hand the dreaded *LSD*, the letter of suspension and disfellowship he had been given for delivery by the secretary general of the Southern Caribbean Conference of Seventh-Day Adventists, headquartered at St. Augustine in Trinidad. He had had to rest the letter down on Ramrod's center table and quietly and respectfully leave behind at the house in Roxborough not just the *LSD* but also a Ramrod mute of malice, for the ex-pastor would not respond to Anatol Leonce's ardent offer to visit and pray with him from time to time, beginning there and then.

"You know as well as I do that, with the issue of that LSD, I wouldn't be able to let you come into the church, but there's nothing that stops me from coming to meet with you and pray with you at this difficult juncture, wherever in Tobago you may be, my brother."

Ramrod stared out through the window and would not reply.

"Well, don't you think it would help?"

Ramrod stared out through the window again and would not reply.

Pastor Leonce left, truly sad about the predicament of his former colleague, whose nineteen-year-old domestic help had, on her deathbed, identified him as the father of her unborn child.

The women raised the head of Vanessa's mum by placing a second pillow under it, and then they applied more bay rum to the mold of the flaying head. Observing that there was no immediate result, one of the women shouted, "Smellin' sarlts, smellin' sarlts, mo' smellin' sarlts!" Out of nowhere, two smelling salts phials appeared and were thrust, one each, into the mother's nostrils. Strictly following the tried-and-trusted medical procedure applied by the villagers in such circumstances, one of the women boxed Vanessa's mother hard, which is to say that she opened the palm of her right hand, drew her outstretched arm as far back as it would go, and then, swinging the arm forward, brought the open palm into violent contact with the left side of the patient's face. Vanessa's mummy took a deep, involuntary breath, shook her head briskly, and came to. But not for long. Looking about her, she saw the forlorn faces, reheard in the wind the devastating news of her daughter's death, and promptly fainted again.

"Put mo' bay rum 'pan de moul' ah shi head. Put mo' bay rum 'pan de moul'!"

The body was going to be brought to the house the following day and put on ice in a larger version of the box we used on special occasions to keep our ice from melting for as long as possible so we could enjoy our drinks cold. The box would be made of wood layered with tin sheets inside to minimize leaking, and the ice would be covered with sawdust to hold back the melting. While some were attending to the task of constructing and preparing that preservation box for the body, one of the men would select appropriate lumber (a pile of which the brothers each always kept in a corner under his house), plane and smoothen it to perfection, shape it, and build and varnish the coffin. The day after that would be the funeral.

"W'at about de service?" one of the men asked that same night as they sat in the streaming moonlight, at the bamboo patch near

Gra'ma Millie's house, sipping coconut water and speaking only sporadically. "Shi breed outa wedlack. Buh Pastar Leance goh still do it. If nat, ahwi goh 'affoo goh ah Goodwood lakka Ort'nel famaly?"

"'E goh do am. 'E-ah wah good man, nuh lakka Ramrad," came a response.

"Well dat ah de fuss t'ing ahwi 'affoo check out, eh." There was a murmur of acceptance.

"Look," one of them said after a long silence, "dis t'ing cyah ge' complicated, eh. It carl fooh cayful handlin'. L'ahwi tark to Teacher Aaron. L'ahwi leh *he* handle dat."

The others agreed, and together they declared, "Dat mek sense."

The following morning, Pappy came at four as usual to awaken Gobo and me to go and get the grass from the estate for the cattle, but I don't think he noticed my uncharacteristically brisk response, the result of having slept hardly a wink all night, lying awake instead, as I had been, trying to come to terms with the fact that Nessa was really dead. By and by Gobo stumbled out of his sleep, rubbed his eyes with the back of a hand, and mumbled something surly and not quite decipherable.

"Arright!" Pappy said. "Up, up, up, up! Arl t'ree ah-ahwi ah goh fooh grass dis marnin'." Then, ignoring the pitch-blackness of the predawn hour, he urged, "Ahwi 'affoo do quick. Sun n'aly down arready!"

As we headed for the grass piece, Gobo and I, as usual, had to be running to keep pace with his giant steps, and even so, he had to wait for us for a minute or more at the foot of the breadfruit tree where we would leave the plastic milk pails until our return with the precious guinea grass. When we did get back, he left us to do the rest of the daily cattle chores.

"Arright, ah leavin' alyuh to milk de cow an' feed de animals, arright? Ah haf to go an' si Teacher Aaran about de service an' ah haf to come back an' buil' de carff'n."

With that he sped off, moving so fast it was as if he were halfway up the hill by the time the last word left his lips.

"Vanessa rayly dead, bway!" I all but screamed at Gobo, who was understandably taken aback by a hint of inexplicable aggression in my voice. It was almost as if I was accusing him of having caused her death. He opened his eyes wide and looked me up and down.

"Yeah," he replied, looking at me quizzically, "shi dead… young, young she!"

That is all the conversation I have ever had about Vanessa's death, one of the most momentous happenings of my life.

\* \* \* \* \*

When Pappy got to the house at Sheep-Pen Ridge where Teacher Aaron now lived with his widowed mother, he had no need to call out to the former headmaster. It was around six on a fair morning, and it was certain that he would be working on the adjacent land for nearly two hours before grabbing a quick breakfast and heading off to meet the first student-driver of the day at the corner of the Windward Road and Sheep-Pen Ridge opposite the school, next to Derrick's shop. Pappy entered the yard of the house and peeped down the hill, down which the fertile land gently rolled away from the house and the plateau on which it stood. There, as he fully expected, was that formidable man, in the middle of the fruits of his hands, molding gushing green tomato plants.

"Morning, Teacher Aaron," he called out, ever fastidious, when circumstances required it, to avoid the everyday practice of substituting an *a* for an *o* in any word at random.

"Teacher Aaron! Morning!" It was evident that the committed farmer, driving-school proprietor, and village guru had not heard the first greeting.

"Oh, Mr. Brougham! Good morning. What brings you here?"

"Vanessa. The funeral service."

Teacher Aaron knew Pappy well, and he knew that if Pappy came to see him at that hour of the day, he had come about something of the utmost importance. He thought he had a good idea what that something was. He immediately put down the hand shovel and made his way up to the plateau where Pappy stood in the yard outside the house, his eyes fixed on him as he climbed. Presently, they were standing next to each other.

"Good to see you, Mr. Brougham, even though in such sad circumstances. You've been to see Pastor Leonce?"

"No, not rayly, not yet, Teach. Buh wi t'ought dat is betta wi ask for your assistance just in case."

"Oh, because of what happened with Othnel?" Teacher Aaron half-asked and half-exclaimed.

"He is a much betta man dan Mr. Ramrod, but wi cyahn be too cayful."

"Leave it to me. I'll get back to you before midday."

"T'ank you, Teach."

Teacher Aaron was now more settled in his existence. Jenny had made a successful application for a job as a junior loans officer at the Bank of London and Montreal (BOLAM) in Trinidad. At the interview, she had sensed that her high complexion and her francophone background would serve her in very good stead, and returning to Tobago to await the outcome, she had instinctively begun to prepare for migration to Trinidad. When the appointment letter came, she was all but ready. Her one worry was accommodation. Where was she going to live? She would now be a working woman, married and about to be divorced—living as a long-term houseguest of the Lestrades in Curepe was completely out of the question. She walked to the nearest telephone booth, which stood just outside the compound of the post office in Pembroke, and called the administrative assistant who had signed her letter.

"Sanks wery much, I 'ave received your letter. I vill start on ze fifteenth, yes?"

"Yes, yes, of course."

"I 'ave only eleven days to find a place to live."

The AA, confirming she was the Mrs. Harriette Francois who had signed the letter, gave her the name and telephone number of a widow in Woodbrook who had notified BOLAM of a room she had for rent. After speaking with the widow, Jenny sent one of her two boys to Sheep-Pen Ridge to tell their father that she was taking the boat to Trinidad that evening for another brief business trip and would return by another overnight boat trip setting out from Trinidad the following evening. So it was that Jenny secured a room much like the one that, years earlier, Aaron had lived in at St. Joseph—except that Jenny did not have to use the outdoor bathroom facilities but, rather, being a woman of high color and about to become a loans officer at a bank, was permitted use of the main bathroom.

The divorce had followed not long afterward, but although Teacher Aaron lived at Sheep-Pen Ridge, he continued the tenancy of the house on George Street, mainly so that Jenny's exercise of her right of access to the boys would never interfere with the quiet of his life. He employed an older lady from the village to work half-day every day on weekdays looking after the boys, and he dutifully went to spend evenings with them, having dinner with them and seeing that they paid sufficient attention to their schoolwork. A reasonable, self-confident man of simple, elegant taste, he found his income from working the land and conducting his driving school enough to allow him to support the boys and enjoy a satisfactory living—even to save something for a rainy day, something to fall back on in the event of sudden or dire need, whether on the part of himself, the boys, "or even *Jenny at arm's length*," as he once said.

He had, of course, stopped attending the church at Glamorgan and had, in fact, jettisoned the proposition that the worship of God could properly take place only in a Seventh-Day Adventist church: he was going thenceforth to worship in any church, indeed in any holy place, and on whatever day of the week that might apply to any holy place in question. He experienced a feeling of awesome liberation.

By now, on the sparse occasions when he did go to church, it was to the Methodist church in Goodwood. So it was that, as Pappy turned to go back home to embark upon the construction of Vanessa's coffin, leaving in the reliable hands of the former headmaster the matter of the arrangements for the farewell service, Teacher Aaron took a quick wash, changed his clothes, and set out for the neighboring village to meet with the accommodating Reverend Granderson.

"Aaron!" the priest exclaimed, opening the front door himself. "Come in, come in. Come right in."

"Sorry to trouble you, Rev, especially this early in—"

"Come on! You and I know only too well that you wouldn't unless it was necessary. I'm here to help."

"It's about the girl… the girl who died…"

"The funeral! Leonce refused?"

"Preemptive, a preemptive step on my part. He hasn't been approached yet."

"You can count on me. Just alert me the moment it's settled."

"Thanks."

"Some Milo, a cup of Milo?"

"Thank you, but I must head for Roxborough. Thanks."

Pastor Ramrod's previous housekeeper hailed from the little subvillage of Ten Chains, near Delaford, and she would walk home after work on evenings, staying back and sleeping in the maid's room only on the rare occasions when he was ill and might need attention during the night. But it had been different with the one who had recently died: she was from Charlotteville, and not even so strong and formidable a creature as a Tobagonian woman of that era would have arranged matters in such a manner as to include a journey home on foot at dusk, at the end of the working day. There would be no public transport available, and the possibility of a lift in a private or government vehicle, even if you could program your life around that, was perilously close to zero. So the nineteen-year-old who died in childbirth had been a live-in housekeeper who had somehow managed to conceal her pregnancy until the very day she had been rushed to the hospital.

At that hospital in the capital, Scarborough, the only one in the whole of Tobago, there had occurred, some time before the crushing (*en ventre sa mere*) of the fruit of Pastor Ramrod's loins, the death of a thirty-year-old married woman eagerly awaiting the arrival of her first child, and it had been nearly a year since the authorities had set up a commission of inquiry into it with a mandate to report in forty-two days. In neither case had the baby seen the light of day ever: in both cases, the babies were overdue and the women were, in each case, weeping as the baby died, the final words they themselves ever heard being, "Push! Push! Nobady cyahn do dat fooh yuh. Push!" Even years later, though, when news of the notion of the cesarean section reached the shores of Tobago, it took time for suspicious villagers, comprising almost the entire population of the island, to stop regarding pregnancy as a sort of terminal disease.

It is from that terminal disease that Vanessa died. Her predecessors in death, though, had encountered no problem with their rites of passage to the other side. The married woman, a Seventh-Day Adventist from Lowside in the southwest of the little island, who had been married for nearly eight months at the time of her decease, had never had to face the hard evidence of her having had sex outside of marriage, and the pastor's pet belonged to the Moravian church in the neighboring village of Speyside, where the doctrine followed was that all had sinned, judgment was God's and God's alone, and no man had had delegated to him the power to judge another and consign her to the everlasting bonfire.

"Hello, hello?" Teacher Aaron called out again as he stood on the steps of Pastor Leonce's house; still, there was no reply. But he was not going to give up; the Ford Cortina motorcar was parked on the road outside the house, and the pastor could not be far away. In fact, for all he knew, the man could be catching a late sleep. He turned to go back and sit in his car for a while and was rewarded with the sight of the holy man, clothed in a bathrobe, crossing the road, heading home. He had obviously just enjoyed the delight of a morning swim. Some sad thoughts of Teacher Aaron's late good friend, Pastor Ellington Pascal, one of Pastor Leonce's more enlightened predecessors, filled his head as he recalled how a vibrant, progressive young man, just past thirty, a very good swimmer, had drowned right there at that beach across the road, his body found three days later half-devoured by innocently unthinking fish. And two pastors later, there had been Ramrod.

"Good morning, Pastor." Teacher Aaron spoke first.

"Ah, my lost brother! Welcome back into the fold."

"Alone, or accompanied by all my sisters and brothers who have sinned or otherwise fallen short of the glory of God?"

"Come in, Brother Millington, come in," said the pastor, taking the front-door key from his bathrobe pocket and opening the door. "Do have a seat while I get dressed."

Teacher Aaron set himself down and, resting his elbows on the curved side rests of the Morris chair, clasped his hands together and summoned his fingertips, pointed upward, to support his chin as he leaned slightly forward.

"Hope it's nothing catastrophic," Pastor Leonce called out from the bedroom.

"Beyond the death itself, I hope not," Teacher Aaron replied.

"Ms. Brougham? You've come about Ms. Brougham? You're related?"

"No, no... well, not by flesh and blood, but as poor pilgrims together passing through."

"Well, my brother?" the pastor queried as he emerged from the room and sat down in a Morris chair next to Teacher Aaron's.

"It's the funeral service for her... you know, not long ago... Othnel Nurse... you must have heard... you surely know about that... you understand?"

"He had been on suspension, I recall?"

"Yes."

"And Ms. Brougham? She's not on suspension. Is she... I mean *was*... was she?"

Teacher Aaron declined a response to the rhetorical question and instead took pleasure in the pastor's trend of thought.

"Nor, as far as I know, has she been disfellowshipped. Yes, there've been rumors, but it would be unseemly to let them, without, er, process, survive her untimely passing. In any event, my brother, my core responsibility is to save souls, not to take it upon myself to damn them on any pretext that presents itself to fiery folk."

"That's a mouthful, pastor. I am humbled and delighted by your wisdom."

"So three tomorrow afternoon? Would that be suitable?"

"I'm eternally grateful."

"See you tomorrow, then."

Not long after Vanessa's funeral, an anonymous petition was received at the headquarters of the South Caribbean Conference at St. Augustine in Trinidad demanding that Pastor Leonce be forthwith disfellowshipped for having held a funeral service for someone who had had sex out of wedlock and had, indeed, become pregnant to prove it beyond all doubt. Thinking about all I had been hearing all my life about dedication to the pursuit of sexual pleasure in the villages of Tobago, I was certain that the real sin ever entailed in these cases was the commission of a pregnancy coupled with an unpardonable failure to marry before the virgin's belly began to show. The Conference held firm to its policy of ignoring anonymous allegations.

## Chapter 18

"*You* cry de mos' w'en Tanty Nessa did dead," Shirley said to me on a moonlit night about six months after the funeral.

It was true. I had been quietly and morosely grief-stricken from the moment I had learned of her death, constantly shedding silent and profuse tears whenever I found myself alone. But at the graveside I had been loud and openly inconsolable. In the days that followed, as I looked back at the expressions on the faces of some of the adults while I bawled, it was all but crystal clear that they had settled upon some reasonable explanation for my deep distress. But I cared nothing.

"Yeah, mih behn' cry plenty. In fac', mih behn' barwl like a cow. Mih miss shi baad. Mih miss shi baad-baad."

Shirley did not pursue the subject. Instead, she drew up her knees, lifted her buttocks off the crocus bag on which we lay, pulled off her panties, straightened back her legs, and uttering not a word, took my left hand and placed it gently where she liked to feel it most.

"Yuh have *me* now," she said after some soft moments of silence.

"Yes."

It was a Wednesday night, and a special Wednesday at that, as it was Easter week, and almost everybody in the Pint had gone to the church in Glamorgan for the midweek service. I had been left behind to take care of my two youngest siblings, and quite by chance, Shirley had come by. Electricity would not, for countless years yet, come to the Pint, and the outdoors under the gentle light of the moon always insistently beckoned. Marginally southwest of Gra'ma Millie's house, and more or less side by side with ours, there flourished the little wild coffee (or *myamarl*) field, whose plants, at maturity, reached up some five feet above the ground. My toddler charges were asleep, and I knew I could clearly hear them cry were they to wake up and need me, so I felt no sense of irresponsibility when we strolled into the field with our crocus bag, found a satisfactory clearing amid the myamarl plants, rolled out the bag, and lay on our backs admiring the wonder of the heavens. We had kissed and cuddled and, her right hand in my left, had fallen into an enjoyable silence only after she asked me about the overabundance of my tears at the funeral. Over time, she had taught me a great deal about physical expressions of love, all of which, as she freely admitted, she had learned, and had been learning since she was just past nine, from her primary school teacher, a circumstance that, though I viewed her as nothing other than the unfortunate victim of it, often made me recoil and fathered and nurtured within me a gnawing sense of abiding equivocation about any possibility of an enduring relationship with her. Thoughts of these things stole into my head, without consulting which my left hand lifted itself off her *pupu* and went across and took ahold of the right, and then, clasped together, they came to rest on my stomach near the level of my navel.

"W'a 'appen?" she asked in alarm.

"Nutten," I dissembled.

She turned onto her right side, reached over, burrowed her head beneath the back of my neck, drew me toward her, and kissed me long and sweetly. She resumed her supine position and took my left hand and put it back just where she—and I, I supposed—wanted it to be.

"Arl mih eva do ah tell yuh de trut', eh. Mih like yuh baad, bway, but… look, leh we jes' do rudeniss nuh, boy! Yuh doh want to do rudeniss?"

Those idle thoughts I have mentioned stole away just as swiftly as they had come.

# Chapter 19

INSIDE A DAY OF THE principal's announcement of my success in the trial-run London University ordinary level examination, almost every soul in the cluster of villages along the Windward Road, from Mt. St. George to Charlotteville, had heard of it. And each and every one of them, it seemed, had become an instant authority on the details of the results, each expostulation being, nonetheless, remarkably different from the other, all of them wildly exaggerated. The one ingredient that the narratives had in common was an alleged declaration by the principal that I was an absolutely 100 percent certainty for a *house schol* in the upcoming Cambridge University school certificate examinations in December. One good effect of all this was that it seemed somehow to stop the exaction of the *no-tap-up* tax I had been paying to Pepe and Doyle. The great disadvantage was that the principal took no steps to set the record straight regarding the alleged house scholarship declaration, thereby pushing people to pressure me to walk on air, a method of approach to life and living that did not hold, nor has ever held, any attraction for me.

"Brougham," the principal said to me one day at the end of the Additional Mathematics period, just before recess, "let me see you in my office."

That had come clean out of the blue, as far as I could make out. I had long ago finished my daily anger-management sessions with him and begun to appreciate how amazingly effective they had proven to be. I recalled how apprehensive I had been when he first required me to attend them after I'd hurled my chair at him when my form 3 mates had ganged up on me, wilfully setting me up to be punished for something I hadn't done, and he'd decided at first that it must be I who was the untruthful one. He'd said then, after catching the chair like an expert goalie saving a bullet penalty kick, that he had a sacred duty to save me from the gallows, a declaration that, to me, smelled then far too much like a sneaky way to subject me to penance. As the years went by, though, I would come to marvel at his wisdom. As for being subjected to penance, in the ordinary course of school life, I was always way beyond that and, indeed, later, as prefect, could, in certain circumstances, award it myself.

"Yes, sir. Coming, sir." I got up and followed him right away.

"Take a seat, son. Look, you and I know very well I didn't say you're *certain* to win a house schol. Matter of fact, I can't say that. Nobody can. But…"

He got to his feet, went to the back of the chair on which I was sitting, and rested a hand, palm down, on each of my shoulders.

"But let them talk—it's good for you and it's good for the reputation of our school. All I want from you is that you do your best, always. Go enjoy the rest of your recess."

I took it that, inevitably, he had heard of my many complaints about the stress I was under because of the much-mouthed expectations of me in the villages, when December was just around the corner.

"I understand, sir."

"Good."

Jacinta was at the rival school on the day of the proclamation, but from that same afternoon, she started calling me, whenever she could whisper it for my ear only, "my house-schol boyfriend," an endearment that soon enough became abbreviated to "my HSBF," and later, simply "my HS." We had become much closer since our adventure on the bed of dry leaves at Bamboo Patch. At lunchtimes we would sometimes meet by the seashore and have our meal together, sitting on the trunk of a fallen coconut tree, and we would almost always find ourselves in the same group walking home at the end of the day. Often, a vehicle would pull up alongside our group, offering lifts, but having room for only three or four of the eight to ten of us; at any time that we couldn't both be accommodated, we would gladly opt to give way to someone else so that we could keep walking along together.

It was some considerable time after the adventure of Bamboo Patch that I—as our remarkably creative grown-ups used to designate this matter—*put question to her* again. We were holding hands as we almost always did as soon as, reaching Mango Tree, we broke away from our group, or what was left of it by then, and took the Pint's own dirt road home, sometimes, if we felt it unlikely that somebody would come along and surprise us, stopping for a kiss and caress, and perhaps even a touch at our special spots, too; but nothing more, both of us, I think, surely restrained by the memory of the mess we had had to face that other time.

I remember the first time when we ventured to touch those spots, too. There had twice along the Windward Road been some heated arguments between a pair of boys over some matter that seemed very important to them, and in each case, the whole thing had culminated in an extremely vigorous exchange of fisticuffs (a tool of aggression that we, inheriting the incurable predilection of our communities for abbreviation, called, simply, *cuffs*). As these disagreements and settlement procedures, involving many starts and stops, had slowed our march home, it was early dusk before we got to Jacinta's gap, where the tributary said goodbye to and ran away from the main dirt road down to her grandfather's house. It was our second kiss-and-caress stop that evening, but this time, for long seconds, she didn't release me from her embrace. Presently, she set me half-free, using her left hand to lift her skirt while she guided mine to her special spot. Both of us standing awkwardly, she nevertheless leaned forward and engaged my lips with hers.

"Dis ah heaven se'f!" she whispered as, trembling with excitement, she briefly interrupted the kiss. "Ah heaven sé'f, HS bway!"

Her words reminded me of what Doyle had once declared when we boys were alone together, discussing the joys of life as, having so often absorbed the contents of the coded conversations of unsuspecting adults, we saw them then. Hear Doyle on the burning subject of sex: "If Gard mek anyt'ing sweeter, betta 'e keep am up deh—

down-yah, dat goh kill ahwisuh dead!" But her lips reclaimed mine in a flash, and all I could offer in response as my body burned was "Mmmmm!"

This happening served to cure me of the restraint and to embolden me for the next time the touching seemed to be on the cards. Still, I was not alarmed by the fact that it was taking an eternity for us get back to that point. Girls were strange people, and even your own mother could weep bitterly one day when your father had *boofed* her by the fireside and try to inveigle you the next to say you didn't want to continue at high school. Even so, when the day for the repeat came, it brought only disappointment. Jacinta and I would often talk about it and giggle as we lay in bed after we met up again in San Fernando some five or six years later.

# Chapter 20

My marriage to Shirley had not lasted long. Truth is that I had never enjoyed our relationship completely without equivocation. I had some idea why, but I was never absolutely sure about it. There was something more than a little bit unsettling about the way she seemed to have no remorse whatsoever about having started to have sex at such a tender age, and, at that, with her primary school teacher. More than that, not only did she not hold anything against this teacher, she even seemed to be elatedly grateful to him for the world of ecstasy to which he had introduced her. It was not that she said anything specific; it was just the casual, natural way in which she spoke about these things and the sweetness in her voice and the light in her eyes that seemed to go with it. *Of course,* I told myself, *you know you can be seeing all that the wrong way!* What was not disputable was that, at one and the same time, I hated all that and loved her for being such a free and open soul. It bordered upon torture. With her, with this particular female person, I somehow didn't feel obliged instantly to embark upon a careful analysis of all possible motives and intentions that might inform her every word and action and, even after that, to make sure and keep looking back over my shoulder.

I thought I was beginning to understand a little all those girls in the villages all along the Windward Road who seemed to like only the bad boys with nicknames like Cutouter, Slice, Boulderman, and Gunslinger, with whom we, the goody-goodies, couldn't compete for their attention. Perhaps it wasn't the badness at all that was the attraction; perhaps it was just the freedom of the soul, the self-confidence, the fearlessness, the *machismo*, a primordial sense (scent, even) of certainty that these were men who could feed them and protect them from all evil, these were the men that mattered. Was that not the sort of reason that what seemed a majority of women, at one time or another, displayed an otherwise irrational weakness for a man in uniform? Shirley forged a me totally free of guilt for the love of that ultimate intimacy.

"Is jes' me an' you now," Shirley would say, and then, remembering she was now a monitor at the primary school and was expected to speak properly, she would make an amendment after a brief pause. "It's just me and you now, Jakey."

"Now? Why the *now*?"

"Why de *now*? Tanty Nessa garn ah heaven, and dey sen' back Rooks ah Trin'dad."

I fell silent. I couldn't bear the pain of hearing Nessa's name again, and I remembered with distress that I didn't even know when they had spirited Rookmin away to Trinidad to live with relatives. I'd never seen that move coming, nor, I felt sure, had Rooks. True, she had told me that her mother had taken to questioning her, "W'a' it is dat rayly ah goh arn between you an' da' Brougham bway?" And she had gone on to issue a dire warning: "Yuh betta tell mih de trut' an' doh leh yuh farda fine out t'ing an' kill yuh dead pan de spat right in front mih two eye an' dem."

Even after Nessa had eased me out of the intimate part of her life and gone into a less unequal and more mature relationship, Rookmin would come by to visit her from time to time and she would somehow contrive, whenever barely possible, to allow us time alone together. Rookmin would tell me that her mother would, every now and then, return to the questioning about me, but like me, she had thought that, at worst, they would stop her from visiting Nessa and then we would have to work out how we would meet up. I should have read the signs. One day not long before her disappearance, the mother had been very specific, very pointed, as Rookmin described it to me.

"Shi seh how she fin' mih lookin' biggish-biggish an' mo' an' mo' like a big ooman every day."

"She said that? Bad, dat bard, bard!" I paused. "More and more like a big woman?"

"Arlways tarkin' dese days 'bout mih breas' an' dem an' mih hip an' dem."

That was the last time Rookmin and I were together before she disappeared. It was a Sabbath Day, and Nessa was in the outdoor kitchen, pretending to be busy putting some lunch things together while Rooks and I were lying on the bed in her room, just two months or so before she passed away. During the weeks that followed, Nessa had kept her promise to me to look out for Rooks anywhere that she might be, but she had never been able to set eyes on her. She had had some idea of the questioning Rookmin's mother had been subjecting her to and did not think it wise to make any inquiries in the little villages for fear of raising suspicion as to her role in the whole affair.

"Deh mus' be sen' shi back ah Trin'dad," she had told me. "Yuh haffoo fooget *she*... w'at about you an' Shirley, how alyuh goin'?"

"Good."

"Arright, buh remember yuh cyahn bring shi here an' kerry arn—she is mih niece."

"Mih know."

Soon after Nessa's funeral, Shirley had received a condolence card from Rookmin. The envelope bore a circular stamp that read, "Couva Post Office," but there was no return address. There was a note inside, though:

*Dear Shirls,*

*I so sarry Nessa ded. Ma sen' an' tell mi an' mi cry foo so becar shi woz ah good, good fren to mih. Ma an' dem did pick mi up jes' suh an' sen' mi back down hay. Mi miss Tobago foo so an' you an' Jaykee too. How Jaykee? He an' Nessa binna good, good fren too. Mi bin like de too ah dem foo so. Ba-bi foo now.*

*Rooks*

"Just me and you now," Shirley repeated, "me and you alone… alt'ough mih t'ink mih affoo watch Jacinta."

"Who Jacinta dat?"

"Doh try dat!"

"Try w'at?"

"Eyy! Mih neva goh ah high school, but please don't forget, sir, that I'm bright enough to be a monitor—soon to move up to pupil-teacher, if you please, and then… who knows?"

# Chapter 21

After the Cambridge school certificate examinations in December, Jacinta went to Trinidad to spend Christmas with her uncle Albert, a taxi driver. He lived at Cocorite and plied his trade from that village, along the Western Main Road, through St. James and Woodbrook, down to Salvatori Building at the corner of Frederick Street and Marine Square North in downtown Port of Spain. He would then go past the Cipriani statue and make a double right turn to get on to Abercromby on his way back to the Western Main Road via Duke and Edward. Almost directly south of Salvatori Building, on Marine Square South, stood the Bank of London and Montreal, where Mrs. M now worked.

Notwithstanding the failure of her marriage to Teacher Aaron, Mrs. M never stopped asserting that Tobagonians were really nice people and that she felt very comfortable with them. That explained why the taxi driver with whom she used to travel to work was certain to lose her custom for good the Thursday after the long Easter weekend that same year.

If Albert had not been a Tobagonian, she might well have forgiven Rohan as she had grudgingly done earlier in the year, on the second of January, when, too, he had gone AWOL and had not bothered to contact her until the end of the day. This time, he had let her know in advance that he had promised his wife and children to take them to Tobago for the weekend and that they were going up by the SS *Tobago* on the Wednesday night and returning by the SS *Trinidad* the following Wednesday night, landing at the Port of Spain wharf at about 4:00 a.m. on Thursday. He had explained that he would have liked to take the boat from Tobago the Tuesday night but that he had booked for the Wednesday night months in advance in order that he could relax and be comfortable at Buccoo on the Tuesday and enjoy Tobago's traditional Easter Tuesday *Great Goat Race* and *Crackling Crab Race*. The trouble was that, when Thursday morning came, Rohan was AWOL again.

Mrs. M was fuming as she flagged down Albert's route taxi, but she quickly calmed down when, the car having pulled up next to her as she stood on the pavement, the driver smiled, emerged from the vehicle, greeted her by name, and held the back door open for her. Hardly more than a minute later, the only other passenger in the car exited the front passenger seat as Albert drew up outside her workplace, Republic Bank on Tragarete Road. It was then that Mrs. Millington gave in to her curiosity.

"Ziz I hear you say 'Morning, Miziz M'?"

"Yes, ma'am."

"Ho… how… ?"

"Ma'am, my title is *Pilgrim*. Ah have family in the Pint, frien's of dem Brougham an' dem."

"The Broughams! So you know Mr. Manny Brougham and eez wife, Emmy?"

"Yes, ma'am!"

"And zeere son, Zhacob?"

"Yes, ma'am, de whole family. Ah know de whole famaly. An' Ah know you, too, ma'am—from two time w'en ah did come fooh harvis in Glamargan, an' w'en ah did come fooh Ort'nel Nuss funeral."

"You went up twice for zee 'arvest vestival at zee church?"

"Yes, ma'am… and ah did see you deh de two time."

"I fear I'm going to be a bit late. Can you hurry a leetle, please?"

"W'ere to, ma'am?"

"BOLAM… zee bank."

"Arright, ah wouldn' stap for no mo' passenger."

"No, I can't…"

"It's okay, ma'am."

Off Tragarete Road, he turned onto Richmond Street, then left onto Park Street and right onto Frederick. As he drove by Salvatori Building, turning left onto Marine Square North heading east, he politely, if, perhaps, somewhat presumptuously, declined her request to be let out of the car and to be able to walk across the road to Marine Square South and her workplace.

"It eez nearly eight sirty. I'm going to be late. I can zhust run across zee road."

He merely speeded up in response.

"It drizzling, ma'am. Wih arlmos' dere. Ah jes swinging down dis street here an' den Ah will jes' tun right' an' wih right dere!"

Indeed, hardly had he finished the sentence than there she was, opening the door of a completely stationary vehicle right in front of BOLAM. Over her shoulder she called out to him to pick her up at four thirty in the afternoon, and bypassing voice, he responded with a thumbs-up. He dutifully collected her in the afternoon and again at eight o'clock the Friday morning, and they quickly developed a rapport that robbed Rohan of an erstwhile permanent passenger.

By the time Jacinta arrived in Trinidad to spend the Christmas season with her uncle, through the combined efforts of Mrs. M and her landlady, Mrs. de la Granade, an interview for Jacinta (a sufficiently light-skinned girl, judging by Albert's appearance and by oral certification passionately articulated by him) for a position at BOLAM had been secured. Jacinta later reported that, in her "humble opinion," she had passed the interview with flying colors. Be that as it may, she went back to Tobago after Christmas only to collect her belongings, and as the celebrated Tobago saying goes, bright an' early January marnin' (which is to say, early on the morning of the second of January, the first not counting for these purposes, being a public holiday), she started her job as a teller at BOLAM, a development that was, when she learned of it, a source of great elation to Shirley.

"Suh yuh gyal ge' wah big bank wuk ah Trin'dad?" she said to me when we met up at the traditional Sports Day held at Roxborough on Boxing Day.

"Who gyal?"

"Yuh nuh affoo play chuppid again yuh-nuh. She garn, dat done, dat dead an' garn. Jes' l'ahwi get together tonight an' celebrate nuh bway."

"What!"

"Girl," she mocked herself, "you're a monitor now, so speak properly, you hear me?" Then, turning to face me directly and look me straight in the eye with complete confidence, she continued, "Boy, please screw the life out of me tonight in celebration, I beg you."

The image that those musical words conjured up excited me unbearably, and to hide the bulge that appeared at the front of my trousers as we sat on a wooden bench in the shade of a cluster of bamboo trees, I bent over and very slowly untied and, to give the bulge more time to adopt acceptable behavior, retied and again untied and retied, the laces of my white *watchekongs*.

The people of the Pint hardly realized that the only important things they lacked were running water, electricity, and a proper road to replace the mile-long dirt track that hustled away, if surreptitiously, from the junction of the Windward Road and Mango Tree right down to the last house, which was Pappy's, ours—and even beyond, through Mr. Young's estate, to the secluded beach. We did our own chickens and our own eggs. We did our own cows and our own milk and our own butter and our own beef. We did our own sheep and our own goats and our own mutton. Living hard by the sea, we caught our own fish. From our lands we got all that we needed to eat, including fresh condiments and seasonings and cooking oil from our coconuts. We really needed money only to buy our "good clothes," *pitch oil* for our *bols de fer*, and schoolbooks and Bibles, and to pay tithes and offerings and school fees. The source of such money as we did have was the proceeds of sale of our surpluses and the wages from the laboring *tasks*, or *day-wuks*, that the men did from time to time cleaning the two English-owned estates that locked us in and choked us on all sides, even denying us access to the sea except, by ceaseless, unrepenting trespass, through one or the other of them. Still, of money we had but little.

And so it was that the burning ambition of your parents for you after you got through secondary school was to see you pass the civil service entrance examination and secure a permanent civil service position in order to ensure for yourself a salary at the end of each and every month and a monthly pension following your retirement at the age of sixty. Some unusual bird letting the right seed fall into your eager, unfallow mind, you might rather have envisioned yourself as imperious as the seemingly everlasting Mango Tree or the unsmiling calabash tree bearing no visible arms yet somehow conveying a conviction of constant readiness to protect and defend Gra'ma's house and person or the immortal *cedars of Lebanon* they spoke about at church. As it was, I indeed felt little attraction to the civil service, which seemed to me a place of semiservitude in which, in those colonial times, there was little or no chance of your ever becoming your own man, the man in charge, the nearest thing to that being possibly becoming a middle-level administrative officer position at a point of your life at which, clutching the handle of some *crook-stick* in its turn grasping in its V-shaped extremity the roots of a nearby clump of submissive guinea grass, you are desperately striving to keep your feet from slipping on unstable ground that, heedless of your desperation to hold on, lies, cruelly neutral, right at the edge of your yawning, hungry grave.

At all events, life expectancy did not extend much beyond sixty, if it did at all, and the period of payment of the pension you devoted your entire life to securing would scarcely prove longer than the life of an eyeblink.

"Bway," said Pappy, "dat is de bes' yuh cyah do?"

"Pa, de civil service pay is eighty dollars ah mont'. W'at ah getting dere is one forty."

"Yes, buh no pensian, bway, no pensian!"

"Pa, ah rayly feel ah too little to start to t'ink *abor* pensian."

I was mischievously borrowing the *too-little* defense from Man-Man. I had often overheard Pappy talking, with a kind of astonished half-amusement, about the way Man-Man had gotten away with it. Man-Man, though not disfellowshipped, was on a sort of permanent suspension from the church, and he accepted that when he died they would have to church his mortal remains elsewhere. But Man-Man, it was obvious, was not overly worried about that detail. "Mih na'ah goh cry if dem nuh chu'ch mih, as lang as dem bade mih dead bady befo' dem bury mih" was all he would say whenever this or that anxious friend or relative urged him to do the right thing and make his peace with the church and with God, almost always adding, "Yuh si me an' fooh-me Gard, ahwisuh peaceful, peaceful."

Man-Man was tall and slender and good-looking and, in a few of the villages, people winked and nodded about a child here and a child there said to be his offspring. I never heard of any comment that he had ever been accused of making on the subject of these loud, though seldom verbalized, allegations. But he always admitted to being the father of Verna's two teenage boys. Pastors and church elders, too, did not concern themselves with any other but these two children; in any case, with all the *shoo-shooing* about other children people seemed sure that Man-Man had fathered, nobody ever said that even one single one of their mothers was a Seventh-Day Adventist, so that was not the holy men's concern. *Let the dead bury their dead.* The pastors and elders insisted that Man-Man should marry Verna (and so get the suspension lifted), and Man-Man, who was pushing fifty and still lived at his parents' house six buildings down the road from the church and the school located on its ground floor as the road ran west toward Pembroke and Goodwood and, ultimately, Scarborough, the island's capital, would never say no. "Buh mih too likkle to married now. Jes' now suh, w'en mih ge' big, m'ah goh married to shi." Man-Man's parents were influential folk, and the second boy was already more than seven years old when the church bosses, finally accepting that they were being had, suspended Man-Man pending celebration of the wedding.

Pappy replied to me, "Too little, eh? Y'ah play Man-Man?"

He lifted his eyes and his open, upturned palms toward the heavens, as if in supplication, and declared, "Up to dis day Man-Man nuh married Verna yet!"

# Chapter 22

Alejandro Moreno had never considered entering the civil service himself, but before the entire class, he would often say how important it was to work hard and pass the school certificate or, better still, the higher school certificate, examinations and get a safe and secure job there. For the five or six of us whom he saw as "top class material," he would separately say, "The civil service—good for the plodders, not for you! In any case, it pays very little." He would have been disappointed if I hadn't accepted the teaching job at the college that he offered me, and once I had done as he fully expected, he would not have wanted to pay me anything less than the one-forty I now earned.

"So we are both teachers now, Mr. Brougham, except that I'm a little senior since I started out before you, eh?"

Shirley was relaxed and smiling out of both corners of her mouth as we lay on the crocus bag in the twilight shade at Bamboo Patch still catching our breaths. It was our first time at Bamboo Patch, and we were able to go there only because her erstwhile competition was safely slaving away ("like a good girl," in Shirley's words) at BOLAM in Trinidad. Shirley had insisted that Bamboo Patch was where she wanted us to be. It was, I thought, nothing short of the exorcism of the spirit of Jacinta. I saw no need to reveal that I had seen through that, to let on that I was beginning to feel inside me the stirrings of an incipient comprehension of her bright and bushy-tailed, confident female mind. Instead, I quietly agreed that it was a great occasion on which to satisfy the raging, unbearable curiosity she swore she had always had about that place.

"You're senior in other matters, too, Ms. Wilson!"

"Nasty! Nasty! Truly nasty! But, Mr. Brougham, one thing you must never doubt, I will always, *always*, be fait'ful to you."

"Truly trut'ful, if you ask me!"

"Yeah—dat I'll *always* be fait'ful, right?"

That special, that promising, that inviting, salacious grin of hers appeared like a lightning flash, and it weakened my knees and my elbows yet another time—and perhaps my tongue, too, for I could make no reply.

It was the sight of that same grin that made me deliriously happy when she turned up at the little guesthouse at Oxford Street in Port of Spain on the first Monday after the Easter school break. Those were the days when the school year coincided with the calendar year and the breaks were at Easter and at what, ignoring the bulk of July, people used to call the August holidays or, later, absurdly, as the northern hemisphere unrelentingly imposed its will upon all the world, the summer vacation. There was, too, to be sure, the Christmas break.

"Weh de hell, weh de… w'at yuh doin' here?"

"Yuh bex o' yuh glad?"

"W'at yuh doin' in Trin'dad?"

"Mr. Brougham, let me repeat myself, Are you angry with me, or are you beside yourself with joy to see me?"

"Mih glad fooh si yuh."

"Good. Well, yuh know de Anglican school pan Duke Street by Dandanal' Street carner? M'ah teach deh fram today!"

"That's not Dundonald, I think it's…"

After teaching at the high school at Roxborough for a single school year, I had, through the generosity of Mr. Moreno, left Tobago to attend the prestigious St. Mary's College in Port of Spain to prepare for the Cambridge Higher School Certificate examinations the following December. The little guesthouse on Oxford Street, owner-run by a middle-age Venezuelan lady whom we called *Ma Rondon*, not only was a warm and friendly hearth, where we were provided with basic necessities at manageable cost, but also practically bordered upon the schoolyard, daily rubbing shoulders with it and eliminating the transportation expenses. There, the lone noticeable discomfort was that there were two double-decker beds and four boys to a room; but it was still a steal at the price Ma Rondon charged.

"Buh ahwi cyahn do nutten yah!" Shirley said, taking me completely quite by surprise.

"Eh? W'at?"

"Yuh cyahn ge' no privacy yassuh!"

Ever slower than she in these matters, I needed that elucidation to help me grasp her point.

"Where are you staying?"

"Nuh tark suh nuh, bway. L'ahwi tark Tobigonian becar ahwi neh know who ah listen."

"Arright, aright."

"Mih ge' wah likkle room ah Belmont—own bartroom an' shower an' everyt'ing. Yuh goh affoo come deh."

"Wark arl de way deh, gyal?"

"Since w'en Tobigonian 'fraid wark? Look yah, bway, yuh warnt it or yuh nuh warnt it? Ah fooh-you own, yuh nuh—lack, stack, an' barrel… it's all yours, sir."

The widow who owned the house in Belmont had her hands full with her three vibrant, self-assertive teenage daughters, the eldest of whom was teaching at a private secondary school at upper Henry Street, while the twins were in the sixth form at Holy Name Convent. Their father had reached the lower levels of the administrative grade in the civil service, a grade ordinarily the preserve of white people sent by the Colonial Office in London, and they had grown up with status.

They loved the exclusive house parties that, in those days, young people of status would organize among themselves for their private fun and enjoyment. Prohibited things often happened, and parents, especially widows with teenage daughters, were constantly anxious, staying awake until their daughters' dates dropped them back home after the parties. Even if, in surrender, you admitted to yourself that you probably couldn't stop them from stealing some sex, you knew you would be sunk if, God forbid, one of them should get pregnant.

The landlady was far too concerned with her own fears and apprehensions to bother about what a girl of doubtful status, and from Tobago to boot, wanted to do in her room. In fact, that was exactly why, after her husband died and she decided to rent that out-front room to get a little money to supplement the widow's pension she was getting from the civil service, she had used a part of the veranda to add on the toilet and bath. All she wanted was her money. Well, and some reasonably good manners from the tenant.

Shirley was happy. She had feared it would be otherwise, that the landlady, widowed, perhaps with dribbling tongue hanging out, unable to fend off the ache of longing for male company, would watch her, would watch any young woman, like a hawk, just to make sure she did not get any either.

"Wih haf to celebrate. Yuh warnt to come every night?"

"You're insane. I have exams to study for!"

"Okay, a compromise—every other night."

"As a monitor, you have exams too. Yuh haffoo mek pupil-teacher, and then study to make full teacher, right?"

"Okay, sir, we'll see how it goes."

In the August holidays, Mr. Moreno would give extra lessons to help his charges prepare for the upcoming December examinations. That was one of the school's traditions. Part of the arrangement for his financial support of me at St. Mary's College was that I would return to teach at the school during that period that year. Of course, the school year and the duration of each term of it were the same throughout the system. It came as no surprise to me that, although Shirley had been uncertain of her travel date, she just happened to be on the SS *Tobago* on the same trip that was taking me home for the holidays. What did surprise me was that she had been able to pay for a cabin instead of having to endure the overnight journey sleeping on the metal deck chairs.

"Bway, yuh nuh look comfortable pan dah chayr deh at arl," I heard her voice behind me saying. She had come out of the blue from somewhere, and I hadn't seen her approaching at all. I was, I suspect quite visibly, startled.

"Nuh jump," she teased, her Delilah smile at the corners of her lips again. "Ah jes' me... *ongly* me... come, fallow mih."

Both the first and the Easter term had been exciting ones: We had studied hard and still found ample time to nourish our relationship. We were both new to Trinidad and had no other long-standing friends to distract us, and her landlady seemed scarcely aware that I frequently slept over on Friday and Saturday nights. The three midweek nights could be trying. We would not walk to her place together after school. I would go home and change out of my uniform, grab the old grocery paper bag I kept for that purpose and put into it the books I needed for the evening's labors, and then head for her little room. Exiting the little guesthouse on Oxford Street, I would go east to Frederick Street and, turning north, would go past the Royal Victoria Museum on my left and Memorial Park on my right and then head east again to Jerningham Avenue, through to Erthig Road, and finally to my destination at Industry Lane, which I always felt must certainly be the narrowest paved street in the world. She would have just come out of the shower, and I would go straight in.

The evening trip back would be in the cool of the nine o'clock hour and would take place only after a disciplined attention to our books followed by a relaxation hour, the bread and butter or biscuit and cheese we had for dinner having been washed down with Milo or Ovaltine during our study period. And although I sometimes became quite morose thinking of all those things she said she had learned from that exploitative teacher and which she would patiently teach me, we had grown closer and closer together.

"Fallow yuh? Weh yuh mean? Ah weh ahwi ah goh?"

On my feet now, I tried to keep my volume at whisper level while the rocking of the boat churned up my poor stomach.

"Mih ge' wah cyabin," she said, walking away with me in tow.

"Cyabin?" The question came out far more quickly and far louder than I had intended, much to my mortification, mortification that deepened precipitously as she turned sharply and cast a severely disapproving glance at me, before placing two fingers onto her lips. We were soon at the cabin, and I followed her into it, slammed the door shut, and stood with my back against it, facing her as she looked back at me. The Delilah smile appeared, and I stepped across and held her tight and kissed her.

"Better than a deck chair, sir?"

"Weh yuh ge' de money fram?"

"Thrift, sir, pure thrift!"

I awakened her at three, an hour or so before landing time.

"T'anks, bway. Eyy, dat was sooo good… wait, weh yuh grip?"

"Oh, Lard, ahwi didn' bring in mih grip, gyal!"

"Eh-heh? Suh w'a's dat over deh?"

"Weh de!" I started to exclaim, for there, to my astonishment, was my suitcase lying on the floor of the cabin.

"Mih wait till everybady ah sleep an' mih goh far am… you yuh-se'f behn fars' asleep—yuh farl asleep wan time, bway, *wan* time!"

It was far too overwhelming. I somehow felt as if my manhood was being undermined. I began to dress and said nothing.

It was nearly five o'clock when we set foot on solid ground at the Scarborough Jetty. Mr. Moreno, who now lived in the capital town instead of at Kendal, the tiny coastal village extending a mile and a half or so westward from its border with Roxborough, had told me to relax and not worry about transportation to his house near to the top of Young Street, that we would work something out. For all the years, whenever Alejandro Moreno told me not to worry, I worried not. So I was not surprised to espy him through the morning half-light standing there on the wharf next to *Rolling-Home*, doubtless Tobago East's most famous taxi driver, reputed to know the history of Tobago "lakka de back ah 'e han'." Al Moreno forever insisted that you could learn a lot from anybody who was not a complete fool, so you should shun nobody; your friends, though, should be people whose company you easily enjoyed, and that should be the only qualification. And Rolling-Home was one of Al Moreno's friends. At first, I was delighted at the sight of them, but suddenly, I felt my heart sink.

*Shirley!* I thought. *What about Shirley? What will Shirley do or blurt out?* I rested down my grip on the bare wharf concrete, rubbed my eyes, and looked straight at her.

"Look! Mr. Moreno! 'E come to pick me up!"

"W'ere?"

"Ova dere!" I all but screamed as I sought to conduct her eyes with my right index finger toward Mr. Moreno and the taxi driver.

"So?" she asked offhandedly, as I skinned my own eyes wide and wordlessly scrutinized her face, looking for reassurance that she at least understood what I was trying to say.

"Or-huh! Ah 'fraid yuh 'fraid! Yuh 'fraid yuh own teacher? Leave it up to me."

I bent down and picked up my grip and began to move. We couldn't keep standing there and not be conspicuous when all the other passengers were hustling to get out and go home. My fervent prayer that she should dissipate completely on the spot was not answered. She was shoulder to shoulder with me as I approached Rolling-Home and Al Moreno.

"Good morning, sir. Morning, Mr. Rolling-Home," I said as I got nearer to them, my voice sounding to me like somebody else's altogether, while Shirley was as chirpy as a *blue-jean* bird.

"Hello, Teach! Hello, Mr. Rolling-H!"

*Rolling-H?* I screamed inside. *Where on earth did she get that from?*

"Morning, good morning," said the teacher and the taxi driver together, sounding relaxed and chirpy.

"She's with you?" Mr. Moreno asked rhetorically. "Come, come, let's get going."

*So he meant it, then!* I mused. He used to tell me in particular, and the older ones of us students in general, that romance and sex are the currants and the raisins and the sugar in—and perhaps even the icing on—the cake but that they are not quite the cake itself. "Still, what kind of cake would that be without them, eh?" Then he would go on to another subject. Big-people rumor had it to say that he really liked the ladies, and we older students, having examined the matter carefully, could find no evidence to belie that, but we cared not, for he was a delightful teacher. At one point or another, he would teach, at any level, any subject on the curriculum; he told the sweetest jokes and had a honeyed sense of humor; always he displayed an extraordinary commitment to our physical as well as to our mental well-being.

All that and ladies too? Some of the girls had their own views on the matter, but we lads held him in uncomplicated awe, period.

Doyle was the most eloquent of us when referring to the part about the ladies. He had his standard, well-worn commentary: "Tell dem leave de man alone. 'E-ah wuk hard an' e' deserve w'a'ever recompense 'e cyah get fram w'erever, an' mih tired seh if Gard mek anyt'ing sweeta dan 'ooman leg." *We did have our euphemisms.* "Le' 'E keep am up deh. Ahwisuh cyahn handle nutten sweeta dong yah."

"There's only one bedroom available," Mr. Moreno said apologetically after Rolling-Home drove off, turning to Shirley and unwittingly dangling guinea grass before a hungry heifer. "Is that all right with you? Can you manage with that?"

Shirley turned and looked at me, and you could see the struggle in her eyes and on her lips: she so badly wanted to burst out laughing. Truth is, I wanted to burst out laughing myself.

"Yes, Teach," she said. "I think I can protect myself!"

# Chapter 23

Bright and early September morning, we were back at the grind in Port of Spain. For both of us, school began again on the fifth, the first Monday in the new school term—she as monitor and I as sixth form student facing the HC exams in December. We went down on Sunday night, and as usual, the boat docked in the wee hours. This time, though, at her insistence, we had pooled our fares and booked a cabin with a double-decker bed, confessing only by an exchange of winks and a deployment of her impish, devastating grin that we well knew that very likely one of those decks, as narrow as they were, would all the same be destined to remain unruffled throughout the journey.

"Ahwi goh save some ah yuh ticket money fooh pay jetty taxi nex' marnin', sweetheart."

*Sweetheart* had, over the vacation period, somewhat surreptitiously installed itself as one of her preferred names for me, and I soon found out that I had accepted it.

"Okay, Shirls, anyt'ing you like."

"*You* know what I like!" This monitor and aspiring schoolmarm was daily proving herself to be deliciously incorrigible.

During the vacation, I lived at Mr. Moreno's house, while she spent most of the time at her mother's house at Belle Garden. She wanted to spend Saturday nights at her aunt's house at Government House Road, but that didn't quite suit me. On weekdays, I assisted Mr. Moreno at the school, and I dutifully left Scarborough on Saturdays in time to get to my own parents' place in the Pint at a reasonable time after sunset. In that way, I avoided the straightjacket of a strict observance of the Sabbath from sunset Friday to sunset Saturday. No doubt for the avoidance of undue awkwardness, no one ever made the matter of my set arrival time the subject of conversation in the house while I was there.

Every Sunday evening, though, Shirley would find herself on the late bus to town, which was my means of transportation back to Scarborough for the week's teaching ahead. She, too, had a little job—giving midafternoon lessons to older students at the Belle Garden Anglican school preparing to sit the school leaving examination, some of them earnestly hoping to become monitors themselves. But she would get back in time for that on Monday afternoons. Mr. Moreno, for his part, played blind, or, perhaps more likely, cared not a hoot, and never behaved as though he knew we spent Sunday nights together under his roof. Sometimes I felt as if I were witnessing an unspoken conspiracy between the two of them to bind me to her for good.

Even Pappy seemed to soften, which was rather curious. I mean, the girl was not even a Seventh-Day Adventist, yet he actually said she was a nice girl! In the face of that, I couldn't help remembering again the time when Miriam's mother said, as if speaking to herself but, so as not to let the soliloquy go to waste, loud enough for Pappy to hear, "Mih hayr Miri-she ah seh how shi want to married jes' now. Hmm!"

Pappy, fully aware that Miri's boyfriend at that time was none other than his own son, responded immediately, "Shi warnt to married jes' now? Well, when yuh fin' out who shi warnt to married to, nuh fooget to invite me an' mih *famaly* eh!" The thing is that very early on, in reference to Miriam, he had asked Gobo, "Sh'ah Seven-Days?" and, raising his eyebrow at the response in the negative, had completely moved on from the subject after a rather sharp "No?"

On the bus headed for Scarborough on the late afternoon of the first Sunday in August, we had just stopped giggling at some really good joke some other passenger had made when she suddenly turned toward me in her seat and asked, "Yuh tekkin' Wednesday arf, of course?"

"Yeah."

"An' yuh comin' Belle Gyarden, of course?"

"Of course!"

"Tuesday five o'clock, Bamboo Patch?"

To that rendezvous she brought a small cake, some ginger beer, two plastic cups, and some paper napkins. As we settled ourselves on the carpet of dry bamboo leaves, she lifted the cake out of the old book bag, carefully freed it from the protective embrace of the grease-proof paper, broke off a piece, and brought it to my lips.

"Eat," she said, that smile about her lips again. "This is my body… made by my own fair hands."

I hesitated for a fleeting moment before responding, "Blasphemy!"

"Taste it. It's for our birthday—all three of us!"

"Buh wait nuh…"

In response to a gentle shove from her fingers, the cake was fully inside my mouth in no time at all. I could see that *she* could see the satisfaction on my face.

"Da' is only ah tas'e, bway. Mih have de big cake home. Mek showre Pappy deh home lunchtime tomarrow."

This girl was not a girl to be trifled with. Not only was he *Pappy* now, instead of *cousin Manny*, not only did she keep very much in mind that Wednesday would be his birthday, too, and not just hers and mine; she was going a big step further and planning something for lunchtime.

"Fooh w'a'?" I said, feigning incomprehension.

"Doh play doltish fooh mih nuh, bway. Mih done season fish an' goat meat arready. An' de ginger bayr weh mih mek nice-nice. Heh, tas'e am!"

She gave the icy-hot a brief but vigorous shake such that I could hear the sound of the little blocks of ice jumping in the grassroot drink. She poured some into a plastic cup and, lifting it to my lips, said with jocular solemnity, "Drink!"

On the birthday, the following day, the tenth of August, her sister Gillian in tow, helping her with all she was bringing along, she arrived at noontime. She hugged Pappy, kissed his cheek, and handed him a birthday card, urging him to open it at once. It was an attractive card, and observing the satisfaction with which he was viewing it, she lined up a cheek about his lips, and he, hardly having time to think, dutifully placed a peck on the cheek. She grinned gleefully and said, "Happy birthday again, Pappy!" Finally noticing my mother standing there, next to the carpenter's workbench below the house, she hurriedly turned toward her.

"Cousin Emmy, mih bring some rayly nice food. Fram de time mih get up dis marnin', mih deh-deh ah cook—mih hope yuh like de food."

We went into the house and sat down to eat at the dining-cum-ironing table in the *gallery* with its whitish pinewood floor. At first, Mammy was a bit taciturn, undoubtedly thinking, as adults in the Pint were wont to do in such circumstances, *Dis little woman over-fappish an' farward*. But in time everyone became relaxed and, well, jolly. In the end, Mammy even joined with Pappy in declaring the food delicious and the ginger beer really special. No question arose as to whether any of the cooking had been done by this heathen girl in any pot also used for the cooking of pork and crab.

As the SS *Trinidad* was docking, we woke up to realize, with little surprise, that we had had a sound sleep on one deck of the double-decker bed and were each ready to face our day. The taxi driver made it clear that if he had to fulfill our wishes and go to Industry Lane first and then return to drop me off at Oxford Street, there would be an extra charge. So we jettisoned that noble notion, and leaving the jetty, he let me out where Abercromby met Oxford and then continued north toward Belmont in the half-light, with Shirls his only passenger. The following evening, we resumed our regular dinnertime study sessions, the frequency of which abated a great deal after mid-November, as my examinations would begin on Tuesday, the twenty-second of that month, and run until Thursday, December 15.

From the middle of November onward, to be alone in a corner and study in peace and quiet, I would, every now and then, repair to the public library at the corner of Pembroke and Knox, this latter barely separating the library from the now-famous University of Woodford Square, lying just south of it. One fine afternoon—I think it was the last day of November, a Wednesday—I was deep into *Pepita Jimenez*, the novel by the nineteenth-century Spanish professional diplomat and writer Juan Valera, trying to deconstruct what seemed to me a somewhat-sordid mental picture of the twenty-year-old widow's previous three-year forced marriage to her rich eighty-year-old uncle, when I felt a gentle touch on one of my shoulders and heard a greeting, uttered ever so softly: "Hi!" That voice was familiar, my mind said to me, but could it really be Jacinta's?

Leaping off the chair, I turned to look at her and found myself breathless at the sight of the accomplished-looking young woman before me, splendidly outfitted in the dark-brown skirt and cream top of BOLAM's uniform. The sight of her looking like that made me feel quite ordinary at first, and it took some stern internal soliloquy for me to secure the recovery of my composure and resettle my self-confidence.

"Hey, lady, you look great!"

"Thanks, my friend. You…"

"God! And you're so grown-up, a real big wo—"

"*Goddess*, if you must," she cut in, smiling with mischievous self-satisfaction, "but seriously, at the bank they teach you how to *groom*, as they call it—oh, and Mrs. Millington kinda tek mih in han', too, eh."

My heart skipped a beat at the mention of Mrs. M, but what really concerned it was that it felt itself being drawn relentlessly toward this new and improved version of this girl with whom its owner once held hands daily, and perhaps, surreptitiously, even beginning to falter, just a little bit, in its commitment to Shirls.

"Suh, suh… suh w'at yuh doin' here? An' w'at yuh doin' beside wukkin'… in yuh spare time nuh?"

"Study. Evening sixth form school in St. James. Maths an' econ… an' w'en is yuh big day?"

"Exam? Las' day, fifteenth December."

"Nuh dat, stupid—de rayly big day!" Something in her voice made me uneasy, very uneasy. There was a strange, accusatory tone in it that made me feel, for more than one chilling moment, scared.

"Ah weh yuh rayly ah tark 'bout, gyal?"

"Look, ah haf to go, mih afoo run right now! Mih wark up de road fram de bank to buy brown shoes, unifarm shoes. Uncle Albert mus' 'e ah look fooh mih arl-now-suh, jes' acrass deh, 'pan Frederick Street. Mih garn!"

Jacinta disappeared just as suddenly as she had materialized into my presence, leaving me in no state to go on to analyze, in preparation for my Spanish literature examination paper in a few days' time, the evolution of the mind-set of the trainee priest as he observed a fifty-five-year-old man, who had fathered him some thirty-three years earlier, single-mindedly pursue the hand of the baby-widow.

Unsettled and unable to concentrate on my schoolwork, even after I had made my way back to Oxford Street, I took a slow, pensive shower and then headed out to Industry Lane.

"She hasn't come in yet. You can sit in the gallery and wait for her. My girls went back out—net ball practice." The landlady was always kind and helpful—that is, whenever she ever put her mouth into your business at all.

"Thanks a lot, Mrs. Hull."

"You walked all the way here. Would you like some juice?"

"No, thank you."

"Have a seat," she invited me, motioning to one of the vintage Morris chairs in the gallery.

I said "Thanks," but remained standing.

"How are the exams going? You're concentrating okay?"

I thought that to be a curious question, but I did my best to conceal my surprise and sound nonchalant in my reply.

"Oh, yes. Tough, but I'm managing."

I noticed myself beginning now to feel conscious of my hands, and I soon found that I definitely didn't know what to do with them. It was almost as if I had just discovered, for the very first time, that I had hands. What did I do with them all this time, if I had them? I nearly shoved them into the pockets of my trousers but decided that that would look disrespectful and rude. Instead, I plaited all my fingers together and rested the resulting parcel behind me just atop my buttocks. But I very soon afterward untied the fingers and let my arms bring them back in front. Hardly aware that I was doing so, I took two steps toward one of the Morris chairs and lowered my body into it.

"Sweetheart!" In general, I didn't like, and perhaps I even hated, being called that in public: for some reason, it made me feel extremely self-conscious. But this time it was music to my ears, because by then I had each hand cupping a knee and still did not quite know yet where to put them.

"Shirls!" I realized that I had all but screamed out her name (well, the name by which, as I had lately discovered, I now called her), but who could help that when the relief brought by the sight of her was so great?

"Take care, you two, take care!" Mrs. Hull said in a soft, motherly voice as she withdrew into the main house.

As we entered Shirley's room, I could sense that what had earlier seemed to be her enthusiasm to see me had evaporated. She now seemed more than a little withdrawn and esconced deep into her shell.

"You all right?"

"Yes, buh w'at yuh doin' here, yuh doh have ah paper Friday morning?"

"Yes, but—"

"Look, we is big people, we haf to be respansable!" she scolded, leaving me feeling like a wet fowl locked out of the coop on a rainy day.

No doubt noticing signs of deep despair etched on my face, she offered me Ovaltine with biscuit and cheese. Inside, she was doubtless overcome with feelings of guilt, knowing, as full well she did, that the delivery of that scolding had been no more than a desperate, unplanned, preemptive act of self-defense. She had been so happy that exam time had come along to prevent us from spending a lot of time together, even if she had pretended that that was merely necessary sacrifice that would be ever so painful to her. Now she had to do what she had to do, heartlessly or not. Deep within, she was glad that I had refused to eat, and she did not take the chance of repeating her offer of food.

"We have to be responsible!" She returned to her theme. "We is big people!"

Despite what seemed on the surface to be some kind of implacable logic, something did not look quite right. My arms folded across my chest, I grabbed ahold of her eyes with mine and pierced them in search of whatever they were trying to hide. But not even a shadow of it could I see. Offering no comment, I rose from the edge of the bed and headed home to Oxford Street.

# Chapter 24

In *Pepita Jiminez*, the trainee priest, surprised and overwhelmed by the great love and understanding his father was showing him, opined, "En el amor paterno hay algo de egoista; es como una prolongacion del egoismo."

You always knew when Pappy found a girl to be attractive or, perhaps more accurately, when a young woman he wanted to identify by word was one physically pleasing in his sight. Never was she anything if not tall and dark and slim and smooth-skinned with curly hair and a nice nose and proud white teeth. Everybody knew about this foible of his, except he; he didn't even know when he was in its grip. So when I discovered that he had actually been heard in the village to say that Shirley was a very nice girl who had cooked us a great meal for our common birthday, I didn't have to inquire what else he had said, seeing that, in any event, she fairly well fitted his favorite picture. That consideration emboldened me quite beyond reason, and I came to believe genuinely that I would be able, on a fine Saturday night eight days before Christmas, to give him, perhaps even in a slightly off-hand manner, the news of what had befallen Shirls and me. When the moment arrived, however, I hastily decided that it would, quite obviously, be better to do the thing by letter sent by post from Trinidad.

Shirls was not even a Seventh-Day Adventist and so did not meet the core qualification. True, in her days as a student at Belle Garden Anglican, people referred to her as *ah pretty likkle girl*: that had been reserved for her, any other of her peers being *ah nice gyurl* or *ah good-looking chile* or even *ah cute one*. But that high compliment, in certain quarters, meant, if you were not a Seventh-Day Adventist, that you were a Delilah-in-the-Making. Though Shirls had frequently come from the main village to the Pint during her school days, no adult there would have noticed her heathen beauty. At all events, a beautiful heathen was just a Delilah.

"Pappy blood tek mih!" she had said, almost wistfully, that early September Sunday night in the cabin as we headed back to Trinidad. "Ah did see dat since ahwi bort'day lunch, an' every single time 'e meet mih after dat." It wasn't news to me. It was past midnight, and she had just turned and nodded before switching off the lights in the cabin. I could almost hear myself snoring already as I kissed her lovingly on the forehead and whispered "Good night."

Pappy's reply to my letter was a relief: it was scathing, but the compassion and the undying love could find no place within it to hide from me. "At de end ah de day," it concluded, "ah fooh-you life. You decide wat it is yuh want to do with it—yuh can mek one salid brick-wall outta yussef or yuh can mek flour-pap. Ah fooh-you chaice dat-deh. You decide." El amor paterno: I knew him well enough to know that what he was giving me was not a choice, but an order.

Shirley had come to Oxford Street just before seven on the day of my final paper. It was Thursday and also effectively the last day of school for her before the Christmas break: the following day was Christmas Treat Day, and that would be over before one.

"Yuh ready fooh dem, sweetheart?"

That *sweetheart* again! I wasn't self-conscious about my hands this time and desperately in need of a savior, and I instinctively cast my eyes about to see if anybody in the little guesthouse could have overheard it.

"I hope so... weh yuh doin' here?"

"Yuh exam ah done today. M'ah cook somet'ing nice dis evenin'. Mih garn!"

The girl was truly special. It was not just that you could see her standing there in her sparse shorts and, braless, her totally diaphanous skin-colored top, obviously newly showered. In that small room, with that little tabletop stove and two tiny pots, she had prepared a *callaloo-soup* starter, a beef pot roast, pigeon peas stewed in coconut milk, and scalloped sweet potatoes! And she unwrapped, to top it off, a bottle of inexpensive Portuguese wine. Observing my eyes open wide in disbelieving admiration, she deployed her familiar bewitching smile and motioned me to sit down.

"Is it okay?" she asked, gloating at her *coup de cuisine*, keeping in place, unsheathed, the sword of her smile.

"Just about," I returned as I tried to dampen my earlier reaction, take back control, and put on show for her a more balanced display of appreciation.

"Well," she said as she continued to prepare my plate, "mih hope arl ahwi goh be happy in the en'," adding, as she set down my plate on the little table, "Open de wine nuh."

As far as I could make out, anything to eat prepared by her hand was delicious. Dinner was delightful. For an hour or so after, we sat and chatted about this and that, how the Christmas Treat planning had gone, whether I was confident of a good exam result, what we thought of the prospects for the fledgling West Indian Federation—while we finished off the bottle of wine. Presently, she rose and, plates in hand, got to the sink just about half a step away.

"It hot today, boy. W'at about tekkin' a quick shower w'ile I do dis?"

"Good idea!" It was exactly what I'd just been thinking.

"I'll go after."

"Doh want help?"

"T'ink ah cyan manage two likkle plate by mihself'."

For what felt like the thousandth time, I tried in vain to whistle a happy tune. I never did learn to whistle. But to *me*, at any rate, I was a great bathroom singer, and I amused myself a lot as I showered, not a little encouraged by the water warmed in the pipes by the all-day sun. Still singing, I slid the shower door to the right and was emerging, towel wrapped around my hips, when I saw it. As if automatically reacting, too, the knot holding up the towel loosened, and I made a hilariously clumsy and needlessly desperate attempt to grab it before it hit floor. Ever the agile one, Shirley was right next to me in no time at all, wearing nothing but her ensnaring smile. She picked up the towel and, with a completely serious mien, began to retie it on my hips, as meticulously as if she were dressing me for an appearance at some big, important event.

"Yuh naked!" I told her, as if I had just made some earth-shattering scientific discovery. *Eureka!*

"Is in de shower ah goin', bway. Is de fuss time yuh si mih naked?"

"Wait! Wait! Yuh pregnant!"

As a matter of chronological fidelity, it must be made clear at this point that it was the manifest signs of the pregnancy and not those of the mere, familiar nakedness of her that had brought my private cantata to its abrupt end and demanded of my towel that it fall and present to her my bared, compliant loins.

"It real hot dis evenin', bway. Mih rayly haffoo bade," she said calmly, swiftly going past my surly loins and sliding the shower door shut behind her.

These are the matters of which, in retrospect manifestly in some moment of total loss of lucidity, I had thought I would casually make mention to Pappy two Saturday evenings—or, more correctly, in the circumstances, two Sabbath evenings—before Christmas, when thoughts of the Savior's birth and of his eventual ultimate sacrifice would more than likely be those mostly on his mind. I had insanely let myself believe that, at some appropriate point in the middle of a jolly conversation, I would just blurt out, almost as an aside, the news that Shirls was pregnant and that on the Friday morning after my last exam, we had stuck up wedding banns at the Red House on St. Vincent Street in Port of Spain.

It was not that I was feverishly waiting for Shirley to come out of the shower or that the objective room temperature had changed all of a sudden. The reason the towel lay on the floor, to which it had fallen again, and I was sitting at the edge of the bed pressing the heels of my palms into the mattress to keep my torso up straight, sweating and cold as I used to be in my primary school days after a midmorning post office errand, was simply that the thing had begun to sink in and I was terror-stricken.

"Weh ahwi goh do, bway?" she asked me as she approached.

In some strange way, the fact that she, too, was terrified brought me some relief from fear. I had half-thought she would emerge from the shower with the killer smile and fake-breezily announce, "Bway, look lakka ahwi haffoo married. Mih pregnant fooh true!"

I felt my lips part to permit me to answer her question, but hard as I listened, I could hear no words escaping them, just a faint hiss of barren breaths. I urged myself then to admit that that question that she had posed was itself no less a declaration of what our next step had to be than would have been the announcement I had feared.

"Yuh warnt to… ?" I managed before she locked away the rest of my words, lowering her body onto the bed next to me and pressing the huddled fingers of her right hand firmly against my lips.

"Shhhh," she said, then removed the fingers, turned and embraced me, and kissed my lips. "I'm a monitor in a denominational school," she went on, "moving up to pupil teacher soon. We can't spoil my whole life."

"Yeah, but if—"

"Yuh know m'ah show arready. People know! If mih t'row it 'way… yuh know how dem people stap. If wih married an' mih bring it, dey doh min', buh if mih t'row am 'way o' if mih bring am widdout marriedin'…"

Back in Trinidad early in January, as I sat down to write the letter and found my arms shaking out of control and my fingers quite unable to grip the pen properly, I could not help asking myself, again and again, what had ever made me think that I could discuss these matters with Pappy face-to-face. Before heading for Tobago for Christmas, I had asked Ma Rondon to allow me to stay on in the little guesthouse on credit for a month or two until I got the job I was expecting as a third-class clerk in the federal civil service, and she had agreed: the other young men, all from South Trinidad, had gone home to their parents' houses for the holidays and to await their invitations for job interviews, and the place would be empty anyhow.

"*Bueno.* Okay, but some *plata*—a leettle money for the…," she had said, pointing to her open mouth.

"*Quecomeres?*" I replied superfluously. "Food?" She made no reply.

Shirley's school would be reopening on Monday, January 9, and our boat had docked in the early hours of that same morning. She was going to ask for time off on Friday so that we could spend the day together at the Normandie Hotel after our marriage at the Red House at nine o'clock in the morning, before the deputy registrar general, officiating at the civil ceremony, got into the really serious business of her day's routine.

The taxi driver again put me down at Abercromby and Oxford, and Ma Rondon, up early as usual, had hardly let me in when I threw myself onto the bed. When, awakening and rubbing my eyes, I saw that it was minutes to eight, I panicked for a moment before quickly realizing, with relief, that I no longer had any school to be late for. That short-lived moment of serious apprehension gone, however, a new one immediately took its place as I remembered that I had the letter to write to Pappy.

I have always believed that when you are terrified deep inside, your best refuge, that place where your privacy is more or less ensured, is the bathroom. I sat up on the bottom bed of the double-decker, swung around to rest my feet on the floor, leaned forward to reach my grip and draw it closer to me, and got out my bath towel. The indoor bathroom was for Ma Rondon and her family, so I headed for the one at the back of the guesthouse, where I let the water run down my body for long as I wrestled to call up words suitable for the letter to my father. In time, I was back inside, lingering over the cup of chocolate tea and the slice of margarined bread Ma Rondon had kindly given me, struggling still for words.

The letter, when I had finally managed to write it, said that I was happy he had taught me to do the right thing no matter what the circumstances and that I was letting that sacred rule guide my life and would always do so. There was something I had to tell him while up home for Christmas, but at the last moment, I had gotten cold feet. He knew, I wrote, that Shirley and I had become good-good friends, and he would remember how well the girl could cook. Well, all the time I was going to school down there in Trinidad, I had had many delicious meals, day and night, at her place in Belmont, which was within walking distance from where I was staying, and I didn't know how I would've survived without her care and kindness. And then, after a time, things had begun to happen between us. And then something really serious happened, which meant we now had to get married. The bad part was that she was already four months gone (although she wasn't showing too bad yet), so we couldn't wait too long. In fact, we were going to get married in the Red House Friday coming, which might even be before he got my letter, which was really bad. I would beg—in fact, I was begging, in advance—for his forgiveness.

It was a great relief to get that letter, those words, out of me and down on paper. Now, however, it would be torture's turn: night and day, I would be visualizing, in unceasing agony, all of Pappy's various possible reactions, none of them in my favor. All the same, suppressing those negative thoughts, I got dressed, bought and addressed an envelope a few hundred yards away at the People's Drugstore on Frederick Street, and headed down to the post office on Marine Square, where, turning my head to one side, I rounded off the deed by thrusting the envelope into the mailbox, onto the stream of no return.

"Who yuh writin', shi modda?" It was unmistakably Jacinta's voice, and I spun around as if I had been caught doing some very shameful deed.

"Hi, Jacinta… w'at, w'at yuh doin' here?"

"Mr. Brougham, why do I get this feeling that wherever you see me, your first question to me is what am I doing there. Dis nuh fooh-me country too?"

"Sarry, sarry! Mih wrang!"

"Of course you're wrong, sir. BOLAM deh jes' up ah road deh-suh. Half-pas' eleven ah mih lunchtime. Weh wrang wid you, bway?"

"Mih seh mi sarry, weh mo' yuh want?"

"Nutten. Is okay. Suh yuh good?"

"Yeah."

"Well, exam done now, suh w'en is de big day?"

There she was again with this big-day thing. I felt more than a little confused. At first, my heart had skipped a beat or two as I thought that she must somehow have gone to the Red House and seen the wedding banns we had stuck up. But it was then that I quickly recalled that she had asked the same question the day she had come to confront me at the library, when, as far as I knew, no wedding had yet been planned and, certainly, no banns had been published. So what was this big day she was harping on? I decided that my only escape was into innocence.

"Oh, the interview! I don't know yet."

"W'a' interview y'ah tark 'bout?"

"Federal civil service. Mih apply. Interview should be any day now."

"Is play yuh playing do'tish o' shi rayly ain' tell yuh shi pregnant?'

"Eh?" To hear her say it startled me, and I could feel the rest of my body physically jump about inside my skin, completely without my permission.

"Look, mih cyahn was'e mih whole lunchtime wid you nuh, bway. Mih garn!" she declared, hurrying away.

"Wait, wait!" I pleaded, thrusting both arms forward and clutching at the air that now filled the space that she had only just occupied.

I didn't go to see Shirley that evening. I was preoccupied with not only the possible outcome of the deed I had done in the morning but also the realization that Jacinta (and heaven knew who else!) was calmly in possession of my deep secret. I taxed my gray cells heavily, demanding that they urgently offer some plausible explanation as to how she could have come by such carefully suppressed information, but they paid me no mind. My thoughts turned to Pappy and the letter. This one was serious business, nothing like the puppy love one I had written to my cousin Gemma in Manzanilla years before and then later foolishly and irrationally tried to disown when he confronted me with it. *How very pathetic!* I heard myself say as I lay on my back on the top deck of the bed, ridiculing myself, aloud.

It was dusk by then. Coming to after Jacinta had skipped away, to help me forget that the girl knew what she obviously did and stop my brain from frying itself trying to figure out who else would know, I had gone to the library near Woodford Square to bury my head in a book with the idea of brushing up on my chess play. That wasn't a success: I found myself stuck for long on the same page, having to reread every paragraph twice or three times in order to be able to move on. My system had had a similar response to the rock cake and maubey I had bought at the little *parlor* on Abercromby Street just north of its junction with Marine Square. I had taken the rock cake, wrapped in a bit of brown paper, and the glass, filled more with ice than with the precious liquid, and gone to and sat at the lone little table drooping in a corner and topped by its years of accumulated grime, a rusty, creaking fan hanging from the ceiling just above it, spinning at what looked like one yard an hour. I took three tiny bites of the rock cake but, in the end, left it right there on the grimy table, resting on its brown paper base, as indeed I abandoned the generous helping of ice after sucking out with the straw the little drops of maubey that had been running around its cubes, slowly diminishing them. In the library I gave up on the chess book, sneakily tried the comic section, and eventually got stuck with Shakespeare and the goings-on on the battlefield in *Julius Caesar* up to the husband's definitive acknowledgment of the death of Portia: "No man bear sorrow better—Portia is dead."

I wasn't overly concerned that Shirley was not going to see me that evening. She knew well, and accepted, my dedication to the pursuit of full and proper sleep. If I traveled on the boat by night, in either direction, be it by deck chair, be it by cabin-presented double-decker bed, the next night is, as a rule, mine and my sleep's alone. She would reasonably half-hope that I would come, but that would be it. Leaving the library, as it was closing at six, I headed home. One of Ma Rondon's sons-in-law, Rolo, was there with two of his five children, as always begging me to play a game of chess with him. I would have played if I'd been in a better state of mind, unconcerned about the fact that he had beaten me comprehensibly each of the seventeen times we'd played before. Instead, I had a very quick shower and climbed into bed and lay there in the darkness, letting my thoughts go around in circles. I did hear the college clock strike the half-hour at eleven thirty, but I have never ever been able to recall having heard the midnight chime that night.

"Suh, w'a 'appen las' night?" She well knew the answer to that question. Asking it in feigned seriousness was merely a means of putting me on the defensive and softening me up generally.

"Weh yuh mean by dat?" I retorted, joining the game.

Still, half past three on a hot Tuesday afternoon is probably never a good time to play a game like that. It would be far less so if the object of your prank had been morose all day reliving a future moment of his own recent creation when his father would receive a certain letter he had written to him and, too, a future moment of his own creation when, trembling, he would say "I do," on Friday, in three days' time. She recognized something of that sort in the acidity of my tone.

"Boy!" she exclaimed, changing the subject. "It rayly hot today. Yuh warnt to bade an' come by me later?"

"Sarry, gyurl," I apologized for the acidity, "pressure, pressure!"

"Neva min', coulda been wuss," she said, mollifying me, as she darted through Ma Rondon's front door onto Oxford Street, continuing on her way home at the end of the school day. "Ah t'ought yuh did ketch col' feet and put foot!"

"Eh-eh. Mih 'trang... I'm strong... mih deh yah still."

Although it was not yet six o'clock when I got to Industry Lane, it was already getting dark, and the lights were on in her room. Casting my eyes about, I could see that dinner had already been cooked and was waiting patiently in the pot, under the transparent lid. That being so, she should have been lying in bed, showered and smiling when I gently pushed open the unlatched door. Instead, she sat glumly at the little table, poring over what seemed to be a letter, and did not leap up to greet me.

"Is fram Rookmin," she said without raising her head.

"Rookmin? De same Rookmin? Weh shi seh?"

"L'ahwi eat fuss."

The girl was a real genius. I could never understand how she could make dining on a simple thing like a chicken *pelau*, with a green salad and homemade dressing by the side, feel like the glory of some sort of banquet. I supposed it was just one of the numerous surreptitious gifts she seemed possessed of, and as usual in such matters,

I savored the thought and left it at that. This evening, too, even the un-iced ginger beer delighted. How did she always manage to make it taste different? We enjoyed dinner, but once again, she stubbornly would not let me help her wash up.

"Yuh haf to come back tomorrow," she said as she bent over the sink. "Wi haf to get ah witness."

"W'a'… w'at? W'a' witness?" I had almost forgotten she was there, there in her own place, where I was but a visitor, and I had been staring straight ahead of me, thinking, now about Friday itself, now about Pappy reading the fateful letter.

"Me mihse'f behn fooget: yuh cyahn married widdout witness."

"Oh mih gard, yuh right! Ah how yuh remember?"

"Rookmin letter."

"Rookmin letter?"

"Look am 'pan de shelf deh. Shi was livin' by shi uncle in Couva, shi mudder bredder. Deh is weh deh did sen' shi to get shi 'way fram you in Tobago—"

"Wait, wait, wait, stap right deh! Get shi away fram me? Ah dat weh yuh seh?"

"De uncle use' to constantly interfayr wid shi w'en 'e wife garn out, *abuse* shi," she continued, completely ignoring my hollow protestation. "It happen now dat one day 'e younger bredder ketch 'im *francomen* in de act. An' yuh know weh 'e do to save 'e skin? 'E tell 'e bredder tek some too!"

"Oh mih gard, nasty! Nasty! An', Shurley, dat mek yuh remember witness?"

"Yuh hurry or w'a'? Nex' t'ing yuh know, likkle bredder ah get married, an' big bredder want *she* fooh goh as witness. Shi put foot one time, an' garn goh live by a nex' uncle. Buh shi live by shise'f right now. Ah dat weh mek mih remember 'bout witness."

"Jesus Christ! By de time sun down tomarrow, Friday marnin' reach arready!"

"Ahwi haffoo arks Ms. Hull. Yuh haf to come back yah tomarrow."

"But—"

"Shhhh," she uttered, placing her right index finger to her lips, "ah didn' tell yuh nutten, buh is a good w'ile now shi tell mih shi know mih pregnant an' ahwi cyah depen' 'pan shi for any assistance."

My legs were lazy as I walked home, and also, I was sure there was an invisible ton of something of really high density bearing down upon my shoulders. I worried that just ahead of me there surely lay another night of sleeplessness. And if I mostly lay awake again on Tuesday night, would I have my wits about me when we met Mrs. Hull on Wednesday evening? It was more than bad enough that I had not known before this evening that she was aware of the pregnancy, never mind she was empathetic, but suddenly, to have to face her seeking a favor from her in connection, so to speak, with it! My head was a shambles. It was still in that state and condition when Ma Rondon shook me awake minutes (if not seconds!) past nine the following morning.

"Get up, Brougham, somebody come here. He is telling that you have to sign ah paper."

"Ma Rondon? Who come? Sign w'at?" I managed, rubbing my eyes.

"Rapido! Rapido!" Ma Rondon replied without empathy as she headed out of the room. "Hurry up!"

I jumped down from the upper deck of the bed and finished rubbing my eyes in front of the mirror hanging from a nail on the wall above the backless dresser. Satisfied that I was now clear of *yampi*, I took my comb off the dresser and ran it quickly through my hair twice. Out of the living room window I saw the van bearing, encircled, the unmistakable official sign: FEDERAL GOVERNMENT OF THE WEST INDIES. I knew at once that that could mean only one thing and, in sharp contradiction of the reality, felt as if I had slept soundly all night.

"Mr. Brougham?" the clerk more declared than inquired as he emerged from the front passenger seat, leaving the driver in the van.

"Yes, sir."

"Please sign here," he required, handing me a pen and then holding out the delivery book toward me with both hands.

I promptly did as commanded, and he handed me the brown envelope with the letters OFGS printed on it in very bold type. He went further: he told me my interview would be at eight forty-five the very next morning and explained that it was due to the short notice that the letter had been delivered by hand rather than posted, though he had to confess, he said, that that kind of thing happened rather often. Somewhat overwhelmed, I uttered with great passion a few staccato words of gratitude, the identities of which I absolutely cannot now recall.

When I arrived for the interview, the orderly took my name, spoke into his telephone extension receiver, and motioned me to the lone chair in a corner near his booth, assuring me, with the aid of an adverb with which, as a member of the federal government service I would presently become familiar, "Mr. Mohan shall be down momently, sir." While he was on the intercom, I could see from the clock on the wall across from his cubicle that the time was somewhere between eighty twenty-five and eighty thirty and that I was well on time, which gave me satisfaction. In short order, there appeared the same clerk who had delivered the letter to me the previous morning.

"Mr. Brougham," he said, holding out his hand as I hustled to my feet, "I'm Mr. Mohan. Please follow me."

Somewhere along the line, someone had stuck it into my head that people ought not to introduce themselves with handles attached to their names unless the handles were necessary to explain why they were present where they were at all. Strangely, perhaps, when big things annoy me, I just smile and let them pass, but when seemingly small things get on my nerves, I tend to react, but without overt sign of aggression.

"I'm Mr. Brougham," I said deliberately and quite unnecessarily.

"You should put your best foot forward." Clearly, what I solemnly viewed as my carefully conceived and executed attack on him had been a complete waste. I determined I would try again.

"Which one is that?" To be sure, I knew full well that success at the interview in no way depended upon him.

Mercifully, right at this point, we got to the waiting room just outside the interview chamber, and motioning me to a chair and acknowledging my thanks with a slight bow of the head, he left.

The wedding was a simple affair, duly witnessed by Mrs. Hull, all in a morning's work (in fact, all in a miniscule part of a morning's work) for the deputy registrar general. When we had met Mrs. Hull on the Wednesday evening, after all the tension had eased a bit, she had offered to take us out to brunch after the marriage (she'd almost said *wedding*!) ceremony, but we had declined, disclosing that we had arranged lunch and an overnight stay at the Normandie. She quite understandably did not accept our offer to join us at lunch, and the taxi we had hired and into the trunk of which we had already secured the grip with our nightwear and clothing change, went back to Industry Lane to deliver her home before we headed out to the hotel.

To my considerable discomfort, when we went to the reception to carry out the check-in formalities, I came face-to-face with David Yung-Kow. David had been a close colleague at CIC, and I had on occasion had a meal with him at the Normandie, which must have been one of the reasons that, at my instance, Shirley and I had, almost automatically, chosen that hotel, another reason surely having been its location in a quiet corner of St. Anns. But it was not the day and time that I preferred to run into David. How could I have been so unthinking as not to foresee that he would definitely be around there somewhere, working in the family business until he went off in late August to the Massachusetts Institute of Technology to pursue his studies in actuarial science?

"Mr. Brougham," he said with the hint of a smirk and an invisible wink, "I hope you have a very pleasant weekend with us. You're still at Oxford Street, I take it?"

"Ye… yeah" was what I intended to say, and I must have succeeded, but I don't know how he made it out, because I myself couldn't make any sense of the faint, pathetic sound that came out through my lips when I attempted the respond.

"In that case, just sign here. I'll fill in the rest." I could see the wicked fetal smile battling in vain against the corners of his lips, demanding passage for its birth.

"Thanks," I managed, steeling my nervous fingers to grasp the pen.

"Enjoy your stay, madam," David said, hardly looking at me as he took the card from my hand.

I don't know if David, perhaps passing along the corridor outside our room, had earlier overheard our spirited discussion on the matter of our mode of travel from the hotel, but when we had done with the midday checking-out formalities the following day, he quite casually offered to have one of their drivers do the honors for us. In any case, he knew by then that for us it wasn't a weekend but a single night, and he wouldn't have needed one of those complex mathematical equations he had so mastered to work out why. I found myself very quickly reliving the morning's matrimonial discussion.

"Look, Shirls, never min' it might feel mo' like ah one-night stan', is still yuh honeymoon. Mih cyahn traipse out ah road jes' suh wid wah grip ah mih han' ah goh look fooh ketch taxi fooh goh 'ome. Wi simply *haf* to hire ah car!"

"Mr. Brougham," she replied, confidently mounting her high horse, "a route taxi would cost us twenty-five cents each. Hiring a car would be five dollars plus a fifty-cent tip. We just cannot afford that."

"Suh, wi come in style, an' wi goh sneak out t'rough de back doe?"

"No, no—"

"Plus! David boun' fooh ketch ahwi flaggin' down taxi waitin' fooh wan wid room fooh two"

At the checkout counter now, a sweet smile on her face, she cut in briskly, denying me any ghost of a chance to respond to David's offer. "No, thank you, sir. We have other plans."

"*You* kerrin' de grip, right?" I demanded later, livid, barely out of David's sight and hearing.

"Mih know yuh blue-bex, buh jes' now ahwi haffoo buy baby clothes," she responded, snatching the little suitcase from my grasp. "M'ah goh tote de grip!"

It was the fourth or fifth route taxi that we flagged down as we stood incommunicative by the roadside that, having room for two, stopped. We came out at the Jerningham Avenue corner, and she said testily, "Yuh cyah goh straight home if yuh warnt!"

Mute of malice, I proceeded along the avenue at a pace with her in tow. Presently, I looked back and saw her, unsmiling and purposeful, striding along after me. She put up no resistance when, having stood and waited for her, I took the little suitcase from her hand, saying with medium-gentle affection, "Gimmih de grip."

Shirley had hardly inserted the key into her door lock when Mrs. Hull, sounding a bit breathless, called out to her, "Doh light no stove, mih dear. I have food for y'all. You can cook your stuff for Sunday lunch."

Responding to the landlady's offer extended when we had met with her the previous Wednesday evening, Shirley had seasoned a couple of chicken thighs the following night and given them to her to keep in her fridge until we returned from the hotel that day. Shirley pushed the door open, and I left it so as I followed her into the room. After her usual fashion, she sat at the edge of the bed, propped up by the heels of her palms, while I pushed the grip into the bottom of the little clothes cupboard and sat down at the table. Before we knew it, Mrs. Hull reappeared, bearing on a wooden tray two bowls single-mindedly shooting steam.

"Cowheel soup!" she announced, as if in triumph, turning my mouth in an instant into a flourishing spring. Just that self-same Wednesday evening before the fateful Friday, she had learned from us how much we loved that delicious dish, especially for Saturday lunch. As we set about the meal with gusto, I particularly enjoyed the baby green figs and the firm little dumplings, some of them long and slender and others round like a kaiser ball. It was not just because of the lovers' quarrel that we spoke little or not at all.

As she washed the bowls at the little sink, Shirley, without looking back at me, said gently, "Yuh doh have wuk tomorrow. Wih jes' married. Wark acrass to Oxford Street an' le' Ma Rondon know yuh sleepin' hayr tonight." I quietly got up and did as I'd been told.

It was a great and pleasurable night. Just over a month later, though, at midmorning on a sunny Saturday, together with three other newly minted federal civil service third-class clerks, I left for Up-Park Camp, Kingston, Jamaica, where the West India Regiment was based, and after that, for some years, I would share a bed with Shirley for only one more night.

## Chapter 25

The Williams sisters, both in their middle to upper twenties, were seven to eight years our seniors, but that didn't stop those three, uninhibited by marital status and impending fatherhood, from wondering aloud, when we were out of sight and hearing of the sisters, about their probable attitude to "adventure": for they seemed to all of us to be lively, attractive, independent, outgoing young women who loved life and would doubtless be disposed to what Nizam called new explorations. Mere months separated us lads in ages, but in physique as well as in looks, Froix fairly towered over the rest of us. So Michael was designated to test the waters, and he did so at dusk one fine evening. The report he brought back was not promising, though: they were awfully sorry that they were busy that evening, but we could all join them for Saturday-afternoon tea at four the following day. Nizam and Vishnu leaped up in glee, but their widening grins of anticipation survived only as long as it took for Michael's sober response to thrust their feet right back onto the ground. Even I had been moved to a little excitement and had risen from my seat, onto which I now sheepishly lowered my person.

"Fellas, take it easy, eh. Ah didn' reely ge' de impression dem gyurls takin' we serious! In fac', ah have a feelin' we not goin' to enjoy dat tea too much!"

Copying me, the others now slowly sank back onto the waterproof cushions that spared our backsides direct contact with the metal seats of the chairs that surrounded the table planted underneath the ackee tree.

"Weh yuh mean, weh it is yuh mean?" demanded Vishnu.

"W'a's dat man, w'a's dat?" Nizam queried.

"Come, come, man, yuh goin' an' talk sense or not?" Vishnu came back.

Those were all rhetorical questions of despair, but Michael, forever compassionate, chose to reply all the same.

"Fellas, to be trut'ful, ah t'ink deh was jes' laughin' at we!"

"How yuh mean, Mike, jes' so?" I put in.

"Look, *I* was talkin' night limes, plenty night lime, an' *dem* jes' watch one annoda an' smile an' invite we to Saturday-afternoon tea! And only one, eh… if you get my drift, gentlemen!"

"Fellas, Froix mekkin' plenty, plenty sense," I offered, breaking a deep, dark, and heavy silence.

"Yeah," Vishnu agreed, "afternoon tea my backside! Is jes' ah latta bull!"

"Gentlemen, gentlemen!" Nizam, who more than once had claimed to be *the only rational one*, opened his palm and raised his right arm with a benevolent imperiousness. "Let's not speculate: we don't know what may be in store for us. Look, one evening back home, I propositioned an older lady, and in due course, she invited me to her place. I absolutely salivated in anticipation. At her house she motioned me to sit on her couch while she disappeared to 'get comfortable.'" He inserted the inverted commas by the use of his index fingers. "Emerging from the bedroom, she poured two drinks and came and sat beside me, offering her glass for a clink. I took one sip of my drink and, a whisker short of immediately, leaned over and sought out her lips with mine. She pushed me away gently and admonished, 'Yuh want to spoil everyt'ing now! I invite you home not to grable me, but in the hope you would elegantly seduce me, so would you please, *please* just give that a try.' So, gentlemen, let's just go tomorrow and relax, have some tea, and see what the afternoon brings!"

It didn't bring much for the rest of us. But before we knew it, Michael was married. When he first mouthed his intention to engage in the holy sacrament, the other three of us fell silent, because the man simply sounded as if he wasn't joking. He was a handsome six-footer with high complexion, an athletic body, and "good hair," who, most of the time at any rate, seemed as tough as John Wayne, though every so often, before our very eyes, he would morph into a softie and a huge big-baby. Trinidadians with his physical characteristics, even if without his academic achievements as at date or his clearly classy upbringing, did not, as a rule, end up marrying people of Claire-Marie's pigmentation. It was true that it was definitively accepted by us, as indeed, as far as we could tell, by practically everybody else who knew her, that it was not every day that you would meet someone nearly as beautiful or full of class. The thing was, she was fully qualified for the name of what self-deprecating folk would call *tar-baby*. The thing about Mike, though, was that he was handsome and not only full of class but also brimming with self-confidence. He was not a sufficient slave to the mores of the place to succumb to the surrender of his own judgment and substitute for it that of others in any matter whatsoever, far less in so important a one as this.

"Go for it, Mikey boy! Live fast, die young, make a pretty corpse!" Nizam sounded nonchalant, but in truth, I for one couldn't tell whether he was sad, scared, disappointed, or honestly just plain unconcerned. But I had met Froix's parents and his sister, his sole sibling, at their St. Augustine home, admittedly only once, before we'd left for Jamaica, and I judged him now to be, even if utterly his own man, essentially the softie and the huge big-baby, well brought up in a home headed by a kindly GP who had undergone his medical training in faraway Ireland and known mindless discrimination and unrelenting hardship.

"Yuh serias, Mike?" I asked him.

"Yeah."

"Yuh rayly feel yuh know shi good enough arready?"

"Well, yeah, good enough."

"Yuh si *me*," said Vishnu, who paused briefly, as if waiting for some kind of response to his nonquestion, "yuh si arl de play I playin' man, w'en time come fuh me to married, is arrange dey arrangin' dat, *oui*. I cyahn come to Jamaica, meet ah 'ooman somew'ere, an' jes' jump up an' seh I marriedin' she!"

"De good t'ing about dah system is dat yuh always have somebody to blame if de damn t'ing doh wuk out!" I offered.

"Blame?" Nizam asked rhetorically. "It ain' have no room fuh blame in dat yuh nuh. If it ain' wuk out, all yuh can do is cut de 'ooman arse mornin', noon, an' night!"

The tea had been an elegant affair. Although the sisters had warned us to "dress appropriately," all of us except Mike could have done much better in terms of chosen attire. As instructed, we were on site for 3:50. There was a table, laid for twelve, standing in the shade of a cluster of bamboo at the edge of a massive meticulously manicured lawn that eased away eastward from the house. Nearby was another table, on which lay what were obviously the goodies and paraphernalia required for afternoon tea, including some sort of equipment connected to convenient electrical outlets, all guarded by two middle-aged ladies of pleasant mien wearing well-starched aprons. The sisters complimented Froix on his appearance and then, as if rehearsed, together bade us, "Welcome all!"

"We've invited six intelligent young ladies, who'll be here at four," said the elder sister. "We do feel confident that you'll be on your very best behavior, gentlemen."

"Now," said the other, "there are five chairs on each of the long sides of this table. *We* will, of course, sit at the other ends, and two of you guys will sit next to me and two next to her. Let's take our seats."

During the two minutes immediately leading up to four o'clock, three cars containing two young ladies each successively pulled into the driveway that bordered the lawn at its western extremity. We all rose to greet the first, and there was barely time to allow us guys to introduce ourselves but insufficient to chat, even for a bit, and we had no opportunity to resume our seats between the arrivals. Every member of that group of six was different, but they were all very attractive. Unfortunately for the rest of us, none of them seemed to have eyes for anybody but Froix. True, we all had dates by the following weekend, but only Michael and Claire-Marie hit it off. The others of us had explanations for that outcome: Vishnu and I had no wish to "press on" (as we were wont to put it), the one because of what Nizam, who, as we would say in the villages of Tobago, had no cover for his mouth, described as *oppressive cultural considerations*, the other because he was, remember, recently married and on the verge of fatherhood; and Nizam viewed the entire notion of "becoming affixed to one sole woman" as "self-abnegating, inhuman, and an abomination." Froix reveled in the self-abnegation and inhumanity and, in fairly short order, made the vows and slipped on the ring, while the rest of us had many and varied other dates and enjoyed Jamaica—until the referendum of September 19 spelled the end of the Federation of the West Indies.

The late father of the Williams sisters had been, from as far back as anyone could remember, an ardent promoter of the vision of West Indian nationhood and had passed away soon after the federal elections of 1958, as legend had it, with a smile of deep satisfaction on his face.

Mr. Williams had been the managing director of a large insurance company, while his wife, now a widow pushing sixty and on the verge of retirement, had risen through the ranks to become the principal of a prestigious secondary school. For by far the better part of their lives, they were well-placed in the society, and they had lived well and had brought up their two daughters accordingly. It was in these circumstances and to pay homage to the realization of the federation that, at the request of the federal authorities, we had been welcomed as paying guests in the Williams home. Mrs. Williams would often tell us young men, after the referendum, "I'm very, very glad my husband died peacefully before this West Indian tragedy, because, otherwise, he would, more than likely, have died of grief or a massive heart attack on the night of September 19."

I cannot forget that fateful day, for on the nineteenth of September 1961, the baby was exactly four months old, though it would not be until little Uriah was some seven and a half months old that I would first set eyes on him.

# Chapter 26

Ms. Rousseau's family enjoyed high standing in society, her parents having first come to Jamaica from Haiti to take up jobs as French teachers in a secondary school and having later moved on to establish prosperous businesses as merchants of French wines and perfumes. But to them, a man of Michael's combined physical and mental properties was still a really good catch. The Williams sisters fully understood these things, and when the older one approached the Rousseau parents to suggest that the small classy wedding be held at the Williams mansion, she had no apprehension about the likely response.

"Yes, yes, of course!" cried Mrs. Rousseau, grasping her husband's arm with both hands and arresting his eyes with hers, demanding from them, if not from his lips, some confession of unbearable elation. Her effort was not in vain, but rather yielded for her the sight of a grin of gleeful satisfaction.

Ms. Williams said, "You know the priest—"

"Yes, yes," Mrs. Rousseau said, cutting her off. "Father Gayle will officiate, and... and..."

"What I was going to say is that he... that Father Gayle would gladly come to our house for the cerem*ony*," Ms. Williams explained.

"*Mais oui!* Oh yes... *oui*! Yes!"

The wedding took place in the shade of the bamboo stool standing at the eastern edge of the lawn at four o'clock on a Sunday afternoon sixteen days before the referendum, the result of which everyone knew well in advance. The Thursday before, Froix had sent in his resignation by telegram, but it was a purely perfunctory act, and he felt no need to rub feverish palms together awaiting a response, which, in any event, was never going to be forthcoming.

The foreseeability of the outcome of the plebiscite notwithstanding, on the day following it, Vishnu, Nizam, and I were, as they would say in the Pint and the Windward Road villages, "lakka fish outta warta," for we had formulated no plans or made any inquiries about what we were to do next.

As for Michael, he was gone: three days before, on Sunday, September 17, he had left with his brand-new bride, bound for Florida, where they were to embark on their university studies on the twenty-fifth.

The Rousseau family had used their wealth strategically. The husband's younger brother, Louis, had gone from Port-au-Prince to study in Miami, and from Jamaica, even when confined to the income of a mere high school teacher, Mr. Rousseau had supported his sibling to the hilt. Later, as he began to make money from the wine and perfume businesses, he had become a significant benefactor of the university itself and had, in course of time, constructed a five-unit condominium for himself not far from the campus. For his part, Louis had spent his whole academic life at the university and had risen to become a senior dean and chairman of the scholarship committee, with considerable discretion under the rules. Long before the Saturday-afternoon tea in the shade of the bamboo stool on the edge of the lawn, Claire-Marie had secured a comfortable bursary for study at that university, and when the elder Rousseau called upon Louis, Louis was able to "work out something" for Michael. Following the wedding ceremony, the young couple had gone on a nine-day honeymoon at a resort in Ocho Rios, and when they came back, Michael had spent the next four or five days with us at the Williams mansion, during which he was mostly very pensive and a little withdrawn. That was perhaps the time at which the rest of us might have discussed our possible postreferendum futures, but I think the general atmosphere must have gotten in the way of that.

We dutifully reported for work at Up-Park Camp and found our bosses, in impeccable British Army uniforms, passionately pretending to be busy, only to look like busy mannequins that, finding themselves inexplicably alive and mobile, were dancing to some ethereal music only they could hear. A staff sergeant asked us about the whereabouts of Michael Froix, and at first, there was only silence. It was I who then chose to reply, "He *mus'-bi* somewhere, looking for a job!"

"Man, it ain't have nutten to do here," Nizam pointed out to the staff sergeant, who was our immediate supervisor. "Can we go?"

"Go where?"

"Not to Englan', baass man. Dey mightn' let us in anyhow!"

We had, very soon after our arrival, discussed among ourselves the apparent education and intelligence levels of the noncommissioned soldiers who seemed to enjoy the right to lord it over us, and we felt very strongly that we were facing a grave injustice. Much to our colonial surprise, we even were convinced that we spoke the queen's English better than they, not to mention at all the woeful way in which they wrote the thing. We were extremely resentful and could scarcely bring ourselves to feign respect.

"No, they will not," the boss man said with great emphasis. "*You* stay put, too. Army discipline!"

"Yes, but *we* are not soldiers."

"Dismissed!"

We spent all day playing a game—trying to outdo one another in our choices of adjectives appropriate to describe fully and fittingly our various superiors from the British Army. Mrs. Williams happened to be at the front door when we got home a few minutes before five.

"You seem exhausted, gentlemen," she observed, looking a little puzzled. "You would think it would have been otherwise. Did they overwork you lads today?"

We all had a great liking and great respect for Mrs. Williams, but in the context, we didn't think her question quite merited a response. I more than suspect that resentment toward the said superiors, general mental and emotional exhaustion, and apprehension about our futures would mainly have come into play. I vaguely remember forcing a weak smile onto my face to try to reassure Mrs. Williams that we did very much appreciate her and her genuine concern, but I didn't think she noticed.

"Come, gentlemen," she said, cuddling us with a maternal tone and pointing to the table standing at the far end of the veranda, set for four. "Go have a quick washup and let's have some tea."

All the tension left us.

"Not boasting or anything like that, but I'm proud of my coconut drops and my ackee tarts—hope you like them. And you have a choice of Ceylon tea or good Jamaican Blue Mountain coffee. Enjoy!"

Her offerings were indeed delicious, and no further words sought to intrude and distract us from the business at hand, until her smartly attired helper began to clear the table and *she* cuddled us with her tone again.

"So are you boys going to stay here or go back to Trinidad?"

Nobody replied. None of us had even realized that staying in Jamaica was an option.

"You two," she said after a brief pause, gesturing in the direction of Nizam and Vishnu, "will probably have some sort of family business in Trinidad to work in for a while until you find yourselves new jobs…," before her voice trailed off.

"All *my* famaly have," Vishnu declared, "is a vegetable garden, a little old truck, and a stall in de Chaguanas market!"

"That is plenty, Mrs. Williams," Nizam put in. "That is plenty-plenty. With me now, is something different. Ma died young, and Pa took it hard. Since then, he completely dedicates his life to the promotion of the economic advancement of Mr. Toolsie, who sells spirituous liquors by retail. When she was alive, we had a little roti stall just outside the Couva magistrates' court, and a lotta time, when lunchtime reach, even the magistrate used to send somebody to buy roti for him."

"Okay, so you boys prefer to stay here. Right now, at my school, there's a vacancy for one undergraduate teacher."

"*I'* goin' back home for sure," Vishnu confirmed. "I'm the eldes' chile of de famaly, and dey expec' me to come back home an' be dere wid dem."

"Six a' one, half a dozen a' de other for me," Nizam all but merely soliloquized; so low was his reflective voice.

"Mr. Brougham, are you here with us? You haven't lost your tongue, I trust. Would you like to have the job at my school?"

"Yes, thanks, Mrs. Williams."

"Okay, Mr. Hosein, if you're interested, I think I can find you one at another school. Enjoy your evening, gentlemen."

As we watched her erect frame disappear, Nizam studiously fiddled with his trademark goatee.

# Chapter 27

IN THE INTEREST OF THE preservation of your good health while waiting for a decision from a government department on a matter of the greatest importance, it is essential that you learn to be calm, patient, and understanding and to hone to a fine point your capacity to identify productive ways of occupying your time for the whole duration of an unrelenting hiatus. All three of us failed on each of these counts, but the saving grace was that, unlike Mr. Hosein *pere*, opting for the advantages of economies of scale, we did not purchase our substantive prop by retail, even though payment of our emoluments had not stopped. The red tape problem was not lack of money; it was that at the time the federal budget had been passed, no provision had been made for procedures to be adopted in the event of an unfavorable outcome of a possible plebiscite, and the result of that little oversight was that, although it would have been infinitely cheaper to fly us home fast than to maintain us at Crossroads in Kingston, no one had the authority, or the interpretative ingenuity, to spend federal funds on three one-way economy-class tickets for travel from Kingston to Port of Spain.

Time wore on, and we eventually landed at Piarco at just past four o'clock on Christmas Eve. That was a Sunday and not a business day for the SS *Trinidad* and the SS *Tobago*.

An hour or so before touchdown, I sensed that we had, all three of us, including the studiously phlegmatic Nizam, become somewhat solemn, somber even. We had effectively done just about one-half of our expected one-year tour of duty and had then spent the next three months or so floating around, like so many rum-loving ghosts, in induced high spirits. But here we were, heading fast for the landing strip and home, on Christmas Eve, with nothing to show for our erstwhile-celebrated overseas assignments. For me—and, I suspect, for Nizam, though he would never admit a thing like that—the realization that there would be no open arms of relative or friend waiting outside the terminal to encircle me did not help matters.

Unlike Nizo, though, when the moment came, I encountered a somewhat pleasant surprise. As confidently anticipated by all of us, there were two dozen or so relatives and friends waiting to welcome Vishnu, and we knew that, right there on the spot, they would each require, on average, two minutes to greet him properly. Nizo, not given to sentimentalism, quickly stole away, but I, feeling that any rapid and unempathetic departure from the welcoming proceedings would be inappropriate, stood by, notwithstanding that none of the *dramatis personae* paid me any attention at all. I resolved that as soon as a decent number of minutes had passed, I would go and queue up for the POS/P'CO/POS bus and hope that, Christmas Eve or not, Ma Rondon would prove true to her word that anytime I was stranded anywhere in Trinidad, her "lowly leetle 'ouse" would be open to me.

"Jaykee! *HS!*"

I jumped out of the insidious reverie that had sneakily enveloped me and almost taken me completely away from my physical surroundings. Jumped out, or was I still its submissive captive? Let it be what it might be, that sweet, excited voice was distinctly familiar, and I instantly forgot Vishnu and his welcoming party, craning my neck this way and that in ardent search of the lips that had unleashed that cry of joy.

"Jaykeee!" she passionately cried again. "HS!"

And this time I saw her.

"Eez so gooode to see you!" said Mrs. M, rushing toward me with open arms as I approached the two of them. Then, having, more patiently than I, awaited my release from that chillingly unexpected embrace, Jacinta planted a kiss on my cheek, with lips that felt far warmer even than the season's pervasive glow.

"Uncle Albert waitin' somew'ere outside dere wid 'e taxi. Oh," she added in answer to my unspoken question, "dey said in de papers dat alyuh comin' home today at las'. Was big, big news."

"Vell, eets Chreestmas Eve, and you cannot get to Tobago, but you 'ave family 'ere. Cinty and I, *vee* are your family—at least for *zisse* Chreestmas."

"Buh, buh, buh... but ah was really goin' to Oxford Street... Ma Rondon." I felt rather overwhelmed and, almost gasping for air, seized as firmly as I could the first opportunity I had had since landing to prove, mostly to myself, that I hadn't altogether lost the gift of speech.

"Buh, HS," Jacinta said, "Ma Rondon know yuh comin'?"

"Weh... weh... well, nah rayly, but..." I stammered.

"HS, Christmas Eve an' yuh warnt to jump up an' goh to people house jes' suh?"

"Shi did tell mih dat anytime..."

Jacinta and Mrs. M raised their eyebrows, furrowed their brows, cast wide-eyed looks at each other, and then turned their gazes toward me, wordlessly demanding that I should try to see sense.

"Broughamie! Ahwi bway!" Albert pulled up and was out of the car in a flash. He put his arms around me as if we were really tight. I felt some shock, some relief, and a feeling of great appreciation all at once. There are circumstances in which people grow close to you in your absence and build a pedestal to put you on.

"Dat ah fooh-you grip dat deh?" Albert asked, no doubt rhetorically.

I confirmed that the suitcase standing on the floor next to me, which he had pointed at, was indeed mine, and he grabbed it and turned and deposited it into the belly of the boot.

"*You* siddong in front," Jacinta turned to me and offered in a tone of glad deference, many seconds after we first noticed ourselves standing around outside the car like a pair of awkward mannequins.

"Buh, buh, buh..." was the entirety of my immediate response. The truth was that I could hardly summon the will to formulate, could scarcely divine the logic to support, even perfunctory protestation.

Mrs. M stepped in and, this time, for once, rescued me. She explained, "Meeziz de la Granade eez prep-paar-ring a gooode Chreestmas Eve dinner, and you are 'err guest. 'Ow zoz zat sound to you?"

It sounded fantastic, and I said so.

"Alber', you'll come in for a glass of ponche-a-crème?"

"Yes, ma'am."

"So how's the job goin', Cinty?" I asked, making no effort to turn and look at the two ladies in the back seat of Albert's taxi. I sensed with relief that I was finally beginning to wind down a little.

"Good. I'm in San Fernando. I got transferred to our High Street branch."

"So all dat travel yuh haf to travel, gyurl?"

"No, no! Ah live in Sando now… spen'in' Chris'mas with Mrs. M. You know, dis young lady—an' de odder payin' gues' too, in fac'—shi gone home, gone home to Moruga fooh Chris'mas. An' Tanty Harriette even have ah room fooh you an' arl."

"Ah, Mr. Brougham!" Tanty exclaimed when we got to the house. "I've heard so much about you! Come, come, have a seat. Make yourself completely at home."

"Thank you, thank you very much."

"You must be tired after the flight. But you must taste my ponche-a-crème even before you have your shower. I'm very proud of my ponche-a-crème, Mr. Brougham."

"Tanty Harriette," Mrs. M put in, "and one also for my goode friend Alber'?"

"Oh my god, I almost forgot you, Mr. Albert, er, Mr. Pilgrim. I'm so taken up with this returning son of the soil. Would you have some of my ponche-a-crème? It's delicious, take it from me!"

There was absolutely no denying that the drink was delicious, and when, afterward, Mrs. de la Granade left the living room and headed for the kitchen with the glasses on the tray, leaving me in less formal circumstances, I found myself passing my tongue around my lips, determined to capture all residual froths, aromas, and vapors. Albert got up and asked to be excused and headed for the front door as Mrs. M quickly rose to go and see him out.

Jacinta seized the opportunity. She turned toward me, and my heart leaped at the sight of the grave expression I saw on her face.

"Yuh know de picknee nuh fooh-you own!" she half-asked, half-proclaimed.

"Pi… pic… picknee'? W'at!"

Just then, the two older ladies came back into the living room, but neither of them sat down.

"You'll surely want to have a shower, Mr. Brougham. Let me show you to your room—it's really my guest room, it's self-contained. Ladies, do gimme a hand in the kitchen!"

It was just the four of us, and Mrs. de la Granade removed one of the chairs from each of the long sides of the eight-seat dining table, now set so we could sit facing one another, Cinty directly across from me. I politely skipped the hostess's "special recipe" ham starter and had a slice of baked turkey instead.

"You drrink rhum and vhisky, but you don't 'ave pork, eez zat right, Zhacob?" Mrs. M, Catholic again following her divorce from Teacher Aaron, teased.

Cinty stopped trying to tell me things with her eyes and gleefully let her lips giggle at me. She clearly wasn't noticing that the question caused me no alarm, or even discomfort. I turned to my right and faced the ribber.

"I guess," I said, "the difference is that I was never tempted to taste pork."

At first, I could find no explanation as to why Mrs. M, sitting on my right, would have jumped and appeared startled, but I quickly settled upon one when I looked diagonally across to Mrs. de la Granade, where she sat facing Mrs. M, and found a like expression on her face. I decided that my reference to the tasting of pork had brought to their ready minds the double entendre in each of two of our most loved songs—"Ah Want Ah piece Ah Pork Fuh Mih Chris'mus" and "Sixty Million Frenchmen Cyahn Be Wrong." Then, wondering whether I might not be completely wrong about them, I quickly chided myself for being unduly naughty now, if only in my thoughts.

"And now you're dreaming of...?" Cinty asked in genuine innocence, making me start and realize that my saucy mind had moved away from all of them and the table.

"Oh, that drink, that great ponche-a-crème!" I replied and then quietly patted myself on my mental back for what I considered a far too infrequent piece of quick thinking.

For that, too, Cinty, who knew me so well, gave me a big thumbs-up with her loudly laughing eyes and her smiling lips.

The taste of the lamb roast was unshakable testimony—though, truly, no more was needed by now—to the kitchen craft of the hostess, and there wasn't a great deal of talking done as we ate. The thing of greatest moment to me, though, was when Mrs. de la Granade looked to her right and asked—or commanded—Cinty, "You're coming with us, of course?" just after she had reminded Mrs. M that they were going to midnight Mass in Diego Martin. Cinty reddened a bit and reserved her verbal response for the short while when we were alone at the breakfast table rather late the following morning.

"Bway," she said, "mih cyahn tell yuh how bex mih behn bex w'en dis 'ooman tell mih dat. In any case, since w'en Mrs. M tu'n back cyartalic? Me seh Tanty Harriette ah goh goh ah chu'ch by shise'f an' Mrs. M mighta farl asleep eena shi room home-yah—oh, gash, look sh'ah come!"

After the main course at the Christmas Eve dinner, we went back to the comfort of the living room chairs and the dessert of traditional Christmas black cake with its ingredients, in substantial quantities, of fruits presoaked for several months in good Trinidad rum and of more live rum added later for good measure.

"Okay," said Mrs. de la Grenade presently, getting to her feet and omitting to wait for any response, "I have to get some quiet before church time. Shall we have a quick drop of a little something now? How about some fine Jamaican Blue Mountain coffee liqueur?"

Not only had I never tasted this fine brew before, it had also never remotely occurred to me that anybody in the Caribbean ever produced beverages other than rum and some beer. But I rather liked it. We all of us emptied our liqueur glasses fairly quickly, and to my mild astonishment, the hostess all but ordered me to bed, saying,

"Mr. Brougham, you look a bit tired, understandably. We'll see you in the morning. Do have a good night." I went to my room, brushed my teeth, and on the evidence of what I beheld in the mirror when I woke up next morning, went to sleep in my underwear.

Mrs. Hull tracked me down in San Fernando on Wednesday, just two days later. Christmas Day and Boxing Day were both public holidays in Trinidad and Tobago, and both the Monday and the Tuesday were off-work days. Wednesday started off the last three working days of the year.

"Yuh in trouble, HS bway, plenty trouble!" Jacinta said to me in the gravest of tones when she returned to her Cipero Street apartment from the High Street bank at the end of that working day. Up to that point, I'd been in high spirits, waiting for her to come home to hear the news about my interview at Paradise Pasture earlier that afternoon. I had no idea what trouble I could possibly be in, but my heart sank all the same, and I sensed something that felt much like an instant headache. I supposed she quickly perceived that I might well collapse right there and then, I didn't know, but she took pity on me and explained.

"Well, Mr. Brougham," she said with mock formality, "I have information that your darling wife is frantically searching for you—suh yuh in big, big trouble, bway!"

When, upon awakening on Christmas morning, I had observed my scantily clothed body in the full-length mirror, I had instinctively, and quite before I realized what I was doing, rushed to the door of the guest room to check if I'd locked it at some stage before falling asleep the previous night. If it was already past nine as my watch declared, it was altogether conceivable that one or other of the ladies, concerned that no sound of life was emanating from that quarter, might have tried to push the door open to satisfy herself that all was well with me—and then, unless she was Cinty, quickly retreated at the sight of me lying on the bed in my drawers. To my relief, I found that I had, indeed, secured the door. I immediately got into the shower and was able to leave the room at about half past nine.

"Merry Christmas, HS. Mih rayly glad fooh si yuh. Yuh know how lang mih deh out yah ah look out fooh yuh. Mih seh yuh dead!"

"Merry Christmas! Yuh good? How come ah you wan deh out yah?"

"Ah t'ree a'clack ahwi come back fram chu'ch. De ol' people an' dem nuh get up yet… yuh wan' some charclite tea?"

Wondering whether or not it was by accident that she was sitting on the love seat, I nevertheless moved deliberately to set myself down beside her. Before I had properly done so, however, she had her cup pressing against my lips.

"Heh, tas'e fooh me own. Tas'e fooh me charclite tea."

"Good, good, it rayly good," I approved, and misjudging her action as invitation to get cozy, I turned toward her and added, "Come gimmih ah kiss fooh Christmas!"

She was, if you can imagine it, at one and the same time very firm and noticeably gentle as she pushed me away and got up and headed for the kitchen.

"Yuh want am jes' lakka fooh me own?"

"Yes, just like yours, thank you, ma'am."

Presently, she returned with my cup of hot chocolate as well as a fresh one for herself. She handed me mine and moved determinedly to sit across from me at one end of the three-seater couch.

"Dah picknee deh rayly nuh fooh you own, eh!"

"Who seh suh? *You* see am?"

"Mih si am, aye! Mih-ah tell yuh ah nuh you-own!"

Her eyes followed mine to what, by my personal calculation and logic, was surely the liquor cabinet, and she was almost on her feet already when I asked if she could get me a glass. At that time of year, say, for the ten or so days sandwiching Christmas Day itself, it was perfectly acceptable to have a drink of your choice at any time during any twenty-four-hour period that you fancied. It was a purely individual choice. Cinty went to the kitchen and came back with a whiskey tumbler half-filled with ice.

"Is Christmus, Tanty Harriette nuh goh min'."

"T'anks. T'ank yuh, t'ank yuh, t'ank yuh!"

"Doh do nutten schupid, eh. Wait till yuh si am yuhse'f!"

Mrs. M emerged from her room just about then, looking resplendent in a cheerful, strapless flowered dress, her hair left free to tickle her bare shoulders and the back of her neck.

"Merry Chreestmas, Zhacob. Already I veeshed Cinty… and vat eez zat in your hand, visky? Vell zen, today you must also eat zee ham, yes?"

"Yes, Mr. Brougham, you haven't ever tasted ham, so how do you know you don't love it? Merry Christmas! Mr.… may I call you *Jake*?" put in Mrs. de la Granade, filling up the living room with her somewhat imposing presence as she bustled out of her bedroom.

"Yes, ma'am!"

"Jake, tell me, before you tasted whiskey, did you know if you would like it?'

"I felt I would, ma'am. With pork, I feel quite the opposite."

I think she had somehow expected me to be speechless and was utterly surprised to find that it was she who now could produce no verbal response. She sought refuge in the demands of duty.

"Okay, folks, breakfast in half an hour. Come, Jenny, let's get to it."

"Tanty, can I help?" asked Jacinta unconvincingly, still miffed, as she told me when they were gone, about having had to go to church with them the previous night.

"No. You keep Jake company, my dear."

"Mih hope yuh charclite tea still warm?"

"Warm enough. Suh ah w'en yuh did si de… ?"

"Yuh si dah suh'noo deh, lef' am right deh till yuh si de picknee yuhs'ef;mih ge' suh'noo betta fooh tell yuh."

"Naparima Callege ah San Fanando advatize fooh ah andagraduate Spanish teacher. Look am right yah," she rejoiced, holding up to me the newspaper clipping with the ad, from which she now read, "Interested persons should attend for interview at the college at 2:00 p.m. on the twenty-seventh day of December 1961."

"Buh… buh… buh weh m'ah goh… ?"

"Cinty, help mih set this table, girl," Mrs. de la Granade said, briskly and purposefully entering the living room, grasping a lively,

Christmassy tablecloth with both hands. She was about to spread the tablecloth, but Jacinta was at her elbow before she knew it.

"No, Tanty, let me do that," Jacinta said as Mrs. de la Granade promptly released her hold.

About ten minutes into our late breakfast, counting from the moment Mrs. M had wished us *bon apetit*, our hostess broke our dedicated silence.

"Hope it was worth the wait, Jake. Look, after Christmas dinner, say, around six thirty, I'm going off to visit some relatives, and these two lovely ladies will go with me."

I began, "Mrs. de la—"

"The younger ones who don't call me *Tanty*—from French *Tante*, I'm sure, Millie... of course, you took French at St. Mary's, Jake!—well, they just say *Ms. Harriette*. Suit yourself. You were saying?"

"I think I'll go by and see Ma Rondon, where I used to live when I was attending St. Mary's. I think she'll expect to see me."

Ms. Harriette asked a question with a raised eyebrow, and Jacinta replied to it.

"Oxford Street, almost right inside the college yard."

"Oh, that's good, then. You'll take a front-door key with you." It seemed that Ms. Harriette never said anything that was not the final word on any matter whatsoever.

"Yes, ma'am... er, thank you, Ms. Harriette."

"Tanty, I'll do the dishes," Cinty offered, and as Ms. Harriette rose, so did the rest of us. Cinty began the clearing of the table, and Ms. Harriette, seeing in my eyes signs that I was wondering if I should help her, motioned me with her head toward the three-seater couch, where she, too, set down herself almost simultaneously with me as I sat. Mrs. M chose the love seat.

"So," said Ms. Harriette, "I hear you have an interview on Wednesday? I hope all goes well."

I was startled. For some reason, I didn't expect Mrs. de la Granade to know that; I could see how Mrs. M might, but Mrs. de la Granade!

"Oh, I hope so, too, Ms. Harriette." I was feigning complete equanimity—at any rate, as best I could.

"Zhake, eet may be better if you stay at Cinty's place tomorrow night… be fresh for zee interview zee next day," Mrs. M suggested.

"But, Jacin—"

"Oh, she would be very glad to accommodate you, don't worry," Ms. Harriette ruled. "It's so sad they cut you boys adrift in Jamaica for more than four months. It was all over the news the last few days. Before that, the public had no idea that that was going on!"

"We managed. What we worried about was what would happen if our salaries simply stopped coming and we had no tickets to come home."

"'Ow ziz you boys spend your time, Zhake?"

"We went to work—well, to the workplace—every day and had our evenings to ourselves as usual."

"You wouldn't have lost much, then, if you could land that job on Wednesday," Ms. Harriette rounded off.

We were only two candidates there on Wednesday afternoon. The other one arrived late, wore his shirt outside his trousers, smelled as if he had had a couple of prelunch drinks, and as he entered, quite without noticing it, put a frown on the face of the principal's secretary as, sounding awfully desperate, he asked her for an ashtray. This was Naparima College, a premier Presbyterian high school, and I felt that these manifestations would not serve my competitor well. I felt no sorrow for him. On the contrary, I was convinced that if that was all they had to compare me with, it would probably be my lucky day, especially considering that the beginning of the new school term on January 8, 1962, was just around the corner, and with the New Year holidays coming in between to boot, they would very likely take on one or us.

"Mr. Ragoonath, this way, please." She disappeared with him in tow, leaving me to enjoy exclusively the small, if pleasantly decorated, receptionist's cubicle, where, she gratuitously offered, she was merely holding the fort only for the day.

Objectively, I was less than half-concerned that they were calling him in ahead of me although I had arrived before him, and on time. Still, in some way, that development made me a little uneasy; I mean, suppose he was from a well-known Presbyterian family right there in the south land and practically had the thing sewn up? I could be wasting my time and abusing my self-confidence.

"Mr. Brougham," she called out, reentering the cubicle after a few minutes, "the form you filled out earlier is quite comprehensive. We're just making a couple of routine random checks. The other candidate's details were very scanty—oh, and then his application was received before yours, you understand?"

I felt instantly better. And then my confidence leaped sky-high, because there was my competitor, let free in less than ten minutes, passing by in the corridor just outside the glass wall of the cubicle, looking a little dazed, perhaps even forlorn. Now he would definitely want, if not need, a rum and Coke, I said to myself—to my everlasting shame, completely without empathy for him.

The substitute secretary went back in and, reemerging, said it would be only another five or six minutes or so before I was called in. When I finally went in and encountered the three men sitting in a row on one side of the interview table, the one in the middle motioned me to take a seat on the chair directly facing him.

"So how was the experience in Jamaica?" asked the chairman.

"Well, sir, nothing happened after the referendum, or even during the months leading up to it. But we had to go to work every day—army discipline."

"Oh, were you in uniform, then?" asked another.

"No, sir, but the rules applied all the same."

"We see you've had some teaching experience?" the chairman came back.

"Yes, sir. I do like teaching," I said truthfully, but not without some anxiety fueling fear that that could be seen as merely a self-serving, platitudinous declaration. Pausing for a while, I added, "There aren't many things quite like watching the joy of discovery on the face of a student, be it good student or not-so-good student." *Oh my god, am I making matters worse?*

"I see, I see," the chairman responded, unblinkingly piercing my eyeballs with his, without a doubt in search of confirmation of the seeming earnestness.

"Anything else, gentlemen?" he said, looking to his right and to his left.

His colleagues each replied in the negative with a shake of the head. Still, I didn't immediately stop wondering when the hard part of the interview would begin, and I just about held my breath.

"The term begins on the eighth of January," the chairman advised.

"I know, sir."

"Congratulations. The secretary will be in touch with you," he said, rising.

"Thank you, sir."

I sailed back out of the room on cloud nine and, returning to Cinty's apartment, continued to revel in my state of elation—until she came home from work and gave me the news about Mrs. Hull's call to her.

Ma Rondon was really happy to see me when I got to the little guesthouse on Oxford Street just before seven on Christmas evening. I had been lucky to get a taxi on an evening like that practically as soon as I came through the door of Ms. Harriette's house and had gotten off at Green Corner, walked east along Park Street, and headed north on Abercromby. Loud voices and *parang* music coming through from a dedicated radio station were in stiff competition as I appeared through the open door.

"*Mama mia*! Brougham, is you? Goode, very goode! You know I looking out for you since last night! What happen?"

She hugged me, let go of me, looked me over as if to satisfy herself that I was all in one piece, and then hugged me again. "From lot of things I hearing long time, I frighten-frighten you no come back from Hamyca—you and the others!"

Reminiscent of the situation at Ms. Harriette's, all the schoolboy boarders had long left for the holidays, yet the little guesthouse was teeming with people. Ma Rondon held me by the left hand and led me through the crowd and the din to a table standing at the far corner of the living room weighed down by bottles of drinks of every kind. "Help yuhself, yuh at home, *mi casa tu casa*—you know that, Brougham!'

I knew quite a few of those present, starting with Ma Rondon's two married daughters, one of whom lived right there with her husband and five children. Then, visiting from Venezuela, there were her youngest sister, Clementina, and her husband, Rodrigo, whom I had met earlier on one of their trips for the annual carnival. Also, there were one or two former patrons of the little guesthouse, Ma Rondon's "sons" (as she called us), including my good Tobagonian friends Khari and Norris.

Whenever I talked for long in circumstances like those, in which you had to scream to be heard and also keep pretending that you were indeed hearing what was being said to you, I would end up with a stubborn headache. So now I mostly walked around with my glass in my left hand and shook people's hands or patted them on the shoulder, as appropriate, and said, "Merry Christmas. How are you?" and smiled broadly and moved on, hardly waiting for their shouted, inaudible replies. Presently, I noticed an empty chair next to the table with the drinks; I moved gradually through the crowd toward it, sat down, and deliberately avoiding any more alcoholic drinks, dropped a little piece of ice into my glass and poured myself some sorrel drink. No one, I think, noticed when I slipped out half an hour or so later.

"We're back!" Cinty announced, although she surely must have known that I had heard the three car doors slammed shut and the key turned in the front-door lock. They entered the living room, where I sat reading the previously untouched Sunday papers (none had been delivered on Christmas morning), and Cinty and Mrs. M, both, one after the other, kissed me on the cheek. Manifestly in high spirits, Mrs. de la Granade, no doubt intent upon keeping under full control a voice certain otherwise to come out far jollier than usual, said with force-ripe solemnity, "I hope you had a swell time, Jake."

"Yes, thanks, Ms. Harriette," I replied in a proper tone.

"Well, Tanty, eet's a shower and off to bed for me, if you zon't mind," said Mrs. M.

"Mind, my dear? What you think I am going to do?" Mrs. de la Granade replied before she turned toward Cinty and me, adding, "You two may want to try some coffee and black cake before turning in, I dunno... oh, to be young again!"

Still on her feet as we were left alone together, Cinty looked at me and asked, "Yuh warnt carfee an' black cake?"

Sensing mischief in her voice and seeing plenty more of it in her eyes, I responded correspondingly, "M'ah tek anyt'ing yuh gimme dis Chrissmuss, love!"

Ever committed and true to the rules of the play of love, she instantly pulled back. "Arright, carfee an' black cake fooh yuh!"

As she headed off to the kitchen, I asked, "Need help?"

"Nope."

I returned to the lead story on page 3 of the paper I'd been reading before they came in. STRANDED CLERKS 3 HOME THIS AFTERNOON was the headline. It was arresting; its font looked like forty-eight-point Gothic bold. But all I could think of immediately was that they could have left out the *3*: clerk 3 was the entry level. They could have just said clerks; what did it matter what level of clerks? Still, I was amazed at the furore our predicament in Jamaica (or Hamyca, according to Ma Rondon) had provoked back home. In the article, one opposition member of the federal Parliament was quoted as having asked scathingly, "If you can't find a way to return four suffering clerks 3 to their frustrated families, not even in time for Christmas, how can you run a corner grocery not to talk of a federal government?" According to the article, the minister of finance, Mr. Bradshaw, an unsmiling man of erect posture with a bristling handlebar moustache and a tremendous fondness for words, when asked for a comment on that observation, told the journalist, "With your kind permission, I would respectfully decline to lend respectability to it by seeming to take any notice at all of it."

Standing just outside the door of the kitchen, Cinty called out to me, "HS, how yuh warnt de... ?"

"Brown... little bit ah milk, one sugar... t'anks."

Presently, she was setting down the half-plates with the cake and the cake forks at the extremities of the coffee table standing in front of the three-seater couch, on which, on their return, they'd found me sitting with the Sunday papers. She made the trip back for the coffee cups.

"One ah mih gyurlfren an' dem fram de bank have ah Baxin' Day party ah Sando tomarrow, y'ah come wid mih?"

# Chapter 28

The moment at which the chairman of the interviewing panel was reminding me that school would start on the eighth of January was the same moment, more or less, at which Cinty, picking up her extension on the second ring, first heard the unfamiliar, if friendly, female voice at the other end of the line.

"Jacinta Pilgrim. Good afternoon. How may I be of service?" she said, following the standard answering format prescribed by the bank, complete with the regulation smile in her voice.

"Good afternoon. I'm Barbara Hull… I am Shirl—"

"I beg your pardon? I didn't quite get your name…," Cinty responded, her tone interrogative, largely because she was sure she had heard that name somewhere sometime before but could not immediately place it now.

"Mrs. Barbara Hull, Shirley Brougham's landlady—you know, Jake's wife!"

"Yes, yes! Oh, yes, Mrs. Hull. How are you, Mrs. Hull?"

"Very well, thank you. And you? I hope you had a good Christmas."

"Yes, thank you. Very good, thank you."

"I'm calling you because I'm trying to help Shirley get in touch with Jake."

The telephone receiver almost fell out of Cinty's left hand as, feeling the pen slip out from between her thumb and right index finger onto the blotter on her desk, she struggled with the onset of a very sudden headache.

"Jake? Oh, yes, yes. You know, I think he had a job interview in San Fernando today."

"You're in San Fernando. Any chance you'll see him later?"

"Yes, yes. I expect to see him."

"Good. Shirley would like him to know she's coming down on the boat next week Friday. I wonder if you can please give him that message?"

"Sure, Mrs. Hull," Cinty replied as she rested the backs of her hands on the blotter, fingers interlaced, and buried her forehead into her open palms. It was not only in search of relief from the headache that she did so, but also in an attempt to try to temper the agony of her astonishment at the realization that Shirley's landlady had reached to her, just like that, while her HS was, even if, so far, ever so innocently, a sleep-in guest at her apartment.

"Thank you ever so much! Shirley would be forever grateful to you."

The mortification in which this unwelcome conversation had enshrouded Cindy had subsided a lot by the time she got home. Think as she might for the rest of the afternoon, she had not been able to decide what words she should use to relate that telephone exchange to me. A long time later, in describing the whole experience to me in excruciating detail, she would certify that the words she had eventually used that afternoon had, as she faced me in the apartment after work, formulated themselves and escaped her lips entirely of their own accord—even if, in the very instant of their escape, she had consciously adopted them and claimed maternity of them, making them hers.

"Your darling wife is frantically looking for you," she said again.

"W'a! Weh you ge' dah towry deh fram? How *you* know dat? How yuh know dat? Weh yuh ge' dat fram?" I challenged, speaking with the relentless rapidity of a man who was afraid to stop talking and thereby give somebody a chance to say something he might not want to hear.

"Well, aryuh lan'lady carl mih."

"Mrs. Hull carl yuh? Weh shi carl yuh, ah-wuk?"

"HS, ah wuk mih behn deh. Mih nuh behn goh noway else! Weh yuh expeck shi fooh carl mih?"

"How shi fin' yuh? Wehmek ah *you* shi carl?"

"Bway, ah weh y'ah arks me? How *me* suppose' to know dat?"

"Mih jes' cyahn anderstan' how—"

"Yuh si me, leh mih goh an' tek arf dem wuk clothes yah. *You* tek yuh time an' wuk out fooh-you stowry dem."

"Ah wah 'towry y'ah tark 'bout? Wah towry y'ah tark 'bout, Cinty?"

Cinty disappeared into the bedroom without inclination to respond. She undressed and lay on the bed on her back, naked, her eyes closed, just thinking, thinking.

It bothered me a lot that I couldn't, for the life of me, figure out how Mrs. Hull could have found me there, a virtual needle in a haystack, a virtual common pin in a bundle of guinea grass. I got up from the couch forming part of the three-piece living room set and headed to the kitchen to search through the little cupboards in vain: I could find not a single drop of any alcoholic beverage, or even some cousin of it, anywhere. "Nat even a likkle end se'f!" I said in audible exclamation to myself, exasperation bordering upon bitterness almost overwhelming me, before I went back and sought relief in lying again on the couch, my head on one armrest, my crossed feet resting on the other. I tried again to see if I could figure it out.

*Shi neva meet Cinty in shi life, nat to tark 'bout Mrs. M. Shi doh know Ma Rondon... ah who shi know, bway?* I interrogated the deepest recesses of my memory.

Unable to keep the rest of my body still for long while my head was whirring, I swung my feet and legs off the armrest onto the floor and sat up. I then scratched my head.

"Tea!" I said aloud, as if addressing some invisible person. "Tea!" Then, with rapidly depleting enthusiasm, in unspoken words, I said to myself, *De onlies' t'ing mih know, mih showre Jacinta nuh ge' no charclite tea yah. Mih goh affoo drink green tea.*

I was soon lifting the whistling kettle off the stove and was about to pour water onto the expectant teabag when Cinty's voice surprised me. "Mek some tea fooh me too'."

I turned to look at her then instantly turned my attention back to the bottom of the cup standing in front of me on the kitchen counter. Just like that, I felt myself in the throes of a barely controllable excitement, which was making my right hand shake. I briefly glanced at the patient teabag that somehow seemed to be quizzically looking up at me and, so as not to frustrate its legitimate expectations, briskly tilted the kettle and slowly scalded it at first, and then I tilted the kettle even further and drowned it. I was still struggling to conceal my erection when, out of sheer necessity, I turned slightly in her direction in order to reach the tap and replenish the kettle.

"Have mine, I'll make another cup," I offered.

"Every time trouble tek yuh, yuh does fooget how fooh tark prapa Tubigonian an' yuh does start to tark fareign," she replied, and then mocked me. "Oh, 'I'll make another cup.' Ha! Mih know exac'ly w'a' happenin' to yuh *dingaling* right now, buh yuh betta cool dong. Mih come out yah eena mih badiz and bloomers jes' because dat ah weh mih feel fooh put arn, nutten else, nutten else! Suh cool yuhse'f, mister-man!"

When I had made the second cup of tea, I followed her into the living room and deliberately sat right next to her. She took a sip of her tea, put the cup down on the coffee table in front of her, and without turning to face me, spoke.

"Mih showre dah picknee deh nuh fooh-you own!"

Unable to find anything to say, I resorted to a source of solace that I hadn't pressed into service for quite a little while. I began to bite and strip my left-thumb nail.

"W'a 'appen, yuh tu'n moo-moo? Yuh fooget 'ow fooh tark?"

To me, the silence that descended and would not go away after that seemed to give flesh and blood to the air about us, which, it would surprise nobody to learn, made its easy passage through the normal pathway to my lungs all but impossible. Much as I dreaded what the dear Cinty would say next, though, it came as a relief when she broke the silence and destroyed the body it had gratuitously given to the air, and thus freed up the ether and the oxygen.

"Mrs. Hull… the lan'lady seh yuh wife ah come down back dong hayr by the boat nex' week Friday night."

"Nat dis Friday comin', nex' week? Fooh-she school goh open the eighth, too. Nex' week Friday ah de fif'."

"Yes, ah dat mih seh. Ah nex' week Friday mih seh!" she scolded me for the unnecessary interruption, clearly caring nothing that it was obviously born of my deep, dark, and disobedient anxiety.

"Providin' yuh cyah be'ave yuhse'f, yuh cyah stap yah till Tuesday night. Buh when Wednesday come, bright an' orly Wednesday marnin', is betta yuh goh 'ome by she, goh 'ome by yuh wife—or yuh cyah goh ah Oxford Street an' stay by yuh ol' gues'-house till shi come. Mih nuh wan' no trouble!"

"Gosh, Cinty, you're so kind to me!"

"Yuh si, yuh garn faereign again! Yuh rayly frighten, bway! Ah 'ow yuh frekken suh? Yuh name Frekken Friday now?"

There was silence once more as we left each other alone to think our separate thoughts.

As children growing up in the Pint, neither Cinty nor I knew anyone—except for Mr. Short and Mr. Young, the two Englishmen who were the respective owners of what were, especially in the context of a tiny island such as Tobago, vast expanses of land, known respectively as Richmond Estate and Belle Garden Estate—who actually had a telephone at home. Telephones were things you would go to at public booths or faraway exchanges, much as how you would go to church or school. The making of a telephone call to some official or business place entailed an elaborately planned and carefully executed visit to some distant public booth—unless, by some quirk of a benevolent fate, it proved easier, on an odd occasion, to get to the exchange in Scarborough. It was noticeably different in Trinidad: there, people like school principals and senior government officials and certain business owners had them right inside their homes. Mrs. de la Granade, Mrs. Hull, and Ma Rondon all had telephones at home. I wondered once more, almost idly now, how Mrs. Hull had come to track down Cinty at the bank and telephone her there.

"De mo' mih t'ink 'bout am," Cinty said decisively, draining the teacup and getting to her feet. "De mo' mih showre seh dah picknee deh nuh fooh-you own."

That seemed to me to have come right out of the blue, and it physically startled me and made my flesh jump up and down, in some disarray, upon my seemingly inert, unsuspecting frame. I made no verbal response, had no time for any, as she wheeled around, dropped off the teacup in the kitchen, and went back to her bedroom. Presently, though, I knocked at the bedroom door. As there was no reply, I gently pushed my way in, and there she was, lying naked on her back again, staring at the ceiling. She lifted a thoughtful hand and waved me away. I went back out into the kitchen, took out the seasoned chicken I had earlier seen in the meat compartment of the little fridge, and proceeded to cook the pelau I had gone to talk to her about in the first place.

"See you later," she called out to me as she bolted out through the door on her way to work the following morning. I was sure, as I lay there on the couch, that she knew I was only pretending to be fast asleep, but I was grateful all the same that she obviously wasn't waiting for any kind of response. She had told me more than once after we'd finished our pelau dinner and she'd complimented me on my "kitchen skills" that I was free to share the bed with her. "Jes' suh langse yuh be'ave yuhse'f." In the end, my only response to her generous offer was to ask for a pillow. I had unbearably mixed feelings about choosing the couch over the bed and being beside her, but in the end, the desire to be alone and try to sort out my thoughts won the day (or the night, if you like). She had looked distinctly puzzled, if not a bit hurt, as she handed me the pillow.

When it was safe to be wide awake, I got up and showered and made myself some breakfast. Later, I walked up to Coffee Street and bought myself a *Guardian* and a *Bomb* from a wayside newspaper vendor. Back in the apartment, I spent the day with my rather harrowing thoughts, at the same time finding space to read, from cover to cover, first the daily and then the fresh, new edition of the weekly scandal sheet. It was a few minutes to five when she pushed the front door and came in, her handbag over her left shoulder and a plastic bag in her right hand.

"How yuh do, yuh arright?" she asked, hardly looking at me and heading straight to the kitchen. But in no time at all she returned, rested the handbag down on the couch between us, sat down, and swung in my direction her tight-knit knees sheltered by her open palms.

"Yuh gi' dem mih wuk number? Yuh nuh tell mih nutten 'bout dat!"

"Dem who?"

"De school secretary carl. Yuh ge' de wuk! Mih rayly glad!" she exclaimed truthfully. Then she rose, took a step to the end of the couch where I sat, bent down, took ahold of my chin with both hands, jerked my lips upward to hers, and kissed them hard. As if she had just exhibited the most normal behavior in the world, she resumed her position on the couch, looked over at me, and smiled brightly.

"Deh seh deh have a Ol' Year's Nite party Sunday night an' yuh mus' come an' collec' yuh invitation—fooh you an' ah gues'."

"Who, de school?"

"Deh seh ah de Ol' Bwayz Associatian."

"Y'ah come wid mih?"

"Buh wait nuh, ah who else yuh wan' fooh kerry? Yuh ge' somebody else fooh kerr'?"

My spirits had therefore begun to soar long before, within a minute or two, she told me next that she had bought a flask of White Horse whiskey for us to celebrate my success in getting the new job.

"Chaser! W'a' 'bout chaser, yuh buy chaser?" I asked.

She wouldn't answer; she just sat there with an endearing smile on her face, silently looking at me, her knees now completely unknitted. I had immediately returned the favor. As soon as she told me about the whiskey, I rose and went across and bent over her. I opened my palms wide and clasped her face between them. My intention was to reciprocate with the warm, puckered kiss of a good friend—until I felt her burning tongue searing out a pathway through my pursed lips.

"We still need chaser," I said as my palms released her face and my own face kept trying not to betray any acknowledgment that what had just happened had happened.

She laughed out loud and stood up, then grabbed me in a brief, if extremely vigorous, embrace. Then, setting me free forthwith, she said, "Bway, ah wehmek y'ah tark fareign? Yes, mih foohget the chaser. Mih cyah goh far am if yuh too egzarstid arready. Weh yuh warnt, soda or coc'nut warter?"

"Egzarstid? Who egzarstid, *me?*"

I knew very well that I should continue keeping my cool, but, in all the circumstances, the notion of my being exhausted, especially after having spent all day in the apartment while she was at labor at the bank, seemed to have inside it components and insinuations highly subversive of my manhood. That was no excuse, I thought: if that were indeed so, and if it was her needling intention that it should be so, that would be all the more reason that I should keep my cool. I was going to keep my cool now. I put on a smile that spoke of consternation.

"*Me* eva seh yuh egzarstid? Mih seh *if* yuh egzarstid mih goh goh fooh de chaser. Yuh cyahn anderstan' English or w'at?"

"Sweetheart, *me* ah goh far am. Mih t'roat dry-dry an' de White Harse deh-deh ah suffa. Weh yuh warnt, soda o'—"

"Coc'nut warta. Enough fooh tomorrow night, too. Mih wan' fooh stap right home yah frah tonight an' res'-up fooh Sunday night."

I could hear the shower running when I returned, but almost immediately afterward, the sound of it was gone. I called out to her.

"Shall I pour one for you?" I asked, observing at the same time a couple of helpless medium-size sweet potatoes being tamed on the stove inside a merciless pot of water gleefully bubbling at the boil intent upon turning them into food for us. I thought, macabrely, idly, about how much I liked mutton and how it could conceivably have been two young sheep that I was looking at, if it had been a big wedding pot and we had untethered the lambs, just as the potatoes had been severed from their vine, and washed them, just as the potatoes surely had been washed and put unpeeled into the pot, and placed them into the boiling water, live, to reduce them to food for our satisfaction and pleasure. The sheep would surely have been bawling like hogs being slaughtered, never to be silenced until their voice boxes, sliced through and through, succumbed. Suppose, even now, the sweet potatoes, pleading to me with their eyes, were screaming and bawling and I couldn't even hear them? I meant to say, were they not right there before me, jumping around, as if they were living things, in the boiling water?

"Bway, w'a' it is wid you rayly? Wehmek y'ah tark fareign again?" she called out, bringing me abruptly back to the business at hand and making me realize that I was, in fact, in a state of subdued, explosive excitement without admitting it to myself, being, indeed, scarcely even conscious of it.

I felt I had a duty to tame it.

"Mih arright. Mih jes' tusty."

"Bade fus'. M'ah come out ah de bart'room now."

Presently, she entered the kitchen with her towel wrapped around her hips and, pretending she was wholly unaware of her erect nipples pointed at me like a pair of John Wayne pistols, sent me to the shower.

"*You* go-arn, goh bade. *Me* goh mix de drinks an' dem," she mock-commanded with a sly grin.

Through impeccable timing, or by happenstance, she was just outside the bathroom door, two glasses in hand, when I emerged dressed just like her. She smiled and handed me my scotch and soda, and when she wheeled around, I followed her, not through the adjacent bedroom door as seemed logical to me, but to the couch in the living room. She took a sip of her drink, and then a gulp of it, and got up and came over to me where I sat and kissed me hard, just as she had done before. The towel, like some self-unwinding sari, loosened itself and fell, and as my eyes opened wide at her nakedness winking down at me, she hurriedly put that lone item of apparel back into place and headed for the kitchen, saying only, "Perhaps later... for dinner we'll have barbecued beef ribs with garnished sweet potato and red wine."

I had no idea where she had discovered this business of garnished sweet potatoes; boil, roast, bake, fry—those were the things that I knew people did with that delightful root crop. Garnishing was an entirely new thing to me, and not even in the Williams household in Jamaica, where I had learned a thing or two about preparing and presenting food, had I, as far as I could recall, come across it. But whatever it was, it was good. And dinner on the whole, a delight to the palate, and with its simple elegance, and in towel wear and by candlelight, was awesome.

## Chapter 29

I COULD ONLY VAGUELY RECALL having met Felix Rodriguez at the Dhandoolal Boxing Day fete, but Sonya, cool as cucumber, was now introducing him, almost offhandedly, just above the din of the chatter level at the Old Year's Night party, as her "very good friend."

Cinty frowned and then seamlessly set about the studious removal of an imaginary bit of flint from my jacket collar whilst whistling into my left ear, through her front teeth, "Nuh le' shi fool yuh. Is shi man. Felix ah shi man!"

If you can picture it, there was a certain ferocity in the whisper, which at first unnerved me but which, quickly afterward, gave birth to a little smile (invisible to the naked eye, I hoped) of satisfaction, painted, perhaps, by a wispy brushstroke of apprehension. We had, up to that evening, had a joyous weekend alone together in her apartment, and neither of us had seemed since to be entertaining any second thoughts about what had gone on there. Now, even the flash of my incipient apprehension about what appeared to be her proprietary instincts fast went out like a light and, in no time at all, had become but a dim memory: for I had turned and looked at her again, her shapely body still adding grace to the delightful black dress she had earlier collected from the seamstress, around midday on that same Sunday.

"Wehmek yuh seh dat?" I heard myself saying without conviction.

"Suh mih nuh know shi, mih nuh know dem? Mih-ah tell yuh ah shi man!"

As luck would have it, I found a genuine reason to drop that line of conversation. The face of the man leaning against the wall across the room definitely seemed familiar, and either I was imagining it or he was staring at me intermittently. To make matters more intriguing, there was something about the appearance of the woman next to him that set off clanging memory bells in my head. Who on earth were these two people? Try as I might, I could find nothing in my recall to help me place them.

"W'a 'appen, yuh tu'n moo-moo or w'a'? Yuh nuh have nutten to seh? 'E was right deh. Dey doesn' kerry-on in front ah shi mudder, buh if yuh eye an' dem behn open, yuh woulda si fooh yuhs'ef dat da' is shi man!"

"Wait!" I exclaimed. "Is Vishnu! Jeezas Chri—is Vishnu!"

"Well, I'll be… Yuh mean arl dat tark *me* deh yah ah tark to yuh arl dis time, *you* nuh hayr one single word weh mih seh? Ah who Vishnu y'ah tark 'bout now?"

"Vishnu nuh. Yuh did si 'im ah de ayport Christmas Eve."

Seeing no light of comprehension on or about her face, I hurried to supply some further and better particulars. I said, "Jamaica. He was one ah de fellas an' dem who was wid me in Jamaica. Yuh an' Mrs. M did si 'im wid 'e famaly w'en alyuh did come an' meet mih in Piarco!"

"Jeezas! Yuh right, ah he se'f! Buh da' 'ooman 'tan'-up nayr am deh, how shi look lakka Rookmin suh?"

"Oh, shit! Ah Rookmin fooh true. Arl de time m'ah watch de 'ooman, m'ah tell mise'f seh mih know dah face deh somew'ere 'bout, buh mih min' neva run pan Rookmin."

"HS," she said with unexpected tenderness, "since w'en you does use dem kin'a dutty word deh, bway?"

"Sarry, gyul. Mih behn rayly, rayly surprise. Sarry."

"Hmm! Arright, mih forgive yuh. L' ahwi goh an' tark to dem."

Vishnu hardly noticed as we approached them, but Rookmin's eyes were a pair of blinding torchlights trained on us, even as her facial expression betrayed a deep confusion, if a confusion that survived only up to the moment before I took her into a tight, warm embrace.

"Rooks, is you?" I asked rhetorically, loosening my hold a little and throwing my head backward and intently scrutinizing her face. "Is rayly you, gyul?"

"Yes, ah me se'f, Jakey. Ah me se'f!!" she said as I watched Vishnu start visibly for never having heard her speak quite like that before. "Hi, Cinty."

"Brougham!" Vishnu exclaimed when he had recovered. "W'at de hell yuh doin' here? How yuh get here? It look like I is de onlies' stranger in dis company!"

"Small world, Vish! But what de hell *you* doin' here in a Ol' Year's Night fete wid Rooks by your side?"

"Real small world fuh true, Brougham!"

"Ah starting to teach here w'en school open nex' week. Da's how ah ge' de invite."

"Oh-ho! Dat make sense.... Well, you know I's a Naps ol' boy, right?"

"Dat make sense. Meet Cinty. Tobago school days friend. Working in Sando these days."

"Hi, Cinty. Nice to meet you."

"Me too you."

He turned back to me. He didn't, he said, want to tell me Rookmin's business, just before proceeding to do so. She was his cousin (her mother was his father's sister) and, after coming back from Tobago, had lived with his family for a couple of years before she got some London GCE passes, completed a typing course, got a job in the civil service, and started renting a place of her own in Barataria. When her parents sent her back from Tobago, she had gone to live at her mother's sister's place, but that hadn't worked out: her uncle-in-law... He trailed off and then said abruptly, "Look, le' Rookmin tell yuh dah part shiself, yes."

To kill the awkward silence that followed, and also to acknowledge the cousin's earlier greeting, Cinty said, "So, Rookmin girl, how are you?"

"I'm okay, girl, I'm okay."

"Good. So is somebody going to get us girls a drink or what?"

As previously remarked, Naps was a denominational school, owned by the Presbyterian Church, and, like all the other schools of that kind, belonging to the various religions, received a yearly grant from the government to help defray expenses. All such schools, unlike most of the state-owned ones (whose results, in general, did not encourage their students to celebrate), boasted former students who were very proud of them and could safely rely for material support upon vibrant old-boys or (for the products of all-girls institutions, who tended to be allergic to the word *old*) past-students associations. These associations would raise funds by running carnival and Old Year's Night (in time rechristened as New Year's Eve) and other fetes with good returns from the sale of spirituous liquors at two or three points on location. It was, at Naps, a rule of some antiquity that such points of sale at the fete location should never be described as *bars* (a word that exuded a connotation of decadence), and that rule was always strictly observed. So it was that Vishnu and I, without needing to ask the girls their choice of drinks, headed for the nearest of the three sets of electric lights persistently winking out loud the words DRINKS STATION.

"Allyuh good, yes!" I grinned at Vishnu as we moved along. "Ah know police station an' railway station, even stations of the cross, but what de hell is a drinks station?"

"Boy, don' min' is dis school ah did atten', eh, buh I's a Hindu and dem t'ing deh hard for poor little me to understand, yuh annastan'? But watch good, is premium scotch dey have, eh!"

By now we were at the station in a queue, the length of which seemed to us to be far too great for just after half past nine, a circumstance that made us unhappy and somewhat taciturn.

Back at the spot where we had left the two ladies by themselves, Rookmin turned and faced Cinty. "Sorry I gave Mrs. Hull your... did you get a call from a Mrs. Hull?"

"So is you!" Cinty returned. "Is you who put shi on to... but how did you know where—"

"Take it easy, Jacinta. Lemme explain."

"Go right ahead."

"Next week Monday, I may—ah ain' make up mih min' yet!—I may start out as a nongraduate teacher at St. Augustine Girls' High School. In any case, up to Sunday, I'll still be a clerk at the Ministry of Public Utilities in Salvatori Building, straight across the road from BOLAM."

"Or-hoh! So…"

"Ah have mih account in BOLAM."

"An' yuh neva even—"

"Two-t'ree time ah try to ketch yuh eye, buh like yuh neva mek me out. I gave up. I stopped trying."

"Suh jes' suh yuh ups an' decide I's some Ms. Uppity, right?"

"Well… anyhow, Christmas morning, breakfast done, me an' Vishnu siddong talking about hi' time in Jamaica. Ah ain't tell Vishnu not'ing, but ah realize for sure Jakey was in Jamaica too and came back together with Vishnu. I didn' go Piarco Christmas Eve w'en dey did come back… an' w'en Boxing Day come ah gone straight Industry Lane in Belmont t'inkin' ah goin' by Shirley to check dem out."

"And… ?"

"Not a soul, only Mrs. Hull, their landlady."

Mrs. Hull told her that I had indeed been in Jamaica with three other young men from Trinidad and that I must have come back with the others on Christmas Eve. It had been a big story in the papers, but the papers had never put the names of the lads, but she was sure I had come back. Shirley had gone to Tobago with the baby for the Christmas holidays, promising to get to a telephone and call to let her know the exact day of her return.

"Perhaps," said Mrs. Hull, "you and I can exchange telephone numbers, and if either of us find out where… By the way, did you check by Mrs. Rondon?"

"Mrs.… ?"

"Rondon. The guesthouse."

"No, ma'am. Don't know her."

"Okay, we exchange numbers. I give you my number and you… well, your work number. If anything, we call each other?"

Back home in the early afternoon, Rookmin persuaded Vishnu that they should stay home and rest rather than go to the fete they had planned to attend. Although Felix Rodriguez was a Presentation College old boy and a good Catholic who had once, before meeting Sonya, almost answered the call to the priesthood, Vishnu counted him among his best friends. As soon as Felix had realized from newspaper stories that Vishnu would be home for Christmas, he had bought a welcome-home card and had Sonya write a note in it inviting "Vish and Guest" to the fete.

"Yuh never even met this Sonya person, Vish. Is only since yuh gone Jamaica Felix pick up with she."

"Buh Felix is mih dead pardner, gyul."

"Say w'at? Ent yuh goh see dem Ol'-Year's Night."

"Arright, good point."

All Rookmin wanted was to have enough time to get from her cousin sufficient details about his arrival at Piarco on Christmas Eve to see if she could figure out where I would have gone, little realizing that the easiest way to find me would have been to attend the party at Sonya's house. But in the end, she struck gold. She got a good description of the two women who had come to meet me at the airport as well as of the taxi driver, and she thought she knew exactly who they were. Bright and early Wednesday morning, as soon as she had signed on at her office in the Salvatori Building, she headed across the road to BOLAM. The lowdown was not long in coming. All that remained was for her to call Barbara Hull and give her the pointer: "If you call BOLAM in San Fernando and get on to Ms. Jacinta Pilgrim, you may get some news for Shirley."

"Bu... But who...?"

"Oh, she's an old friend of theirs... from Tobago school days."

# Chapter 30

SHIRLEY DID NOT HAVE ANY baby in her arms as she descended the gangplank of the SS *Tobago*. Nor could I see anyone near to her holding one. Yet I had time to wonder, idly if you like, what used to happen to people traveling with babies in the days, not too long before, when the boat used to drop anchor far out in the sea in Tobago and passengers would have somehow to get into and be brought ashore, brought to the jetty, often by wildly rocking pirogues, baby in arms or not. When she reached the foot of the gangway, she stepped to one side, away from it, and put her grip down on the bare concrete of the wharf, and I wondered, rather briefly as it turned out, if, in the pre-dawn lighting, she had been able to see me standing amidst the little group of waiting friends and relatives. In an instant, though, much like a calf making its single-minded way through a field of guinea grass to the taut udders of its mother, her body was, as if pushing aside the fading darkness of the dawn, heading for mine directly. When she reached near enough to my body, she leaped onto it, threw her arms around its shoulders, her legs pointed backward from the knees, and said, "Mmmmm!" Then she kissed me with pleasurable ferocity.

"Happy New Year!" I said as she let go of my body and her feet hit the concrete.

"I love you."

"Where is the baby?"

Her smile faded at the speed of light, much faster than the pace of the early-morning darkness, and I quite understood why: my use of standard English to make an inquiry of that kind was a happening of unpleasant portent, it being notice of an attitude of strict formality and rigor. It seemed to take forever for her to reply, but presently she did.

"Mammy keep de baby. We have to talk."

I followed her to the grip and picked it up as she stooped and was about to do so herself. She followed me in turn to the front of the taxi rank just outside the compound. I called out "Industry Lane," and seeing the grip in my hand, the driver opened the trunk to receive it. I opened the door for her and went round and joined her in the back seat. As soon as we got into the studio apartment, she headed straight for the shower and, emerging fully clothed in shorts and cotton bodice, did not look directly at me when she spoke for the first time since our exchange about the baby.

"Mih bring fry-jacks, fry-bakes, an' charclite barls, yuh warnt any?" she asked as she opened the suitcase.

Even had I not been hungry, the promise of fried jackfish, fried bake, and fresh *chocolate tea* would have been far more than enough to make me so.

"W'a 'appen to de baby?"

"Mammy keep am. Ahwisuh haffoo tark. Me an' you affoo tark. Goh bade an' in de meantime m'ah goh mek yuh brockfuss."

I promptly obeyed. The shower was the perfect place of refuge from her alluring presence and the bellicose feelings of apprehension and unmuzzled passion to which, unerringly, it effortlessly made me prey. Away from it now, naked beneath the spray, I thought only briefly about the seven-month-old, before my mind's eye became transfixed upon the image of her body, on its back, bare and begging, outstretched on the bed. Still, I was not idle in the interim: I had been conducting the business of showering and had almost finished drying myself when she knocked gently at the bathroom door.

"Yuh finish? *Everyt'ing* getting' col'."

I barely resisted the temptation to say, "Everyt'ing? Yuh showre?" and opted for a reply less playful, less suggestive.

"Less than a minute," I promised.

The girl was blessed with a sweet hand, and as usual, the meal was a total delight, and while we ate, the only sounds to be heard were barely audible grunts of deep satisfaction. She got up as soon as she had finished. I myself had uncharacteristically devoured my share completely moments ahead of her and was just sitting there, looking at her with my deep-seated old admiration of her and her guileless, unrehearsed honesty, doubtless grinning, as I did so, a bit like the famed Cheshire cat.

"M'ah goh an' brush mih teet' an' den m'ah goh 'tretch out likkle bit. Y'ah come?"

"Eh-heh, m'ah come. Buh mih lef' mih grip by Ma Rondon, an' mih nuh ge' no toot'brush wid mih."

"Doh worry, mih bring wah new wan fooh yuh. It deh eena mih grip deh."

*What do you do,* I asked myself, *when her cooking is outstanding and her presentation of both the main course and the dessert leaves nothing to be desired, and her honesty flows easy, and her spirit and yours just simply mesh?*

# Chapter 31

When she opened her front door in response to my knock, Jacinta didn't bother to feign surprise; she just smiled briefly and took my grip from me and headed for the bedroom. Presently, she was back in the living room and stayed standing there, looking me up and down, as I sat there on the couch as if to satisfy herself that I was free of physical damage. I was in no great mood, and I simply returned the compliment. In time, she smiled broadly and then spoke.

"Mih-ah cook wan ah yuh favorite—cowheel soup."

"Enough fuh two?"

If my voice happened to sound raspy, it was not because I was not impressed and thrilled and hankering; it was just that I found it almost equally irritating to have been so confidently anticipated, and to such a nice point. None of this was lost on her, and it scarcely came as a shock to me that she turned and walked away and spoke again only after she'd been in the kitchen for some minutes.

"I've set the table, HS… and even if I say so myself, the soup smells really good. Yuh comin'?"

Of course, the proper thing for me to do in response was to become even more irritated and to put together in effective sequence a word or two in conspiracy to reek of biting sarcasm. Instead, I began to be overwhelmed by the delicious smell of the soup (which I definitely hadn't noticed before and of which I was, indeed, not yet cent-percent certain) and to allow the waywardness of my mind's eye to bring back before me certain things that I had seen and still not seen, up to that point: the minute pair of stylish shorts, the braless-ness peeping out from beneath the diaphanous skin-colored blouse, the arresting shade of the lipstick, the careful faux wildness of the hair, the arresting shapeliness.

"Well, I *am* hungry, as it happens," I said, struggling to keep my voice from betraying the pretense. "I'm coming."

I didn't fool her one bit. As I was about to pull the chair and sit at the little dining table, she came up to me, took ahold of me, pulled me close, and kissed me.

"You're going to enjoy this soup, I promise you, HS. A lot of love went into its preparation."

By a very long stretch, it was not an overstated promise: I had had many a bowl of cowheel soup before, but this one was outstanding. I told her so.

"All for you, HS." The formality of language and the seriousness of mien made me start a little and drove me to want to move away from that subject.

"Think I've overeaten, though."

"Goh back 'pan de couch. Siddong likkle bit an' le' yuh belly settle. Den yuh should goh inside an' lie dong. Le' mih wash up de wares… Is Saturday today. Yuh have yuh clo'se ready fuh wuk Mond'y?"

"Mm-hm. Mih ge' enough clo'se eena mih grip fooh de week. Mih nex' grip still deh by Ma Rondon."

"Mih goh affoo iron yuh shut and dem fooh yuh."

She had to wake me up when she joined me on the bed. I used to say to friends that if, at the same time that I needed sleep, the whole world decided to set about collapsing about me, I would go to sleep fully committed to examining the resultant ruins as soon as I awoke and to doing thereupon everything I could to help repair all damage. At the matrimonial apartment in Belmont, I hadn't slept well at all the previous night. I knew I loved Shirls all the more for her awesome honesty, but by daybreak, I had decided that it was not a situation I could handle. I had had to face the fact that, by contrast, I didn't even have whatsoever it took to tell her straight and clean that I was leaving. I always ran away from emotional confrontation. At once hating her and loving her and feeling wholly unworthy of her unvarnished commitment, I had, clutching my pathetic little grip, sneaked out while she still slept, hiding underneath the dawn's sneering darkness as I fled.

Kneeling over me and leaning forward slightly, her body supported by the heels of her hands, and mine a compliant prisoner of half sleep, she brushed her lips against mine, twice moving her head from left to right as she did so. I rubbed my eyes, looked up at her, rubbed my eyes vigorously, and briskly propped up my trunk by the elbows.

"Cinty!"

"Aha! Bet yuh did t'ink binna Shirley! Yuh know weh yuh is right now or yuh too sleepy to know? Well, ah fooh-me bed yuh leddown ah sleep in eh!"

"Shir... Cinty, weh arl dis fah?" I asked in a semistupor, not quite knowing myself what I was talking about, but Cinty's only response was to divest herself of the pair of minishorts and the diaphanous blouse and to cast a sharp, conspicuous glance at the only item of clothing I was wearing, thereby prompting me to haul off my jockey shorts.

"Suh shi tell yuh de trut'?" she asked in time, breaking the satisfied silence.

"She always does!" I returned, somewhat sharply.

"Oui, papa, yuh garn fareign again. Mih know weh dat mean... Buh jes' tell mih, shi tell yuh or shi ain' tell yuh?"

"Tell me what, for God's sake, Jacinta?"

"Seh dah picknee deh nuh fooh-you own, becarze ah nuh fooh-you picknee dat deh, HS. Ah nuh fooh-you own at arl."

She got up and walked to the kitchen and came back bearing a bottle of wine and a corkscrew.

"Mind opening this?" she said, holding out her hands toward me. "I'm going back for the glasses."

I sat up and opened the bottle of chilled Chilean white.

"Well," I said after my second sip, "yes, she did tell me everything. She's very up-front. What you see is what you ge..."

A rain cloud—or something that looked like one to me—darkened the expression on her face, and it struck me that she must have found those words of appreciation of Shirls, especially considering the context, definitely far short of inspiring. I told myself that I hadn't been exactly chivalrous.

"I think both of you may have something in common there," I scrambled to offer, without ever having given the slightest thought to any such comparison.

"Thanks," she responded dryly, just before uncharacteristically gulping a mouthful that nearly emptied the wineglass.

"Since m'ah likkle picknee mih behn fin' out seh 'ooman conniving—arl kin'a 'ooman," I pronounced, adding quickly, taking great care to exclude her, "buh nuh you an' Shirls—ahyuhsuh different."

"Shi tell yuh who ah de picknee pooppa?"

"Yes. As I said, up-front and not conniving."

"Yeah, after shi ge' ketch!"

At the end of my first day on the job, the principal, Dr. Jimmy Sieunarine, invited me to his office for a cup of tea. I took a sip and said yes, I had found the first day fulfilling and that no, I didn't anticipate any problems settling in. No, I said, I hadn't found suitable accommodation, but I was staying with a friend. No, it wasn't a young man my age, as he supposed, but a young woman, an old school friend of mine from Tobago, er, Belle Garden… er, more precisely, the Pint.

"The Pint?"

Not surprisingly, he was puzzled, and he rather abruptly adjusted the lie of his bristling eyebrows. I saw that he was scrutinizing my face with some intensity and shifted uncomfortably in the chair. In an instant, though, I accepted the suggestion of my inner voice that the relief from the onset of hyperventilation lay in my own hands (or, properly speaking, on my own lips).

"Well… er, it's a kind of family village, sir."

I explained that it was a kind of promontory, a little piece of land, jutting out into the sea between Richmond and Belle Garden Estates, each consisting of vast acreages owned by Englishmen by virtue of grants made to them by the Crown. Although Belle Garden was more or less a proper village, Richmond was a kind of subvillage inhabited only by the Short family and their long-term workers from Trinidad, while you might call the promontory was a sub-sub-village under Richmond, inhabited solely (or almost solely) by the Broughams.

"I understand… I think. You're looking, I suppose?'

"I beg your pardon, sir?"

"For accommodation."

"Yes, yes… yes."

In the evening, when I related these matters to Cinty, she was quite clear about the significance.

"'E know somet'ing!" she all but shouted out. "Yuh t'ink 'e carl yuh fooh tea becarze 'e like yuh? 'E know ah yah yuh live!"

I felt quite the *chupiddy* to realize that I had had to wait for her to show me the obvious. I put down the rum and soda she had poured for me as soon as she'd come home and dropped her handbag onto the couch and buried my face into my open palms.

"Ah how 'e fin' out?" I said aloud to myself.

"Y'ah arks me?" she demanded, but almost immediately afterward adding, in a voice grown warm and tender, "Ah wah likkle place weh ahwi live in, HS. Sando ah wah likkle, likkle place."

"Suh yuh t'ink… ?"

Cutting in, she reminded me that the tenant in the apartment next to hers would be moving out at the end of the month. She had, she pointed out, shared that information with me before but had not pursued the matter further, not quite knowing what my domestic plans were. Things seemed, she declared, a little clearer now.

"An', too besides, I right here, babes. Yuh goh ge' yuh food cook, yuh clo'se iron, everyt'ing."

The next day, Cinty telephoned her landlady and made the inevitable appointment to introduce me to her. We met the landlady at her High Street store at closing time at noon the following Saturday, and I made a small deposit on the rent for February, as a nonrefundable binder, an outcome that seemed to put Cinty into high spirits and that rendered me more than a little introspective.

Cinty and I left the apartment together on Sunday morning, she bound for church, I headed for Ma Rondon's to collect my other grip. Neither of us mentioned it, but it was understood that there was no way I was going to go into town without stopping by to see Shirley.

Barbara Hull had raised three daughters who were endowed with both brains and beauty and who, knowing that, were brimming with self-confidence and were independent-minded to an extent closely bordering upon the rebellious. She knew and understood many things as she had weathered many a storm with them while managing to remain at once firm mother and faithful friend.

"She's not there, she's gone to church," she called out, startling me as I knocked for the third time at the door of the studio apartment.

"Thanks, Mrs. Hull… er, good morning, Mrs. Hull. Er, thank you… thank you… er…"

"She should be back any moment now. Come sit for a while. Would you like some coffee?"

I was relieved that she had so saved me from continuous babbling, and I wondered just how many more times I would have gone on expressing my thanks—-and for exactly what, I wasn't even quite sure—if she hadn't so kindly come to my rescue.

"Thank you… er, and yes, thanks… the coffee… er, thanks very much."

"My three ones have gone to church, too. Me, I've done my bit, God knows," she offered, sitting me down on a chair and wheeling around and heading for what I presumed would be the kitchen.

When she came back out onto the veranda bearing two steaming mugs, she handed me my coffee but remained standing and, in between sips, looked now at me, now up and down the length of the street, Industry Lane, below.

"I think she went to church just about every day this past week… I think she's pining."

Quick as a flash, she gently eased the mug out of my hand, the moment I had reacted to her words by emptying it in a single gulp. Her obvious empathy prised open, in quick succession, my soul and my lips.

"We have a huge problem… I… she…"

"She told me. You don't have to talk about it… shouldn't, in fact… oh, good, here she comes!"

"Oh my gosh! Jakey, you're here! Hi, Mrs. Hull!"

"Hello, Shirley. Let me leave you two alone. You need time together."

I was right behind Shirls as she turned her key in the lock.

"Yuh want anything? Lemmih goh an' tek arf mih chu'ch clo'se an' dem. M'ah come back jes' now."

I looked around for a moment or two after she disappeared and almost, out of habit, sat on the edge of the bed, but then thought better of it, regarding such a procedure as inappropriate in the circumstances and an act far too intimate and too fertile with capacity to father unwelcome misunderstanding. I sat on one of the two chairs at the petite dining table. *I just came by to say hi,* I practiced silently. *Mih rayly come een tong to ge' mih grip fram by Ma Rondon, buh mih come fooh si you fuss.* I had started a third round of practice when her voice interrupted me.

"Yuh wan' brokfuss, yuh hungry?"

"Nuh, mih arright."

"Yuh warnt anyt'ing?" Was it my imagination, or was there, in fact, a suggestion of an invitation in her tone?

"Mih arright!" I replied at a decibel level distinctly higher than necessary, as if I were really addressing somebody harder to convince than Shirls. *What you're doing,* I said to myself paternalistically, *is screaming, "Get thee behind me, Satan."* And yet, in the throes of the conflict, I somehow found time to think, idly, *What's the feminine of* Satan, *anyway? Guy never had a woman in his life, anyhow!*

"Mih rayly come een tong to ge' mih grip fram by Ma Rondon, buh mih come fooh si you fuss."

I thought it was a good thing that I had rehearsed that speech.

"Yuh nuh behn bong fooh come. Ah me weh wrang. Ah me weh mek de big, big mistake. Dah man, mih own teacher, tek mih maid w'en m'ah wan' likkle, likkle gyurl, an' 'e break mih een. Den 'e come rong an' ge' de monita wuk fooh mih—'e t'ink 'e pay mih back wid dat. Den, when mih realize yuh n'ah come back ah Tobago, ah he mih behn goh an' beg fooh ge' de transfor suh mih coulda come down yah fooh wuk nayr yuh. And den, w'en mih behn deh-deh ah help am out an' mek ah likkle bit ah money fooh mihse'f Argas'-time, he beg mih an' beg mih an' beg mih. Oh gard, gyal, jes' wan las' time, jes' wan las' time…"

Her eyes filled right up, so much so that I felt as if I could almost taste the brine, and her lips began to tremble uncontrollably. Unable to bear the sight of her in that state, I got up and went to look out of the window over the sink. I could not think of anything at all to say, and it was she who broke the long silence that ensued.

"I doh blame *you*, Jakey. Ah doh' blame you at arl. Du wey yuh haf to du. Ge' yuh divorce. Buh if after dat yuh ever decide yuh wan' fooh come back to mih, mih goh deh yah still ah wait 'pan yuh… I love you, Jakey, I love you!"

I had an almost overwhelming urge to hold her and reassure her and make love to her, and I might well have done it if the grinning face of the evil primary school teacher, already now risen to the heights of headmaster, had not then and there appeared before my mind's angry and frustrated eye. What I did was walk back over to Shirls where she stood, kiss her on the forehead, and leave.

## Chapter 32

There was a Catholic church in Ten Chains and one in Goldsborough, these two villages being among the many miniscule ones lying along the south coast of Tobago separated by the Windward Road from the sea. If Tobago had nothing else, she had churches and, with a population numbering just under 1 percent of that of a country like, say, the United Kingdom, possibly had the most in the world *per capita*. Every Christian denomination you had ever heard of was represented on the island, but throughout her checkered history, her leering conquerors had been Protestants, and the Catholic Church did not have an overwhelming presence there. The Pilgrim family was a Catholic one that had migrated to the Pint from Les Coteaux, a little village in the hills toward the southwestern extremity of our little island, but the Catholic churches at both Ten Chains to the east of the Pint and Goldsborough to the west of it were too distant for the comfort of folk who would have to get to them by foot. The priest for the Parish of St. David, where of yore they had worshipped, had, through the years, consistently and with fervor, whenever he ran into a member of the family, expressed his deep sadness at their inattention to Mass and, concomitantly, the continuing grievous potential for the loss of their souls.

"Not necessarily the old man with his wooden leg," he would say, "but why can't the rest of you take a leisurely walk to Ten Chains or Goldsborough to attend Holy Mass on a Sunday morning—either way, it can't be more than three or four miles, can it?"

"Farda, ahwi goh be stink an' sweaty lang befo' ahwi reach chu'ch, an' even if ahwi come, by de time ahwi reach home back, goh be jes' time fooh ahwi to jes' leddong an' sleep," they would repeatedly explain, and he would drop the subject—until he set eyes on one of them again.

For Cinty, a memorable encounter with him took place when, after a particularly enjoyable carnival, right there in San Fernando, she went to the Catholic church on Wednesday, the fifteenth of February, to get some ashes on her forehead. Long afterward, she often found herself still wondering what her life would have been like if she had accepted Mrs. M's invitation to spend the carnival in Port of Spain and attend Mass there early on Ash Wednesday morning before heading to work in the south land. She felt that that encounter with the priest had, in the end, radically changed the course of her life.

When I had gotten to Ma Rondon's that sad Sunday morning in mid-January, the place was very quiet, and I feared at first that there was nobody around. I was relieved when Rolo, her son-in-law, poked his head out of a window, greeted me, pulled his head back in, and went to open the front door. Ma Rondon and her daughter and her five grandchildren, all Rolo's offspring, had gone to Holy Mass at the Cathedral of the Immaculate Conception right next door and would be back home soon, according to Rolo, "After mih mudda-in-law manage to say howdy to every living soul in sight. Coffee?"

"No, thanks. Just enough time to collect mih suitcase and catch a bus back to Sando. You can get it for me, please… the suitcase?"

"Yeah, sure. Ah know exac'ly where it is."

Cinty met me at the door and took away the grip from me, explaining, "Yuh lookin' rayly beat, HS." She had been peeping out, looking out for me ever since she returned from church and started to cook. Lunch was ready, she said. "An' mih showre yuh hungry!"

For the next four weeks, though technically having separate apartments, living together for all practical purposes, we enjoyed each other's company fully, even if, every now and then, the recurring vision of Shirley's tear-filled eyes on the day we last parted caused me severe heartache and made me distant and uncommunicative. Was her sin really mortal and not merely venal? After all, she had been ruthlessly exploited by an older man she trusted—her primary school teacher, no less—and she had tried no subterfuge on me. Even at the carnival fetes Cinty and I were attending, sometimes when there was a lull in the music, a vision of her streaming tears would come back to trouble me. Still...

We showered as soon as we got home on carnival Tuesday night and thought we would lie in her bed and rest a little before putting together some kind of quick little dinner, but it was clear when we looked about us in the morning that we had simply fallen asleep the moment our bodies hit the bed. Schools had the day off on Ash Wednesday, but not the banks, and certainly not BOLAM. Cinty would have to stop by and get her ashes in church before going in to work. I was happy that, as a Seventh-Day Adventist, I didn't have to suffer pangs of conscience over ashes—only over the rum and the dancing—and I have no doubt that I was deep in untroubled sleep when Cinty got out of bed and showered and dressed and left.

Days after Ash Wednesday, the curate, fully frocked, knocked on Cinty's door at just past eleven. When she peeped through the jalousies and saw who it was, she scampered into her bedroom to discard and replace the extraordinarily skimpy shorts she had on, leaving me to decipher the meaning of her somewhat mystifying direction. "Quick! Put am fooh siddong 'pan de couch deh 'til mih come back!" Waiting for elucidation of some sort, I watched her for one or two openmouthed seconds and then, for at least another second, examined futilely the space through which her frame had just passed, almost forgetting to attend to the door itself. And then I rushed out of the kitchen, where I had been sitting chatting with her as she added more fresh seasoning to the cowheel for our Saturday soup.

"Good morning to you. I'm Father O'Donovan. I am looking for a Ms. Pilgrim."

I felt my lips silently leaping about like a buoy at the mercy of some raging sea, but coming up just behind, Cinty spoke up and saved me.

"Oh, good morning, Father. Please come in," she said, guiding him to the couch, where they both sat down.

"If you will excuse me," I said, at one and the same time pointing at, and moving rapidly toward, the kitchen. Once safely there, I finished Cinty's seasoning job and then sat down at the little table, idly leafing through the copy of the *Catholic News* that she had brought home on Wednesday and which would, in normal circumstances, in all probability, have received no further attention from anyone at all.

At the church on Ash Wednesday, the priest had furrowed his brows and looked her up and down at least a couple of times and had eventually gone up to her and asked her if she was a Pilgrim. She had been quite young when the family had left Les Coteaux, and he seemed quite the stranger to her. She, in turn, screwed up her face and, before she knew it, was asking him, "A pilgrim? If I am a pilgrim?"

"No, no, no. Not a *pilgrim*, a *Pilgrim*... the Pilgrim family... Are you from Tobago?" he returned, no doubt realizing she couldn't actually hear the uppercase *P*.

"Yes, Father."

"Okay, then. Hope to see you here again soon. Have to get on with Holy Mass now."

As fate would have it, near midday that same day, he went to the bank to draw out some cash and couldn't help calling out her name as he laid eyes on her. "Ms. Pilgrim!" He introduced himself in rapid detail and explained that he had spent many years at the St. David Parish and had been transferred to San Fernando some six months previously. She gave in and gave him her particulars.

"Good. I'll be in your area at sometime over the next couple of days. I'll stop by to see you, if it's all right."

"Of course, Father."

All this I was hearing for the first time as she rolled or twirled the dough into shapely dumplings for the cowheel pot bubbling away on the stove.

"An' now 'e ah come yah an' arks mih if mih married an' who *you* be!"

Father O'Donovan clearly found that I looked far too comfortable, far too much at home there, to be nothing more than a friendly visiting neighbor, and it just so happened that afterward, his duties took him frequently to her area, and he would drop in each time and talk to her about the "eminently resistible" temptations of the flesh and about mortal sin. In short shrift, communication between Cinty and me had lost all subtlety, and all the little nuances and double entendres from which I had derived so much pleasure were gone. Even the rich language we had grown up with in Tobago had now, as the older ones in the Pint would say, put foot. In their place had entered the banality of "What are our plans for the future? Are we going to just go on living in sin?" These developments significantly upset my equanimity and also often made me angry and withdrawn.

# Chapter 33

For some time, later on, almost every time that, on a leisurely weekend drive in our Morris Minor motorcar, we passed by the old barbershop on Tragarete Road not far from Barclays Bank, I would find myself remarking to Shirley that for four months an apartment at that location had been my home. I never did it again, though, after the Saturday when Shirley's son said, in all innocence, but with an unmistakable emphasis on the last word, "Dad, yuh tellin' we dat *again*!" It hit me immediately how unwelcome to Shirley's patient ears must have been those repeated recalls of my association with that place. *And to think,* I thought, *that her only response had always been to flash that smile of hers that had never stopped testing the sturdiness of my knees!*

"Shirls, yuh okay?" I asked lamely, as a way of apologizing.

"Bway, yuh know dem t'ing deh suh doh badda me!" she replied, compassionately accepting the apology.

It was the year of independence from Great Britain: for Jamaica, it was going to be the sixth of August, and for Trinidad and Tobago, the thirty-first. The constitutional conferences had taken place earlier in the year, and by the beginning of August, the British Parliament had passed the two independence acts and Her Majesty had duly signed the orders-in-council. But quite properly, neither of the two fledgling countries would await these formalities to begin organization of its inevitable foreign ministry. Because of this, a whole new opportunity now presented itself to me.

Easter Sunday that year fell on a date that was also otherwise very auspicious for every awake member of our body politic: it was on that date, the twenty-second of April, two years earlier, that we had, as the calypsonian later put it, "marched in the rain with our premier" to press the United States to return Chaguaramas to us—all part of our striving for full control over our own destiny. The following Tuesday—without regard for the dedicated crowds, including tourists hailing from all over the world, concerned mainly with the goat and crab races—was the first day back at school in Trinidad, following the two-week break. My lunch intermission came, and I quickly disposed of the two *doubles* and the small bottle of guava juice I had bought at the little food stall standing at a distant corner of the school grounds. Leafing through the daily newspaper I found lying on one of the couches in the staff room while some of my senior colleagues, as was their wont, were seated at three different tables, passionately surrendering their all to their bridge games, I saw the advertisement for "candidates with a strong mathematics background, some competence in French and/or Spanish, and some experience working in accounts."

I immediately began to draft my application in my head. Applications, said the advertisement, were to be addressed to the administrative officer V attached to the Foreign Affairs Advisory Committee (FAAC) located at the former Federal House (now Trinidad House) on St. Vincent Street, Port of Spain. A successful applicant would, after a brief training period, be subject to posting abroad at one of our new diplomatic missions. The deadline for submission of applications was Thursday, the twenty-fourth day of May 1962 (that date in the yearly calendar by now no longer celebrated as Empire Day). Thus, it was that on the fourth of June of that year I found myself entering the old Federal House again to take up duties as a public servant. By the end of September, I was on duty at the brand-new high commission in London as financial attache.

There clearly had not been an overwhelming response to the advertisement, and the interview the Saturday week seemed to me to be altogether perfunctory. The previous afternoon, as I was having some pigeon pea soup in my little veranda, a policeman in uniform called out to me from the street below. At his invitation, I hurried down to meet him, and after I had first signed his delivery book upon demand as evidence that I had received that which he had not yet given to me, he presented me with an official-looking brown envelope.

"De job yuh apply for, de interview is tomorrow—ten o'clock," he said and turned and went away.

There were two interviewers, both of whom seemed throughout as if their minds were actually elsewhere, concentrating on more important matters. One of them asked me two or three questions, none of which I could ever remember, before inquiring from the other if he wished to ask me anything. His immediate response was no, but then he turned toward me and said, "One thing, can you start on Monday—if you get the job, that is?"

"Ye-yes, sir."

The interview over, the thought of visiting Shirley crossed my mind briefly before I dismissed it. What were we going to say to each other, anyway? I didn't like the idea of going straight back to San Fernando, either; by now, Jacinta and I were, consciously or otherwise, doing our best to avoid each other, and I hadn't quite made any real friends in the place yet. I thought of going to Strand or Globe cinema to see a movie but recalled that my claustrophobia almost always got the better of me during those twelve thirty shows, and so I jettisoned the idea. In the end, I went window-shopping on Frederick Street. There, wandering about in J. T. Johnson Dry Goods Store, I saw this familiar figure. I was quite sure that I knew her, but there was something about her that put me offtrack. I agonized over it a little and then said to myself, almost aloud, *Is de dress or w'at? De hairdo? Ah-hah! De polish, de polish!*

"Rookmin?" I called out tentatively, throwing my voice at her in the distance, and to my relief, she spun round.

"Jakey?" she half-inquired, knitting her eyebrows, and my only response was to rush forward and, quickly covering the space between us, take her into a friendly embrace.

"Gosh, so good to see you again, Rooks."

"Hey, boy, yuh look real good. Like Sando agree wid yuh. Wey yuh doin' in tong?"

Upstairs one of the shops on Marine Square, just west of Frederick Street, was where Hong Wing Chinese restaurant, with its reputation for providing a tasty fare at reasonable price, sat waiting for its customers. I'd often been there and enjoyed it, and it came directly to mind now, but I didn't mention it right away.

"Wey *you* doin' in tong?"

"Window-shoppin' today, buh in any case, ah livin' in tong now—ever since ah ge' de job in de ministry."

"Me too—window-shoppin', nuh… buh, ah t'ought yuh was goin' to teach at St. Augustine Girls'?"

"I said I might. Ah change mih min'. Ah didn' goh no way, becar ah like tong… Talk de trut'! Yuh gone by Shirley an' she ain' home, right?"

"Nuh really. Yuh mean you ain' hear wih done!"

"For true? Al-yuh done?"

"Long story. W'a 'bout some lunch? Chinese? Hong Wing restaurant right down ah road deh."

At the restaurant, I told her all about how things had gone between Shirley and me and the real reason I was in town that morning. She said it was a pity my marriage hadn't worked out but that such things happened in life.

"Buh still, wid all dat, w'en yuh married somebady dat yuh know good, dat yuh know fram lang time, yuh always stan' ah better chance; aryuhsuh shoulda be arright."

Instead of making some sort of response to that last remark, I began trying studiously to wrap some wayward noodles around my fork. Rooks would have none of that; she rested down her knife and fork on her plate, pointedly planted both elbows on the table, turning them into stilts for her open palms, put her chin into the open palms, and called my name.

"Jakey, yuh doh agree wid dat? Yuh doh agree wid w'at ah jus' say?"

Looking her straight in the eye, I said, "Yeah, I suppose so…"

"Orh-hoh," she said, retrieving her eating implements and turning back to tackle the mixed vegetables afresh. "T'ink you'll get the job?"

"Well, yuh neva really know, buh ah expec' suh. One ah dem arks me if I can start Monday. Only t'ing is, I doh know if dey arksin' everybady dat."

"Good. Ah haf to leave de place w'ere ah rentin' now. Ah fin' a place on Tragarete Road. Ah tek it although the rent kinda stiff. Buh is a two-bedroom. Weh yuh t'ink?"

"Well, yeah… if I get the job."

"Obvious!"

As it happened, the following morning, before Cinty could return to her apartment from Sunday Mass, the same police officer who had brought the interview letter came back and delivered my letter of appointment on probation. *These people are really serious,* I thought and wondered if working hard on weekends would be part of the deal for me.

Along the whole length of the east side of the four-apartment building, at both the ground and the upper floor levels, there ran a narrow veranda, cut in half, at each level, by a steel-bar partition, each half half-furnished with a five-piece plastic patio set. I had had three beers at lunch while Rooks fought with a single rum and coke, and that, followed by a cold evening shower, had made for a great Saturday night's sleep. On getting out of bed, I went into my kitchenette and prepared my breakfast. Now I sat at my plastic patio table, enjoying my poached eggs with sliced, minimally salted, fresh tomatoes and cucumbers going down well with my *fry-bake*, which I happily washed down with chocolate tea, musing upon how rapidly, and without any notice whatsoever, big things in life can change. When I had gotten the job at Naps and later rented the first-floor apartment rubbing right up against Cinty's and she and I were having most of our meals together, it seemed past clear that my life was settled for the foreseeable future. Now, all of a sudden, all that settled mental edifice was ashes, resulting mainly from the flame of Father O'Donovan's priestly ardor.

"HS!" I heard, as from a voice way in the distance, and, turning my head sharply northward, beheld, unsurprisingly, the only person who ever called me by that name.

"Yeah! Hi! Hi! Ho... how was Mass?"

"Bway, is de turd time ah carl out yuh name! Yuh jes' deh-deh ah daydream or w'a'?"

"Could be."

The thing was, she seldom, if ever, went out onto that little patio, and sitting there looking east, my view unobstructed by the flat, single-level houses before me as far as the eyes could see, I felt as secure in my privacy as I would be while lying, of a dry and sunny midday, under a verdant, many-handed mango tree or on a dry-leaf mattress in the shade of a bamboo patch.

"Suh y'ah arffer mih brockfuss?"

"Doh tell mih yuh rayly t'ink yuh goh appreciate dis kin'a basic vittle after yuh wafer an' wine!"

"I'll pray for you, Mr. Brougham!" she promised severely as she turned sharply and retreated into the bowel of her own apartment.

At lunchtime on Monday, I walked across to the Ministry of Public Utilities at the Salvatori Building. I had wanted to telephone her as soon as I got into Trinidad House but felt it would be unwise to seek to use the office telephone for private business in my first moment on the job. When I got to Rooks's office, somebody there told me she had already left to go out for lunch. I felt more than a little disappointed and slowly headed back to the elevator, but as I stood there waiting for it to appear, it was Rooks who did so first.

"But dey tell me yuh gone for lunch arready."

"Yep, but just stopped by the washroom... is obvious yuh get de job. Congrats!"

"Feels good!"

I can never remember, to this day, anything about the use to which they put the top floor of the building on Tragarete Road. Even when, in time, Shirley and I and the two children would drive by there in the Morris Minor and I would spiritedly mention that I had once lived at that address—even on those occasions—it was in vain that I would attempt to call to mind a memory of any single event connected with that top floor. Nowadays, some silly something keeps whispering into my ear that it was probably a meeting place for some Masonic lodge or other, but I really have no clear recollection or idea. What I always loved and cared about was the high white-painted wooden ceiling hovering over the ground-floor apartment shared by Rooks and me, our bedrooms situated on opposite sides of the passageway that, beginning at the northern wall of the little living room, led right down to the kitchen and the bathroom to the back, which together occupied the full length of the northern side of the building, separated from each other only by the laundry room.

"So when to expec' yuh?" she had asked, almost casually, as we sat down for lunch for the second time in three days at a table at Hong Wing's.

"Depends."

"Depends?"

"Suppose mih lan'lady insis' dat ah live out the month as well as gi'e she one month's notice?"

"I goh be dead by den—wid dah high rent ah facin'. Talk to shi. She might be very reasonable, yuh never know. *And* don' fo'get yuh goh be savin' travel money if yuh live in tong… an' travel hassle to boot."

As it turned out, my landlady was reasonable to a fault. She congratulated me on landing "such an important job" and said that she wouldn't dream of standing in the way of such an ambitious young man just starting out in life. In any case, by the grace of God, her apartments were always snapped up and never remained empty for long; she was always good to her tenants and was on her knees twice a day every day and constantly received God's guidance and abundant blessings. He would never let her down—unless, by some chance, she did not do right by young people like me. To help me out, she would give me back half of the rent I had paid for the month of June, and in the meantime, I was free to leave whenever it suited me. Hustling back south at the end of my first day on the job to meet her at her store before the six o'clock closing time had been more than worth it.

"Yuh si w'at ah tell yuh! Yuh si how reasonable shi was!" Rooks pronounced with great satisfaction when I met her at lunchtime the following day.

"An' yuh know w'at? Ah write out mih resignation letter an' Jacinta agree to le' de bank messenger drop it over by Naps for me."

"Good. Yuh was on probation, an' 'either side may terminate this appointment without notice,' right? Mih know de jargon."

"Yeah, dat tu'n out rayl good fooh me."

"Suh w'en yuh comin' in? Yuh cyah start to save pan travel money wan time."

"Well…"

"Me an' Vishnu tark. 'E seh he glad ah wouldn' be here alone. He can pick yuh up straight from work any day yuh like an' carry yuh Sando for yuh t'ings an' bring yuh straight back."

That evening, shortly after Father O'Donovan had left Cinty's apartment at the end of one of his frequent calls, I went by and explained to her that I would be moving into town that very Thursday. Irrationally, I felt almost horned, just because she looked relieved instead of sad.

The whole situation at the apartment was a bit awkward at first. Everything had been so nice and easy when we met at J. T. Johnson's, and even when we had gone off to lunch twice and sat at a discreet corner table in Hong Wing's dimly lit dining room and talked with barely disguised gushes of enthusiasm about sharing the apartment. Now that the sharing had become a reality, we were both looking really nervous and behaving as if we wished we could simply undo the whole thing.

On our way from San Fernando, Vish (as I resumed calling him now) had thoughtfully stopped in Couva, where we bought three shrimp rotis and three red Solo soft drinks, and he stayed on to have dinner with us that first night. We found ourselves alone in the apartment for the first time when, at just past eight o'clock, Vish headed home. She stood at the front door, pretending she was watching over him until the car was out of sight, but even so, she had evidently added a lagniappe to the time needed for that. Then she came and rejoined me at the dining table set at a corner of the living room. She fidgeted with her hair and her ears and her nose, and now and then, she pulled on the end of her blouse or of a leg of the pair of the shorts she was wearing. Finally, she spoke.

"Yuh want anyt'ing else... ah mean, yuh satisfy? Ah mean, de roti was enough? Yuh, yuh...?"

"I'm okay, Rooks. Yuh takin' a sho... ah mean yuh does bade before... ah mean, yuh know, I does bade every night before I go to be... to sleep... I mean, before ah go in an' lie down."

"Retire?"

"Yes, yes, *retire*... nice word... before I retire for the night."

"Me too. You go first."

I don't remember what movie I saw, but the following day, I took in the four thirty show at the Globe Cinema at Green Corner. We had taken the same taxi to work, and I had done on foot the distance between Salvatori Building and Trinidad House. At the lunch break, using the office phone for the first time, I had called and told her about my plan for lunch and for the after-work show. I went out and bought a cheese sandwich and a soft drink at a parlor on Queen Street and resisted a temptation to fill up the rest of the lunch hour by walking along Marine Square toward her workplace to see if, by chance, I would run into her.

As I exited the Globe not long after six o'clock, I followed my nose eastward along Park Street to what turned out to be, as the sign said, the Fry Chicken Shoppe and, feeling that I couldn't possibly go home with only one dinner in hand, bought two chicken-n-chips. I had sensed a hint of unhappiness in her voice at midday at my mention of the show and was glad now to see her eyes light up as she opened the apartment door for me.

"HS!" she exclaimed before regaining control of herself and saying in a less effusive tone, "We haf to cut a key fuh you. You is a big boy, right?"

"Ah bring two fry-chicken fuh dinner."

"An' yuh know I buy two roti misself," she said with a smile, with a certain look of contentment on her face, "buh we can eat dem tomorrow. Yuh want to eat right away?"

"Nope. Ah rather tek mih shower before dinner."

"Okay, goh-arn," she said, easing the plastic bag out of my hand. "*Me* bade arready. Wih goh eat after."

Over dinner, we agreed that, together or otherwise, on working days—at any rate, most of them—we would have lunch at some presentable sandwich place and share preparation of simple home-cooked dinners in the evenings. On most weekends, too, we would share the cooking. I extended my hand toward her plate as she emptied her glass of the fresh, homemade lemon-juice drink, but she gently pushed it away, explaining with a smile, "I will handle dat."

I had finished brushing my teeth and was drying my lips with my hand towel when she pushed open the bathroom door, saying, "Oh, sorry!" while studiously looking anything but.

"Oh, dat's o—"

Cutting my last word in half, she pressed her pursed lips against mine, pecked them loudly, and then backed away, looking at me impishly.

"Yuh finish?" she asked as if nothing at all had happened. And then, "Do you think I can do my teeth now, please?" she inquired *in foreign*.

Over and over after that, almost daily, she would tease me in every way and excite me but deny me fruition, and that soon began to irritate me, if ever so slightly. When, on the last Thursday of the month, as we sat at our dinner table, she offered to take me out to dinner the following evening, I replied with a contrived sternness, "Ms. Rookmin, how do I know you're not just teasing, taking me for a ride?"

She seemed shocked and a little hurt, and we finished the meal in silence. When I pointed out that it was my turn to do the dishes, she took them up and brusquely declared that she would do them; and she did not go near the shower until she was quite certain that I had retired to my room. All that caused me severe pain, but I could not find it in me to feel regret at the action I had taken.

Come four o'clock on Friday afternoon, the extension on my desk rang, and putting the receiver to my ear, I heard, "HS?"

"Hey, what's the matter, Ms. Rookmin?" I asked, and then, fervently wanting to be quite contrary, and recalling my "military service" at Up-Park Camp, I noted with doubtful relevance, "It's 1600 hours, you know!"

"Sixteen what?"

"Hundred hours—you know, soldier-talk for 4:00 p.m."

"Orh-hoh, yuh gone back to Jamaica? Jakey, yuh goin' home straight from work?"

"Yes. Why?"

"Nutten! See you later."

Getting home within the hour, I could hear the water running and knew she was having a shower. It was a hot June afternoon, and I was in the kitchen, next to the fridge, with a bottle of cold water poised over a glass encircled by the fingers of my left hand. She rushed out of the bathroom in a frenzy, screaming, "Ah lizard, ah lizard! Ah big, big lizard in de bartroom!"

First the glass, and then the bottle, in orderly, split-second sequence, fell from my hands—I supposed the one responding to her screams, the other to her stark, entrancing nakedness. She grabbed me by the left arm and led me briskly toward, and then cautiously into, the bathroom. But the big lizard had already disappeared, leaving us free to fill in the predinner time without lingering apprehension and in such manner as we chose. By seven o'clock, we were dressed and ready to go out.

On Tuesday, the fourth of September, three months to the day from the date on which I had assumed duties, the AO III called me to her office. She was an unmarried, no-nonsense woman of Chinese descent whom everyone, including the AO V, seemed to fear and who, in a later year, took early retirement after she had been bypassed for promotion in favor of a less senior AO III who was male and of another kind of ancestry.

"Good morning, ma'am," I greeted her desperately as her secretary ushered me into her office and shut me in there alone with her.

"Good morning, Mr. Brougham. And how are you getting along?" The superfluous *and* was a staple in that office, used by superiors in that sort of context to stop you from forgetting who was who. I never failed to be irritated by it.

The question was a huge question, and I was far from sure about what she wanted to hear. However, I quickly decided that she really didn't care to hear anything at all from me, and I accordingly responded, "Okay, thanks," and was not surprised that I saw no evidence that she had heard any of it.

"You know that in accordance with the terms of your letter of appointment, you are subject to overseas postings?"

"Yes, ma'am."

"Very well. Be prepared to depart for the high commission, London, on the twenty-ninth of this month. Please check with head admin for further details."

When I got home to give Rooks the news, she was howling at me before I could properly open my mouth.

"Oh my god, HS! HS, I'm… I'm… I'm—"

"Pregnant? Oh my god! Oh my god! Rookmin, I'm *not* your god!"

On the next day but one, after exhaustively discussing the matter, we went to the Red House and stuck up the banns, and we returned to the Red House for the marriage on the fifteenth of September, with Vishnu for witness.

The marriage, as it turned out, was not idyllic. Following the lizard demarche, the occasions of teasing had multiplied, only that now fully half or more of them yielded fruit. Even so, the fruit fell distinctly short of perfection, and there was always, on her part, a certain notable insufficiency of physical as well as mental surrender or, short of surrender, at least total commitment to the loving.

"Look," I had said once from my heart, "you don't have to if you don't want to. It's either for both of us or nothing. Either we are transported to the seventh heaven together or we just remain earthbound, separately—it's the way I've always seen it. It's why I can never comprehend rape—except as an act of terminal violence akin to homicide."

"Rape, eh? Mih uncle did rape me!"

"Whaat?"

"Plenty time, HS. Every time mih tanty—hi' wife—goh out to de market, o' anyw'ere, is rape 'e rapin' mih."

"Doh tark schuppidniss! Yuh own uncle?"

"As dere is ah Gard above," she replied as she kissed the back of her right hand to underline the truth of her declaration. "Dah's w'y ah had was to go and live by mih nex' uncle—by Vishnu an' dem. Vishnu farda is mih rayl uncle."

"Wait, wait, wait, wait, wait… w'a's de stowry? W'ah's de rayl stowry hayr?"

When I had heard enough of it, I asked her to stop. When, in order to prevent any unwanted liaisons maturing out of her visits to the Pint, her parents had had her spirited away from Tobago back to Central Trinidad, where the family hailed from, she had gone to live with her mother's sister and her family. There she soon noticed, with great uneasiness, that her aunt's husband could not take his eyes off her, and she was not surprised when, one fine day, when her aunt was out and they were in the house alone, he molested her. After that, whenever her aunt was going out, leaving her husband behind, Rooks would, on one pretext or the other, beg to go with her aunt, but always in vain, as taking her would require her aunt to pay an additional route taxi fare. Rooks was finally able to convince her parents, without telling them or anyone else the truth about her ordeal, to let her go and live at the home of Vishnu's father, her mother's brother. There she had found a haven, and before this, the only person she had told of her tribulations (as she put it) was Vishnu himself.

"Now, is only you, me, Vishnu, an' dat nasty man know w'at I rayly gone t'rough. An' now every time ah try to do dis t'ing, every time ah try to do a likkle rudeniss, ah does see dis big, nasty man in front ah mih eye an' dem an' ah does jus' clam up, jus' freeze up! Ah jes' cyahn help it, HS!"

"Okay, dah enough. Ah doh warn' to hear nuh muh. Goh in yuh bed, goh in yuh bed. *Goh in yuh own bed.*"

I didn't feel good about myself after she meekly turned and walked away. What she needed at that point was empathy, and I had failed her. You mean I wasn't made of sterner stuff than that? I didn't sleep well that night and for many a night afterward, and for quite a while, in my relationship with her, most probably overcompensated considerably.

When we arrived in London on the morning of the thirtieth of September, we were taken to the Carlton Tower Hotel, where we stayed for a couple of weeks, until I located an apartment for us in Hampstead, in North London.

The baby came in the middle of May. Soon after he appeared, the midwife, opening and briskly applying to some part of his person the skilled palm of her right hand, had induced him to scream, and he presented us with a wholly inscrutable face. You could understand if he'd seemed upset or angry, but what he was, was inscrutable. I could hardly bear the blank gaze, so irrationally asking myself if it was because of anything I had done, I looked away. I told myself that the only sin I could have committed, if sin it be, was to have been, of late, in a state of almost constant irritation at the absence of relaxed and enjoyable intimacy in the marriage. Much as I had tried to fool myself by telling it that it was probably because of the pregnancy, it would not believe me.

"Babe," she would say, surreptitiously taken to calling me that, "ent ah did explain de problem to you. God hear, ah does try mih bes', buh no matter how ah try, all ah does see in front ah mih eye is mih mudda sister husban' and 'e big, nasty self. An' is numb ah gone numb, one time!"

At first, I had managed to show some empathy, but in rather short order, my standard response consisted of getting dressed, abruptly heading to the kitchen for a rum on the rocks, and stretching out on the couch in the living room until I was certain she had fallen asleep. At all events, time was to prove beyond reasonable doubt that it wasn't the pregnancy at all.

It was from this boy, though, my precious little baby, son of a Seventh-Day Adventist father and a Hindu mother, that Father O'Mally, the priest of St. John's Wood, would resolutely withhold the opportunity for the everlasting life that he himself held to be attainable only through the Holy Catholic Church. In the end, Shivnarayan was, simply and without complication, a very happy Hindu.

## Chapter 34

"Suh yuh happy?" Shirls softly asked, extending her arms across the table, pivoted at the elbow, and placing her hands, palms down, each on the back of one of mine.

If the place hadn't been so dimly lit, my senses could have added the look in her eyes to the softness of her touch and the tone and texture of her voice and so created a kind of *app* capable of guiding my brain's computer with ease to understand her question definitively.

Cousin Conrad was the blood brother of Paapa Milton, one-time reputed husband of Gran, that one of my two maternal grandmothers who lived atop the cliff by the sea at the farthest extremity of George Street from the school in Glamorgan, and that paternal great-uncle of mine had passed on shortly before my scheduled departure on the posting to London. Supposedly, they made us call him *cousin* because trying to fit him snugly into the family tree in a way that children's minds could assimilate would have proved to be an excessively demanding and, indeed, altogether unnecessary, task.

When he died, I made a two-day trip to Tobago to attend the funeral and to bid farewell to parents, siblings, and close relatives. At an earlier time, I had given Pappy notice (absurdly brief though it was) of my then-impending marriage to Shirls, and as I have shown earlier, to do that had taken courage; of my marriage to Rooks, though, I had offered not a single word of information. Yet I was ever conscious of the reality that I couldn't very well get up and go off to London for years without going to Tobago first to say goodbye to the family while, at the same time, I could not see how I could very well go to Tobago to visit the family and compound my sin by making no mention at all of Rooks. In time, I had decided that my best course of action would be to make a quick one-day trip and try to explain away that procedure by passionate references to the pressures, both official and domestic, of preparing to proceed on a posting abroad—knowing full well that such an approach would fall quite short of taking care of the dilemma that I faced. That cousin Conrad should die just about then and put a mere one-day visit out of the question increased my worries manifold. In the end, there was no choice left to me but to go and face the music.

The funeral service at the Goodwood Anglican Church was set for three o'clock, and I timed my arrival in such a manner as to help delay for as long as possible all opportunities for a substantive face-to-face conversation with Pappy.

"An' yuh wife, how shi du?" he had asked when the occasion barely arose, right in the middle of our initial exchange of greetings.

Now, nearly three years later, back in Tobago for another funeral, there was Pappy, the moment we found ourselves alone together after the service, asking me the same question.

"An' yuh wife, how shi du?"

It was Teacher Aaron's funeral now, and ignoring murmurings and grumblings, the Glamorgan SDA Church pastor had, as chairman, used both his original and his casting votes in the management committee to authorize him to "permit the occurrence at the church" of the funeral service for this backsliding—though well-known—brother, and also to conduct it himself.

When Shirls and I got out of the minibus that had brought us into Scarborough from Crown Point Airport, we were lucky that she quickly set her sharp eyes on the last two available seats in Rolling-Home's five-passenger route taxi, declaring as we entered, "Glamargan an' Belle Gyarden," as indication of our different intended destinations. We had decided in advance that Shirls would not attend the funeral. There was no doubt that Mrs. M and Cinty would be there, not to talk about a whole host of inquisitive people from Belle Garden as well as Glamorgan and all the other nearby Windward Road villages. Though unimposing in physical stature,

Teacher Aaron had been a quiet, reserved, firmly towering figure, and even the junior supervisor of schools and TACODEF member, Uriah's father, would probably be present at the funeral. It could prove uncomfortable for Shirls and me, but it was not a funeral that I myself could—or would—even think of skipping. So while Rolling-Home put me down at Glamorgan to go first to the house of mourning and pay my respects and then to the church for the service, Shirls continued on to her mother's house at Belle Garden.

In the churchyard and in the school area on the ground floor, as we exited the church at the end of the service, I greeted many people whom I hadn't seen for years, all the while considering ways and means by which to postpone, for the longest possible time, the moment when Pappy and I would be alone together and he would, in some one of his inimitable ways, inquire about a certain detail of my domestic life. Presently, I took the bull by the horns and approached him. The churchyard crowd had begun to thin out noticeably as some people headed home and some embarked on the walk along George Street toward the site of the graveyard rites.

"Pa, yuh know ah was close to 'im, ah warnt to goh arl de way wid 'im. Ah warnt to goh to de graveyard."

"Goh-arn, buh come home quick after. Ahwi haffoo chat little bit."

"Yes, Pa."

As always on these occasions, in far too many of which I felt that, for my age, I had already been involved, the concerted sound of the gravediggers' relentless shovelsful of earth falling on the unresponsive coffin lying inert six feet down kept pursuing my hapless ears as I headed for the Pint after the graveside ceremonies. That man in particular, that man nailed up in the wooden box covered up forever down there, left alone straightjacketed for all time in that buried box, had always meant a lot to me, and those gravediggers, though having nothing to do with his death, were, to my exasperated mind, no more than happy hangmen.

There were other mourners about me walking along George Street on their way home, most in silent single file, no doubt thinking their own thoughts about their own, immediate or remote, future. In my own head, competing for space with the hammering of the coffin by the hangmen's clay, there played out many rehearsals of my coming encounter with Pappy. By the time George Street reached its junction with the Windward Road and I looked to turn right on my onward journey, it hit me that I was alone, that no one else from any place east of Glamorgan had gone to the graveyard, which, in the falling darkness, caused me a little disquiet. Still, I all but jumped out of my skin when Mrs. M approached me, as if from nowhere, put her arm around me, and said, "You 'ave always been a very goood boy, you and I, vee know zhat. You vill be all right, you vill get 'ome safely."

"Ta... t'anks, Mrs. M, t'ank you. I have to hurry."

For the first couple of hundred yards, I did not walk; I ran, ran away, actually.

"An' yuh wife, how shi du?" Pappy asked.

For reasons never altogether clear to me, Mammy believed fervently in marriage, but she also believed with equal fervor that there was no requirement for any of her sons to stay with any woman who failed to *treat him right*. It followed that she would not encourage anyone at all to present me with any awkward questions relating to any action I might take to rectify any such situation. She hadn't come to the funeral and had instead stayed home and made pot-fresh cornbake, *buljol,* and lime-bush tea for dinner. After the meal in the pinewood-floor family room, with the usual kerosene lamp for light, she had my siblings walk across with her to the kitchen to help her "mek *two buldifay* an' clean up de place."

"Arl-yuh farda warn't to chat wid 'e big son," she explained.

On the long walk from the graveyard to the house in the Pint, I had recalled the unforgettable exchange we had had, years before, after cousin Conrad's funeral. When he'd asked after my wife, I was startled, and I jumped and was completely speechless for more than a fleeting moment. Recovering now and wondering if he'd heard about my marriage to Rookmin and what his next question would be, I said, simply and with general applicability, "Shi good."

"An' de Indian 'ooman mih hayr dey seh ah goh ah Inglan' wid yuh, how *she* du?"

The senior Mr. Brougham, for flexibility much more like Father O'Mally than like his spouse, most decidedly did not believe in divorce and remarriage. I should have known; often in my younger days had I heard him, whenever he'd heard a heathen talk of divorce, passionately quote the Bible as saying, "What God hath joined together let no man put asunder." Marriage was made in heaven, and divorce was an evil man-made, which manifestly made divorce a huge sin. I wondered whether it was a good or a bad thing that for us, as Seventh-Day Adventists, there were no formal categories of sin.

Before the divorce was pronounced by the court, Shirls studiously shunned the use of the word *marriage* and obviously related ones. However, by unrelenting deployment of other expressive words backed by generous demonstrations of genuine caring, she ceaselessly said that we belonged together. Sometimes she would mention Uriah and say how much she loved him "arlt'ough 'e come out ah de biggis' mistake mih eva mek eena mih whole life," after which she would pause, turn, and engage my eyes directly with hers and add, "Jakey, mih cyah neva, neva love anybady else."

By now she had sailed through all her monitors' exams and been promoted to what was designated, somewhat inelegantly, as untrained teacher class 3. No matter the title of her new post, the salary was better, and it represented upward movement in the profession. More importantly, it meant that she could now afford to bring Uriah from Tobago to live with her. Mrs. Hull was generous. The room that Shirls was renting from her was obviously too small to accommodate a double-bed or even an extra little one, and the landlady at first contemplated extending it by enclosing the portion of her veranda that was adjacent to it, an idea that, for one reason or the other, she very soon jettisoned. Then she remembered her friend, Mrs. Mendes, a widow like herself.

"Shirley, I've decided against enclosing your section of the veranda as I had mentioned—wouldn' look too good, not worth it! But I have a friend just down the road. She might have just the thing for you."

"Oh gosh, t'anks, Mrs. Hull. T'anks."

Mrs. Mendes's house was practically a replica of Mrs. Hull's, complete with that separate entry room that was such a common feature of middle-class family houses in that area and elsewhere in Trinidad built in a certain period. The difference was that at Mrs. Mendes's, the portion of the veranda adjacent to that special room had previously been enclosed for her son Ronaldo to move in there with his wife immediately after their honeymoon; and now, three years on, with Melissa pregnant for a second time, the couple had just moved into their new home in an apartment building in Newtown just outside the Port of Spain city center. Even before Shirls could settle her new living arrangements with Mrs. Mendes, Mrs. Hull went further and offered to help out with Uriah whenever she could. "Shirley, you're a very promising young woman. It would be my privilege to assist," she explained.

"Fits the bill beautifully, Mrs. Hull," Shirls commented after the showing of the room. "And thank you, Mrs. Mendes."

Sitting next to me on a Queen's Park Savannah bench under a solemn, overcast sky on a July afternoon, Shirls was adamant. "No, no rudeniss for now, Jakey. Wih haf to do t'ings right dis time. If wih goin' an' coat'n, leh wih do it right."

"*Me* arks yuh fooh rudeniss, Shirley?"

"Suh w'en yuh tell mih fooh come by you an' spen' de night... ?"

The divorce came through on the first court day in October, the beginning of the Michaelmas term, following the two-month "summer" break. Shirls had carefully suppressed her undoubtedly keen interest in the progress of my petition, and using her own pretense as shield and cover, I had, in my turn, kept her in the dark regarding the date of the hearing. That evening, I went home directly after work, had a shower, and set out for Industry Lane to see her.

When our stay at the Hilton as taxpayers' guests ended, Rooks went back, as planned, to live in Central at her uncle's, Vishnu's father's house. South of the Western Main Road in Carenage, and sandwiched between the road and the sea, there thrived an opulent residential settlement called Bayshore. I found myself a modest two-bedroom apartment at School Street on the northern side of the road, where, in time, Shiv would come to live with me. Soon after I moved into the apartment, and before Shiv came, I had asked Shirls to come by and let us cook a nice dinner together, and I had suggested that, since the day I had proposed was a Friday, I could accompany her home the following morning and we could make a good Saturday cowheel soup at her place.

"Take it easy, Jakey. We need time to settle down."

"W'a' language yuh tarkin' in dey, Shirls? Yuh garn fareign pan mih jes' suh?'

"Mih cyah come during daytime an' help yuh put 'way yuh place, buh mih na'ah tek arn da' sleep-out business deh."

Failing entirely to grasp the full significance of the expression *sleep-out businesss* as she intended it, I felt a surge of excitement, sufficient to force me to have to struggle to lower the speed of my heartbeat. For fear that a tremble in my voice would betray me if I spoke too quickly, I let some seconds pass before I replied.

"Suh w'a' 'bout Saturday, yuh cyah come Saturday?"

"Yeah, ah could du dat fooh you, Jakey."

She did come, and she did a great job helping me set up my apartment, but she laughed at every subtle and unsubtle attempt I made to guide our exchanges, verbal and nonverbal, into the direction of pleasurable acts of the ultimate intimacy, and she talked a lot, instead, about how much she missed Uriah, how clever Uriah was, and how it was important for Uriah to have the advantage of growing up under her watchful eye.

"An' w'at about Shiv?" she would put in. "Wid ah farda like you, mih showre *he-suh* mus'-be bright like ah bulb!"

"Yeah, 'e arright."

"Tark de trut'. Edderwise Gard goh sin yuh. Mih showre 'e bright like ah bulb!"

"Ah true. 'E rayly bright fooh true."

"Arright, yuh place well put 'way now," she declared, having secured the confession. "Mih affoo goh 'ome. Mih feel fooh wark. Y'ah wark mih 'ome?"

At her place in the late afternoon, my further attempts to induce intimacy knew only failure. It seemed all she wanted to concern herself with was the future of Shiv and Uriah, Uriah and Shiv, apparently—it did not escape my notice—with equal fervor. In the early evening, still a bit sullen even after the delightful fried breadfruit and buljol dinner, I walked to the corner of Duke and Abercromby, where I caught a route taxi back to Carenage.

As hard as it was to do so, I suppressed every urge to make contact with her over the next few days, and I heard nothing from her either. Until Friday. On Friday afternoon, I checked the time when the front desk attendant reached the telephone extension on my desk, and found it to be exactly one minute to four.

"A Ms. Shirley here to you, Mr. Brougham. Shi say she is ah frien' ah yours."

The passage of time without contact had, by now, become almost unbearable, and my ego made me happy that she had surrendered just in the nick of time and spared me from doing so. Yet I dissembled.

"W'at happen, problem?" I asked while trying to steady the rate of my heartbeat.

"Dis marnin' orly mih mek some good chicken pelau, wid pigeon peas an' coc'nut milk. Mih bring some fooh yuh."

"T'ank yuh, gyurl, t'ank yuh!" I responded gleefully, then, completely misreading her intentions and barely restraining myself from licking my lips, added, "L'ahwi goh home by me an' eat am nuh—an' den ahwi cyah mek some good roas'-bake fuh brockfuss tomarrow marnin'."

"Ah fooh you mih bring am. Fooh-me-own deh 'ome by me," she replied, in full control of herself. Pausing only for a second or two, she added, "An', by de way, Mammy ah bring down Yuri by de boat nex' week Friday night.... W'en *you* gettin' Shiv home by you?"

As was her wont, she had, without even risking offense, made herself crystal clear, ably eschewing, without effort, the ordinary words that, in similar circumstances, others would have used to do so. If this was going to be the last Friday night before Uriah went to live with her and she was not going to spend it at my place and she was needling me to get Shiv from Rookmin, what plans could she possibly have for a little bit of intimacy between us? I asked myself.

Finding no satisfactory answer to that question, I felt something much like desperation set in.

"Well, wan day nex' week yuh cyah come by me an' ahwi cyah cook ah nice dinner—an' yuh cyah bring yuh wuk clothes fuh nex' day wan time?"

Even if I hadn't known the answer to that question before I began asking it, well before I was halfway through it, I saw the reply written clearly all over her face.

"If yuh doh min', Jakey, de nex' time m'ah come by you, m'ah bring Yuri."

I loved my father dearly, but on the evening of Teacher Aaron's funeral, when, reaching the house after my long, lonely walk from the graveside in Glamorgan, he asked me, "An' yuh wife, how shi du?" I couldn't help but chuckle thinking of the pickle into which his principles and perceptions could plunge him. When, some three years previously, after the service for cousin Conrad, he had asked me the same thing, I had replied breezily, foolishly expecting it to be a perfunctory inquiry, "Shi good." But the Pint, let it be remembered, was a kind of subvillage of Belle Garden, Shirley's home, where, as in all the villages that dotted the coastline along the Windward Road, there were no radios, no electricity even, and gossip was a major pastime. And well should I have known how probable it was that all and sundry in BG would be apprised of my quiet divorce and my subsequent marriage to Rookmin. And he had, completely without mercy, proceeded to ask me about the woman who would be going with me to England! I chuckled now, wondering what he would do on this occasion when I gave the same reply "Shi good," because although Shirley insisted that whatever happened, we were going to have a small unpretentious church wedding at the earliest, we had gone to the Red House in mid-December, less than a month after the issue of the Decree Absolute, and got married again, the kindly Mrs. Hull once again our witness. So who was my wife now? I would have Pappy in a pickle.

Full of self-induced satisfaction, I gave Pappy the same answer as before. "Shi good."

"An' yuh son modda, how *she*?" he speared me.

Which son? Which mother? Who was in the pickle now? He was effortlessly vindicating my frequent avowals that whatever little brains I had had been passed onto me through him.

Shirley did not, as she had threatened, bring Yuri the next time she came to my apartment. On the very Monday after she had declared that that was how it would be, she came to my office at lunchtime bearing a homemade roast beef sandwich and expressing satisfaction that she had caught me before I had gone out anywhere to get "somebady else cancacshan fooh nyam."

"Wan t'ing yuh know fuh showre, *me* neva gi' yuh no chuppidniss fooh nyam!"

"Eh-heh. Mih know dat. Mih *affoo* gi' yuh dat."

"Mammy na'ah bring Yuri again. Shi seh school ah close mont'-en' an' since m'ah goh 'ome fooh de lang school 'alidays i' nuh mek sense... shi right! Mih 'gree."

## Chapter 35

Shirls was in very good spirits, and she looked at me for only a split second before taking the initiative and answering the attractive waitress herself. The waitress had been looking at us with barely concealed curiosity from the moment she first laid eyes on us, and it had taken me some time to give myself a reason why. Now that I had settled upon a reason for it, her confusion tickled me: she would have to spend a long time yet figuring out why neither of the boys looked quite as if he was the joint product of both of us. Scrutinizing us while hardly being aware of doing so herself, she had, almost distractedly, asked, "Tea, coffee?" At the end of the following split second, Shirls said, with her eyes firmly fixed on me rather than on the girl, "No, no. We'll do that at home," the gaze and the texture and the promise of her voice stirring me to great anticipation.

We had both taken the day off, and in the morning, the boys had gone to Industry Lane with us in the relatively small but sufficiently spacious moving van we had hired. The driver and the loader both helped us pack her belongings into the van, and it wasn't long before we were ready to embark on the journey back to Carenage.

"Wait!" Shirls had said. "One more thing." She rushed back inside and quickly came back out carrying an aluminum pot held in her firm grip by its two semicircular side handles, its lid firmly in place. "Our lunch!" she told me, with a huge grin and a wink of satisfaction.

Come midday, we took a break from the unpacking and the reorganizing of the apartment and we, all four, heartily enjoyed the delicious oxtail soup eventually yielded up by the aluminum pot. When, at the end of the meal, I followed Shirls into the kitchen to help with the washing-up, she turned and swiftly took ahold of me and, receiving my full and ready cooperation, thoroughly tongue-kissed me.

"Mind you, Mr. Brougham," she said as she released me from her firm embrace, "that's just a little show of appreciation and is no excuse for you to misbehave at this time!" Then, half-abandoning the mock-sternness in her voice, she added, "I strongly suggest that any misbehavior that may take place should await the hours of darkness!"

The attractive waitress at the Italian restaurant on Park Street had looked us up and down one more time before disappearing to fetch the bill. As we were so many, all of four, rather than wait at the corner of Park and Abercromby, hoping to get a route taxi with enough empty seats, we walked to Green Corner, where almost all passengers traveling on the Carenage route would disembark at that hour, and we would pay for the fifth passenger seat if need be. It was not long before, a taxi all to ourselves, we were on our way home. Back there now, as we sat together, Shirls and I having our coffee while the children savored their Milo, Yuri, addressing me directly for the first time ever, said, "T'anks fooh de dinna, Uncle. Mih enjay it." Not to be outdone, Shiv said his piece. "T'anks, Dada. De food was rayly nice."

It had been nearly five o'clock by the time we were done with the apartment. I could sense that we were all a bit exhausted and that it wouldn't do at all to expect anybody to have to prepare dinner. At all events, the two boys had done their bit and deserved a little treat.

"Why don't we go out for dinner? Anybody for Italian?"

"Yeah, Dada, yeah!" Shiv shouted as Yuri turned anxiously and looked at his mother with eyes that urged her to hurry up and confirm.

"Nope! Still a Tobago country bookie, buh mih… but I trust your judgment," she replied, pulling herself up a little when she remembered our decision to speak more English (*mo' fareign*) when the boys were around. After everybody had had a quick shower, we had walked down School Street to the Western Main Road and, after some time waiting for one with room for four, caught a route taxi to Green Corner on our way to the restaurant.

It was past nine by the time we finished our coffee and Milo. In the course of rearranging the apartment, Shirls and I had shown Uriah his single bed at the other end of the second bedroom across the floor from Shiv's. They would be sharing the clothes cupboard. Shirls and I now glanced at each other, and then she turned to them.

"Okay, boys, bedtime! But not before you brush your teeth. You go first, Shiv."

I was altogether taken by surprise at the awkward silence that descended on us when Shirls and Yuri and I suddenly found ourselves alone together. I practically panicked and had to scold myself quietly, amazed that I hadn't pictured that scene before and prepared myself for it.

As for Shirls, she was glancing, somewhat uneasily, now at Yuri, now at me. I understood that I absolutely had to say something.

"You okay, son?"

"Yes, Uncle."

"You boys worked hard today. You should have a good night's sleep."

"Yes, Uncle."

As I kicked myself within for hardly knowing what next to say, I was relieved to see Shiv emerge from the bathroom, to which Uriah, looking equally relieved and springing up from the chair and asking to be excused, now headed.

"Mih 'ope 'e start to carl yuh Dada lakka Shiv. Yuh goh min' dat?"

"Me? Min' dat? Fooh w'a'?"

"T'anks, Babe. Mih showre 'e ah goh start to carl yuh dat jes' now, doh worry. Fooh now, w'a' 'bout a likkle misbehavior later, babe, yuh able?'

"Try mih, nuh!"

"Ah warnt ah quick shower. Come and scrub mih back foohmih nuh."

As she lay in bed beside me later, the last words out of her mouth before she slipped into deep sleep were "Suh yuh t'ink yuh ready fuh misbehavior every single night fram now arn? Ah lang time now yuh lef' mih yah ah suffer!"

The easy rhythm of her breathing forbade the intrusion of any attempt on my part to reply.

Just about that time, as I was to discover later on, Shirley was still keeping to herself two pieces of information that she fully meant to share with me but that, as she would tell me in time, she feared I might take, singly or in combination, somewhat badly.

It was good that schools were on the Christmas vacation and she would be at home all day, helping the boys settle into their new environment and, importantly, establishing her relationship with Shiv. Wednesday, Thursday, Friday—each day, as they all greeted me at the front door after work, I could sense that things were going well, that we were likely going to be a good family unit. On Friday afternoon, though, she suggested that we take the boys to the Savannah to play and probably watch the inevitable football game that would be on until darkness fell, "especially if you an' me cyah lime an' jes' watch them fram ahwi favorite bench!" We four were, on this occasion too, the only passengers in the route taxi on our trip back home, and the driver agreed to wait as we stopped off to buy some soursop ice cream, a flavor to which I had introduced the boys and which they were now pleading for.

Back in the apartment, she set about warming up the dinner she had prepared for the family in midafternoon, while I, doing my bit, laid the little dining table standing in a corner of the living room, just outside the kitchen door. When the boys finished their ice cream dessert, they set out together for the bathroom to brush their teeth. Rising to clear the table of the dishes, Shirls, with her famous grin supported by a mischievous wink, said to me, "If yuh wash up de wares, ah might le' yuh scrub mih back fooh mih later."

She somehow managed to let the word *later* contain and convey, all by itself, an overwhelmingly ecstatic sense of limitless promise. Add to that that the references to the scrubbing of her back had, by then, attained the hallowed status of code, and so understand why I mock-leaped to my feet, barely forbearing to salute, and replied, "Yes, ma'am. I'll definitely do the dishes, ma'am."

"Dah wasn' ah bard idea, eh… de Savannah?" she said later as we lay on our backs, breathing evenly.

"Yeah, deh praparly enjoy dehse'f. Dey hit it arf good, eh?'

"Yeah. Two nice, nice bways. Ahwi couldn' ah arks fooh betta… excep'…"

"Excep' w'a'?"

"Jakey, yuh does eva t'ink about it—me an' you ha' two nice picknee. De two ah dem ah ahwisuh picknee, buh me an' you nuh ge' none *together*. Wey *you* t'ink 'bout dat?"

In truth, it was not a matter that I had never thought about, and hers was not a question that I did not know for sure she would pose frontally one day. Yet for some reason, I demurred. Shirls rested the pile of dishes back down onto the table and sat down again.

"Yuh know, Jakey," she said, breaking the silence, "mih feel yuh 'gree. In fac', mih arlmos' showre yuh 'gree. Fram orly, arlmos' fram day 1 Tanty Nessa behn tell mih seh yuh is a rayl good bway an' dat if you an' me hit it arf, mih mus' hol' arn to yuh fooh good, no matta w'at."

"You an' Nessa tark dem kin'a t'ing deh 'bout me, Shirls?" I demanded firmly. "W'en? W'en aryuh did du dat?"

"Was only good t'ing ahwi behn tark, Jakey… an' plenty good t'ing, eh. Tanty Nessa did rayly, rayly like yuh, bway!"

"How *you* know dat? Aryuh tark 'bout me plenty, plenty, den?"

"Jakey, after ah time shi did ge' to realize mih behn know good-good weh behnah goh arn between you an' she…"

"W'aat!"

"Wan day, me an' she wan deh eena de kitchen deh. Shi tell mih ahwi affoo tark. Shi start to tark. Shi tell mih shi know dat me know 'bout certain t'ings she does du wid you buh dat she know t'ing 'bout me too—'Like weh ah goh arn between you an' yuh teacher'—da's weh shi tell mih."

"W'aat!" I screamed, but Shirley did not hear me.

"Shi tell mih to fooget 'bout mih teacher. Shi tell mih she shise'f have a big bwayfrien' now an' shi warnt me an' you to frien' an' dat how shi warnt mih to treat yuh rayly good. Den shi arks mih weh ah t'ink 'bout dat."

"An' nobady nuh arks *me* nutten!" I protested, weakly now.

"Jakey, bway, to tell yuh de trut' eh, w'en shi done tark mih behn glad-glad. Ah lang time befo' dat mih behn like yuh, an' now mih own tanty behn deh-deh ah tell mih fooh like yuh, de bes' gif' shi coulda eva, eva gi' mih!"

"Gyal, *you* rayly did like mih fram lang time? *Me* behn like yuh fram lang time too, gyal," I replied, at once happy and cautiously thoughtful, before I added, "Buh Nessa, she was so smart, ah bet yuh shi did well know arl de time seh me an' you mus'-be did deh-deh arl de time ah eye wan anneda, eye wan anneda, eye wan anneda."

Briefly abandoning words altogether, Shirls rose from her chair and walked around to the back of mine. Standing behind me as I sat there, still, she rested her arms on my shoulders, just below her elbows, and stretched them forward; then, dropping her clasped hands onto my chest, she kissed me on the crown of my head. And now she reached back to speech.

"Jakey, mih pregnant... de fuss Friday night mih sleep hayr after yuh divorce did come t'rough."

As I made to get up from my chair, she sharply withdrew and reclaimed her hands and arms before stepping backward, as if fearing my displeasure.

Rising at last, I turned toward her and took her into my arms in a long, tight embrace. Presently, I would release her and, looking deep into her smiling eyes, kiss her lovingly on her relieved lips.

"Would you mind, ma'am, if I did the dishes *after* I scrub your back?" I solicited.

Instead of giving voice to an answer, she abandoned words again; she held my hand, and I was all too happy to let her lead me, like her sheep, into the shower. The washing of the dishes took place on the following morning.

Early on Saturday morning, Shirls came out to join me at the kitchen sink. She sneaked up behind me on tiptoes and kissed me on the back of my neck, thus blessing me with a delicious tickle.

"Good morning, Big Daddy," she greeted me as I turned to face her. "Let's do this, too, together. The joint effort last night was simply out of this world."

"How does a man not love a woman like you?"
"He doesn't!"
"W'aat? W'at yuh mean?"
"*My* Jakey doesn't *not* love a woman like me... of whom, incidentally, there is only one!"

"What a wonderful playmate you are... in every way! Look how nice yuh fondle an' play up wid dem word an' dem deh. Nobody else would do, as the song says... Paul Anka... was it Paul Anka? Doh matter... wan ah dem fellas!"

"Ah who dat deh? Ah who Parl Anka yah tark 'bout? Ah how *me* goh know he? Anyhow, good time to tell yuh mih nex' secret."

"W'a's dat?"

"M'ah goh ah Mausica September!"

"Mausica?"

"Teachers' Training Callege!"

"You're a bloody genius," I replied, holding her in a tight, possessive embrace.

My back to the kitchen sink, I found myself looking over her head at the far wall. My mind roamed back to the time of our divorce, and I began to stroke my hairless chin as it purred in response to the concerted attentions of my thumb and middle finger and forefinger.

"I could have lost you," I said quietly, almost unwittingly, as if addressing the wall and taking it into my confidence.

"W'at!" she responded, waking me from a half-dream and making me lower my line of vision and look back at her.

"I went, and I came back. You were always there, solid as a rock... open, straightforward, no matter what... always showing your love... you never tricked me!"

"Wait, wait! W'a' s arl dis ole tark? An' in fareign to boot! Yuh arright, Jakey?"

"Yeah, mih arright. Yuh know, w'en ah was growin' up, plenty big *'ooman... famaly* an' arl—who shoulda be helpin' mih... yuh doh know ho' much ah dem try fooh trick mih wid arl kin' ah chuppid t'ing."

Shirls stepped forward, and we encircled each other with our arms, uttering, for many moments, not a single word.

"Ah lang, lang time now m'ah fight up, fight up wid missef ah try fooh l'arn fooh trus' ooman!" I soon said.

I told Shirls my other secret, too: I had applied to start evening classes at the university in St. Augustine come September. She was delighted. She had worried, she said, over telling me about her selection for professional teacher-training, no doubt fearing, at least subconsciously, that I might see her as taking strides in life quite ahead of me, with the possibility of some kind of future detriment to our relationship.

"We can move to Curepe, nearer to Mausica, practically in St. Augustine se'f," she offered.

"Yeah… easier fooh me to travel to wuk in tong from dere."

We spent a great deal of the August long vacation looking for our new home and, in time, found ourselves a compact three-bedroom bungalow, forming part of a commercially constructed residential compound on McInroy Street called Sinanan Multi-Family Complex, named for the developer. To top it all off, we also got the boys enrolled in a kindergarten right in that area.

Little Emelina, the newest member of the family, had arrived early in July, shortly before the start of the school holidays, and the third bedroom of our tiny bungalow came in handy as rescue to Shirls's mother from the canvas couch that until then had been her bed in the apartment living room.

# Chapter 36

WE WERE BEYOND DELIGHTED THAT, after all our countless ups and downs, things had at last gone so well for us. But I was ever conscious that there was one little outstanding matter that demanded my attention: I had no doubt at all that my next duty was to arrange, preferably without too much delay, the church marriage ceremony that Shirls had, every now and then, carefully let slip that she would always want.

An attractive sign on a building on Agostini Street in Curepe invited all to enter and meet with the pastor of the Holy Tabernacle of the Faithful Few. We went in, and my disappointment was complete and immediate, for the pastor and proprietor turned out to be none other than he who was now Apostle Anatol Wellington Leonce (formerly Seventh-Day Adventist pastor resident at Roxborough in Tobago), who had since established his own church. He showed no sign of recognizing me. We told him we would get back to him.

By and by, we found ourselves another pastor who, hearing (without the details) that we had already been blessed with three children, instantly became committed, heart and soul, to do all in his power to help us "do the right thing." Dr. the Very Reverend Bishop E. Isaiah Nicholson, founder of the Church of the Trinity of the Living God, explained that the main temple at McCarthy Street at St. Augustine was booked up for marriage ceremonies for the ensuing six months. He explained with passion that there were far too many one-parent homes in the country and that that was a cancer eating away at the heart of the society. His church, cutting the officiating fee in half, was on a mission to alleviate that situation, and by the grace of God, they were succeeding admirably. Unless we wanted to wait that long (which, "in the circumstances," he definitely would not recommend), our ceremony could be conducted at his other temple, in Barataria, by Pastor Savitri Manmohansingh-Nicholson, his wife, who was responsible for ministering to the flock at that branch.

Pastor Manmohansingh-Nicholson was a lady of considerable charm. In the delightfully furnished Interactive Relationship Room (her secretary called it the IARR) discreetly located out of sight behind the altar, she welcomed us with great warmth as she took Emelina away from Shirls and cuddled her, saying, "What a sweetie she is! She's *beau-ti-ful*."

"Thank you!" Shirley said, so dryly, it appeared to me, that I wondered if this meeting would rival for duration the one we had had not too long before with Apostle Leonce, leaving us still to search for someone suitable to conduct our religious marriage ceremony.

On our entry into her little office just outside the IARR, the secretary had welcomed us pleasantly and was in the process of inviting us to hold on for a minute when the lady pastor pushed open the IARR door and took control of the proceedings.

"Oh, Mr. Brougham, Ms. Wilson!" she gushed. "I was expecting you. Bishop told me about you... oh, and that *baby*!"

I could tell by the look on Shirls's face that she heartily detested some aspect of all this—perhaps either being gratuitously called *Ms. Wilson* or the excessive attention being showered on her precious baby girl or both.

"Very happy to meet you, Pastor," I said as soon as I found a little speaking space.

"Come in, come right in," she urged, motioning with her ample chin to the door leading into the IARR, through which she had just emerged. "Raveena, do bring us some coffee. Would you like some coffee, Mr. Brougham, Ms. Wilson?"

Mrs. Brougham bristled.

Over coffee, the pastor told us what a pleasure it would be to conduct our marriage ceremony and what a privilege it was for her to be the one to help such a wonderful couple do the right thing. She said that that was exactly in keeping with one of the main missions of the church as enunciated by the founder, the Right Reverend Bishop. She hoped that as we cultivated and nurtured our marriage life, we would always be sure not only to hold a place in it for Jesus but also to put Jesus first.

Mrs. Brougham bristled again, but again, Pastor Manmohansingh-Nicholson did not notice.

"I myself was born a Hindu and grew up as a Hindu. Even after I met Bishop—well, to tell you the truth, he wasn't a bishop yet, eh—I continued for a long time to be a Hindu, as I had promised my pundit and my parents after, finally, they agreed, very reluctantly, to our marriage. Mind you, I loved—in fact, still love—being a Hindu, but now I've found Jesus, too, and believe me, it's a real joy, I tell you. It is a real joy… a double joy, you could say!"

"It is we who are privileged, Pastor," I said, "to have someone like you officiate at our wedding. We feel ourselves truly blessed. We have known pastors with far less heart and soul, we have."

"Pastor," Shirls said crisply, "I want to second that. We feel blessed."

Exchanging vows for the third time, we celebrated our church wedding on a quiet Sunday afternoon in mid-September. Shirley looked gleeful and happy all through it.

As we exited the temple, a light coming through from somewhere shone onto the boys' faces, Emelina chortled, and I could feel a silly grin fully in charge of my face.

The End

# About the Author

Hollister Horace Broomes was born on the tiny, almost wholly rural, island of Tobago—part of the two-island nation of Trinidad and Tobago—specifically, on a promontory not far from the coastal village of Argyle that, years later, would produce Winston Duke of *Black Panther* fame. He was born in 1941 and is the father of seven children, five of them male.

Being the eldest of the eight children (six of them male) of his parents' nuclear family of somewhat unspectacular means, he branched out on his own in his midteen years and has been high school teacher, journalist, diplomat, and for the last thirty-odd years, attorney-at-law.

He is the holder of a bachelor's degree from the University of the West Indies and a law degree from the University of London, United Kingdom, as well as certification as a barrister-at-law from Gray's Inn, London, one of the four venerable English schools of law.

He gets supreme pleasure from the imagery and expressiveness of the peculiar idiom of Tobago, in which his dialogues abound.

He has been forced to give up tennis (in which, in any case, he never showed sign of genius), and his only pastime now is bridge.

Lightning Source UK Ltd.
Milton Keynes UK
UKHW041550280419
341740UK00001B/63/P